ENDLESS TIDES

First Published in Great Britain 2012 by Netherworld Books an imprint of Belvedere Publishing

First edition: 2012

A copy of this work is available through the British Library.

ISBN : 978-1-909224-18-6

Netherworld Books
Mirador
Wearne Lane
Langport
Somerset
TA10 9HB

Endless Tides

By

Sam Leeves

Netherworld Books

Chapter One

The benevolent, almost smiling, moon of that night spun a pool of light in the desert. Far beneath the sky the wind swept up flocks of sand making them waltz as if to a lament.

Three men stood in the pool of lustre, locked in their struggle.

The thief's hands moved slowly to the pocket of his brown garbs, checking his loot was still there. It was, although he knew not for how long it would stay.

The man in the crimson coat rested the blade of his katana on his shoulder; the blade, black, even in such magnificent, haunting light, seemed as stoic as the smiling man holding it. The hilt, as crimson as the man's coat, gave an air of arrogance to the weapon. Two red ribbons swam from the hilt in the breeze.

The third man, wearing a blue coat, was stood next to the man in crimson. His sword remained sheathed, yet something in his face whispered to the thief that he would use it more readily than his companion.

The men were silent. Their thoughts were muted, mere images running in the reflection of a flowing mind.

A lone black cloud crept across the sky obscuring, at first, only the stars, then, as it seemed to swell with night air, the moon. The pool of light disappeared leaving the men in darkness – a veritable nothing in the nothingness of the desert.

The man in the crimson coat moved his shoulders wearily before tilting his head to the man in blue.

"You want to kill him, don't you, DeFlare?" he said. His voice was frivolous, yet a deep and soothing baritone. It shattered the silence instantly.

DeFlare nodded.

"We have our orders." He placed his hand on the hilt of his sword.

The man in crimson tilted his head back to the thief. The thief observed as the breeze blew his enemy's chin length blonde hair, causing it to shroud his face. In the already thick darkness he thought it must have impaired the man's vision at least slightly, though the thief knew not how to take advantage of this. The man in crimson ran his fingers through his hair, clearing his face of obstruction.

'So much for that advantage...' thought the thief.

"Do you know who we are?" the man in crimson said.

"You're Captain Laike Skyheart of the Fourth Division, although, I don't know your associate."

Skyheart smiled.

"Actually, it's Division Four," he said. "But I'll allow the mistake to go unpunished just this once. At this point the identity of my associate is unimportant." His smile faded. "I assume you know why we're here?"

The thief nodded.

"Give it to us," Skyheart said, "and you're free to leave."

"We're wasting time," DeFlare said.

Skyheart held his free left hand out to the thief. The black cloud continued on its journey, washing the men in light once more.

The thief didn't move.

"You're making this harder than it needs to be," Skyheart sighed.

Lieutenant DeFlare began a slow, heavy walk over to the thief, his footsteps singing out, serenading the silence. The imposing figure constantly growing with shrinking distance caused the thief to shiver, though he told himself it was the cold. Unknowingly, he placed his hand in his pocket, grasped the jewel and, in a smooth sweeping motion, threw it to the Captain.

Skyheart caught it in his free left hand, his sword in his right still resting on his shoulder.

"Thank you," the Captain said.

DeFlare continued his advance. A glint of steel shone out in the desert and the sword being drawn from its wooden scabbard screamed. The blade cut through air, then man, then air once more.

The thief fell.

"We had our orders," DeFlare said, sheathing his sword and neatening his short brown hair.

"Indeed we did," Skyheart replied, "although, I never was one for following them."

DeFlare turned and looked back towards to younger, yet higher ranking, man.

"We've a long walk home," he said. "We'd best start now if we're to be back by morning."

"And so ends another adventure," Skyheart said, placing the jewel in his pocket and sheathing his sword. "How long must we wait until the next?"

The two began the long walk back to Thieron, paying no mind to the dead thief, his blood colouring the sand a familiar shade of red as the viscous fluid seeped into the grained ground, as if at the request of the leaving men; their silhouettes shrinking in the distance, their long leather coats swimming in the breeze.

*

The sun reigned down on the island; their island. The only inhabitants were a mother, her young son and his pet baby turtle. They sat on the beach looking out at the calm sea doing nothing other than being.

The boy named Paccon stood.

"I'm ready now, Mama."

She looked up at him smiling. He was wearing the tall pointed straw hat she had made him and his grey rags. His face was practically non-existent under the shadow of the hat's rim, yet still she knew he was smiling.

He clambered into the fishing boat and she passed him the fishing-rod.

2

"My first time fishing alone," he said, beaming. "What an adventure."

"You be back by dark."

"I will, Mama."

"And if the waves get too strong you come back straight away."

"I will, Mama."

She kissed him and pushed the boat out, sending him on his self-deemed "adventure". She waved as he rowed further out. He waved back and set the rod out, waiting for his catch.

The woman saw he was consumed with his fishing and returned to the hut. The adventure could begin.

He felt a tickling in the pocket of his rags and reached in. The baby turtle was revealed as he pulled his hand out.

"Franklin!" Paccon said, elated by his pet's presence. He laughed, leaned back and lay in the boat.

He lazed the hours away doing nothing. He exhaled gently and the warm air from his body met the cool air of the sea, creating perfection. He sat up and checked the line. Nothing had bitten. He sighed and lay back down, looking to the sky. It was perfectly clear. Franklin clambered over Paccon's chest eliciting yet more laughter from the boy. After a few minutes the combination of the peacefully buoyant sea and perfect temperature led Paccon into a deep darkness. A deep nothingness. A deep sleep.

Back on land, the woman stepped outside of the hut onto the rocky beach – a collage of grey against the blue of the sea. She looked to see him, but instead saw the sky's new blackness. Heavy clouds had drifted in from the north. She ran to the shoreline but still she couldn't see him. She screamed out for her son to return but her voice fell silent on the air. She screamed again but was masked under a symphony of thunder. Rain crashed free of the clouds. She ran back to the hut, praying to any deity that might be listening to bring him home safely.

He woke to the sound of thunder; an antagonistic, violent roar from the heavens ripping through his ears. The seas, before so pleasantly buoyant, now attacked the fishing boat with visceral impact. The whining wind, winning in a contest against the terrified boy, caused the boat to spin in the apocalyptic waters.

"Mama!" Paccon screamed.

He reached for the oars only to find they had long been blown or swept away. Franklin clambered back into Paccon's pocket finding what little sanctuary there was. The boy screamed again.

"Mama!"

The wind made its final assault, lifting the boat, boy as well, from the sea and carried them further into the night.

*

The flowers had long been blooming in the garden. Blossoms of pink and white sprouted from the soil beds and high bushes, obscuring her garden from prying eyes.

The young woman placed a bouquet of red blossoms onto the first of three graves.

'Here lies Lawce Harmoire,
Beloved husband and father taken in The Mineral Wars.
He is dearly missed.'

She moved onto the next, placing blue blossoms.

'Here lies Farr Harmoire,
Beloved mother who took her own life in The Mineral Wars.
She is dearly missed.'

She moved onto the next grave, removing a previous wilted bouquet of ambiguous origin and replacing them with black blossoms.

'Here lies Kote Venar,
Beloved fiancé of Myri Harmoire.
May we finally be wed in time, my dearest?
When next we meet, perhaps fate will be less cruel.'

She stood facing the ground for a few minutes experiencing a familiar itching behind her eyes. A feeling she had felt so often as a child and on days like that one. A tear made its way to the outside. More followed.

Myri fell to her knees and clutched at her heart, with every will and intention to tear it out. Alas, she could not. She knelt there shrieking lightning in the graveyard garden. A garden in full bloom of life yet containing an equal amount of death. And that death was growing.

"How long?" she asked her fiancé's headstone. "How long until we are reunited? Have the Gods not toyed with me enough?"

Tears turned to a river, birthing from her eyes.

She heard thunder approaching her town of Port Fair. Consumed in her sorrow she continued to cry, mourning the long dead and new dead for as long as she could bear or as long as she could before she was stopped. Stopped before it was her time to be mourned.

Chapter Two

Thieron stood in the middle of the desert; an iron fortress outside, a decaying city within. The walls towered many metres high, shrouding the inner city from view. The metal on the gates was starting to wear from centuries of sandstorms, beginning to rust merely from age. In the dawn's sun it was a tired home to a tired people and two tired soldiers approached from the north, bearing a jewel planned to rejuvenate the forgotten power.

Skyheart and DeFlare reached the North Gate and waited. It had been a long walk on an even longer night, as long a night as Skyheart could recall. Eventually, they were seen by a guard somewhere in the wall. The hissing of pistons and turning of cogs caused a caustic cranking forcing the gate to slowly creep open, gradually revealing the Old District; the oldest quadrant of Thieron, once known as the 'Industrial District', now worn down to the homes of thieves, whores and drunks. It was fast becoming known as 'Vice District'.

The two men stepped through the gate and onto a street with metal shacks on either side. A putrid smell invaded their nostrils. Skyheart removed a bottle of brown liquor from the inside of his coat, took a swig and held the bottle out to DeFlare. The Lieutenant refused with a wave of his hand and a superior expression. Skyheart shrugged and placed the bottle back in his coat pocket. He looked up the road, seeing only prostitutes making their early morning rounds (a shift he thought strange, but, having used their services on more than one occasion, could hardly disparage), stalls selling (what he assumed were) illegally acquired goods and drunks stumbling to the next bar. In the distance was their destination: the Monument, a towering gold skyscraper shimmering with desert heat. They went on their way.

Those they passed were aging, decaying like the quadrant of the city they lived in and had once loved, now just there as a convenient melting pot for them to begin to die in. A fading life in a broken part of the city, erased from the memory of the world.

Old men drank as they attempted to wipe their younger selves from their mind, hoping that if they could just forget they could start a new life with the time they had left. Yet still the young men in their minds taunted them in their drunken dreams. No stupor could kill them. So old men had to live with who they were then and who they were long ago.

The women were festering sexual relics. Not wanted by their clients but the best their clients could get. Once, they were brightly shining virgins of youth and their innocence was a viable currency for nearly anything they required or wanted; then they were unavailable. Now they were very available but unwanted, scorned. Pilgrims that had travelled too far and too hard through the valley of age to come back to, or even remember, what they were.

The people of the Old District had been promised that the industrial revolution wouldn't leave them behind, that the steam factories would still be fuelled, used and that the people wouldn't lose their jobs. The saddest thing was that the government hadn't lied. There was just no money to put into the district. The Old District still had the most technologically advanced machinery in Thieron, but the city run on steam was being left behind. It stood as a monument to the old days and, like the old days, Thieron was very much in the past.

"Why don't they leave?" DeFlare asked, looking at the squalor and those who lived in it.

"They love their land," Skyheart said. "Besides, where else would they go? The Housing District certainly doesn't have room for them all."

"Disease will be here soon," DeFlare continued, ignoring his captain.

Skyheart didn't reply – he was busy observing a people to whom disease would be a welcome respite. As they walked through the quarter they attracted more attention. Whispers crawled between the people of the Captain's presence. Men and women pointed at him, smiling and waving, trying to meet the eyes of the famed Crimson Captain. He smiled and waved back theatrically, as an actor at the end of a successful performance.

DeFlare scoffed. "Is anything not a show to you?"

Skyheart's smile broadened.

"Not an awful lot," he replied.

A young girl in ragged, once white, clothing approached them. They stopped and allowed her to walk to them. Her face was covered with dirt and grime, her hair slicked back with grease. She coughed weakly as she walked and stopped directly before the Captain.

"Excuse me, Captain," she said. "My mother wondered if you would consider selling your sword to us." She blinked a few times in quick succession and swivelled on her feet. "We don't have very much and couldn't offer you a lot for it, however if we sold it on, it might at least see us through the rest of the year."

A grin pulled on Skyheart's mouth. DeFlare looked at him disapprovingly causing the grin to widen further.

"My reputation precedes me," the Captain said. "Run along little girl. Your mother and you have no need for swords. I suggest you leave such thoughts alone."

They continued walking.

"I don't see what there is to smile about," DeFlare said.

"All the more reason to smile," Skyheart replied.

Soon they reached the Central Gate; the iron lattice that separated the Districts from the Monument. The guard saluted as they walked through into a courtyard of pure white stone. In the centre was a statue of a man in a coat not dissimilar to Skyheart's, he looked not altogether different, though perhaps rather less effeminate. Upon sight of the statue Skyheart grimaced, though DeFlare couldn't trace the emotion that caused him to do so. A path of black stone led to the skyscraper itself. They walked along it and entered.

Thirteen men sat in the President's office on the top floor of the Monument. President Kylar sat in his black suit with six men in white hooded robes either side of him. Behind the men was a great window, encompassing the entire back wall, facing out over the New District. If steam powered the old Thieron then war would be the new economy. The President watched as soldiers were drilled and trained. He turned back and sat at the table.

"They have returned?" he asked.

"Yes," replied a voice from under one of the twelve hoods.

"With the Diamandé?"

"Yes. Although our preparations are a little behind schedule."

"When can we commence with Operation Shell?"

"No later than in two days' time."

"So be it. We wait."

"We are surprised. Are we not?"

The President sighed.

"He may be arrogant, gentlemen," he said, "but Captain Skyheart is more than reliable."

Silence ran throughout the room, drifting from man to man lending prominence to the President's final words of the meeting.

"Send for Skyheart, DeFlare, Thean and Okain when preparations are complete. It's best that they know nothing for now."

The men's hoods shuffled as they nodded in agreement.

The powerful looking man sat before them studying the jewel with a severe expression. Skyheart wondered exactly what he was looking for; he was a general, not a jeweller. He turned to them rumpling his black uniform in the process. He looked up at Skyheart and raised an eyebrow.

"The thief?" asked General Wraste.

"Dead," Skyheart said, moving his eyes sharply to DeFlare.

"So, nobody knows that we have it?"

"Nobody knows," Skyheart's eyes moved back to the General. "What exactly does it do?"

"I'm sorry?"

"The jewel. I assume it does something other than sit there looking pretty, otherwise you wouldn't have ordered us to retrieve it."

The General's face became even more severe.

"You know better than to ask questions, Captain," he said. "You'll hear from me in the next few days."

He pointed to the door and the two men from Division Four left. They walked up a sterile corridor and into the steam-powered elevator. Skyheart leaned against the back wall as DeFlare pulled a rusty lever to the ground floor setting, causing the same hissing sound as when they entered the city.

"Why did you ask?" said the Lieutenant.

"Because, DeFlare, I wouldn't be me if I didn't antagonise the General at our every meeting."

"And if he informs your brother?"

Skyheart sighed. "Emaina's made it quite clear that I'm a Skyheart only by name. The Captain of the Second Division may be my senior, but he is no longer my brother."

"Still, you have a habit of annoying powerful men."

The elevator stopped and the doors opened revealing the lobby. DeFlare gave Skyheart a questioning look which he ignored and walked out. DeFlare followed him.

"You know what the jewel is, don't you, Captain?"

"I have an idea and so should you, you know the scripture better than me," Skyheart stopped in the archway leading to the courtyard. "You drill the men for the next few days. I've business to attend to."

With that he left. DeFlare saw not which gate he exited through.

The stream was flowing gently beside him. He put a hand in it and let the cold fresh water wash past and through his fingers. The cherry blossom tree he was using for shade had long been flowering and was in the midst of one the most impressive blooms he had seen. The sun made its way through different branches and the breeze danced with the tree.

He sighed, knowing what was coming. The advancement of the westernmost power, Mandra, was constantly being matched by that of the easternmost power, Genko, and, inevitably, they would meet in the middle of the continent: Thieron.

He was aware that the Assembly were continually making countermeasures to skew the efforts of the two super-powers, but he doubted they would work and he knew he would soon be involved in one of them. Indeed, he already was. Collecting the jewel – a mere prologue of an operation to follow; he was sure of it.

Thieron was a match for neither of the powers. Both countries were proud warrior nations left far stronger after the Mineral Wars that had started thirty years previously, six years before Skyheart was born. Not only this, but their armies were many times the size of Thieron's. Since Thieron's failure in the Mineral Wars they had avoided war. The six year conflict had almost left Thieron bereft of an army, despite the fact that they had made the most progress south. However, upon turning north to return to Thieron they had been ambushed by both Mandra and Genko, although the two powers had never intended to aid each other in such a way. The defeat was of great shame to Thieron, although Skyheart, at only the verge of birth when the war had ended, struggled to see why Thieron carried this with them. However, he could not deny that the current situation was severe. The army of Thieron was barely one thousand strong with two hundred and fifty men in each division. It was more for ceremony than war, although the Captains and Lieutenants were regarded as world-class swordsmen. Swordsmen, not soldiers. They were more closely considered to be artists; artists who used death as a canvas. Skyheart thought it a distasteful comparison.

He sighed once more. A blue butterfly flew softly above him. He took his hand from the stream and stretched it into the air. The butterfly landed on his index finger and appeared to rest. Silence in the garden but for the stream. He flicked his finger and the butterfly went on its way.

"Now wouldn't that be easy?" he said to himself.

His reply came in the form of a door opening and footsteps approaching his sanctuary of shade and solace. The interrupter leaned against the tree, wearing the black uniform and white leather coat of a Captain of Thieron.

"Still sporting the crimson coat I see," said the figure. "Well you wouldn't be the Crimson Captain without it, would you?"

"Hello, brother," Skyheart sighed.

"How long has accessorising uniforms been permitted?" Emaina waited for the younger sibling to answer but carried on when no reply came. "I thought you didn't live here anymore?"

"I'll be sent on an operation in a few days," Skyheart said, standing up. "The garden relaxes me."

"Why so sure you'll be sent?" Emaina asked, his brown eyebrows contorting into a frown, framing his eyes in the manner of an unwelcome apparition.

"Because, brother, I'm Captain Laike Skyheart of Thieron's Division Four," his smile betrayed his earlier thoughts of war. "Who else is there to send?" He began to swagger down the white stone path.

"Such infallible confidence," his brother said, tauntingly. "Such infallible confidence from a careless, fraud of a Captain."

Skyheart exited the garden with a casual, yet performance-worthy, gesture of a hand waving his brother's words away.

'Yes,' a quiet, melancholy voice in his head spoke, 'Captain Laike Skyheart of Division Four. He of such complacent, arrogant, unassailable confidence.'

His walk took him away from the Housing District and to Division Four's barracks in the New District. This was not where he had intended to go, though once there he thought it only proper that he put in an appearance. His men greeted or saluted him as he walked passed, but to him they were mere shadows – shapes to be ignored.

He sat in his office, a rarity for him (as such there nothing in there save for the chair and desk). He closed his eyes. The sound of DeFlare drilling some selected troops drifted in from outside. The haunting voice of the Lieutenant gave the proceedings an aura of mysticism.

Skyheart heard a knock at the door, followed by its opening. An old man in a Captain's uniform sporting wild white hair entered.

"Well this *is* a rarity," he said. "Captain Laike Skyheart in his office."

"Captain Thean," Skyheart said, smiling. "What brings you here?"

"I came to congratulate you on your latest exploits. The retrieval of the jewel sounds like quite an adventure."

"I'm afraid not," Skyheart said. "The adoring Thieronian public will have to wait for a tale of true adventure." His smile disappeared. "It is what I think it is, isn't it?"

"So it would seem," Thean said, also becoming serious. "They're running tests on it currently."

"Who would have thought that the Diamandé actually exists?"

"People still believe in Thiera, present company excluded, of course."

Skyheart looked up at the old man.

"Some of us know better," he said.

"Don't let your brother hear you say that. Or your Lieutenant, for that matter."

"Although we may say what we wish to Ryden."

"Yes. Though make sure it doesn't get to the Assembly."

"Speaking of the Assembly, what do you know of the Operation that's coming up?"

"Only that it involves the Diamandé, us and our Lieutenants."

"I feared as much," Skyheart said, slumping in his chair. He hadn't slept since he returned from the desert and was struggling to stay awake.

"I'll leave you to your sleep," Thean said, reading Skyheart's body language. "But remember 'On the battlefield on which the forces of Seph and Pycra faced one another raged a fierce fire. The ashes and flames of which created Cendré – a mighty and powerful sword of black and crimson.' You know best of all how right the Scriptures were about that." Thean looked at the hilt of Skyheart's sword. "The Diamandé is mentioned in the Scriptures too."

"Your point?"

"I've seen you do things with that sword I didn't think possible. Perhaps it's you, perhaps it's Cendré. The Diamandé's power is described as 'unimaginable' as the shard of a sword long lost, compressed of the coals of that fire – a sword the blade of which is diamond."

"I still don't see your point."

"My point is that not everything in the Scriptures can be dismissed so easily, especially with the existence of Cendré. If the Diamandé is as powerful as the Scriptures say..." He trailed off.

"I know," Skyheart said. "You're worried the Assembly might want to use it."

"Yes, although they'll most likely call it a 'deterrent'."

"Well, whatever it is, it had best not ruin my next adventure, or any more to come."

"How cavalier of you," Thean said, smiling. "Though I'd expect nothing less. Anyway, I've kept you long enough. I shall leave you to your sleep."

Skyheart watched as Thean left and closed the door. Then darkness.

He woke after his dreamless sleep with a distinct nauseous feeling. He hauled himself up from his chair and staggered outside of his office. He could still hear DeFlare drilling the troops. He headed towards the noise.

The training ground of Division Four was a large square courtyard between the barracks. The troops were sparring heartily with each other while DeFlare watched. He smiled when one soldier attempted a particularly viscous strike which, had he been using a real sword instead of a bamboo one, would surely have killed his opponent.

Skyheart stumbled groggily into the courtyard, blinded temporarily by the light. The sky was pale, the sun a brilliant white amidst the insipid blue. He raised his right arm to shield his eyes and moved towards DeFlare who was slowly pacing the outskirts of the mock battlefield.

"Good morning, Captain," DeFlare said as Skyheart approached.

"Morning?" Skyheart said. "I seem to have slept for an entire day." He felt himself beginning to rouse. "Admittedly not for the first time." He smiled and rubbed his eyes, trying to force himself awake. "Any word from General Wraste?"

"I'd have woken you if there was," DeFlare said. "When do you think he'll summon us?"

"Later on today or early tomorrow I'd imagine. He doesn't like to keep me in Thieron for too long, which is probably wise," Skyheart said, smile forever widening.

"Perhaps you shouldn't antagonise him so much then."

"I'd abhor for him to get rusty, DeFlare."

"Your brother came to see you," DeFlare said wearily.

"What for?"

"He didn't say, though he seemed rather irate."

"Well my existence has always frustrated him."

"He said he'd be in his office in the Second Division barracks all day and to go and see him immediately. But you won't."

Skyheart smiled.

"Actually, today I will follow this one order," he said. He put the index and middle fingers of right hand to his temple and flicked his wrist away from his head in a casual salute and swaggered away, leaving DeFlare alone with the troops once more.

It was a short walk to the Second Division's barracks and the morning air helped wake him. This pleased the Captain greatly as he was aware he would need all of his wits if he was to face his brother. Emaina was his senior by eight years and, until recently, his closest rival. For Laike the rivalry had become stale and not worth the effort. He would rather have been on a great quest than outdoing his brother in some childish contest. Emaina seemed to believe that the pinnacle of human achievement was to reach the heights of their father, Commander Zenedin Skyheart, however Laike had no interest in that particular pinnacle.

He arrived at the office, knocked and entered. His brother's office was far more furnished than his own. Ceremonial swords hung on the walls surrounded by bookcases full of writings on military strategy.

Emaina was sat at the desk filling out some form of paperwork that Laike didn't recall ever seeing. He gestured for the younger brother to come closer but said nothing. Laike did as he was ordered and stood before the desk. He looked at Emaina and crossed his arms. Eventually, Emaina looked up from the papers and spoke.

"This operation, what do you know about it?"

"Nothing much. Only that I'll be going on it."

"I see. You won't say anything more?"

"I don't know anything more about it."

Emaina gave him a scrutinising look. "Lies."

"Such animosity towards a brother," Laike laughed.

"They're sending you why?"

"I haven't asked. After all, an adventure is an adventure."

"We're done here," Emaina said, pointing towards the door. Laike turned and began to leave. He paused in the doorframe and looked back.

"Brother," he said, "if you've something to say to me, that's fine, but don't waste my time with petty squabbles. I'm an incredibly busy man."

With that he left.

Upon reaching the outside he paused to think of where to go and what to do. It was then he realised he had nothing to do. Apparently he wasn't as busy as he thought. He sighed and began a slow walk in no particular direction.

When General Wraste's messenger reached the barracks of Division Four, Captain Skyheart wasn't there. He found Lieutenant DeFlare and gave him the message that Captain Skyheart and the Lieutenant were to report to General Wraste immediately. Unfortunately, before DeFlare could achieve this he would have to find the Captain. Skyheart already had a reputation as a notoriously poor time keeper and an embarrassment on the Captain was an embarrassment for the entire division.

He asked the men if any of them had seen the Captain. One soldier admitted that after not seeing the Captain for so long even if he had seen him he couldn't be sure of it. DeFlare went to Skyheart's office in case he had since arrived but the office had not been entered since the Captain had emerged that morning.

Captain Ryden Cyan was surprised to see the Lieutenant of Division Four in the Third Division's barracks. Natural curiosity eventually winning him over, he approached the typically sullen-looking DeFlare.

"Lieutenant DeFlare," he said, "having problems?"

"Sir!" DeFlare said, saluting. "Have you seen Captain Skyheart?"

"In my barracks?" Cyan laughed. "Well I suppose Laike does choose some rather strange places to sleep. Though, I'm afraid I haven't seen him. Is there a hurry?"

"We're to report to General Wraste immediately."

"Why don't you send some of the men to look for him?"

DeFlare cursed himself inside his head and thanked Captain Cyan for his time. He should have thought of that himself.

'That's why you'll never be Captain,' he thought.

In a particularly debased and run down area of Old District stood a wooden pub with a sign that read 'Reed's'. A large window allowed outsiders to view the patrons, though, with so many inside smoking, it wasn't much use. At the bar, Skyheart recounted to many of the patrons one his famous adventures. He had garnered the attention of the public and, when news of his arrival at Reed's had spread, the bar was soon heaving with custom.

A thin, plain looking man with a cheap suit stood behind the bar with a large grin on his face. Reed always made good business when Captain

Skyheart visited, which was the main reason the Captain got his drinks for free, which, in turn, was why Skyheart had made Reed's his most visited of haunts.

"I'd been locked in a dungeon for three days before I'd worked my plan of escape out fully," Skyheart said, entertaining those around him. "After the guard's next rounds I ripped the wooden bed from the wall and used it as a lever to... well, lever the cell door open."

A voice in a dark corner laughed and all turned to see who would dare interrupt the Captain. A muscular man was sat at a table drinking and smoking alone. His hair was greying and he looked as if he hadn't shaved in days. His clothes were torn and ragged with the air of a man who never took the easy road forward. He stood revealing he was of no impressive height but could match the average man. He approached Skyheart, the crowd parting exactly in half.

"I don't think you're strong enough to rip a bed from a dungeon wall," he said in a deep, throaty voice. "In fact, I don't think you're strong enough to do very much at all. You're a little effeminate if you ask me."

The crowd let out an audible gasp causing Skyheart to smile.

"Reed," he said, "how much has this man had to drink?"

"A lot," came the reply.

"I'm sober," said the man.

"Do you know who I am?" Skyheart asked.

"Yes."

"Say it."

"What?"

"Say it."

"Say what?"

"Say my name."

"Captain Laike Skyheart." He stopped and the Captain gestured for him to continue. "Of the Fourth Division."

"Actually, it's Division Four," Skyheart said, smiling.

The man grabbed the Captain's coat and pulled him closer.

"Arrogant wretch!"

"I can't fight you," Skyheart said calmly. "I'll be reprimanded." Normally Skyheart would have said this only for his own amusement, however with a new adventure looming he didn't want to give the Assembly or General Wraste an excuse to remove him from the operation.

"Please Captain!" said one voice from the crowd. "It would be a wonderful story to tell my children."

"Violent public conduct?" Skyheart said, before realising what area he was in. "Very well. Hold this." He thrust a sheathed Cendré towards Reed.

As soon as Reed had the sword firmly in his grasp, Skyheart unleashed a hard right jab into the man's chest. He let go of the Captain and took a small step back – he made both actions look voluntary although nobody was quite sure whether or not they were. He scowled and swung a wild left hand at Skyheart's head. The Captain ducked and the hand flew over him. Using this to his advantage, he forced his shoulder into the man's abdomen, trying to tackle him to the ground; however he was met by a hard wall of muscle. The man stayed just where he was and pounded both of his fists into Skyheart's back. Skyheart fell, his breath leaving him with a groan. He took in some sharp gasps of air before the man picked him up and slid him across the bar. The smell of years of spilt drinks invaded Skyheart's nostrils creating a foul stench he struggled to escape from. It was almost a relief when he landed on the hard wooden floor at the end of the bar. Slowly, he stood and moved his neck slightly. An almighty crack echoed throughout the silent bar.

"That's not right," he said.

Remembering the situation, he focused and saw the man rushing towards him; feet pounding the floor as violently as his intent towards the Captain, eyes mad with bloodlust.

As the man reached Skyheart, the Captain dropped and, using the man's own momentum, tripped him. The man's face hit a bar stool, collapsing it with a crack that could easily have been mistaken for bone.

Skyheart took a moment to catch his breath, slightly unnerved by the ever growing crowd. Then he smiled; he'd never dream of disappointing an audience.

The man cautiously lifted himself from the floor, severed leg of the barstool in hand. He swung it a few times to test the weight and force of it. Visibly pleased by the results of his research, he stumbled towards the Captain. His pace had slowed dramatically though the crazed determination on his face remained. He raised the leg-come-bat over his head, though the showboating Skyheart did nothing. As the leg came crashing through the air, Skyheart took a step to the right and the leg (man still attached) went flying past, though the man didn't fall. He took a weak swing behind him – the leg finding a home in Skyheart's grasp.

The Captain smiled. He tugged the leg, forcing the man closer, grabbed the man's wrist and forced the palm of his free hand up through the assailant's elbow joint sending a satisfying pop to travel through the bar.

The patrons gasped.

The man screamed.

In a rage, he swung his still useful arm and connected with Skyheart's temple.

The Captain staggered towards the bar, his vision noticeably blurred. He leaned on the structure trying to shake off the last attack. He groaned in his throat. Reed asked him if he was okay and gave him a shot of whiskey. He downed it but didn't answer the question and turned. Upon seeing the man just before him he sighed, hoping for a rest, and smashed the glass against the man's forehead. Blood streamed from the man's broken skin and down into his eyes. Skyheart thrust a fist into the man's chest as he had done at the beginning of the brawl. This time it sent the man stumbling backwards, good arm swinging desperately to regain his balance. The area of the crowd behind him wisely moved and the man landed on the table he had once been sitting at. The table broke; sending splinters into the air and a painful snapping sound rang throughout the bar. The man's beer then fell on his face. One member of the crowd cheered but apologised and silenced himself upon receiving numerous glares from the rest of the audience.

Skyheart's vision had returned but the blow to his temple had left him dizzy and the nauseous feeling from his awakening that morning had worsened. It was at that point he concluded that entering into this fight had not been the most sagacious of ideas, especially considering the man had been correct – Skyheart's story was indeed a fabrication. He'd actually spent the three days monotonously unscrewing the bed from the wall using nothing other than his fingers.

He groaned as the man returned to his feet.

"You're a tenacious fellow, aren't you?" Skyheart said, forcing a smile. The audience laughed weakly, all slightly fearful to do so, worried the more muscular man could still win the fight.

The man roared but didn't move.

Skyheart charged at him. The light rhythmic padding of his quick footsteps sang to the room; his own battle-cry striking true fear into all who would stand in his way. Some of the less foolhardy patrons moved away from the target, which was standing, gawping, at the ever increasingly close Captain. A smile shot across Skyheart's mouth as he launched himself into the air, forcing his legs out in front of him. The powerful kick collided with the man's chest, sending him flying backwards, smashing through the window and landing on the street with a guttural thud.

Residents of the Old District ran over to see what the commotion was and people from the bar rushed outside to see if the man could continue the fight. They found him to be decidedly unconscious.

Skyheart had landed on his back and was now lying on the wooden floor boards. He rolled over and pushed himself up. Then he swaggered over to Reed at the bar.

"How much do I owe you for the damages?" he asked with a pained voice.

"With the business this ought to get me when the story gets out? Nothing!" Reed rubbed his hands together excitedly.

"Well, don't let it get too far," Skyheart said. "I would so abhor being court-martialled."

He started towards the door massaging his neck with his right hand, when two soldiers he vaguely recognised entered through what was once the window.

"Sir!" one said, saluting. "General Wraste wishes to see you immediately."

Chapter Three

It was a cold day in Port Fair. The storm the night before had ravaged the day of warmth. Still, at least it was clear now. A hard sun surveyed the land from its blue sky kingdom; it saw the small sea-side town withering against the force of age.

Fishing was forbidden while Celisso was at sea and the town was running low on food. The fruit gathered from the woods to the north could only sustain the townsfolk for so long, although nobody was willing to admit that just yet.

Celisso appeared in the seas near Port Fair every few years; the southernmost town on the Southern Continent had never found a way to banish it for longer than that. They weren't warriors and couldn't kill the great serpent themselves, not that that had stopped someone from trying. The situation was made even worse by the fact that they couldn't hire warriors who were willing to do it for them.

Yet, something was different this time. It had never stayed for this long before. She had begun to think it was waiting for something. Or that the challenge her beloved had put to it had evoked its wrath.

It swam lazily in those apocalyptically calm seas destroying any boats it came across. Easy prey for one so large, and so it stayed.

Myri shivered as she sat on the beach. She wrapped the blanket firmly around herself and hugged her legs close to her chest. Out at sea, the red tail of Celisso rose from its watery home and crashed back in, sending skywards a spray of surf and wash. She didn't look, didn't want to see. Such destructive power wasn't worth watching.

She was far away enough from town to be at peace (save for Celisso). There were no inquisitive neighbours checking on her wellbeing, wishing well but doing more harm than good. There she could relax and be at one with her thoughts. Thoughts that could well have been left alone. That dark part of her mind swelled and gorged itself on the happier areas, forcing itself from subjectivity into the forefront: a veritable mountain of horrific memories.

She pushed it back. Today wasn't the day for such thoughts. No day was.

A light wind blew. She sighed and lay in the sand not caring when it worked its way into her pure black hair. She closed her eyes, the quiet whispering of the sea; a lullaby against the otherwise silent nothingness of the day.

But something disturbed her peace. The sound of a gentle sobbing, that at first she thought was coming from her – but she wasn't crying. It was coming from somewhere behind her.

She lifted herself from the sand, leaving the blanket where it fell, and followed the sound of the sobbing onto the grassy landing. She walked back and forth, the unruly grass whipping against her bare calves. The violet dress she wore stopped at her knees, offering little protection.

At one point the sound faded dramatically. She turned and walked back the other way, the sobbing increasing in volume, yet eternally gentle.

She slipped, her foot failing her, sending her back to the sandy beach landing on her side with a gentle thud. She lay facing the sea for a few moments before pushing herself up and brushing the sand from her satin dress.

She heard the sobbing once more, far clearer, far louder than before. She turned and saw a small boy sitting in an alcove beneath the landing with his head in his hands. His entire body convulsed softly with each sob, making the pointed straw hat he wore bob on his head.

Myri approached slowly, wary of scaring the boy. She crouched before him. The change in light made the boy look out through his fingers.

"Hello," Myri said.

"Hello," the boy said, in between sobs.

"What's wrong?" Myri asked.

"Mama's gone."

"Your Mama's gone where?"

"My island."

"She left you here?"

The boy shook his head.

"I went fishing and now I'm here and now Mama's gone and Franklin too." He spoke fast and breathlessly, not pausing for fear of weeping more.

To Myri's surprise he launched himself at her, throwing his arms around her and resting his head on her shoulder. She laced her arms around the boy.

"What's your name?" she asked, her voice blanketing the boy's ears.

"Paccon."

"I'm Myri."

The boy began to cry more fiercely.

"Shhh," Myri crooned. "You're safe now."

A few minutes later Paccon had stopped crying and was sat next to Myri, looking out at the sea. She had found the blanket and draped it around Paccon.

"Where do you think Franklin went?" he asked her.

"Who's Franklin?"

"My pet turtle. He was with me when I came here."

"Well he must be around here somewhere. I'll help you find him."

"Really?" His head turned sharply to her, his smile beaming out from under the shadow of the hat's rim.

"Of course," Myri said.

Paccon jumped up and hugged her, knocking her backwards with joyous enthusiasm. Myri laughed and sat back up.

"Are you ready to find him?" she asked.

Paccon nodded in sure affirmation. He took Myri's hand and they began their search.

He struggled to keep up with her, even when she slowed her pace, his short legs were almost at a run, often tripping over, only kept upright by the firm grip he had on her small, pale hand. He was quiet, solemn, almost mature, if sorrowfulness was an indication of maturity. Myri had come to think that it was. She tried to make him smile that huge half-moon smile he had released before, but all smiles were fleeting with him; disappearing in an instant.

He only came up to her hip, although the hat he wore reached her shoulder, and she had to stop often as he became distracted, sure Franklin was somewhere near, only to find nothing of interest around. He became increasingly sad and Myri struggled to console him, yet he was forever determined to find his beloved pet.

He increased his own pace, practically dragging Myri along behind him.

"He's over there!" he laughed loudly and let go of Myri, running to the tiny blot on the sand in the distance.

"It might just be a rock!" Myri called after him, fearful for his hopes to be raised and dashed in the same instant as they had been for the past hour. She ran after him as she saw him sink to his knees.

"It *is* him!" the boy called excitedly.

The baby turtle had somehow been turned onto the back of his shell, crawling in the air, trying to turn himself over. Paccon did it for him and Franklin climbed onto his owner's hand waiting to be put in his usual pocket. The turtle had had quite enough of an adventure. Paccon knowingly placed him in his pocket and smiled at Myri, but the smile soon faded as he looked back out to sea.

"When can I go home?" he said, although it didn't feel as though he said it to her.

"I'll get you home," she said. "I promise."

This time Paccon didn't smile. He didn't speak. It seemed to Myri as he had decreased in age in that moment whilst still maintaining that mature sobriety.

For the first time that day she noticed a lone cloud stirring from the mountains to the north, past the forest. She sighed at the prospect of a less than perfect day. Paccon turned to her and grasped her hand in his.

It was quiet in town as she led Paccon through. Most of the townsfolk had gone to the forest to fetch fruit. The square was deserted. The stone path lay strewn with dust and the flowers in the Remembrance Garden had begun to wilt with neglect, as ceremony was dropped for survival to be held more tightly. Yet, survival was hardly going perfectly. Myri hadn't eaten properly in almost a week and she knew that the other townsfolk hadn't either.

She opened the door to a small stone house and led Paccon inside. There were no walls separating the rooms. An oven sat at the far end of the house, either side of it a counter and a sink. Two beds were located near the front door on a plain wooden floor. There was little else.

"It's so big!" Paccon said.

Myri looked at him questioningly. "That's a matter of perspective."

Paccon ran over to the other side of the house and opened a navy blue, wooden door. He passed through and found himself in a blossoming garden. New smells, sweet odours and scents he didn't know met him. He inhaled gleefully and his large smile returned. Myri appeared behind him as he began removing Franklin from his pocket and put him on the grass.

"Now don't eat any of the flowers," Paccon said sternly, wagging his right index finger forcefully. It seemed to Myri as if Franklin nodded before clambering clumsily away. She shook it off as her imagination. Paccon turned to her. "It's so pretty."

"Thank you," Myri replied, genuinely touched that her garden had cheered the boy up. She knelt to meet his eyes. "You can stay with me for a while. Just until I work out how to get you home. How does that sound?"

"Great!" Paccon said, almost shouting with joy. Then he unleashed a giant yawn nearly causing him to fall down. He rubbed his eyes. "Sorry."

"When was the last time you slept?"

"I don't remember."

"Let's get you to bed," she said and took his hand. She led him inside and he climbed into the bed furthest from the door. She tucked him in.

"Will I meet the rest of your family soon?" he asked.

Myri paused.

"It's just me," she said.

"Where's everyone else?"

Myri looked away, not sure how to answer. When she looked back he was asleep.

She left the house just as the fruit gatherers were returning from the forest and entering the square. The Mayor led the dejected looking group, baskets only half full of fruit. She approached the haggard Mayor, grey beard obscuring the collar and top of the lapels of his baggy brown suit. He greeted her warmly but his eyes betrayed an anxiousness Myri noticed immediately.

"Hello Mayor," she said.

"And how are you on this fine day?"

The gatherers continued to walk past, placing their plunder in the town hall before returning to their homes.

"I'm fine, Mayor."

"Good, good. Bad news from the Northern Continent again."

"What's that?"

"Mandran and Genkoan forces are both advancing at an increased rate. The entire continent should be under their control within the next few months. Then all that's left is for them to do battle with each other for ultimate supremacy."

"Do you think they'll come here?"

"The Southern Continent? No, no. I shouldn't think so. There's nothing here for them since..." He trailed off realising what he would have had to say next.

"The Mineral Wars," Myri said for him. "It's okay, Mayor. You can say it."

They began a slow walk to the Town Hall.

"Yes, well," he said, "still it stings a sharp wound for us all, does it not?"

"Mayor, I was at the beach this morning and there was a boy there."

The Mayor looked at her sceptically.

"That's not so strange, is it?" he said.

"A boy I don't know."

"Oh, a boy you don't *know*!"

"Yes. He's at my house, sleeping. He was fishing during the storm and I think he got washed up here."

"Quite a predicament," the Mayor said, leading Myri through the Town Hall's entrance. "And another mouth to feed." He surveyed the meagre fruit harvest and placed his basket with the rest. "How is he?"

"Quiet. Although, I suppose that's to be expected."

"Indeed." They walked through the hall, their footsteps echoing with each contact they made with the hard wood floor. "Do you know where he's from?"

"He said something about an island."

"There are so many islands. He could be from any one of them and with the Southern Drift at the moment it's not going to be easy to narrow it down."

"Perhaps if we showed him a map he could point his island out?"

"Perhaps," the Mayor said, opening the door to his office. They entered and sat either side of his desk, cluttered with undone paperwork. "Though we'd have to find a map and an up to date one at that. With most being destroyed during the war that won't be easy. Of course you realise, with Celisso around it would be impossible to take him back from here and with the food shortage he can't *stay* here either."

Myri sat, silently shocked, for a moment.

"What are you saying?" she asked

"He can't stay."

"He can't stay?"

"There's not enough food. The rations are too small as they are."

"He can share my rations!" Myri's voice spanned an octave in the sentence, desperate as she was to change the Mayor's mind.

He gave her a sympathetic look. "He'll have to leave eventually."

"But that's a 'yes'?"

"For now," he paused. "He reminds you of you, doesn't he?"

Myri didn't reply. Instead, she thanked the Mayor and stood to leave.

"Oh, Myri!" he said. "What's his name?"

"Paccon."

"Paccon," the Mayor said in the voice of a man enjoying a fine meal. "I'll have to come and meet young Paccon some time."

From the Town Hall she went out to the pier, modest though it was. In fact, it was closer to a wooden walkway out to sea. It was starting to rot from years of overuse and the fishing boats tied to it were in much the same condition. A woman around the same age as Myri stood at the end of the pier gazing out to the horizon.

"Not the most bountiful of fruit harvests, I see," Myri said.

"That's an understatement. If there's anything there that isn't some kind of a berry I'd be very surprised."

A high pitched roar sounded from somewhere out at sea as Celisso reared its head.

Carre flinched.

"When do think he'll leave?" She flinched again at her own words and turned to Myri, who was looking solemnly down at the boards of the pier. "Sorry, I didn't think..."

"It's fine," Myri said quietly.

Silence washed over them and Celisso roared once more.

"Carre," Myri said, looking up again. "What do you know about children?"

"Enough to get by," she said. "Why do you ask?"

Myri explained about the morning's events. The ever interested Carre, wordless throughout, nodded at salient points. When Myri was finished Carre spoke.

"It sounds like you're doing everything right."

"But I have to get him home," Myri said hopelessly.

"Well, you can't do much until Celisso's gone. And if his island's to the north then you can't do much against the Southern Drift. You'd have to sail from North Port and that's a tough journey. Too dangerous for you and a small child, furthermore I doubt anyone would go with you."

Myri crossed her arms.

"I know," she said. "But what else can I do?"

"Wait," Carre said, shrugging. "There's not much else. Something might come along."

Myri nodded and began to leave.

"Myri," Carre called after her. "How are you?"

Myri turned and forced a smile.

"I'm fine, Carre," she said. "Really."

When Myri arrived back at the house she found Paccon's bed empty and unmade. She tidied it and found him in the garden looking at the gravestones. She approached him.

"Did you sleep well?" she asked.

He nodded but didn't speak. There was something contagious about his silence that Myri felt she had to fight against, but in the surprise of the moment she let it sweep over her. A nothing sound in an ocean forcing those caught in it to the same destination.

She pushed the thought away and looked at the grave of her fiancé; the latest victim of Celisso. The bravest man in Port Fair, or so he was dubbed, and the only man to be killed by Celisso since its return. Myri thought of how often courage and death collided. Her family tree was testament to that.

A soft touch engulfed her left hand. She looked down and saw Paccon gazing up at her.

"I'm sorry," he said.

Myri gave a weak smile.

Somewhere, a bell sounded, calling the townsfolk to collect their rations. Paccon and Myri, hand in hand, heeded the call.

Chapter Four

Captain Skyheart swaggered into the General's office with typical superciliousness, smile strewn across his face, taking his place next to DeFlare, half standing – half leaning against the wall, observing the four impetuous faces, disdainful of his less-than-punctual arrival. As he exhaled he realised he had carried the stench of alcohol from the bar with him. His breath still held the familiar alcoholic freshness of heat and the reek of fermentation. He gave his usual casual salute.

"Did I miss anything?" he said with irrefutable charm.

The General opened his mouth to speak and undoubtedly berate Skyheart, but was interrupted by Captain Thean, stood next to his stern faced Lieutenant, Okain. Okain was a man of average height with few distinguishing features. He had shaved all the hair from his head and made it a point of honour never to be seen with even a small amount of stubble. He was muscular in the blue Lieutenant's coat. Skyheart thought him similar in stature to DeFlare.

"Actually, we were waiting for you," Thean said. "The General was informing Okain and me of your heroic exploits in the desert only two short days ago."

"There were no heroics," Skyheart said. "Merely orders being followed." He glanced at DeFlare who was standing attentively waiting for the General, who was growing increasingly impatient. "But, alas, we have been called here by General Wraste who wishes to gift us with a new adventure." He gestured giving all attention in the room to Wraste, although Skyheart's was the attention that had been wandering anyway.

"As I'm sure you already know," General Wraste began, "The Assembly, with the help of myself and President Kylar, have been devising a plan to halt the advancement of both the Mandran and Genkoan forces. You are all aware of what dangerous times we have found ourselves in and, if we do not act soon, Thieron could very well be destroyed.

"In the Scriptures of Thiera we are taught that the enemy of my enemy is my friend, the main teaching that the Great Philosophers, Seph and Pycra, agreed on. The plan that has been devised plays on this teaching.

"I fear I am getting ahead of myself." He paused. "Needless to say the jewel that Captain Skyheart and Lieutenant DeFlare recovered from the desert is inherent to the plan. A diamond with a sapphire in its very centre. A thing of flawless beauty and, as we are taught, unbelievable power. It is, indeed, the Diamandé."

Skyheart and Thean passed glances at each other across the room.

"I shall refresh you of its origins," continued Wraste. "The Great Philosophers, Seph and Pycra, both taught of our goddess Thiera and were almost equal in following. However, in some places the teachings differed. This caused animosity between the philosophers. Seph and Pycra debated for many years trying to come to some understanding about the teachings. However, beliefs are powerful and hold potent feelings over us. As such no agreement was reached and the two sides readied for war, meeting in, what was then a great plain, but is now the Thieronian Desert.

"The battle waged for days depleting each force incredibly. On the final day of the battle, just as the survivors were beginning to flee, their belief waning, flaming coals fell from ashen clouds causing the plain to set afire, reducing the plain to desert. The coals were sent by Thiera at the horror of her children at war with one another. Both of the Great Philosophers were killed in the raging fire, but all other believers were spared. From that moment the teachings of Seph and Pycra were combined to create the Scriptures and all believers lived in peace within the city they built in the centre of that desert – Thieron.

"After the battle the believers looked in awe as the smoke, ash and fire were collected in the sky creating a sword of incomprehensible beauty and power. This sword is Captain Skyheart's Cendré. The coals were also collected and compressed to create a sword of diamond. The name is long lost and has come to be known simply as the Sister Sword. Thiera sealed war in these swords and for centuries we knew peace. Eventually, the swords found their way into the Trekas family.

"The Trekas family was a noble family in Thieron's Peace Force, now long disbanded; an organisation devoted to keep the peace through political sanctions. But, a new heir was needed in the Trekas family and the brothers Honan and Bortan were both as superior and deserving as each other. But fate is strange and irony is a cruel mistress. The two peacekeepers vowed to settle the dispute through a battle to the death."

"Peacekeepers indeed," Skyheart said sarcastically. "Who keeps the peacekeepers peaceful?"

The General shot him a glare before continuing.

"Honan took Cendré and Bortan took the Sister Sword, from there the two brothers went out into the desert to fight their good fight. At some point in the duel, Honan gained the upper hand and struck a finishing blow, Bortan, however, carelessly threw the Sister Sword in Cendré's path, shattering the sword of diamond and also killing himself. Honan was victorious, for a while. As he prepared to bury his brother, the fragments of the Sister Sword reconstructed themselves before him, creating a diamond encasing a sapphire - the Diamandé. Coals reigned from the heavens once more, killing Honan in a sea of fire.

"The destruction of one of the Goddess Swords released the war it had been holding unto the world. The Peace Force died out, unable to keep peace in a world so destructive. Powers rose and fell until now, where we find our enemies at the peak of their power.

"The Diamandé was lost until the encounter in the desert those two nights ago," the General stopped; his voice tender at the history of his beloved Thieron.

Skyheart sighed. He had always known this supposed 'history', but was dismissive of the involvement of Thiera, or any deity for that matter, though he could not dispute the power of Cendré. However, the idea of an all-powerful being didn't sit well with him. Plausibility said to him that Thiera didn't exist, although he was a minority, being one of the few (and illegal) non-believers in Thieron. He believed the planet itself had a pulse – a life force. To him it made far more sense that the planet would seal war. The planet had to protect itself, as those on it certainly wouldn't; they were too amazingly naïve to know what to do. Skyheart thought that naivety was almost a skill.

Skyheart waved these thoughts away. Currently his mind was needed on matters of war, not religion. No matter how much the two seemed to be connected.

"And yet no plan is explained," said Skyheart, unable to mask his annoyance.

"Pretext is important in such matters," Lieutenant Okain said quickly. "I'd much rather be informed slowly than rush into a dangerous situation blindly, not knowing what's ahead."

Okain was of course referencing Skyheart's reputation of repeatedly engaging in cavalier antics. The kind of heroics that were not planned and merely fell into place as time progressed; action following action, each more offhand than the last. The unsubtle attack on his leadership style caused Skyheart to smile.

"Still," Skyheart said, "if the mission is as urgent as we've been led to believe, I'd like to hear the details as soon as possible."

All attention returned to Wraste. He took two identical jewels from his desk. The Captains exchanged confused looks.

"These, gentlemen, are perfect replicas of the Diamandé and are instrumental in what has become known as Operation Shell," he said. "The plan is simple. Captain Thean and Lieutenant Okain will go to Mandra bearing the gift of the Faux-Diamandé and Captain Skyheart, accompanied by DeFlare, will do the same with Genko. Needless to say you must convince the powers that you are giving them the real Diamandé." The General smiled pleased at the plan.

"If I may speak, sir," DeFlare said. "To what end?"

The other men nodded, agreeing.

"Ah," the General said. "I see this will need further explanation. As I'm sure you know, although the heathen countries do not worship Thiera, the entire world knows of the Diamandé. By presenting both sides with, what they believe to be, the jewel, we can accelerate their meeting. Having allied ourselves with both powers they will fight far from here. During the battle they will both try to use the Diamandé only to find they have a fake. Unable to back down at that point the armies shall fight unaided by the supernatural and one shall emerge the victor, though with a severely depleted force. Wanting revenge, they will inevitably come to face Thieron, at which point we will decimate the once-victorious force with the real Diamandé, ensuring Thieron's safety." He gave them that self-satisfied look once more.

"It took the Assembly all this time to devise that plan?" Skyheart asked, clearly unimpressed.

"It is simple," Thean said. "However, it does seem plausible. The simplicity leaves few places for it to go wrong."

"That is why it's a bad plan," Skyheart said, standing up straight. "It doesn't sound like much of an adventure."

"Captain?" DeFlare said. "Surely Thieron's safety comes before conquest."

"You'll be reprimanded if you refuse to go," confirmed General Wraste.

"I never said I wouldn't go," Skyheart sighed. "I merely wanted my opinion to be known. I may have to improvise a little way down the line."

"And why is that?" Okain said with a violent growl.

"Presentation before prosperity."

"Fear not, Okain," DeFlare said. "I'll be with him."

The two men from the First Division laughed with DeFlare, even Wraste had a slight smile. Though Skyheart didn't notice. He was planning, plotting, scheming – there was an adventure to be had there somewhere, it just needed to be found. He did so long for a quest and it would be his, just as soon as he discovered where in Operation Shell it fitted in. But soon, natural inquisitiveness disturbed the formulating.

"Where is the real Diamandé?" he asked.

"In a safe place," replied the General.

"You won't say?"

"I'm forbidden to."

"Very well," Skyheart said, smiling. "When does Operation Shell commence?"

"Thean and Okain shall leave tomorrow, you and DeFlare the day after."

"If tomorrow we leave then sleep shall be needed and preparations need to be made," Thean said. "With your permission, General, we shall take our leave."

"Of course," Wraste said. He handed the Faux-Diamandés to the Captains. The four men began to leave when he called for Skyheart. "Captain Skyheart you're wanted in the President's Office."

They left and the two divisions parted ways in the hallway. Skyheart made his way to the elevator.

"Say, DeFlare," he called back, opening the wrought iron lattice. "Look after this." He threw the jewel to the Lieutenant and closed the door. DeFlare heard the hiss of the elevator.

He stood in the corridor for a few moments, in awe of the Captain's carelessness in regards to the object that their very lives depended on. Not to mention their careers. If Operation Shell was successful then DeFlare was sure to be made a captain. But what of Skyheart? Perhaps he would be promoted to Commander, finally reaching the heights of his father, not that he would favour such a move. DeFlare couldn't imagine him staying in an office for as long as all that.

'One so undeserving and yet above me because of blood,' DeFlare thought.

He found himself walking in the direction of the barracks. He would hone his battle skills against the troops. This ambitious Lieutenant would be prepared for any deviations from the Captain. He would be sure of it.

He threw quick glances to the twelve men in the hooded white robes; though, each seemed identical to him. He didn't much care for their observing him. Such disturbing white apparitions, all with a hold on him, unbreakable invisible bonds. Their eyes surveyed him, not that he could see the shadow shrouded instruments of sight.

The President shuffled in his seat, waiting for the Assembly to cease their consideration of Captain Skyheart. Kylar no longer seemed as powerful as he once was. The ascension of the Assembly, twelve advisors, shrank his role into choosing which of their ideas were best. An easy job as they generally agreed on everything. Such potent authority he held.

Skyheart scratched the back of his head, his eyes exuding some combination of insecurity and vexation. He sighed.

"You wanted to see me?" he said with a dubious amount of respect.

The Assembly members looked at each other, seemingly unpleased with his remark. Or, if not the remark itself, the fact that he had the nerve to remark anything.

"You have been briefed on Operation Shell?" asked one.

"You know what must be done?" asked another.

"Yes," Skyheart said.

"You also know your history?"

"Such disreputable insubordination."

"Plans not followed."

"Missions attempted alone."

"Incorrect uniform."

"Dishevelled appearance."

"Sending lower ranking soldiers than you for what you dubbed 'easy work'."

"Necessary battles and duels avoided."

"And, most recently, a bar room brawl in Old District. One of your more regular haunts."

"Put simply, Captain: you're an embarrassment."

Skyheart scratched the back of his head again. "I'm aware of my actions," he said.

"Yet you wonder not why you are being sent on this most important of missions?"

"I have no need to wonder," Skyheart said, smiling.

"You are walking a dangerous path, Captain."

"Such disreputable insubordination."

"You are close to being demoted."

"Or worse."

"We have been debating."

"A long debate."

"And still we are unsure of your future."

"To demote you..."

"... to dismiss you..."

"... to imprison you..."

"...or to execute you."

Skyheart's smile uncurled.

"You are lucky the President finds your antics amusing."

"And thank your celebrity status that has gifted you this one last chance."

"One last chance?" Skyheart asked, his voice a shell of its usual self, subdued and muted.

"Operation Shell," came the answer from all members of the Assembly.

"Prove yourself."

"Your celebrity status is in our favour for once – a sign of goodwill, confidence and trust to Genko. Our sincerity cannot be questioned with our sending one so high profile as yourself."

"Do well and you will not be punished."

"Fail and the consequences will be *severe*," the last word echoed throughout the President's office, the eponymous owner of which still remained silent.

"And were I not to return?" Skyheart asked.

"You are not in the position for such ultimatums, Captain."

"And we trust your Lieutenant will ensure your return."

"Such ambition."

"Such dedication."

"Faithful to Thiera."

"Patriotic towards Thieron."

"The perfect Captain."

"And will be made so."

"If it is your position that needs to be vacated for that purpose, so be it."

Silence swept over the room. Skyheart could do nothing more than wait.

The President leaned forward.

"You have been warned," he said and gestured for Skyheart to leave.

The Captain saluted (rather more formally than usual) and entered the elevator. The doors closed and a smile crept across his lips. The adventure had been laid down before him, perhaps even his last. Of course, he did not appreciate their threats, but at least now he had been given the gift of danger. Quest and conquest hung above him. His new exploit now only needed a plan and one had been planted when he first entered the office, when the assembly sent such untrusting glances his way. Such divine machinations he had realised. He pulled the lever for his floor. Not the ground, no, he couldn't leave the Monument just yet. He had somewhere far more important to go first.

The four intrepid minions of Thieron met at the West Gate as Okain and Thean readied to leave the city of their birth and on out into the desert, through the rock plains, hill lands and occupied territory until they reached Mandra.

It was a bright dawn. The sun was a vermillion sphere in a sky of azure integrity, cloudless honesty reigning upon the city.

The Lieutenants were characteristically taciturn, merely saluting and wishing each other good luck. Thean stood stoically, shaking a smiling Skyheart's hand.

"Duty calls," Thean said.

"I do so envy you," Skyheart said. "You seem to have been given the more perilous journey."

"Were it not for orders I would gladly trade. At my age, getting out of bed is enough of an adventure."

The Captains laughed and wished one another luck. Thean approached DeFlare.

"The very best of luck, Lieutenant."

"And you, sir," DeFlare saluted.

Okain saluted Skyheart. "Good luck, Captain."

"Save your luck for yourself, Okain. I fear you shall need it more than I," Skyheart smiled and gave his usual casual salute.

The gate groaned as steam pushed it open, forcing the two iron segments apart, revealing the great expanse of sand and sky before the travellers. Heat contorted the air in the distance, causing it to shape into miraculous waves, swimming forms, constructed and amorphous equally – neither one nor the other. The windless day let the sand rest, obscuring not a fragment of the horizon.

The two men from the First Division began their journey under the regard of DeFlare and Skyheart. The gate closed, first eclipsing the sky and then the sand, the travellers with it.

"Is this plan as easy as it seems?" DeFlare asked.

"You're the more experienced man, DeFlare. You tell me."

"The confidence with which it is spoke would certainly suggest so."

"Unfortunately DeFlare, I would agree. It seems I shall have to wait for a true challenge," he said, smiling. He started down the street with DeFlare following him.

"Still," said DeFlare, "I wouldn't want to be complacent. I've been practising my sword skills."

"Good. Perhaps if we become bored along the way we can spar with one another."

"How long do you think it will take us to reach Genko?"

"With the path I've devised, no more than two days. The continent seems so small these days. My only regret is that we have to wait to leave."

"Are all of your preparations complete?"

Skyheart smiled. "Actually, I do have one more matter to attend to. Meet me at East Gate, tomorrow at dawn."

They parted ways.

Skyheart entered the bar as Reed was boarding up the broken window. To Reed's displeasure the Captain entered through a part of the window yet to be boarded.

"There is a door," Reed said.

"Indeed there is," Skyheart said.

"You *can* use it."

"Indeed I can."

"It is there to be used."

"It seems we are agreed on every point."

Skyheart, flamboyant swagger intact, walked over to the bar and rapped on the wood, causing Reed to follow.

"*What?*" he said.

"That's no way to talk to a customer, is it?"

"No, but certainly a way to talk to a man as bothersome as you. Now, what do you want?"

"I'm going away for a few days and I need a bottle of your finest whiskey to make such an unchallenging journey, as I am about to embark upon, bearable."

Reed placed a bottle of golden liquid on the bar. "Here."

Skyheart placed the bottle in his inside coat pocket. "I see my encounter with that ruffian didn't liven up your business."

"Deserted isn't it?"

"I should say. What happened?"

Reed shrugged. "Old District's got a bad name. The only customers I get are you and the locals. The latter of which only come out at night."

As Reed finished speaking the door opened and an attractive young woman entered. Her hair was curled elaborately and the dress she wore was just as ostentatious. She looked at the Captain and he looked at her. He bought her a drink. Then he bought her another. They spoke briefly and left together. He wasn't seen for the rest of the day.

The sun rose the next day, much as it did any other. DeFlare watched it from the barracks, disappointed at the lack of spectacle. He felt as if a more boastful presentation of his leaving was appropriate. Maybe Captain Skyheart was right and this was no adventure at all.

He took a slow walk to the East Gate through the Economic District in silence. The business men had yet to wake and even then they would remain inside, counting profit and deducting loss. As if it mattered.

DeFlare reached the gate to find he was there alone. Unsurprisingly, Skyheart was running late.

He opened his eyes to find he was lying on his side facing her. Radiant skin hidden under the mess of hair, no longer in the elaborate style, her eyes still closed, breathing warm and fresh smelling air onto his face. She wasn't like the other women in Old District. She hadn't lost what they had, although what that was Skyheart had no idea. Hope, perhaps. Maybe something more. The effervescent bewitchment held by youth had yet to fade and gleamed from her every subtle movement. She stirred and closed her eyes tighter, but she didn't wake. Skyheart smiled.

He thought back to the day before when this alluring demon had led him, stumbling, back to her lair, the sanctuary where the drunken pair swam in the oceans of one another, consuming the other's lust, slowly being washed back to the shore, waking forevermore. He was sober now, but the prospect of her was increasing in demand. Something inside him commanded that he go to her and appease that desire. Yet he couldn't oblige. He had slept late and he knew it as he moved to the window, seeing a sun almost at noon.

He dressed and looked upon her once more, forcing himself to end it, as much as he wished to stay. Now, if only he could have remembered her name. He left her name to her and closed the door behind him. She didn't stir.

He arrived at the gate with a forced swagger finding DeFlare leaning against the gate.

"How long have you been waiting?" the Captain asked.

"Since dawn. What happened to meeting at dawn?"

"Dawn came and went."

"We're running late already."

Skyheart signalled for the gate to open and the slow process began.

"When do I meet her?" DeFlare asked.

"Who?"

"Your latest conquest."

Skyheart caught a reflection of himself in a shining part of the gate. He looked even more dishevelled than usual.

"I just overslept," Skyheart said, stepping out into the desert.

"And I thought that you couldn't wait to leave," DeFlare joked. Professionalism regained its grip on him at that point and he followed the Captain out into the arid wastes.

They went some miles in silence. The sultriness of the desert sun, sadistically and sardonically surging through them. Though they were accustomed to it. Skyheart even thought the day a little on the cold side.

He came to an abrupt stop at the sight of something in the distance. DeFlare stopped next to him. Ahead of them a spiral of sand reached towards the sky, the force of the apparition caused the grains around the pair's feet to begin to rise and dance around them. DeFlare knew that what was before them was the one word in Thieron spoken in the most hushed of tones: sandstorm.

"You knew about this didn't you?" DeFlare said to Skyheart. "You knew that a sandstorm was forecast and chose our path to go right through it."

Skyheart smiled. "I'd heard tell of one."

DeFlare sighed and the two wandered into the fragmented lunacy.

It swirled around them, forever attempting to cut their skin with every particle it possessed. They shielded their eyes with an arm each, Skyheart used his free arm to pull DeFlare along behind him, determined not to lose his Lieutenant. The vehement current of sand swept over them, seemingly endless in its assault. Such an eternity seemed impossible, hopeless in its inception – yet, the greatest of masters can manufacture anything, or so it would seem, so surely nature, the greatest master of all (or perhaps that should be mistress) could manufacture such an incessant incursion. It seemed that way to Skyheart. He marvelled at the intricacy of it. A natural wonder, almost human-like in its harrowing destructive potential, but still beautiful and enticing in its existence.

At that moment DeFlare tripped. Skyheart felt a sharp tug on his arm and saw the Lieutenant face down in the sand, his brown hair all that was visible of his head. Skyheart lifted him to his feet and watched as DeFlare brushed sand from his coat to no avail as the eternal wave swept more onto him.

"Are we almost through?" he called to Skyheart through the howling chaos.

Skyheart shrugged, that was as much of an answer as he had. He grabbed DeFlare's arm and began dragging him once more, at a slower pace this time. They couldn't afford to stop another time or they may very well have never started again.

Soon the shrieking wind died into a whistling and from a whistling into a whisper. Then silence. Peace fell upon the dune-less desert, a new undertone throughout the nothingness.

DeFlare looked to the Captain. "How much further to the plains?"

"I'm not sure," came the reply. "It's not a particularly large desert; the city takes up a significant portion of it. In fact I'd expected to be on the plains by now."

DeFlare sighed and sat down. Skyheart stayed standing and looked to be measuring the distance.

"We're off course aren't we?" DeFlare asked.

"Nonsense."

"We're lost aren't we?"

"Of course not! We're just not exactly where I had planned for us to be at the moment."

"Do you know where we are?"

"Yes. We're in the Thieronian Desert."

DeFlare rose sharply and faced the Captain with a face that spoke fury. "*Where* in the Thieronian Desert?"

Skyheart paused and scratched the back of his head. "Well, I'm not entirely sure."

DeFlare gestured wildly with his arms, took a few paces away from Skyheart and threw himself onto the sand, facing the sky.

"How did you ever become Captain?"

"You remember my inauguration," Skyheart said. "The old Captain and Lieutenant died and I was the best swordsman in the division. Although, if today is anything to go by they perhaps should have chosen someone with a slightly better sense of direction." He smiled to the typically humourless Lieutenant.

"We're lost."

"DeFlare," Skyheart said calmly. "It's a landmark-less sea of sand. As soon as one steps out upon it one is lost."

"So what's your amazing plan?"

"Simple, we just walk east. Then we'll reach the plains," he paused. "I just need to work out which way is east."

The sand around his feet made small jumping motions, turning into a

31

swirling waltz. DeFlare looked at him and Skyheart nodded, an almost crazed smile crawling across his face. He grabbed the Lieutenant and began running in a direction he hoped was correct.

Soon the storm was even stronger than before. A veritable whirlpool of deranged proportions in the golden ocean, far drier than its blue counterpart, but just as unpredictable.

Running blind, the pair made their way through the wall of grain. Every so often DeFlare thought he could hear laughter cutting through the screaming wind, but he couldn't be sure. The symphonic, animalistic roar of natural intimidation swelled around the two, breeding fear in the experienced Lieutenant, although the Captain seemed to be enjoying himself.

It felt to DeFlare as if they rose from the ground, as if a hand made from the desert itself had plucked them and threw them through the storm, spitting them out from the mouth of the sandy beast.

Skyheart landed hard on his back, with DeFlare a few metres from him. Both were relieved to see blue sky and feel solid ground. Skyheart stood and looked back at the desert, the sandstorm now spun away from them. He gave it his usual casual salute and turned to view the new landscape. A plain of dry, cracked mud (or maybe it was clay) met him. At various points it rose into small mounds. Some places held patches of grass but the sight was mainly that of the grey ground.

DeFlare stood next to him. "Are we on course?"

Skyheart sighed. "Apparently not. This should be a plain of vibrant grassland, so either the landscape has drastically changed since last I was here or we're slightly further south than I anticipated."

"How much further south?"

"Somewhere between thirty and forty miles. Closer to thirty... probably."

DeFlare, having lost the will to confront Skyheart sighed. "What next?"

"We go north-east to get back on track."

"Can we rest first?"

"Why not? We'll need all the energy we can muster."

They sat beneath the reddening sun as clouds drifted in from the east.

Chapter Five

Darkness's end was met by more darkness as the gentle kicking in his ribs woke him into a starless, moonless night. DeFlare was stood over him looking disapprovingly at Skyheart. They were still on the cracked mud plain and had not moved since their exit from the desert.

Skyheart sat up but made no effort to stand. He met DeFlare's look.

"Yes?" he said.

"Shouldn't we be moving?"

Skyheart lay back down. "I thought you wanted to rest," he said, closing his eyes.

"That was six hours ago."

Skyheart sat back up and sighed. He stood and looked once more at DeFlare.

"Fine," he said, lurching drowsily into the night. DeFlare followed altogether more enthusiastically.

Skyheart's steps seemed laboured as if he were still asleep or missing his previous state of unconsciousness, eliciting some slight concern on the part of his Lieutenant. Every so often he took a swig of what DeFlare assumed (or perhaps, with the Captain's reputation, hoped was closer) was water. As time progressed Skyheart's walk became more of a stagger and the stagger slowly became a stumble until he finally tripped. He sat there on the ground for a few moments holding his head. DeFlare looked down at him. Skyheart looked back at the Lieutenant but said nothing. He loosely thrust a hand with a canteen wrapped inside it towards DeFlare who took the canteen and sniffed at its contents; he was relieved to smell no hint of alcohol and took a large swig of the water inside.

"You seem to be struggling," he said to the Captain.

"I prefer adventuring during the day," Skyheart yawned. He stretched his arms, then stood and snatched back his canteen.

They began walking again, each step a gentle whisper of a pad. As time went on Skyheart managed to correct himself and was soon back to his usual swagger, an even flow of movement in the monumental barrier of darkness.

The navy blue, almost black, of the night contorted the landscape into a near endless wilderness where each sight was fleeting and each step could hardly be said to have been made. The sun showed no signs of ever rising again, yet still the men continued to traverse the plain. Had it have been night forevermore, would they have known?

Skyheart stopped and signalled for DeFlare to do the same. The Captain was looking at the horizon.

"Do you see that?" he whispered.

"What?"

"Those figures in the distance."

DeFlare squinted, trying to see as far as his eyes could conceivably allow.

"No," he replied.

Skyheart sighed and scratched the back of his head. He shifted his weight from one leg to another, then back again. He took another look to where he had seen the figures. They were still there. They were small and insignificant in the scale of the landscape, but there nonetheless. He looked back in the direction they had come from, seeing only more naval washed vista of indistinguishable range. He knew not how far they had come.

He knelt down and placed the map on the ground. He proceeded to measure distances on the paper with his hands.

"How far do you think a hand is in real measurement?" he asked DeFlare.

The Lieutenant didn't justify the question with an answer and instead asked one of his own.

"Why have we stopped?"

"Because, DeFlare, there are people on the horizon and I don't want to run into them."

"That's uncharacteristically cautious," DeFlare said. He looked to the point in the distance Skyheart had been examining. "I still can't see them. It's too dark."

Skyheart rolled the map up and placed it back in the inside pocket of his coat. He stood and DeFlare observed on him a pensive look.

"The reason for my caution, DeFlare, is that due to our current position those people can only be Genkoan soldiers. If we were to be seen by them, they would search us and take our oh-so-precious cargo, ruining the plan altogether. Furthermore, were we to fight our way out I doubt that Genko would accept our gift. No, in fact upon reaching Genko they would most likely execute us and march onto Thieron."

"What exactly is your plan then?"

"Obviously we go around. However, this being such a landmark-less terrain we can't exactly hide." He looked slightly to the east of the group ahead of them and began walking.

DeFlare followed.

"That thinking was quite complex," he said.

"I like to remain a few thoughts ahead."

"I always thought you made it up as you went and hoped for the best."

"I do," Skyheart said. "But I like to be a few thoughts ahead in my hope."

Their steps became even lighter than before, no longer even a pad and, although this slowed their pace, they were soon close enough for DeFlare to see the group. Skyheart and the Lieutenant crouched and surveyed the group.

"I count six," DeFlare said.

"Seven, there's one lying down," Skyheart said. "They don't look like scouts to me. Seven's far too many for a scouting party." He paused. "Does it look to you as if they're by a pit?"

DeFlare hadn't noticed until the Captain said so, but it *did* look as though the majority of the group were peering into a pit or hole of some kind.

"Well, at least they're distracted enough for us to go on our way," the Lieutenant said, turning to Skyheart. He sighed when he noticed the Captain was grinning. This was not to be as incident-free a night as he had hoped.

DeFlare hit the two pieces of flint together after spending the past hour trying to find a shrub to use as tinder. He didn't understand why the Captain couldn't help, although he was fairly sure Skyheart was asleep.

Finally, the shrub caught light. DeFlare blew on it feeding the flame. It flared and grew, rising in the darkness – the only feature on the landscape. He poured some of the whiskey Skyheart had reluctantly given him on the fire. It gorged itself on the alcohol growing taller once more. DeFlare heard shouts over the crackling of flame as they noticed the fire he had lit as a diversion for Skyheart. He turned and went on his way, leaving the Captain to his latest distraction. He'd promised he'd catch up anyway.

He woke as the guards rushed towards the flame in the distance, fearful that their presence was discovered and determined to stamp out any witness to their existence. And yet, the only man whose interest was piqued at their attendance went unnoticed. Skyheart rose when they had passed and began to walk to the near empty camp, only one sleeping guard remained. Skyheart stepped over him and approached the pit. He peered inside. The guards had lit a smokeless camp fire in the hole to avoid detection.

"Clever boys," said the Captain.

One corner of the pit was still shrouded in darkness. Curiosity still not fully assuaged, Skyheart lowered himself the ten feet into the pit. He landed with a quiet thud.

"Who's there?" said a gruff, throaty voice from the direction of the shadow. Skyheart could see nothing of who was there. He grabbed a stick of the extra firewood and lit the tip in the campfire. He threw the stick towards the shadow. An old man was chained to the wall of the pit. He wore tattered black rags and his face was hidden by a dark grey beard and matted hair of the same colour. From what Skyheart could see of his face the Old Man was heavily wrinkled. He looked at the Captain with small stone-grey eyes.

"Hello," Skyheart said, giving his usual casual salute.

"Hello," said the Old Man.

"Lovely night."

"I'll say."

Skyheart shuffled on his feet and scratched the back of his head. "Would you like me to free you?"

"No."

"No?"

"No."

"Why ever not?"

"You didn't come to free me. Eventually someone will come to free me and I wouldn't want to deprive them of that."

Skyheart looked at the Old Man sceptically.

"That was my feeble attempt at humour. But you should leave me here. We don't want the guards to get suspicious."

"You're not exactly what I was expecting," Skyheart said.

"Likewise," said the Old Man. "Step closer."

Skyheart obliged and took enough steps for him to be fully visible in the light of the fire. The Old Man's eyes widened.

"You're Captain Laike Skyheart of Thieron's Fourth Division."

"Actually, it's Division Four," Skyheart said, smiling. "But, indeed, I am he. Now would you like me to rescue you?"

"No, I know my place in the world. I'm supposed to be in shackles, so I'll remain in shackles."

"What did you do?"

"I don't remember. It was so long ago now."

"Where are they taking you?"

"Genko."

"I may very well see you there then."

"I eagerly anticipate it."

They paused and were silent for a few moments. Skyheart's face wore the expression of a man in pain, as if the Old Man's sadness were osmosing into him. He shivered and said, "Is there anything I can do for you?"

"You could stay a while," the Old Man said. "I don't get much conversation. I'd imagine you disposed of the guards?"

"They're distracted enough for the time being."

The Old Man smiled weakly and Skyheart sat next to him.

"I've a lot of time to think down here, too much time for one man really. This is made worse by the fact that I've always been thinking. Thinking about big the questions and whether I have an answer to them. So, I have to ask you to excuse my conversation topic, but it is one that had been on my mind, recently and forever before that."

Skyheart gestured for him to continue.

"What do you think the meaning of life is?"

Skyheart said nothing and sat, staring at the fire. Who was this Old Man who asked a stranger such questions? He supposed he had been maddened with a life of captivity and, upon finally having someone with which to converse, had finally become completely insane. However, he could hardly deny this ancient lunatic a conversation and, instead, looked to think about that question. When he finally spoke his voice was soft and slow.

"I would certainly hope that it was to adventure. Otherwise my life has been somewhat of a wasted effort."

The Old Man smiled again. "What is life if not an adventure? I'd wager you're on one right now."

"Supposedly."

"Sorry," said the Old Man. "When you get to my age you start to think about these things. The meaning of life, what you've done with the life you've had, when it's all going to end, how and why." He turned his head to look at the younger man. "I suppose you don't think about it yet, do you?"

Skyheart shrugged. "Quite frankly, Old Man, I'm not entirely sure what I think of."

"I've been asking the question for years, 'What do you think the meaning of life is?' and it seems everyone has an answer except me. Either that or I'm just not brave enough to wager a guess.

"I've had a good life, I suppose, what I remember of it. We live in a world of vibrant colour. From the blue of the sky to the green of grass, the red of fire and so on. I've seen more colours in the setting and rising of the sun than I have in anything else, colours I couldn't describe, or at least don't know the name of. I've lived through wars and peace. It seems to me that each brings memories of the other. Wouldn't you agree?"

"My line of work doesn't exactly allow for a great knowledge or experience of peace," Skyheart said remorsefully. He looked into the fire once more. The dancing flames seemed to sway slowly to the Old Man's lament, as if the story were for the fire's benefit. Skyheart could hear the gentle snoring of the sleeping guard.

He looked at the Old Man. Was he wise? He certainly seemed to be too articulate to be as mad as Skyheart had first thought. Perhaps he was neither. He just wanted an answer to his questions. It didn't seem to Skyheart to be so unreasonable a wish.

The Old Man continued. "I once found a place of great peace. I'd like to go back one day, although I'd imagine it will never happen now." He paused. "The Southern Continent is a place of true beauty, great sadness also. The place refuses to let go of its past. An honourable sentiment perhaps, though ultimately futile and demoralising. Their past is a past of sorrow, as such holding onto it breeds yet more sorrow. There is no catharsis in memories and even remembering happiness merely reminds them of what they no longer have.

"Despite this, despite the past wars and sorrow inflicted onto the people of the Southern Continent, there lies the only place I have ever found total peace. In the centre of the continent there is a meadow that spans ten square miles. It is a sacred place, dedicated to a fallen or forgotten God. No birds sing there and even the residents avoid it if they can. Strange really, avoiding such a beautiful area.

"Back on the subject of colour, that meadow held them all, known or otherwise. How I should have liked to see it again..."

"Then let me free you," Skyheart pleaded, his voice cracking slightly with the futility of his argument.

The Old Man seemed not to hear him, as if he was entranced by his memory.

"I spent my life searching for the meadow," he said. "For so long I knew not where it was, but I had seen it in a dream. A dream of my death. I'd imagine one would usually call a dream of their death a 'nightmare', but this had such vibrancy to it, as if life and death were no more different than a man's left and right eye.

"In the dream I was already there, surrounded by the benevolent scents of the flowers. Sweetness, sweetness. I stood for a few moments merely taking in what was there, but one could never fully comprehend such elegance. Man only understands what he creates and what does he create? War and ugliness. That is his legacy." He looked at Skyheart. "That is *your* legacy, even if you don't want it to be. And what of the artist? What of art? Some is remembered, most is forgotten and what is forgotten is so because man has his legacy of war on his mind.

"I only mention this because in the dream, man's legacy was art as was nature's. Man's legacy was enjoying the art of nature. I know this for I was the spokesperson of man and nature was all that there was for me.

"This brings me to my death. Taken in, captivated by the meditating, illustrious heaven around me, I failed to notice another man until he was standing right next to me. No, that's wrong. I did notice him, only I didn't react to him, almost as though I was supposed to meet him there. But then I looked at him. He held a sword, dripping with blood. That's all I remember about how he looked. I saw his face and can't recall it. Or mayhap he had no face. It doesn't seem so unreasonable to assume that he was faceless. Does death have a face? In my mind he wore black but I can't be sure of this either. Conceivably, in the memory I have dressed him in black because his clothes could never match the intricacies of the colours in the meadow. His clothes were manmade, after all.

"It was then I realised that the blood on the sword was mine. Though, he never touched me with it. It was as if my blood voluntarily left my body and made its way over to the sword. A peaceful death, in keeping with the setting. I just collapsed and never rose again. Part of the meadow forevermore."

The Old Man was smiling. It would have been disturbing under normal circumstances but at that moment gave off an air of wisdom.

"You say that you were the spokesperson of man in the dream," began Skyheart. "But how can you be sure that your murderer was not? You say yourself that man's legacy is that of war. What is war if not murder on a grand scale?"

The Old Man nodded as Skyheart spoke. "Indeed a good point," he said, "and one I have contemplated many times. But I know it is as I say for a simple reason. The dream was an invention of my subconscious mind and as such so were the man and my death. Man can manufacture death, as you have pointed out, but the only way to manufacture one's own death is to commit suicide. Ergo, the man was an extension of me, because to die in a dream one must manufacture one's own death."

Skyheart considered the Old Man's words. He didn't dream often and even when he did the dreams were little more than images, often unconnected, strung together in a sea of irrelevance. He had never died in a dream and the subject of dreams as a conversation topic had always eluded him due to their abstract nature. Was there really anything to say?

He looked once more into the fire. The flames had ceased their dancing, now merely flickering – tired of their performance. There was still little noise from above. Clearly DeFlare was doing a good job of distracting the guards.

The Old Man shuffled and his shackles made a quiet clinking noise. He sighed and also looked into the fire. Skyheart saw the fire reflected in the Old Man's grey eyes, not in the usual way. It was as if the fire was deep inside and had crept to the forefront to meet the image.

"When I woke I knew that although I had manufactured the man and my

38

death, I had not manufactured the meadow. No man has such power, subconscious or otherwise, so as to create something of such allure. I knew that the place must truly exist. I also knew that I would die when I found it.

"I'm a man who knows his place in the world. Right now that place is in shackles. When I have to die then I shall die, I have little choice in the matter. If that was the place in which that was to happen I realised I would have to find it – that it was the purpose of my existence. Of course in the dream it was not explained just where the meadow was. My mind could only give me the information I knew.

"I set out to find it that morning. I had no wife or children and no obligation to continue to live the life I had been living before the dream. My approach was simple: I went to highly populated areas and asked if anyone knew of the meadow. The three Great Cities were the obvious places to go.

"First, I travelled to the closest, Mandra. I asked everyone I met in the local tavern, explaining the dream in much the same way I have to you and the patrons listened intently, again, much in the same you have. Drunken men have some wisdom and they are notoriously fond of sharing such wisdom, however upon this subject they fell silent. None knew of such a place and none understood the logic behind my realisation that the meadow must exist. I heard advice only from the barman; to give up my search before it consumed me completely and return home.

"Of course, this was no option to me and I decided to seek out the wisest mind in Mandra. I heard tell of a man named Kalo who lived in a house of mountain rock near the Mandran palace. I found the house with ease and entered. It so transpired that Kalo was, in fact, a child, though none could doubt his sagaciousness. He greeted me warmly, as only a child can, and asked me of my predicament. I told him of my dream and he meditated on the subject. He requested me to return the next day after he had conversed with the planet on the matter.

"I rested at an inn but failed to sleep. My mind was filled with questions. What would Kalo say? What exactly did he mean by 'converse with the planet'? Indeed, I thought it to be a metaphor (albeit a vague one)... Thankfully, my thoughts were interrupted by a messenger from the Mandran King. I fear I have shown just how old I am. Mandra has not had a king for over thirty years. This was twenty years even before that.

"The messenger took me to the palace where the King granted me an audience. He asked to hear of my dream and I told him, however, quite how he discovered my presence is still a mystery to me. After he had heard all that there was to hear he asked me why finding the meadow was of such importance to me. I explained to him that each person has a place in the world and that the dream had shown me my rightful place. To find this place and to die was my purpose in life. A man cannot cheat his purpose if the planet has gifted him vision of it.

"The King pondered on this for a few moments. When he spoke he said to me that he had never found a purpose for his life and asked me why. I told the King that I was hardly qualified to answer such a question but he insisted that I give him my interpretation. All I could think to say was that he had found his purpose in being king, as such the planet gave him no signs to the contrary. He seemed to weigh my interpretation in his mind. He seemed to like it and offered me a job as a royal advisor. Naturally, I declined as I already had found my purpose in life. The King understood but said that the offer would remain open if ever I changed my mind.

"The next day I went to see Kalo. He said that the planet had not told him where the meadow was, but it had told him if I followed the path of my life I would eventually find it. I thanked Kalo and went back to see the King, now confident that I would find the meadow if I took up his offer to become a royal advisor. The King was elated that I had come back so soon and gave me the job.

"Little happened in the ten years that I worked for him. I was essentially the overseer of the building of a great structure atop the mountain, although that is far from important. I became good friends with Kalo in this time. He taught me how to meditate and talk to the planet. Every day for ten years I asked the planet of the meadow, yet it did not answer. Until one day, when Kalo died.

"He was a grown man by this time, but still mercilessly young. I asked the planet why it had taken him. The planet told me it was out of kindness. Kalo had achieved his purpose and it was best to take him in the blossom of contentment than to let him linger on into misery. I asked what his purpose was, but I received no answer.

"Kalo's death showed me that it was time to on with my journey. I left the court of the King and set out for Genko, although Thieron was closer. I hoped to avoid the desert.

"I arrived in Genko to find it much as I had imagined. It is not so different from Mandra, only where in Mandra there are mountains in Genko there is sea. Once more I searched for the wisest mind, but they had no equivalent to Kalo. Only upon reflection did I realise they never could. The people, however, wished to hear of my story and, once told, they wished me luck with my travels. All agreed the meadow exists.

"I decided to stay there, as many travellers go through Genko on their way to the Southern Continent. One day, I met an adventurer by the name of Nitass; he had been to the Southern Continent searching for a lost artefact of some kind for Thieron. Now that I think of it, he never divulged what it was. The townsfolk brought him to me and we conversed. He said he knew not of the place but agreed that it must exist. He promised he would aid my quest by accompanying me. However, he first had to deliver his cargo to Thieron. We agreed that I should wait for him in Genko.

"He left the next day and I was called to see the Emperor. He had heard of my assistance to the King of Mandra and wanted some himself. He asked of the dream. He then said that if the meadow was found, or ever had been found, man would, upon its discovery, destroy it or have already destroyed it. We need only look at the mountains of Mandra. I explained to him that if my discovery of the meadow led to its destruction, it was out of my hands. All that would mean was that my purpose was the destruction of the meadow. He accepted this, though I doubt he understood. I sometimes wonder if I do.

"He then asked me a question I did not expect. He asked me why I was so keen to die. I told him that it was not keenness to die that drove me, but determination to achieve the purpose of my existence. He then suggested that if my purpose was to die in the meadow then in seeking out the meadow I was displaying a willingness to die. I pondered this. Although I had been armed with the knowledge of my death I had merely taken steps to see its fruition as opposed to taking steps to prevent it. The Emperor argued that one with my knowledge could surely live forever. The idea intrigued me and I meditated that night for some time. I then asked the planet. I received no answer.

"A few days later I was called to see him once again, to give him my thoughts on eternal life. I informed him that my conversation with the planet was inconclusive. He asked me what I thought that meant. I told him, it either meant that it was possible, but the planet wished us not to know, or that the planet just wished not to answer so intrusive a question. He asked me to research eternal life with him. Death had been on my mind for so long that I decided to give life a chance and accepted his offer.

"We received word a few days later that Nitass had died in the Thieronian desert after losing his way. I mourned him, but I was so engrossed in my work for the Emperor that I had a pleasant distraction.

"After ten years we had made no progress, but the Emperor was patient and continued to give me the resources I needed. Then the King of Mandra died. I asked the planet why my friend had been taken. I was told he had become too old to achieve his purpose. My desperate lie had killed him. I shared my guilt with the Emperor who sympathised with me and granted me leave to pay my respects. I left him my research and went on my way.

"I arrived in Mandra on the day of the funeral and was surprised to see how many people remembered me. The funeral also marked the ascension to the throne of the current ruler, Queen Rasset, who was then a mere child.

"I stayed in Mandra for some time. I suppose it was guilt. I felt I had robbed him of wisdom and his purpose. I tried to right this by giving wisdom to the Mandrans, but the people encouraged me to complete my quest and find the meadow. It seems my idea of purpose had given them hope and I was to consolidate this with proof. So I decided to on with my quest to Thieron.

"I was lucky enough to be taken in by a group of travelling merchants going to Thieron to sell their wares. This made crossing the desert a far easier task. I left a small monument to Nitass on my way through, more out of obligation than remorse. It was, most likely, too late to mean anything.

"Those in Thieron I told of my dream thought me a madman. Perhaps they were right. Mayhap they believed too fervently in Thiera to comprehend the power of the planet. Yet, just as I was losing heart I was pointed in the direction of a man thought wise by the Thieronians. An old army Captain named Thean. I hear he's still alive. My, he was an old man then, now he must be ancient! He was intrigued by my dream and amazed at my dedication. We often spoke after that. He knew of no such place on the Northern Continent but was being sent to the Southern Continent to play his part in what would later be known as the Mineral Wars.

41

"I'm sure you know of the history. Queen Rasset was being manipulated by her advisors into invading the Southern Continent for its abundant natural resources. As such, Genko had also raced there, not to be outdone. Thieron, then still a formidable power, had to follow in order to retain its pride.

"Captain Thean promised to take me with his small force and, in return for my expertise, he would help me search for the meadow. I did not understand what he thought I could offer him in way of help, but I accepted. He soon revealed to me he was far from comfortable with his part in the war and wanted my reassurance that he was following his purpose. I told him that it was possible his place in the world was to follow orders. He seemed to find some solace in that, though I struggled to understand why.

"I was forced to fight in the war. To kill. To take part in man's enduring legacy. I only did it once. I killed one man, but even that was too much for me. I imagine it was all part of my purpose, to exterminate the man who remains nameless to me. So long ago, yet I remember it as vividly as the dream. Although, now that man is faceless to me too. To say I remember it is not entirely correct. I remember the feeling. A nausea; a feeling of waking when one is already awake.

"My part in the war was small, but Thean rewarded me as he said he would when it ended and joined my search, sending his troops back to Thieron. With the Genkoan and Mandran ambush that followed I must admit, I am glad that we did not follow.

"We searched the continent, but the war had left only two towns; Port Fair and North Port, both of which are small fishing towns. Port Fair mythology told of a meadow, but they knew not where it was, nor did they wish to. Our presence caused them pain and so we left. We walked the Flat Path to North Port where we found slightly more. We had passed the meadow on our way there. Had we walked the Mountain Path we would have found it.

"We retraced our steps finding the northern entrance to the Mountain Path. We walked through the mountains."

The Old Man gasped. "It was just as in my dream! Such majesty, I cannot begin to describe it any more than I already have, for I would omit some detail and could never forgive myself for blighting the image in your mind. Only I entered. Thean wished not to interfere with fate. How wise of him.

"Ready to die I walked the meadow as in the dream, trying to comprehend the lustrous beauty. But something was wrong..."

"You didn't die," Skyheart said, standing and stretching.

"There was no man, no sword. No death."

"What went wrong?"

"I don't know. I asked the planet many times but it refuses to answer. After that day I returned to the Northern Continent."

"And ended up in shackles."

The Old Man smiled weakly again. "That's a story for another day." He nodded to a shadow on the either side of the pit. "There's a cavern you can use to get out that way. Farewell, Captain Skyheart."

Skyheart gave his usual casual salute and began to leave, but the Old Man called to him and he stopped.

"Do you think me so wrong, to try to find my purpose?"

Skyheart sighed. "I know nothing of purpose, Old Man."

"Is there no purpose?"

Skyheart shrugged but did not turn to look at the Old Man. "Who's to say? You seem to know more than me. Though, I can't say that's saying much."

"You care not to have a purpose?"

"Perhaps I'll make my own."

"Do you think you can choose? What if they are already decided?"

"I'd certainly loathe putting my faith in either. Both seem undeserving beliefs, even if they are true."

"And what of Thiera?"

"I've no time for unworthy ideologies, Old Man. No matter how pertinent to my situation."

With that he left, greeted a fond goodbye by the shouting of the guards. He had stayed too long as it was.

Chapter Six

DeFlare found himself on the grass plain, where Skyheart had planned on emerging after leaving the desert, as day was dawning. He had lost the guards some time ago and decided to continue to Genko alone, still somewhat surprised that the Captain's plan had actually worked. Although, he was slightly concerned that the Captain hadn't had quite enough time to explore the pit.

He wandered on, traversing the plain as a light rain began to fall. Soon a thin mist had formed causing DeFlare to re-evaluate his position. He paused to look around and saw a small hill a mile or so to the north. He made a course for it after noting little else that would help him.

Somewhere a wolf howled.

'Strange,' DeFlare thought, 'wolves usually confine themselves further east than this.'

It was only when he reached the zenith of the hill that he could make sense of the sound. Before him lay the Genkoan frontline. A living, surging mass of men and campfires creeping westwards. War personified, readying himself for the battles to come. What victim would that day bring? DeFlare, perhaps, if he was discovered.

He crouched, fearful of being seen, and contemplated his options. His first instinct was to find a way around, although with such a vast expanse of an army to navigate around it would slow his journey considerably. If he was to deliver to Faux-Diamandé at the same time as Thean and Okain he would have to arrive in Genko the next day at the very latest. Of course, he could go through the line, sneaking past and making an ally of the shadows. But if he was seen by anyone he would surely be stripped of his cargo.

He thought of how the Captain would probably have made a decision instantly upon the sight of the obstacle ahead of him and how that decision would most likely have been to walk straight through. The confidence Skyheart exuded would no doubt have brought him more respect from his adversaries than he deserved.

DeFlare dismissed the thought and lay down to observe the lines more clearly, although the action allowed no more intricate an observation than before. Each soldier was merely an expendable blade of grass in the plain. He sighed; change the uniform and that was him.

As he lay, watching, his mind wandered and he found himself thinking of the plausibility of Operation Shell, to date his most important mission. His success or failure would change the world. Whatever came to fruition it would inevitably become history. He wasn't sure of the level of comfort that was brought to him by the fact. Strangely, he did find some solace in the idea that Captain Skyheart was involved. He shuddered. This line of thought held no reason.

His attention returned to his immediate situation. The frontline had begun to move forward. His decision had been made for him. He would be forced to lay there and wait for them to pass.

He walked the total darkness of the cave, arms half-cocked, as a drunkard shuffling his way home of an evening. The thick blackness before him allowed no light; a habitat that no shadow could survive in. He walked the cavern half in sleep, half in delirium – a state he was used to only in times of his most debased activities. Each step caused an echo to ring out; something he had long ceased caring about, in much the same way that he no longer paid any mind to the group behind him. He was aware that they were catching up, but in this land of enforced accursed blindness their numbers counted for nothing, and even if they did, what could they do? He was Captain Laike Skyheart.

He was slightly confused as to why the Old Man had sent him on the same route that the guards would soon be taking. Then again, he doubted the wisdom of the rambling philosopher. He had about him the aura of a man maddened with desert heat, not one enlightened by a sagacious existence. Yet, his story was one of conviction and commitment rarely experienced.

The thought was interrupted as Skyheart walked into a wall. He grunted and followed the wall, wet with dripping water, using his hand so as not to make the same mistake again.

As time passed his delirium grasped him more forcefully. He felt as though he squirmed in the sweaty palm of lunacy, trying to free himself by prying its fingers from him, but for every finger he broke free of two more took its place. To escape, only to have another hand clasp the first shut. What caused such derangement? The small part of him that still held its sanity hoped it was merely disorientation, though a very real fear struck him: lack of alcohol.

When had he last drunk? How long had he been in this cavern? Already he felt as if he had spent an eternity down there. An endless prison of impenetrable darkness, fortified against the tides of luminescence, the prestigious glow of which would extinguish the gloom if only it could find a way in.

He whispered to himself, though it came as a shock. "No," his voice said, barely a breath against the echo of his footsteps, the reverberation of the men behind him and the choirs of dripping water. "No, not like this." He heard himself say it but knew not what it meant. He must have lost control of that part of himself.

The ever decreasing segment of his mind that seemed to hold an entity of some semblance to sense could do little more than hope the men behind him were experiencing a similar possession. Somehow this minute area of Skyheart's brain managed to guide him along the wall.

Malady swept through him. A feeling of waking when one is already awake. Was that something the Old Man had said? He couldn't be sure. Anything before that moment was of ambiguous origin. All he knew was that he had to escape from the cavern and his pursuers. If pursuers they were. Men behind another on a path are not necessarily in a chase. Their destinations may be the same but that could be the only similarity in their journey.

He fell as the wall left him and he was confronted by, what he assumed were, two paths, though there may have been more. In the darkness and his state of questionable control he could not be sure of anything. It was a condition in which he should not have been making decisions and so his frenzy made it for him. Which path he had taken he couldn't say.

He stumbled in the new direction, his mind a mangled corpse of disarray. Shambolic evidence of the ease of man's destruction. He retched, more than once, though, thankfully, there was nothing inside of him. Empty as the cavern, if the cavern hadn't held the Captain and those behind him. Were they aware of his existence? With the noise he had been making they must have. Yet the reverberation from behind had ceased and the demonic echoes had faded into benevolent silence, nothingness absolute. They must have taken another path.

The area of his mind able to think such thoughts (or perhaps just think) was now smaller than ever, but it was there nonetheless. That fragment of clarity clutched at even the most fleeting thought, desperate not to let the man slip into permanent insanity. He wondered how far he had walked and how far he still had left to go, but came to no conclusions.

Was this what death was: a never-ending walk in darkness? Was this even real? His senses were so dulled and frayed the moment could hardly have been said to have existed. When a man commits an act and is unaware of it, could it be said to have happened if he had no witness, or was that moment another refugee in a war won by inattentiveness and senility?

His eyes began to form shapes in the cavern. He could see vague formations in the rock. Were his eyes finally adjusting to the darkness? No. Light. Light had entered the cavern. He lifted his head and saw a hole in the rock. A pale pink light was invading the nothingness he had long been traversing. Such a colour; could it have been dawn? His pace increased and soon he found himself embraced in the lustre. That was, until the ground was stolen from beneath his feet and he fell into darkness once more.

The troops crawled past in the never ending rain. The mist was thick now but DeFlare could just make out the shape of the advancing war machine.

His inactivity had left him tired and he yawned, every so often he was forced to pinch himself to stop himself from falling asleep. The constant rain had left him soaked. He shuffled on the zenith of the hill and tried to find a more comfortable position. Thunder roared, muffled by the progressing army. But to DeFlare the thunder was obscured by yet another sound.

"The Captain won't be happy when he sees we're late back," said a voice somewhere behind him.

"He shouldn't have sent us on the expeditionary mission then," said another.

"Please, he won't even have noticed we've gone," said a third Genkoan soldier.

DeFlare held his breath, trying to decide how best to avoid detection. He pulled himself forward to the edge of the hill and slid down. He looked up and saw the soldiers at the peak. He continued crawling along on his stomach.

"Where is Captain Skyheart?" DeFlare asked himself.

He awoke, shaking and nursing a headache of epic proportions. He rubbed his head and opened his eyes. It was far too bright. He was on a dusty path in a rocky valley. He looked up and saw in the side of the cliff, the hole he had used to escape the cavern.

The cavern. Was that not some kind of horrible dream? Was it real? It couldn't have been anywhere near as traumatic as he remembered. Then again, if there had been any truth in that senseless endeavour, he at least seemed to be back in control of himself.

He sat up and realised he was in the midst of an impossible thirst. He reached for the bottle of whiskey only to remember he had given it to DeFlare. He then reached for the canteen of water only to find it gone. He must have dropped it in the cavern. Despite his drought, he would not re-enter that godless dark.

His shaking worsened. He tried to stand but was forced to lean against the cliff as the blood drained from his head. What was this sickness?

He craved one thing and upon realising this he shrank back to the ground holding his head tighter still, fearful that the throbbing inside would break through his skull – at the time it seemed to be a very real possibility.

"Problem, stranger?"

Skyheart looked up and saw a plump, middle-aged man in olive-green garbs, pulling a wooden cart full of goods.

"Have you anything to drink?" Skyheart asked.

The merchant passed Skyheart a canteen made of brown leather. Skyheart removed the stopper and took a large swig. His eyes widened and he spat the contents from his mouth, coughing gruffly from his throat.

"Are you okay?" asked the merchant.

"I was expecting something a little different."

The merchant smiled and grabbed a bottle of brown liquid from his cart. He passed it to Skyheart and the Captain passed back the canteen. He devoured the contents of the bottle and only stopped when his body refused to accept any more of the alcohol inside. He looked up at the merchant and smiled.

"That'll be five gold pieces," said the merchant.

Skyheart's expression turned from a smile into a scowl. He stood and scratched the back of his head. He looked from where the merchant had come from and then to where he was headed. He couldn't make out either direction as the rain clouds had obscured the sun from view. He realised his shaking had not stopped, however it was less aggressive than before. He took another swig of liquor and looked back to the merchant, his face now softening into an apologetic smile.

"I'm afraid I have no money," he said.

The merchant sighed. "Last time I do something nice for someone." He began to walk away pulling his cart behind him. "You're all the same you travellers," he called back, "never willing to pay your way."

Skyheart walked beside him. "Where are you headed?"

"Ailta."

"Where's that?"

"Just west of Genko."

"Then I shall get you your money in Ailta." He gently pushed the merchant aside and began pulling the cart. "And I'm not a traveller," he said, "I'm an adventurer."

At that moment his legs enfeebled and he fell to a crouch. He took another swig of liquor, confident that it would aid his strength. The warmth slid down through him into his nauseous stomach. It did little more than warm him against the summer rain. He managed to stand but knew he would fail in pulling the cart. He looked to the merchant, not knowing what to say.

"I'll pull the cart," the merchant said. "Clearly you're not strong enough."

They began walking once more, Skyheart holding onto the cart for balance. He couldn't be sure if the alcohol was detrimental to his stability or whether it was the only thing, aside from the cart, holding him up.

"What happened to you?" the merchant asked.

"I'm sorry?"

"Something must have happened in the night to make you so weak."

"Oh," Skyheart said. "I don't remember." He was relieved to find his shaking had stopped almost completely.

"Must have been bad whatever it was. I thought you were dead until you spoke."

"The way I feel that doesn't seem like a bad alternative."

The merchant laughed and stopped the cart. "Why don't you climb in and sleep?" he said. "I'll wake you up in Ailta."

Skyheart shook his head, but then noticed the concerned expression on the merchant's wrinkling face. Reluctantly, the Captain climbed into the cart and downed the rest of the liquor.

The cart began moving again, but Skyheart didn't know. He was already asleep.

He was woken by the shattering sound of a whip cracking. It cut through him and he sat up, his nausea worse but his shaking gone. Behind the cart he saw the guards, forcing the Old Man along. His arms were tied to a piece of wood stretched out behind his head. Every few steps he tripped and was whipped or kicked or spat on by the guards, causing them no end of delight or humour.

The lead guard called for the merchant to halt and he obliged. Skyheart sighed and observed as the lead guard approached. He sneered at the Captain as he walked passed and was greeted by Skyheart's usual casual salute. He grabbed the merchant.

"Where are you going?"

"Ailta," said the merchant.

"Why?"

"To sell my goods."

"Who's he?" He pointed at Skyheart.

"He's sick."

"That's not what I asked."

"*He* can talk, you know?" Skyheart said, rising and stepping off of the cart. "I am Captain Laike Skyheart of Thieron's Division Four."

The lead guard gasped and bowed. "Sorry for any inconvenience sir!"

The Captain smiled. "Strange that an enemy soldier would greet me so respectfully."

"Our countries are not at war yet, Captain. And any man of your repute deserves the utmost respect."

"How true," the Captain said, smile widening. He walked over to the rest of the group with the Old Man, the lead guard following behind. "What do you want with this man?"

"He's a criminal, sir."

"What did he do?"

"Something unspeakable, sir."

Skyheart looked at the Old Man in much the same way he did the night before. The Old Man shook his head, knowing Skyheart wished to free him.

"Carry on," Skyheart said weakly.

"Thank you, sir!"

They whipped the Old Man and began moving again. Skyheart stood with the merchant and watched them leave.

"So you're the infamous Crimson Captain," the merchant said.

"What of it?"

"I always thought you'd be more masculine looking."

Skyheart ignored this, transfixed as he was on the shrinking visage of the tortured Old Man.

"I could have saved him, couldn't I?" he said.

"With your reputation, I believe so. But you must have your reasons. I won't pry. I don't presume to know about war and conflict."

They began walking again, Skyheart's illness waning, a rotting feeling in its place.

They arrived at a small town a short time later. The buildings were made of grey stone with thatched roofs. The street was clogged with mud where a lone warrior defended himself against a myriad of Genkoan soldiers armed with spears. The warrior was dressed in plated black armour, shimmering with rain droplets. He held a katana in his right hand and a wakizashi in his left.

He attacked with skill unparalleled by the Genkoans. Compared to his talent, they were an untrained mob whose cumbersome spears were a hindrance. However, no matter how skilful the warrior was, he was outnumbered and becoming more so with each passing second.

One Genkoan soldier thrust at him with the tip of his spear only to have the strike parried and the tip forced into the mud. The warrior stood on the spear to keep it down and proceeded to parry strikes from the other soldiers, though he could surely only hold on for so long.

As both of his swords had been occupied by two attacks, another soldier thrust at the warrior's chest. Just then a flash of crimson and black struck the soldier's weapon away from him.

"Hello, Myst," Skyheart said.

"Captain Skyheart!" Myst roared happily. "How wonderful it is to see you." He pushed his attackers away with one explosion of strength. "How have you been?"

"Increasingly bored, until I found you. What adventures have you to tell about?"

"Many," Myst laughed. "However, I fear I am currently rather pre-occupied with freeing this town from the evil grip of Genko. Perhaps you'd care to help?"

Skyheart rested the blade of Cendré on his shoulder and sighed. "Alas," he said, "if only I could. However, I am currently travelling to Genko on a matter of urgent diplomacy. Were I to engage in combat against their troops I fear my cause, and words, would be rather weakened."

"Diplomacy?" Myst pondered, obviously amused. "The great Laike Skyheart now sent on diplomatic matters. Such is the warrior's fate in these strange days we find ourselves in. If I remember clearly you defeated an entire garrison of soldiers at our escape from Pale Castle with no help at all. I was rather annoyed to have so little to do, though your good friend Captain Cyan seemed relieved not to have so many deaths on his conscience."

"How very undiplomatic of me," Skyheart laughed, sheathing Cendré. "But, times change and even the most unruly of us follow the occasional order."

"A true pity."

The two warriors had been so engrossed in their conversation, they had only now realised that the Genkoan soldiers had reformed and gathered sizeable reinforcements. Almost an entire division stood at the end of the street.

"Well," Myst said, upon seeing the force, "I suppose I should meet glory."

"I'm afraid I can't let you do that," Skyheart said. "Even being associated with someone who killed so many Genko soldiers could jeopardise my mission."

"Somehow, when you arrived, I had a feeling I would cease to do battle," Myst sighed.

"My apologies."

"Quite alright," Myst said, sheathing his swords with a devious glint in his eyes. "Though, I fear the Genkoans will execute me regardless and my pride would never permit me to retreat."

Skyheart grew more serious, his face paling slightly. "Please don't suggest it."

"Might I propose..."

"No."

"... a battle to the death?"

Skyheart sighed.

"It makes more sense than you might think," Myst said. "If news travels to Genko – a possibility, if not definite – that you have slain me, they will be sure to accept any proposal you suggest. My death is imminent anyway. Even if you were to decline my offer of a duel and I was killed by the Genkoans, you would still be responsible for my death. After all, it was your presence that allowed the troops to gather. Of course, you could die gloriously with me in a charge against their force."

"Are you so resigned to die?"

"It is the way of the warrior."

"Myst, you ask me to choose between the impossible."

Myst smiled. "Very well," he said. "Then I shall make it easy for you!"

With this Myst drew his katana and sliced at Skyheart's chest. The Captain leapt backwards, drew Cendré and parried the second attack that came with the wakizashi. Although impressive, Skyheart had no time to marvel at his own talent as Myst struck at him with the katana once more.

'By using two swords he can attack constantly,' Skyheart thought. 'If I block an attack from one he can still attack with the other. If he feints with one he can cut me down with the other. It would make sense if his attacks with the wakizashi were to distract me from the katana; however, he's too experienced a warrior to use patterns.'

Just as Skyheart finished this thought, Myst did exactly as the Captain had been surmising. He feinted with the wakizashi and, once Skyheart was committed to defending against the attack, launched at him with the katana. Were it not for Skyheart's superior speed he would surely have been killed, however just as the katana was about to strike him he sidestepped and Myst fell forward.

Myst turned to Skyheart and laughed.

"So you saw through that attack," he said.

"It's by far your most predictable," Skyheart said, resting the blade of Cendré on his shoulder.

"You're even faster that I remember."

"Can we stop this nonsense now?"

"Certainly not!"

Myst swung his katana as a feint to attack with the wakizashi. Skyheart, pretending to believe the rouse, parried the katana with enough force to make Myst drop the sword. As the wakizashi neared its target, Skyheart struck Myst's wrist with the blunt edge of Cendré. Myst dropped the sword, losing all feeling in the hand. He knelt to grab the katana only to be struck in the chest in the same way. He fell to his knees.

"Quite a technique," he said. "Instant paralysis."

"It doesn't last long," Skyheart said. "Once I leave you should be able to escape before the soldiers reach you. Run to freedom."

He sheathed Cendré and turned to leave.

"Is there no freedom in death?" Myst said, his words stopping Skyheart. "Let me die with honour. Not escape like some common coward."

Skyheart turned to him. "You are so resigned to die?"

"Such is the way of the warrior," Myst said and bowed his head.

Skyheart drew Cendré and sighed. He had only met the man bowing before him once, though it had been one of his greatest adventures and, without Myst, it could never have been so. Furthermore, it was a human life he had been asked to take.

Eyes closed, he swung Cendré cleaving Myst's head from his body and sheathed the sword in one motion.

Myst's body fell into the mud and from it fell a bag of coins. Skyheart threw it at the feet of the approaching merchant.

"There's your money," he said bluntly.

"That's not the kind of money I want."

"It's only kind of money I have."

"He was unarmed."

Skyheart sighed. "Is there no freedom in death?"

He left Myst's words in writing and tied them to the hilt of his swords which he stuck in the ground for remembrance. The soldiers, upon seeing this, lazily dispersed and, without a word, Captain Skyheart left. Both he and the merchant would reach Ailta alone.

Skyheart arrived in Ailta at around noon and decided not to stay. Genko was only a few miles away and the sooner he got there the sooner he could find the Old Man.

The term 'town' was perhaps too grand for Ailta. Indeed, it was a bustling market where many different peoples came to buy and sell goods, but little else. There were only carts, no buildings. Some merchants had set up animal skin canvases to shield their carts from the elements, although it had finally stopped raining.

He walked through, shimmying past the crowds. However, he didn't go unnoticed. He never did. After a child pointed him out to the rest of the consumers he was greeted by silent reverie and a path was cleared for him.

"Our prayers have been answered!" One woman cheered. "He goes to Genko to engineer our release!"

Of course, she wasn't completely wrong. Operation Shell, if successful, would release them from Genko's hold, though this was far from its primary purpose. As such, the Captain's expression remained grave, but he did try to smile. He was thankful when he had finally left. He had done nothing to receive such a display of affection. Perhaps more ostentatious heroics were in order.

Not long after, he found himself atop a hill. A row of trees trailed down the slope leading to a large shimmering city, cradled by the benevolent ocean. He smiled. Was this his true adventure? The sun beat down pleasing warmth and somewhere a flock of birds sang. He scratched the back of his head and approached the shimmering city by the shining sea.

DeFlare had finally made his way past the troops and had gone thankfully unnoticed. The rain had washed him of the mud, but he was glad the day was now clear. He was finally starting to dry. The plain was pleasingly deserted and he made his way east in peace. He walked with purpose, so close to his destination now that he almost broke into a jog.

His mind went back to the troops. How many towns between them and Thieron? Five maybe, and they would put up little struggle. Would his beloved city face extinction by the force? If any part of Operation Shell were to go wrong then both forces would, most likely, accelerate to Thieron and the city had little chance of defending itself, unless, in his absence, they had completed their research on the Diamandé. It occurred to him that, with a jewel of such power within their grasp, he had been worrying unnecessarily all this time. However, this was no time to relax. He had been given a task to complete and orders must be followed.

It was around the time of these thoughts that he began to see the sea. The dark blue mass stretched out against the pale blue sky (now void of all clouds). He smiled and, in a few minutes, saw Genko. To the north was a hill lined with trees. The city glimmered alluringly. He was slightly early. This pleased him; he could rest and wait for the Captain.

That was when he saw it: a spec of crimson on a landscape of green and blue. The Captain, surely. He laughed and broke into a run. Finally, everything was going to plan.

Skyheart stood by the towering gate of Genko. It matched those of Thieron in height, yet it seemed somewhat more formidable, sturdier maybe. He put this down to unfamiliarity and observed as a running man approached. It could only be DeFlare. The Captain took a swig from a bottle of whiskey he had deftly swiped from Ailta and waited, a subtle smile curling around his lips.

The Lieutenant reached him and saluted. "Glad to see you Captain!"

"Most people are."

"I hope your journey was more satisfactory than mine," DeFlare said, remembering everything the Captain had put him through since leaving Thieron.

Skyheart smiled. "Very satisfactory."

He took a swig of whiskey and DeFlare groaned. "Why are you drinking?"

"Because, DeFlare, I'm rather parched after all this travelling."

The Lieutenant sneered at the insufficient response, but at least he had someone to lead him now. The cavalier and arrogant man would suffice for the moment.

Somewhere within the city a guard spotted them and began to open the gate. No pistons sounded. Steam was not needed in Genko as electricity, a mystery to the rest of the world, was the energy of choice. The gate rose slowly.

Skyheart smiled at DeFlare. "I hope you're ready," he said. "This all ends tomorrow."

Skyheart swaggered into the city leaving DeFlare there, hoping the Captain meant what he thought he meant. He then followed.

Chapter Seven

They rose early that morning as the Queen's messenger woke them for their meeting in the Coliseum. She could not see them at the palace; they had come on an important day, the ceremonial Criminal Executions, which, by law, could not have the date changed.

Mandra was a large city as far west as was allowed by the continent, shielded from the sea by a vast mountain range. The palace had been built into one of the mountains with steps carved out leading up to it. The people's houses were also made of mountain rock, with a view to stand forever. On the pinnacle of the tallest tower stood the Coliseum.

Thean and Okain followed the messenger up the spiralling path. They had much energy; Thean had planned their route meticulously and all had gone as he expected. All that was left was to hand over the Faux-Diamandé. However, Thean was aware that this had been made decidedly more complicated by the day that had been chosen to commence this action. They had been invited to stay for the Criminal Executions and could not refuse for fear of insulting the notoriously temperamental Queen Rasset; were this to happen the entirety of Operation Shell would be compromised. Yet, the longer they stayed, the longer the Mandrans had a chance of discovering their treachery.

Okain gave Thean a grave look, he replied with one of understanding and calmness. Okain wondered if he was worrying more than was warranted. It wasn't as if Thean was anywhere near as reckless as Captain Skyheart. But what if something went wrong with Division Four's transaction? That would have an unavoidable effect on the First Division that even Thean could not fix.

Okain silenced his thoughts. He would just have to be as alert as possible and keep his mind on his part of the operation, no matter how much he loathed not knowing.

Although the Coliseum was at the pinnacle of the tallest mountain, the spiralling path made it a surprisingly short walk and they soon found themselves gazing in awe at the grey stone marvel before them. It towered at least twice the height of the walls surrounding Thieron, as such it blocked out the sun.

The messenger led them around the circular house of combat to the entrance – a great arch. Okain wondered why it had to be so big, was it just for spectacle or was there some practical reason he could not yet fathom? He gave Thean a questioning look.

"Quite a spectacle," Thean said to the messenger.

"Thank you, sir," he said, leading them inside. "Her Majesty would be most appreciative of such praise."

After entering the archway they turned left and climbed a stone staircase, rather plain compared to the rest of the structure, which led them to a great stone door. It stood twice the height as even the tallest man Okain could think of and at least fivefold wide. It took ten guards to open the door, slowly revealing a grand view of the entire Coliseum. Row upon row of stone seats going back as far as the eye could see. In the centre was a large circular pit of sand. The view was only obscured by the back of the Queen's throne, cut from the same mountain stone as the rest of the Coliseum. They entered the Royal Box and were led around the throne to the Queen's presence. A painfully thin young woman, aged far beyond her years, in a scarlet dress, sat before them. She wore an elaborate gold crown, a little too straight, upon her head. Under the crown her hair was ailing, becoming thin, knotted and tangled.

"Captain Hyardretten Thean and Lieutenant Valus Okain of Thieron's First Division, Your Majesty," said the messenger, bowing and motioning for the Thieronians to do the same. They obliged and the Queen smiled amusedly.

"How kind of you to come," she said.

"The pleasure is all ours, Your Majesty," Thean replied.

The messenger left them and two guards in ceremonial dress entered.

"I do hope you'll excuse my security," said the Queen. "My subjects appear to think I'm in constant danger."

"You're an important woman, Your Majesty," Thean said.

"So they say." She smiled the kind of smile that would have been disarming were she not the ruler of an empire, a woman who sent thousands to their deaths each day. She observed as the Coliseum started to fill with an audience. "Ah, my subjects are arriving." She looked at Okain. "What do you think of my Coliseum, young man?"

Okain, not having expected to be addressed, started and coughed.

"I'm afraid Lieutenant Okain isn't accustomed to such refined company," Thean said apologetically, with a hint of sympathy for Okain.

"Indeed, our little republic doesn't hold such grandeur as this," Okain said.

"Ah!" the Queen said. "You've regained the power of speech! Now, do tell me what you think."

"It certainly is quite a spectacle."

"Well," the Queen sighed, "I suppose that shall have to do. It has quite a story behind it. I believe I have time to recount it before the games begin. Would you care to hear?"

"We would be honoured," Thean said. He gave Okain a sideways glance which Okain read as one of nervousness.

"A wise decision. I do so like to have a little pleasure before business; it makes the act of work seem rather less daunting.

"Two hundred years ago my ancestor, the Great King Caloss, was on the verge of death. Yes, it seems the great die too. Who would have thought such an injustice could be true? Yet it is. Unfortunate, perhaps, or maybe only in the act of dying can one become great, although, Great King was his title even before death. Whether or not the people believed him to be great during life we shall never know.

"As I said, the Great King was on the verge of death. He feared for his legacy. He feared that all he would be remembered for was war and the destruction he brought upon his enemies. As much as he favoured his legacy of war (believe me he truly did, all rulers do) he felt as though it wasn't enough. He asked the people what they wanted, but they didn't know. He had made sure they had enough food and money, the average man wants little more than to survive comfortably. So he was left to decide on the legacy himself. Of course, he had a son, an heir, someone to carry on his line, but what of him? He thought that perhaps a statue would be fitting and, for the longest of times, he had decided on this. But what bearing would a statue have a generation later?

"Needless to say, you've surely resolved this anyway, but Caloss decided that his legacy would be the very Coliseum that you stand in at this very moment. However, he died before he could see it completed, or even begun. Nobody knows how or why he chose this, but the fact remains that he did. Of course, some have been so brash to suggest their views; he was delirious is a rather popular one, and in his delirium he knew not what he said. Others say he simply loved conflict. I can reveal to you I give these opinions little weight. He commanded the Coliseum to be built atop this mountain because he knew it would be a feat.

"To say that the Coliseum is built atop the mountain would not be entirely true. In fact, it's a downright lie. The Coliseum wasn't so much built on the mountain as the mountain was removed from around the Coliseum. Yes the Coliseum was *carved* into the mountain. This was the Great King's legacy. More destruction. He ordered the top of a mountain to be ruined in honour of him. The egos of men shall forever amaze me.

"He died earlier than anyone expected. The city had to round up workers as soon as the Great King passed. It came as a shock to all, especially the newly crowned King Elannus. Elannus was a young man, inexperienced in the ways of life. This was his first experience of death and it took a heavy toll on him. The fact that it was his father made it even worse. Upon the news of his father's death he *enslaved* all he could find and forced them to build the legacy. But it was cold in the mountains and many died. Furthermore, these were not stone masons. They were peasants. What did they know of this work?

"Elannus was assassinated soon after. It is believed that one of the workers did it, though it was never proven. Elannus's son, Seruras, took his seat on the throne. A warmonger at heart he antagonised the other Great Cities goading them into war. Yes, it seems that Genko and Mandra have always warred. He used the captured soldiers to continue the work on the Coliseum and, for a time, it was good. Progress was made and the people of Mandra were happy. Until one day, the slaves revolted and were killed by their guards. None were left and Seruras hired a small group of stone masons.

"Many years later, Seruras died and the Coliseum had made little progress. Upon seeing the destruction the Great King's legacy had brought upon previous generations, Seruras's son, Whurst, closed the project and the generations after followed with this idea. Until my father came to the throne.

"King Remm was a man with whom I was very close, but could never fully understand. I imagine this was the reason I loved him so deeply. He was a trusting man who saw no reason for lies or treachery and so decided there were no such things when he was involved. He would appoint commoners as advisors after having only one conversation with them, always feeling as if he needed more help in life than he currently had.

"I remember my father telling me of the day one such man came. He spoke of purpose. The memory has faded somewhat now, but I believe he had some sort of dream and believed his purpose in life was to discover its meaning or the place in which it happened. That may have been it, if not it was a similar variety of nonsense at any rate. My father, trusting and easily influenced as he was, took this man on as an advisor, thinking he was some kind of prophet. My father asked the man what his purpose in life was. The reply came to be king. That decided it. As king, my father decided to give the Mandrans a legacy, not for the Great King's memory – not even for his own – but for the Mandrans themselves. As such, work commenced once more on the Coliseum with those enthusiastic to complete the project. The new advisor watched over the work as foreman and it was completed sooner than anyone expected. Once it was done he left.

"Some years later my father died, content to the end. I'd imagine that's something of a rarity." She stopped and shuffled uncomfortable in her throne. Okain thought it to be a strange movement for one so young; usually he only saw it in the old. The Queen smiled lightly, observing the now full Coliseum. She turned to Thean. "I believe you know the advisor of which I speak."

"I knew a man with a similar story during the Mineral Wars."

"What did you think of him?"

Thean stood in his usual stoic manner, his face held no countenance other than that of contentment. "He put me at ease."

"Much as he did my father. He returned here for the funeral and apparently stayed for some time. Or so I hear. I never saw him. Perhaps he felt guilty..." She trailed off and her eyes flashed with a sudden realisation. "I'm sorry," she said. "You came here on a matter of importance and all I have done is talk of an irrelevant past."

"The past can never be irrelevant, Your Majesty," Thean said. "Without it we would not be where we are presently. Quite literally in the case of your story."

The Queen smiled subtly. "Indeed. Yet it is business you have come here for and business we must commence."

Thean looked at Okain and the Lieutenant drew their cargo from the inside pocket of his blue leather coat.

"The President and Assembly send their regards," Thean said as Okain knelt and handed the Queen the jewel.

"Is this what I believe it to be?" She said, struggling to speak. She took it from Okain and inspected it. "The Diamandé."

"Indeed it is, Your Majesty," Thean said.

"I thought it to be a myth, a silly story told to convince Thieronians of the power of their god."

Okain flinched at the blasphemous words. Thean smiled. Okain thought he would have to pray for his Captain's soul when next he had the chance.

"A jewel of unimaginable power," the Queen mused. "Tell me, Captain Thean; why is it that Thieron wishes to give Mandra this gift. Mandra: the tyrant power that could easily destroy Thieron."

"We hoped for a truce," he replied. "We give you the Diamandé to destroy Genko with ease in one final battle and, in return, Thieron remains as it is; untouched. Of course, there's nothing for a power as great as Mandra to gain from invading our feeble desert city anyway." Thean smiled. Okain was surprised at how sincere the entire speech felt.

The Queen smiled in return. "A welcome gift," she said. "It is just a shame that it has been delivered today."

"Indeed," Thean said. "Although Genko will still be there to be destroyed tomorrow. Today you can simply relax and enjoy the Criminal Executions."

It was only now that Okain realised how long the three had been speaking. Long enough for the Coliseum seats to be filled to capacity with spectators. Long enough for the executioner to ready himself, his equipment and the wooden execution block. Long enough, even, for the Queen's royal guards to gradually occupy the royal box with them. Yet not long enough for the executions to begin.

His breathing became heavy and laboured.

"Oh no, Captain Thean," the Queen said. "It is unfortunate that you have brought me the Diamandé today not because of the Criminal Executions. Far from it. No. You have brought me the Diamandé on the day the war ends."

The guards pounced on the Thieronians, disarming them and subduing them with heavy iron shackles.

"As we speak," the Queen continued, "the entire Mandran navy is in the ocean just off of the coast of Genko, ready to launch an attack and end this foolishness." She smiled. "We have no need for your desert toy." She handed the Faux-Diamandé to a guard. "Dispose of it." He left and she turned back to the struggling Thieronians. "As for the Criminal Executions, well, they could only be today. After all, we had to wait for the criminals to get here. A shame Kylar sent you really, Thean. I should have loved to kill that degenerate Skyheart. But you'll do."

*

General Wraste entered the President's office trying to control his sweating as best he could, though he wasn't doing a particularly good job. The Assembly would never take kindly to the news he had for them. His sweating worsened as he felt the hood-hidden eyes piercing through him.

"Has it been found?" one of the Assembly members asked.

"No," Wraste said quietly. "Our worst fears have been confirmed. It is true, the Diamandé is gone."

The Assembly members muttered amongst themselves and President Kylar slumped in his chair as the dejected ruler of a doomed country.

"Fools," a voice from the back of the office said. The man stepped forward and Captain Emaina Skyheart revealed himself from the shadows. "This is why my brother is never to be trusted."

Chapter Eight

His hand felt the chill of the jewel in his pocket. Despite having had it on his person for some days, it was only now he realised just how smooth it was. He wondered if the replicas had done it justice.

He had spent much of that morning telling DeFlare of his journey to Genko. The Lieutenant made a willing and attentive audience, only interrupting at the point of Myst's death.

"You killed him?" DeFlare asked. "An unarmed man?"

Skyheart nodded.

"How can you stand there with such little remorse? There was no need to kill him."

"I've killed many men, DeFlare," Skyheart said. "So many now that adding one more has only the slightest of effects to my conscience. So many, in fact, that all men, armed or unarmed, have begun to look alike."

Skyheart waved the conversation from his mind. His attention was needed in the present. He was stood next to DeFlare in the Throne Room of the Genkoan palace. The Empress, pseudo-deity, ruler of the Genkoan Empire, descendent of the gods themselves, sat before them in a solid gold throne, impressed, seemingly at least, by DeFlare's plea to her emotions and wisdom. He held out the Faux-Diamandé with the notion of a truce in mind.

Skyheart allowed his mind to wander once more. Before coming to the palace he had searched the city for clues as to the Old Man, but nobody knew anything of him. He had asked to see the palace dungeon, assuming the Old Man, criminal as he had been treated, would be there. Hoping his celebrity status would allow for the exception, Skyheart sauntered passed the guards, only to be stopped and turned back. The trail had died and now he stood in the Throne Room, the Old Man, prophet or lunatic, still a mystery to him.

"I must say," the Empress said, "that I have so longed for a way to destroy Mandra with the simplicity you offer. How could I refuse such an offer? Of course I accept your gift and the terms surrounding it. However, I must say I am somewhat surprised at the silence of the infamous Crimson Captain. Have you nothing to say, Captain Skyheart?"

Skyheart came to at the sound of his name. It was only now that he noticed the magnificence of the room in which he stood. Marble walls encased them, built up from a floor of platinum. Two rows of obsidian pillars led to the throne.

Upon realising he had missed the entirety of the exchange that led to the room giving him the floor he went to what he was normally required to say after hearing his name. "Actually, it's Division Four."

DeFlare rolled his eyes, although the Empress looked amused.

"The Empress was just saying, to those of us with the manners to listen, that she accepts our gift," DeFlare said.

"Then take it to her," Skyheart said. He'd begun to shake again and wished to leave, although he had yet to put his plan into action. Perhaps he should speed up the procession.

DeFlare neared the Empress, knelt, and held the Faux-Diamandé out to her. She took it, marvelling at the legendary jewel.

"It's beautiful," she said breathlessly.

The familiar wry smile shot across Skyheart's lips. "You should see the real thing."

The Queen's head shot up from the jewel and her eyes narrowed at the visage of Skyheart. Guards turned on their heels giving Skyheart nervous looks. DeFlare turned, not confused or even surprised. Skyheart read it as a look of rage. So be it. DeFlare, by extension, was Thieron and Skyheart was done with the desert city.

He drew from his pocket the real Diamandé, the shimmering brilliance of which dwarfed the magnificence of the room in an instant, making it seem dull by comparison. Although shinning, the jewel may as well have cast a shadow on the room.

The Captain's smile grew wider as he watched the Empress raise an interested eyebrow. He held the jewel out to her, although he was some distance away, in an outstretched arm. "Why not take the real thing?"

DeFlare stood, shoulders hunched with tension, clenching his fists. He began the stride towards Skyheart, only to be confronted by two guards who thrust their halberds in his path. He stopped and watched, helplessly. He saw Skyheart glance at him; treacherous miscreant of heinous machinations. What was this plan?

The Empress stirred in her throne. "I hold a fake?"

"Indeed you do," Skyheart said.

"What is the meaning of this?"

"Thieron planned on playing Genko and Mandra off against one another, giving each a fake Diamandé. They hoped to accelerate their meeting only for one to destroy the other having to use force as neither Diamandés held the power to destroy them. The weakened victor, furious at Thieron's treachery, would march on the desert city, only to be annihilated by the real Diamandé."

"And you would give me the true Diamandé?"

"Yes."

She waved an arm and a guard took the jewel from him. The armoured man delivered it to the Empress, his heavy metal skin chiming with each step.

"Strange," she said taking the real jewel, "how something so destructive could be so beautiful."

"Why are you doing this?" DeFlare said, surprising even himself with his calmness.

Skyheart stopped smiling. His expression turned to something akin to boredom. "There's nothing for me in Thieron anymore, DeFlare. It seems I've bested my betters one too many times. The Assembly wishes to execute me upon my return, so I shan't return. Hopefully, this transaction will make them regret their decision."

"You could have just left!" DeFlare shouted. "Why give the Diamandé away? Think of the innocent Thieronians you've killed. To what end?"

Skyheart took upon himself a more familiar form and scratched the back of his head. "I, uh..." he paused. "I hadn't thought quite that far ahead."

With that a thundering crash sounded outside. Followed by another as the wall behind the Empress exploded from cannon fire. The pseudo-deity screamed as a large slab of marble was made free of the ceiling and fell on her. The crushed, lifeless corpse released the Diamandé with some force and it slid across the floor to the Captain's feet. He picked it up and pocketed it once more.

"How unexpected," he said with a smile.

The guards, horrified by the death of their ruler and god, rushed to the corpse, desperately trying to lift the marble boulder. One peered outside the gargantuan hole left in the wall.

"The Mandrans are attacking by sea!" he called.

With that the cannon fire became more frequent, shaking the ground with each target hit.

DeFlare, now unguarded, drew his sword and lunged towards Skyheart. The Captain drew Cendré and parried the strike.

"It's not safe here," Skyheart sang. "We should probably try to get outside."

DeFlare ignored his words and unleashed a flurry of ungraceful, clumsy strikes, all easily defended by the Crimson Captain.

"I've no wish to fight or kill you, DeFlare," he said. "Again, I suggest we leave."

More guards entered through the large hole. "The Thieronians!" One in a gold helm shouted. "Get them!"

The guards, nearing twenty in number, charged towards the two men from Division Four.

"Well so much for not fighting," Skyheart said, pushing DeFlare away and resting the blade of Cendré on his shoulder.

"We're allies," DeFlare growled, "but only until it's safe for us to fight one another."

Halberds were forced upon the Lieutenant but Skyheart blocked their path. He smiled at DeFlare.

"Very well," Skyheart said. He pushed the halberds away with a smooth swipe and charged towards their owners, striking down three guards before being confronted by three more. He made the first move and kicked one away in DeFlare's direction, leaving two standing together. He struck at one but had his strike blocked by the other. The target of his original attack now swung his halberd. Skyheart smiled. His plan had worked. The attacking guard had left himself open. Skyheart forced more weight onto the defending guard, then released and stepped aside. The momentum caused the defending guard to launch himself into the attacking guard's path. The attacking guard's halberd sliced into the defending guard's neck, severing his airway. Skyheart sliced at the attacking guard's chest, Cendré easily cutting through his armour. Both guards fell and Skyheart's attention turned to DeFlare.

The Lieutenant was defending himself against the remaining force in a seemingly endless procession of parries. Only the bravest had gone to be slain by the Captain and DeFlare had found himself against a sizeable force, made worse by the fact that Skyheart had kicked one of his opponents over to DeFlare.

Just as DeFlare was beginning to give up hope of ever getting out alive, the guards fell with identical slashes across their chests. DeFlare saw Skyheart down on one knee next to him, sword hand outstretched. He could have been a statue of a long forgotten warrior.

Eventually, Skyheart took a deep breath and rose. He signalled for DeFlare to follow him and the two ran towards the hole in the palace wall. It took them out onto a rocky cliff above the sea. Although a port town, Genko was actually high above sea level and a slope had been built that led to the harbour. The Thieronians made their way around the palace and into the city.

Some way away the Mandran ships had begun to dock, sending a great force of soldiers into the city. Much of Genko had already been flattened by cannon fire. Skyheart and DeFlare watched helplessly as the soldiers made their way up the slope from the harbour. A small group of Genkoan soldiers charged passed Skyheart and DeFlare and into the Mandrans, colliding with them halfway down the hill. They were slaughtered soon after.

Skyheart turned and looked out to the shimmering sea, now almost free of ships. He smiled and rested the blade of Cendré on his shoulder. The ribbons, tied to the hilt, fluttered in the sea breeze.

"It seems we have a lot to do with death, you and I," he said.

DeFlare could make no sense of the comment. It was almost as if he weren't addressing the Lieutenant at all.

His thoughts were interrupted as the Mandrans reached the top of the hill, leaving the Genkoan corpses behind them. Just as DeFlare braced himself for the charge he caught, in the corner of his eye, the black blade of Cendré slicing through the air, falling towards him. He blocked the Captain's attack, but Skyheart was forever pushing harder.

"I'm not going back to Thieron," he said.

"You need to pay for what you've done here."

The Mandran forces ran past them deeper into the city. DeFlare, now without distraction, pushed back against Skyheart. He knew he was far stronger than the Captain from their many sparing sessions. The Lieutenant's visible muscles contrasted greatly with the Captain's near-feminine physique. Skyheart was thrown backwards and landed gracefully on the edge of the cliff. A less nimble man may have fallen to his death.

Seeing his chance, DeFlare lunged towards Skyheart. However, Skyheart dodged, spinning, and ended up behind DeFlare. The Lieutenant struck behind him and unleashed a slew of attacks.

He had never understood the Captain's speed. Skyheart fought with only his right hand gripping the sword, as if he were using his left for balance. This sacrificed power and, to a small extent, control, giving the impression that his attacks lacked conviction, yet DeFlare knew this not to be true. He had seen the Captain fight more than enough times to understand his style. By using one hand he increased his speed, fighting with swagger from the shoulder and elbow. Each movement was subtle, hard to read and almost impossible to predict. Power may have been sacrificed, but power was not needed if the attack went unopposed. Indeed, were DeFlare himself not such a skilled swordsman Skyheart would have bested and killed him long ago.

The Lieutenant's two handed technique allowed for constant catastrophic blows, however, these were all absorbed by Cendré, not the Captain. His body showed no signs of damage, even from the strain of battle.

Cendré, long for a katana, caused DeFlare many problems. The length made attacking difficult as he struggled to find a way around it. He was also forced to defend closer to himself than he was comfortable doing, causing no end of panic. The ribbons were a constant distraction, tricking DeFlare into thinking the Captain's attack was going in a different direction to what was truly intended.

Skyheart smiled and lifted Cendré slightly. He locked his elbow and swung diagonally down with his shoulder. DeFlare could not parry the attack and instead leaped back, tripping on a raised part of the ground and falling further than he intended. One leg slipped over the edge of the cliff. Skyheart thrust a hand forward and clutched the lapels of DeFlare's leather coat. He pulled DeFlare towards him and threw him away from the edge of the cliff.

Slowly, DeFlare picked himself up from the ground. Skyheart sighed, wearing that bored expression once more. He slipped his hand into his pocket and pulled out the Diamandé, holding it over the edge of the cliff.

"I won't hesitate to drop it," he said. "Then Thieron will be defenceless and Mandra marches onward."

"You want Thieron gone so badly?"

"No. But I can't see you letting me leave without some kind of a bargaining point. This is it. You let me go and I give you the Diamandé. You attack me and I drop said jewel into the watery depths, condemning Thieron to oblivion."

"With so many Mandran soldiers do you really believe either of us has a chance of getting out alive?"

Skyheart smiled. "DeFlare, please. I'm Captain Laike Skyheart."

With that, the apocalyptic boom of cannon fire sang once more as one of the harboured ships shot at the cliff, dislodging some of the ground from beneath the Captain's feet. He threw the Diamandé into the air, not wishing to take it with him. He fell backwards, feet no longer finding the solace of support.

DeFlare dived forwards, not to save the Captain but the Diamandé. His fingertips just made it to the jewel, yet as he tied to grasp it, it fell further from him. It danced from him mockingly and followed the Captain.

'So this is how I die,' Skyheart thought. 'And all I wanted was one last adventure.'

Uncomplainingly his body crashed into the waters beneath, the Diamandé glinting in the morning sun above him.

Darkness.

Chapter Nine

The battle ended soon after the fall of Captain Laike Skyheart. DeFlare took no further part in it, he had collapsed to his knees and merely stared out to sea. He knew not what to do.

The Diamandé, Thieron's last hope, was gone. Washed out into an eternal ocean. The entire city would now fall against the might of Mandra. Of course, the Genkoan front line still stood, but they could, at best, stall Mandra.

Less significant, but still considerably important to DeFlare, was the loss of Captain Skyheart. The man who had been everything to him: leader, hero, villain, nuisance, problem solver, soldier, surrogate brother and more.

It was only now that he mourned the Captain's death that anyone approached him. Two Mandran soldiers walked to him tentatively, spears at the ready as either a threat or insurance. DeFlare didn't pick up his sword. It lay there, unused, next to him.

"He doesn't want to fight," one said to the other.

"Kill him anyway."

"He's unarmed."

"He's got a sword."

"He's not using it."

"He will if you don't kill him."

"He's not even Genkoan."

"Then what is he?"

"I don't know."

"He's Thieronian," said another man approaching from the direction of the harbour. He was large, taller than DeFlare, and wore the red uniform of Mandra. He had many medals, all of which shone in the midday sun.

"General Tegus!" The two soldiers said, kneeling in respect.

DeFlare looked up at the General, sneering. Tegus looked at him in much the same way as a predator looks at prey it has just dubbed unworthy of consumption. Tegus stepped forward and pulled DeFlare up in order to look him in the eyes.

"Playing Mandra and Genko off against one another, I see," he said. "A dangerous game. Ambitious, perhaps overly so."

He threw DeFlare back to the ground. The Lieutenant landed on his ribs with a thud. He made no noise despite the pain.

"What of your Captain?" Tegus said.

DeFlare rose to his knees and slowly pointed out to the sea.

"Shame," Tegus said. "I should have liked the pleasure of watching the Crimson Captain die. This leaves you in a rather awkward position, I'd imagine. After all, Thieron's Fourth Division is no more."

"Actually," DeFlare said through gritted teeth, "it's Division Four!"

He rose, grasping the hilt of his sword, swinging for the General. Yes, death. Death should meet this man. What would that mean for Mandra? Thieron had lost a Captain, but to lose a General...

DeFlare ceased to move, at first perplexed. He looked down to see the bloodied tips of two spears exiting through his chest. His sword dropped from his hand with a metallic ring as it hit the stone ground.

The soldiers behind DeFlare removed their spears from him and he fell, the comfort of standing escaping him.

Each breath was laboured and painful, inhaling what felt like more spears. He looked at Tegus, living reaper of an undeserved future. The General looked down at him, seemingly enjoying the Lieutenant's pain.

Lieutenant Alrous DeFlare turned his head out to the ocean. The navy of the sea paling into the azure of the sky, powdered by clouds lazily thrown across the landscape. The sun, benevolent as ever, glowed, dimming.

'Fitting,' he thought, 'that I shouldn't live long after you...'

With that, the sun extinguished and DeFlare slipped into darkness. A darkness forever fading.

Chapter Ten

Captain Cyan of the Third Division stood in the elevator with his Lieutenant, Rom, and the Second Division's Lieutenant Xenil. They said nothing to each other, all fearing the news they would receive in the President's Office. All had been informed of Operation Shell and the precarious nature of such a mission did not sit well with them. They were all aware that the men that had been sent were more than capable, although they would have been more comfortable if they had gone themselves.

The elevator stopped and Cyan entered the President's Office followed by the two men in blue coats. They took their places before the Assembly. Xenil stood by Emaina Skyheart and Cyan took his place by General Wraste, Rom in tow.

The President looked small in his chair, dwarfed by worry and the twelve Assembly members. "I believe you all know why you are here," he said. "Operation Shell has failed. This morning Captain Thean and Lieutenant Okain were executed by the Mandrans. They had successfully delivered the Faux-Diamandé; however, it appears the Mandrans had no need of it.

"Late this morning the Mandrans launched a naval assault on Genko, killing the Empress in the process. I regret to inform you that Captain Laike Skyheart and Lieutenant DeFlare were also killed, although the exact details of this turn of events are, as yet, unknown.

"The Mandrans have now taken Genko. However, the Genkoan frontline is making tracks back to Genko with the intention of taking the city back. It is, though, doubtful they will be able to take back the city. Mandra has already set up their defences. At best, the Genkoans can slow the advance of the Mandrans. We are surrounded on both sides by the same force."

Cyan and Rom exchanged burdened glances and then Cyan turned back to the President.

"Undoubtedly," Cyan said, "the loss of Captains Thean and Skyheart and Lieutenants Okain and DeFlare are both personal and national tragedies. However, while Operation Shell may not have been a complete success, we do now only have to deal with one enemy force, as per the plan, and we do still have the Diamandé."

Emaina stepped forward.

"Actually we don't," he said. "My brother appears to have doomed us all by stealing the Diamandé from us. His last action on this planet and a decisive one at that."

"What? Why would he do such a thing?" asked Lieutenant Rom.

"Apparently," Emaina said, "the Assembly informed him that he would be executed on his return. It appears the predicament we find ourselves in is his revenge."

"We did not say he would be executed," said one hooded man. "We merely informed him to watch his step. Execution was the worst case scenario."

"I think you'll find that *this* is the worst case scenario," Emaina said.

"Captain Skyheart, we understand that you are upset by the death of your brother..."

"Upset?" Emaina laughed. "Please don't misunderstand. These events are less than fortuitous, but the death of my brother is a personal triumph for me. Indeed, I am considering throwing a parade as opposed to a funeral. However, I am struck by the *considerable* foolishness of the ruling class of Thieron, telling a Captain so immature and cavalier that he was to be severely reprimanded on his return from the most important mission in the country's history!"

"Immature and cavalier the Captain may have been," Wraste said. "Yet, it was not a mistake to assume he was still a professional."

"He should never have been made a captain in the first place. A great swordsman he may have been but he lacked the qualities of a leader. He may have had the family name but a son of Commander Skyheart is not the Commander himself." Emaina waved a hand. "Although we are wasting time. A plan must be devised to safeguard Thieron."

"We still have the army," said Wraste. "Admittedly it is far smaller than the Mandran force we face, but with the Genkoan frontline soon to face the Eastern Mandran force it is expected that they will have losses."

"Yet still they would obliterate our force," said Emaina.

"Not if we were to join forces with the Genkoans. Were we to send our entire army to aid Genko we could decimate the Eastern Mandran force."

"And who would defend Thieron while the army is gone? All your plan does is leave us open to attack from the Western force."

Wraste stood contemplatively. Of course, Emaina was right, yet the General still felt the army was Thieron's only hope. If he was wrong then Thieron had no hope at all.

"Our army may be small," said Xenil. "However, it is far more used to the desert than the Mandrans. Were each division to defend a gate we have a chance of repelling the Mandrans."

"A good plan," Kylar said. "But it requires two more Captains than we have and, if Laike Skyheart wasn't ready for the responsibility, then I fear the same could be said of yourself and Rom."

"Although," Emaina said pensively, "the Mandrans can only attack from the east and west. If we were only to defend those gates and have two divisions at each we could repel the Mandran invasion."

"True," said an Assembly member. "But were just one gate to fall the battle would be lost."

The room fell silent as all eighteen men lost themselves in thought, working each scenario through in their minds. If the smallest of aspects failed Thieron would fall. But how to assure victory? How could the powerless defeat the powerful?

Rom leaned towards Cyan. "You've yet to say anything, Captain. Is there nothing to be done?"

"There is always something to be done, Rom. But finding what that thing is isn't always simple."

"You have no thoughts?"

"One. Although, it is overly dependent on certain factors."

"It can be no worse than what has already been suggested."

Rom returned to his former position, leaving Cyan to ponder what he had said. His plan was less of a risk than what had already been suggested. Less, perhaps even no, soldiers would die. It required only one or two men and he had already decided on who they would be. He cleared his throat. "What if we were to find the Diamandé once more?"

A shuffling sound broke out in the room as each Assembly member moved to look at him. The President looked up from the desk, frowning. The men Cyan was in line with made no movements, yet he could feel something from them. Something like bewilderment.

"What are you suggesting Captain Cyan?" asked Kylar. "That we just wander out into the desert and pray that Thiera made provision for such an event by making a second Diamandé?"

Cyan smiled lightly. "Not exactly," he said. "The last known location of the Diamandé is Genko. Either the Diamandé is still there or the clues to finding it are. In either case, it's not outside the realms of possibility that we can get back the Diamandé before the Mandrans attack. If we send a small force, one or two men, they could even leave today."

"And what if the Mandrans have the Diamandé?" said an Assembly member.

"Then we shall just have to take it back."

"Not exactly diplomatic," said another Assembly member.

"Perhaps not, although now doesn't strike me as the time for diplomacy. Honestly I'd rather avoid conflict altogether, but that's not really an option now is it? Treachery doesn't tend to make your enemies the most reasonable of people."

"It's as good a plan as any we've had," General Wraste said, "and better than most."

"And if it fails?" said the President.

"With all due respect, sir, perhaps that should have been asked of Operation Shell," Cyan replied.

"This is no time for humour, Cyan," said Emaina. "It's a valid question. Have you a backup plan?"

Cyan sighed. "If the plan fails then you have lost only two men and can repel the Mandrans with the army."

"But you don't think that will happen?" Rom said.

"No I do not."

"Because you want us to go."

"I want us to go."

Rom smiled reticently. "If that is what is needed I cannot refuse."

Emaina stepped forward. "If I may speak!" he spat. "May I suggest that I go with Xenil? No doubt the Third Division is more than capable; however one must feel that a more ruthless leader than Captain Cyan is needed in this mission. Were a civilian to have found the Diamandé would Cyan cut him down?"

The President gestured towards Cyan. "Captain Skyheart has a point. Why should the Third Division go?"

"Surely the name 'Skyheart' has had quite enough to do with this issue already," Cyan said. "Also, while one of us is away the other will be needed to lead the army in battle. Surely, Captain Skyheart would be more suited to the job than me."

The President leaned back in his chair. A distant look came upon him as if he tasted Cyan's words more than he was thinking about them. He sat back up and looked to Wraste. "Who would you want to lead the troops in battle?"

"Captain Skyheart has more battle experience than Cyan and is more accustomed to leading a large number of men."

"Who would you decide to send on the mission to get the Diamandé, regardless of whom was leading the army?"

"Cyan would be more difficult for the enemy to find. Skyheart is a rather infamous name."

Emaina grimaced but said nothing. It seemed his brother had damaged the reputation of the entire Skyheart name, not just that of the Crimson Captain.

"So be it," the President said. "Cyan, when can you and Rom leave?"

"Almost immediately, sir."

"Very well. Thiera be with you, Captain."

Cyan and Rom saluted then made their way for the elevator.

"Oh, and Captain," the President said. Cyan and Rom stopped, turning to Kylar. "If you should happen to fail, I shouldn't bother returning."

Rom looked to Cyan, trying to assess his expression but there was nothing to read. Cyan nodded and the two left.

"If I may speak," Emaina said to the remaining men, but looking at the floor, fists clenched, "although I feel I should not have to; I am not my brother. I have avoided having anything to do with him that was not completely necessary. I have never condoned an action he has committed, nor will I ever now. Suffice to say, I thought you all understood this, so I am slightly bemused as to my treatment in the room here today."

"Captain," said an Assembly member, "since the death of Captain Thean you are the highest ranking Captain in terms of division number and are, therefore, the figurehead of the entire Thieronian army. The decision to send Cyan had nothing to do with your surname, or at least not in the way that you think. Cyan is embarking on a dangerous mission, from which he may not return. For this we could not risk you. You have a different fate."

Emaina frowned studiously. "A different fate?"

General Wraste stepped forward taking a place with the Assembly. "You have shown great tactical and strategic knowledge here today," he said. "Superior even to mine. How would you like to reach the heights of your father? How would you like to become Commander Skyheart?"

The steam-powered elevator hissed familiarly and the two men from the Third Division began their descent of the Monument. Rom looked to Captain

Cyan; tall and strong, yet beginning to age. His face was starting to wrinkle and the blue of his eyes had started to grey along with his once black hair. He kept his face clean shaven, always fearing any grey stubble would make him look older.

Rom thought of saying something before deciding that there was nothing to say. It was not the place of this inexperienced Lieutenant to question his Captain, although he was relieved when Cyan spoke.

"Apprehensive, Rom?"

"A little, Captain."

"I see us as equals, Rom. Please call me Ryden."

"I'm afraid that's not appropriate, Captain."

Cyan sighed. "Very well. Why the apprehension?"

"I realise that it's not my place to question, Captain, but do you really think we can find the Diamandé?"

"Laike Skyheart was many things, Rom. But I do not believe him to ever have been a fool. Today he was shown to be a traitor; to all intents and purposes he committed treason. However, upon realising his plan wasn't working, the Laike Skyheart I knew would have made provision to benefit those he knew: us."

"And if he didn't have time, Captain?"

"Then the fate of Thieron has been decided and we cannot change it. Why worry about that which one cannot affect?"

The elevator came to a stop and the two men entered the Monument's lobby. Their preparations were to begin.

They exited through Thieron's East Gate not an hour later.

Chapter Eleven

The ashen black clouds that gave birth to storms and torment rolled into the sky over Port Fair. The townspeople had experience enough of them over the years to know a tempest was coming. As such, the town was deserted, save for him. Not that he didn't know what to expect. He was well versed in storms, indeed he wouldn't have been there without one. No, what made him stay as the clouds released a light rain was what he could see from the square.

The red tail of Celisso rose as if the beast itself was conducting the orchestra of ruin. It was a popular theory in Port Fair. The serpent had caused them so much anguish it was only natural to blame all misfortune that befell them upon it.

The tail rose and crashed in the grey sea, the surf now as black as the clouds overhead. The boy watched, mesmerised, cursing the beast that thwarted the prospect of his journey home.

How long had he been there now? Certainly no longer than a week, in fact it was almost definitely less than that, yet the images of his island home were forever diminishing, as if the visages were in need of support or reinforcement from the real thing.

The rain hardened. He wiped away a tear, although it did no good for the rain had soaked his face entirely, his hat helping not an inch against such force. A bolt of lightning struck out at sea and a memory of the night he was stolen from home flashed through his mind. How many bolts had fallen that night? How far from home was he?

As if to remind Paccon that he wasn't completely alone, Franklin clambered to the top of his shirt pocket peering at the effigy before him. Paccon removed him, placing the turtle on his palm and holding him to his face.

"When will we get home?" asked the boy.

Franklin looked at him vacantly, twisting his head slowly.

Paccon sighed and placed Franklin back in his pocket. He walked towards Myri's house and entered.

Myri woke early, glad to see Paccon was still asleep. He had only slept a little since he arrived and he often woke in the night, fearful for not being home, still screaming from nightmares that tortured him in his slumber, pleading for his "Mama". If only Myri knew where she was. But she didn't and saw no way of finding her.

She rose and dressed, exiting the house into the glorious light of the morning. It was always brightest in Port Fair after a storm, or so it seemed to Myri. As she walked around the square she was thankful to see precious little damage had been done to the town, a rarity with a storm as fierce as those by the sea.

"Myri!" called an old voice. She turned to see the Mayor standing in the door of the Town Hall.

"Hello, Mayor," she said.

"Yes, yes. No time for pleasantries I'm afraid. I have news! Urgent news. Send for the residents. Gather them. Town meeting!" He shouted this last sentence as loudly as his lungs would allow, though, old as he was, this wasn't quite as loud as he had hoped. However, some of the townsfolk had heard and even as Myri left to gather the other denizens some approached the Town Hall.

She walked the square (the only residential part of the town) informing those who didn't already know of the meeting. Eventually, she believed she had found everyone and started making her way back to the Town Hall. She jumped as she felt a tugging on the leg of her dress. She looked down and saw Paccon.

"I thought you were asleep," she said, smiling and kneeling.

"The noise woke me up," he said, rubbing his eyes. He had a look of confusion about him, Myri wasn't sure if that was because of his tiredness or the oddity of the situation. "What's going on?"

"There's a town meeting."

"Town meeting?"

"Yes," she replied, nodding.

"What's that?"

"Well, every so often something important happens and the Mayor decides he needs to tell the town about it in the Town Hall."

"So something important has happened?"

"Yes."

"Like the storm?"

"Well, everyone already knows about the storm so it won't be that." She stood and held out her hand, Paccon took it and they began walking.

"So, how does the Mayor decide what's important?"

"Well, not much happens around here, so if the Mayor finds out something from far away it's probably important."

Paccon nodded.

When they entered the Town Hall every seat was already taken.

'So this is the thanks I get for collecting the whole town,' she thought, though she was only semi-serious. She stood with Paccon at the back of the hall and watched as the Mayor walked up to his podium. 'What's with him and that podium? He doesn't need it; we all know he's the Mayor.'

"Thank you all for coming," said the Mayor. "I received important news from the Northern Continent this morning. I know that you all think what happens there has no bearing here on us. However, when you hear what I have to say you may realise just what important news this is.

"Yesterday morning two soldiers from Thieron entered Mandra and conversed with the Queen. Their aim was to reach a truce, stopping the Mandrans from marching on Thieron. They aimed to secure this by giving the Mandrans a jewel, a weapon of mass destruction, known in Thieronian mythology as the Diamandé.

72

"However, it appears that the Thieronians gave them a replica, keeping the real one for themselves. This was discovered and Mandra executed the Thieronians. Not that this mattered, Mandra had plans of her own for dealing with Genko.

"Later that morning the Mandran navy launched an attack on Genko decimating the city and taking it for themselves. Though, here is another twist. Two more Thieronians were in Genko securing a similar deal with the Genkoans. It appears Thieron intended to accelerate the meeting of the two powers and defeat the one that was left with the real Diamandé.

"But, after the naval assault on Genko it has been discovered that one of the soldiers had the Diamandé on him: the infamous Captain Laike Skyheart."

A murmur broke out in the hall as each resident discussed the name.

"Who's Captain Laike Skyheart?" Paccon asked Myri.

"The arrogant son of an evil and powerful man," she said through gritted teeth.

"What?"

"He's a soldier who goes on adventures. But his father was Commander Zenedin Skyheart who ordered the Thieronian troops into the Southern Continent in the Mineral Wars. He damaged the continent beyond repair and his soldiers killed my father."

"Oh," Paccon said, looking away.

Myri sighed. That was probably more information than the poor boy needed.

"Yes, yes. We all know the name," the Mayor said, banging his gavel. Eventually the room became quiet. "Thank you. It so transpires that he, along with his subordinate, was killed during the Mandran invasion. Needless to say the Mandrans intend to finish Thieron off.

"Yet, the Genkoan front line remains intact and intends to take back Genko. Whether or not they are successful is irrelevant. We should all take great care that we are watching the events of the Northern Continent very carefully. This could be a period of huge change, especially when we consider that the Diamandé appears to be lost once more. This is a dangerous time in the history of our planet. We are caught between the warring Northern Continent and Celisso. Hopefully, we'll be left alone. It's well known that there's nothing left for anyone here. But that's never stopped them invading before. Perhaps the simple act of invasion is reason enough for these people. We know not.

"I tell you this, not to scare you, but to prepare you. You all deserve to know what dark days these are."

The Mayor's speech ended and the room filled with stagnant silence. Eventually a young man in the front row rose. Myri knew him to be a fisherman named Pahr. She knew little else about him.

"Is this all you've called us here for?" he said, his tense posture suggesting he wasn't doing as good a job of hiding his anger as he had intended. "You waste our time with stories of the Northern Continent when we are nearly out of food! Celisso still commands our waters. Tell us, Mayor;

what is being done to end this starvation?"

The Mayor's head dropped. "I merely think you deserve to know."

"Celisso, Mayor," said another young man. "What is being done?"

"There is nothing to be done."

"I say we kill it!" said Pahr. "What is it? A big fish. I'm a fisherman. A fish, no matter how big, is no match for a fisherman."

Excited muttering began amongst the townsfolk as Pahr's words rang throughout the hall. The Mayor seemed to shrink at Pahr's argument. Myri stepped forward.

"You'll die if you try to kill it Pahr," she said. "You've seen it as many times as I have, maybe more. Celisso snaps boats and ships in half as if they were mere twigs. You saw what it did to..." She wanted to say it. She wanted to say her fiancé's name, but she couldn't. So, this was how it would be from now on. She shrank back.

"Yes, I saw what happened to Kote, Myri," Pahr said. "A cruel fate and one a man as good as him didn't deserve. But that won't happen to me. I know those waters better than any man."

"I'm with Pahr," the other man said, standing. Cheers emerged from others who also rose.

"If you're with me, then come," Pahr said. "We shall dispatch the fish now!" Pahr led the men towards the door and left. The remaining residents looked to the Mayor.

"Are you not going to stop them?" one woman asked.

"How?" replied the Mayor. "They cannot be reasoned with."

Slowly, they all left, shooting the Mayor glances of malice.

It had begun to rain as they stepped outside. Paccon gripped Myri's hand tightly and she started to walk him home.

"What's going to happen to them?" he asked.

"I don't know," Myri said.

"They're going to die, aren't they?"

Myri didn't answer.

He'd sent them to their houses to fetch what weapons they could. They returned with battle scarred spears from the Mineral Wars or harpoons they used on an almost daily basis. He supposed that the quality on weapons didn't matter; after all, there were almost twenty of them. What fish could match twenty men?

As they piled into the boats, also showing signs of age, the rain fell harder. The tail of Celisso rose and fell. Somewhere thunder roared. Pahr told the men not to worry. What could the weather do?

The boats set out, unsteady on the buoyant sea. The men inside tumbled, struggling to stand, yet still they went on. Celisso's form grew ever larger in sight. The red tail rose and fell once more, sending even higher and fiercer waves in their path. Yet still they went on.

The tail did not rise again. The men looked beneath them for any sign of red but such a sight eluded them.

Thunder growled once more.

Gradually, the distance between the two boats grew larger as the waves parted the vessels.

Did their presence scare the beast away? Such was the view of one man. He spoke his mind, eliciting smiles from the naïve few who agreed with him.

It was now that Pahr realised his folly. This was more than just a fish. He turned to his men telling them to ready their weapons.

Before he could finish speaking the gnarled head of Celisso rose between the two boats as the creature launched itself into the air. The tail followed, knocking Pahr's boat away and the head crashed into the boat of the other men devouring those aboard. The resulting wave and surf engulfed Pahr's boat, soaking the men even further than the rain had.

As the men were readying themselves for the next attack by Celisso, the finned, marred head rose before the boat. Slowly this time, as if the monster wanted the men to know what it looked like, truly, before it ended their lives. Scars traversed the scales of the red face, giving the impression that, before the life of defence and destruction Celisso had embarked upon, the face was once smooth. Grey plasma covered the eyes, dripping from them, staining the navy of the sea. It opened its mouth, revealing endless rows of saw-edged teeth.

The creature roared and instantly the rain stopped, the clouds fading into the blue of the sky. A now perfect day. The boat rocked to the noise of the beast.

Pahr, upon seeing his chance, struck at Celisso with his spear, desperate to survive the encounter. Yet, the spear snapped against the tough skin of the creature, falling to the ocean, drifting away on the tide.

Celisso sank beneath the sea once more. Each man knew what was coming. They looked back to shore seeing the majority of the town standing there; keen to survey the progress of events.

The tail split the boat in two, sending splinters of wood at the men, blinding some, killing others. Still the tail thrashed, creating surf that once was not, colouring the sea, his kingdom, red.

Celisso, harbinger of death and sorrow, upon finishing his task of destruction, sank back to the depths, allowing those watching on the shore to survey his mighty work. Were hope never to have existed again, would they have known? Such was life on the Southern Continent.

It was a cool morning as she sat there looking at her homemade monuments to the legacies of those she once knew. Some long dead, one still almost fresh, all still on her mind. She didn't remember her parents. She was only one year old when the Mineral Wars ended those twenty five years ago. Although she couldn't recall the deaths of either parent, no scenario in her mind comforted her. She almost wished she had been older when they had died, to have known their faces and the truth. But in the darkness of her mind there was no truth and comfort could not be stumbled upon if there was no solace to discover.

Then there was him; Kote Venar, forsaken love of Myri Harmoire and victim of Celisso. The first to try and defeat the creature. Never less than present on her mind for those weeks since his death. It was then she realised it was only two weeks, though it could have been centuries.

"They tried again yesterday," she said. "I told them not to, but why would they listen to me?" She sighed. "It's almost like they've forgotten about you." A tear trailed down her right cheek. "Why did you go?" she whimpered. "What about me?" She stopped and took a deep breath.

She heard a shuffling behind her and turned to find Paccon there.

"You're crying," he said. "Are you okay?"

"Yeah," she said, forcing a smile and wiping away some tears.

Paccon sat down next to her and she held him. Was that comfort? She wasn't sure, but it felt like it was what she should be doing. There was warmth to the boy and it entered into her. She felt her body sigh, how long ago had that last happened?

"Why do you do it?" Paccon asked.

"Do what?"

"Talk to them."

"Well, I suppose I want them to know that I miss them and that they're always on my mind."

"Can they hear you?"

"I hope so."

"Can you hear them?"

Myri paused. "Sometimes," she said, "if I listen really hard."

"What do they say?"

"They don't really say anything. They just let me know that they're there."

Paccon nodded and smiled. "I think they appreciate you talking to them."

"You do?"

"I think I would."

Myri stood up. "You've a long time before you need to worry about that."

"I know," Paccon said, also standing. "But still, I'd like people to talk to me."

They walked inside.

"They will," Myri said.

"Do you only talk to them in the garden?"

"No, they're always with me. But the garden's peaceful so it's a little easier there."

"Okay," Paccon said. He sat on his bed and looked at Myri, although his eyes could have been pointed anywhere under the brim of his hat.

She wondered what he thought about in those long periods of silence. He would, at times, go for hours without even saying a word, but he was never unsociable. He was just intense for such a young child. She supposed he thought about home, wherever that was. But, uncomplainingly, he stayed in Port Fair, curious about the town.

A bell rang outside and Myri sighed, knowing what they were being called to. She took Paccon's hand and they left.

They were two of the last to arrive at the Remembrance Garden, not that anyone noticed. The subdued occasion didn't allow for taking note on who was and was not there, besides, the townsfolk were already mourning.

Myri took her place next to Carre.

"I didn't think that you'd come," Carre said.

"Why wouldn't I?"

"It's a little... familiar, isn't it?"

Myri said nothing.

Carre smiled at Paccon and Paccon smiled back, his white teeth barely visible beneath the shadow of his hat.

"And how are you Paccon?" Carre asked.

He gave a thumbs-up but didn't reply. Myri expected that, he'd talked a lot that morning.

"Do you know where he lives yet?" Carre asked quietly.

"No. I need to work out which island he comes from." Myri gave a heavy unintentional sigh.

"Are you sure you're okay being here?" Carre asked.

Myri nodded. "I'm fine."

The Mayor stood and took his place before the congregation. He looked small and pale as if the previous day had aged him. His stoop had worsened and standing looked to be troublesome.

"Thank you all for coming," he began. "We are here today to send the souls of the twenty men lost yesterday to the planet. It is important in times like these, concerning as they are, that we do as we normally would. Even with Celisso in our waters, we must remember that if we work together, as a community, we will survive this.

"These brave men died yesterday trying to rid us of our sorrows. An honourable sentiment, which, at the time, was refused and advised not to go ahead. This, however, does not change the fact that they died for Port Fair and it is only right that we honour them. It is only right that we remember them."

Myri watched, pained as the Mayor trawled through the names and their families laid a wreath for each of them. When he was finished with the names, the Mayor laid a wreath and said; "May the planet look after their souls in death, now that we have failed to safeguard their bodies in life."

Myri thought it was strange to see the Mayor mourning the deaths of men he, only yesterday, had a confrontation with. She thought he might have blamed himself. That would certainly have accounted for his appearance. Yet, there was something very impersonal about the mass funeral; one ceremony for twenty men, each getting only the briefest of mentions. It was as if he believed them to have deserved their fate.

Myri felt a tug on her skirt. She looked down and saw Paccon.

"Will you talk to these people?" he asked.

Myri shook her head. "I didn't really know them."

Paccon nodded. "Okay."

They left the garden soon after, the howling Celisso heralding their misery.

That afternoon Myri, Carre and Paccon went fruit picking in the forest. The entrance had been completely ravaged of its bounty, forcing the small group to venture further inside, something the Mayor had once advised against but now insisted upon. Although, this didn't stop them from being apprehensive; if the choice was go far into the forest or starve they knew which they would prefer.

There had always been peculiar stories about the forest. It featured heavily in the mythology of the Southern Continent and new tales of irregularity were being added almost daily. The most worrying of these concerned the apple tree in the forest centre. On a fruit picking expedition the day before, a group claimed that as they reached for the only apple it disappeared. As such, they returned empty-handed.

Myri wasn't sure if she believed the story or not. She had never been far into the forest before and doubted there even was an apple tree, especially one with disappearing fruit. Although, of the stories surrounding the forest, this was certainly one of the most believable, but Myri knew that believable and true were two very different things.

As they neared the centre of the forest they had very little in their baskets, merely a few berries and, since picking them, Carre had voiced concerns about them poisonous.

"Someone in town will know," Myri said. "Just don't eat any now."

They went on, finding nothing else until they came to a small clearing. The shrubbery had died or been unable to grow in such a place, due to the large tree in the centre blocking the sunlight. Myri and Carre looked at each other, both confident of which tree it was. Indeed, it was bearing many apples, all ripe and ready to eat. The shades of green and red gave the effigy an almost mirage-like quality.

"I thought they said that the last apple disappeared yesterday," Myri said.

"The legend goes that when all of the fruit is gone from the tree it will bear a new ripe bounty the very next day," Carre said.

"That's impossible," Myri scoffed.

"I've heard stranger things about this forest that I think are true. Forget the forest, who'd have thought a fish could control the weather?"

Myri didn't answer. Instead she walked towards the tree and tried to grab the lowest hanging apple she could find, but even that was too high for her to reach.

"Want a leg up?" Carre asked.

Myri nodded and Carre stood before her. She grabbed Myri's legs and lifted her.

Meanwhile, Paccon was sat against the tree talking to Franklin. Every so often, he thought he heard something rustling in the brush, but whenever he looked up there was nothing there. He supposed it was just a bird.

After a few minutes of trying to reach the same apple and failing, Carre put Myri back down.

"I'm going to have to get on your shoulders," Myri said.

"We won't get all of these," Carre said. "Why don't we go back into town and get more people?"

"Because I don't think they'll believe us. At least help me get one."

Carre sighed but knelt down and let Myri clamber onto her shoulders. Carre thrust herself onto her feet and Myri stretched her arms out as far as she could, yet the apple still eluded her grasp.

"I'm going to have to stand on you," she said. "Promise you won't drop me."

"I won't drop you."

"Promise me."

"I promise I won't drop you. Or perhaps you'd like it in writing?"

"Maybe later," Myri said, laughing gently. She pulled her right leg up and placed her foot on Carre's shoulder, holding Carre's head for extra balance. She thought she heard Carre protesting but ignored her. Carre grabbed the foot and held it in place, then did the same with Myri's other leg.

Myri let go of Carre's head and pushed herself into a standing position. She stretched out and could almost reach the apple. She knocked it gently with the tip of her middle finger, but it refused to come loose.

"I think I could get it if you stood on your toes," Myri said.

Carre sighed and thrust herself onto her toes. As she did so Myri fell back a little, but managed to regain her balance. She stood breathlessly for a few seconds, trying to calm herself.

"Hurry up!" Carre grunted.

Myri stretched her arms and fingers once more, but, just as she was about to lay a hand on the apple, the tree began to sway in the breeze. The apple remained elusive. Just as the wind stopped the tree returned to Myri's direction and she wrapped a hand around the apple.

It disappeared, instantly disintegrating from her grasp and sight. Myri looked around and saw that all of the other apples had gone too.

"Carre did you see that?"

"I think so."

Carre helped Myri down gently.

"We didn't imagine the apples, did we?" Myri asked.

"Both of us? I don't think so," Carre said. She sighed. "Well, that was a huge waste of our time."

They rested with Paccon for a few moments before walking back into town. Port Fair would go hungry once more.

Chapter Twelve

The desert had been kind to them as they passed through, granting them a safe and clear passage. The plain had been much the same; innocuous and dependable. At least, until this moment. It was now, with the spears of a Genkoan scouting party pointed at them, that Rom realised, perhaps, that his mission with Cyan was more dangerous than awaiting the Mandran troops in Thieron. He had assumed that their presence would be welcomed by the Genkoans, simply for not being Mandran.

Cyan and Rom stood with their backs together just ready to repel any Genkoan attack. All six scouts seemed ready to strike down either of them at any moment. Then again, what were six men to a Thieronian Captain? They were barely a challenge for a Lieutenant.

Cyan heard a familiar metallic chime as Rom gripped the hilt of his sword.

"Don't be so impetuous, Rom," he said. "That won't help our cause at all."

Slowly and reluctantly, Rom released his sword and Cyan felt the tension in the Lieutenant fade away. Unfortunately, the act of peace was not reciprocated by the men with spears.

"What now?" Rom whispered to Cyan.

"We can't kill them. Firstly because it would alienate the Genkoans from us and we need all the allies we can get. Secondly, we've no reason to. I had hoped to use Genko in our plan, though not quite as early as this. Still, under the right circumstances it could help accelerate our advance."

"Are these the right circumstances?"

Cyan said nothing.

Rom turned his head slightly to look at the Captain; he was still looking at the spearmen. Rom had no reason to doubt the Captain. However, as it was now deep into the night he couldn't help but feel that their presence was slightly more suspicious than it would have been during the day. He fought the urge to draw his katana and dispense with the scouting party.

One Genkoan looked to another. "What should we do with them?"

The other approached Cyan slowly; spear pointed at the Captain's chest. "Why haven't you cut us down?"

"In days like these," Cyan said, "the enemy of my enemy is my friend and we are all enemies of Mandra."

The Genkoans looked at each other sceptically.

"Okay," the nearest said. "Take them to the Captain, let him decide."

They were led, rather more forcefully than was necessary, to a tent in the Genkoan camp. The outside was lit by two fire lanterns and guarded by two more spearmen. With all the precaution and security, Cyan thought it odd that he and Rom hadn't been disarmed.

The guards led them in and stood on either side of the tent.

"Thieronians found on the plains, sir," one said.

"How should we proceed, sir?" said the other.

Rom and Cyan looked at each other, exchanging humoured looks. No Thieronian would go to a Captain for such guidance. It was exactly this lack of initiative that had led to Genko's capture. Or, so Rom thought.

The Captain of the Genkoan force, looking over the battle plan before him, waved the guards away. He was a middle aged man with an immaculate brown moustache and neat hair of the same colour. He wore an elaborate blue uniform which creased as he leaned back in his chair. There was something about his appearance that made Cyan pity those under his command.

"I'll get right to the point," the Genkoan Captain said. "I don't know why you were so close to our camp and, honestly, I don't particularly care. To tell you the truth, Captain, I'm just glad to talk to an equal.

"It's an unruly rabble I'm leading. I don't know how it happened, but I'm currently the highest ranking man in Genko, which wouldn't normally be a problem only, as you can see, I'm not actually *in* Genko and I won't be for a few days yet."

"It must be troublesome moving such a large force," Cyan said.

"It's slow and cumbersome is what it is. It's a job for more than one Captain. Don't misunderstand, I'm not asking for your help in this. Frankly, I'd rather die than work in league with Thieronians, especially after all that's happened. But, dying seems rather likely currently, so I'm not sure how long I can hold onto principles like that."

Rom shuffled on his feet.

The Genkoan Captain seemed to contemplate the Thieronians from his chair. "I don't need to tell you that I'm planning to take back Genko. Truthfully, I don't have a choice in the matter. If I don't try, then the men will go alone and I'll be disgraced. It puts me in a rather awkward position, but such is my place in the world.

"I'm not a tactician; I follow orders. I'm not used to leading and planning an attack on a fortified stronghold. As it is, as soon as we attack the Mandrans will destroy us. There are more of them than us and it's considerably harder to attack than defend. Not only this, but I've got to make sure not to kill too many civilians. I'd hate for my first act as leader to be the massacre of my own people. That's not to say I expect no casualties. On the contrary, I'd be surprised if anyone survived." He paused as a fresh faced soldier entered.

"Lieutenant Umana to see you, sir." He saluted and left.

"Excuse me a minute," the Genkoan Captain said. He stood and exited through the fold in the tent, leaving the Thieronians alone.

"I thought he said he was going to get straight to the point," Rom said.

"He's trying to get us to trust him," Cyan said. "He wants us for something, even if he says he doesn't."

"What do you think it is?"

"He wants us to be scouts, fodder or sacrifices. Only he'll make it sound rather nicer than all that and, whatever it is, we'll agree, because it means we can enter Mandra before them and look for the Diamandé. It also means that we can get out before the battle begins and get back to Thieron."

"What if it's not there?"

"Then we kill as many Mandrans as we can and make it easier for the troops back home."

Rom nodded. "Do you think Genko can really win?"

"The Captain's insane, and not in the good way like Laike. Honestly, I believe Thieron to have a better chance of taking back Genko and we're not even trying to."

"How bad do you think it will be?"

Cyan sighed. "They won't even get through the gates."

They waited for a few minutes more and the Captain returned.

"My apologies," he said, sitting back down. "One of my Lieutenants seems to think he's a better tactician than I am. The sad part is, he's not wrong, only I can't let him know that. Unfortunately, his plan had no bearing on taking back Genko. Shame really, I'd much prefer to see him in charge.

"I suppose I should get to the point. I don't want to know why you're so close to our lines. I know that already; you're going to Genko. That's not really a concern to me. You're only two men and you're not allies of Mandra. But, it does raise a question I would like know the answer to. *Why* are two Thieronian soldiers going to a city that will be a hostile environment to them? After all, you double crossed Mandra too."

"The Mandrans may have something we want," Cyan said, leaning forward. "Even if they do not, that something may still be in Genko. It is imperative to our nation that we retrieve it. That's all I'm willing to divulge."

"Ah, yes. The Diamandé," the Genkoan Captain said. "Well, I'm not going to stop you from getting it. I'd rather see the Thieronians have it than the Mandrans, especially if it's as powerful as I've heard. But, I'll need a favour for letting you enter Genko first."

Cyan nodded for him to continue.

"You may enter and find the jewel. You'll arrive a few days before us, after all, two can move far quicker than ten thousand can. However, I need you to disable or destroy the gate. As long as it's open when we get there I don't mind. You see, we have no cannons and that gate is fortified beyond belief. But, from inside, it's rather easier to deal with.

"I'd estimate that if it's closed when we arrive we'll lose half of our force before we even enter the city and that's a particularly optimistic approximation. So, in return for allowing you to enter the city first, you have to ensure the gate's open for us. Are we clear?"

"As the Diamandé itself," Cyan said.

"Good. Now, if you'd like to rest tonight I can make some room in the officers' tent."

"A generous offer," Cyan said. "However, we should on with our journey if we are to have any hope of recovering the Diamandé."

"Very well. The very best of luck, Thieronians."

"No, Captain," Cyan said. "Save your luck for yourself."

Day was dawning as they entered a small town. The air of downcast oppression was beginning to lift, giving Cyan the impression that it was once a Genkoan stronghold. But there was something else in the air. Something familiar to him.

The town was deserted. It had been built on a dirt road that was still clogged from the rain from a few days ago.

"Ghostly, isn't it?" Rom said.

Cyan nodded in agreement, though he wasn't paying much attention. He had noticed a curious sight in the corner of his eye and turned to see it. At the side of the road were two swords sticking out of the mud. One was a katana, the other a wakizashi. A white ribbon waved from the hilt of the katana.

"Myst," Cyan whispered to himself. Slowly he walked over and gripped the ribbon. Someone had written in a barely legible scrawl:

'Is there no freedom in death?'

"Captain?" Rom said.

Cyan seemed not to hear him and continued to stare at the ribbon.

"Captain, what's wrong?"

"I knew this man," Cyan said weakly. "He was a great warrior. To know that he is dead is truly unsettling."

"Sir?"

Cyan turned to Rom. "It's a long story, Rom. One full of blood and death. One I'd rather not recount. Needless to say, myself and this man, known simply as Myst, along with one other we're decidedly more acquainted with, engineered an escape from a place so evil it could hardly be said to have happened. I often doubt that it did. But, having been there, I am cursed to know that it was very real indeed. Yes, I too played my part."

Rom shuffled on his feet. "How did he meet his end?"

"I should imagine he ran into the other man."

"Who is?"

"There's only one swordsman skilled enough to kill Myst." Cyan smiled solemnly, as if comforted by the thought. Though his eyes, removed from the smile, as if of another man, betrayed him. Rom wondered what it was they showed. Fear seemed to be the closest emotion, but even that wasn't completely true.

"Captain Skyheart," Rom said.

Cyan nodded. The colour returned to his face and he seemed much more himself.

"Still," he said, "I've always thought there to be freedom in death. That's what we three decided long ago, though we may have just been trying to comfort ourselves. Besides, you and I will meet our ends in a similar manner, or so I'd expect. I certainly don't want anyone to lament my passing, do you?"

"No, Captain."

Cyan smiled and turned to the swords once more. He untied the ribbon and watched as it floated away on the breeze. "Goodbye, Myst."

They began walking up the deserted street in silence. The glory of the rising sun was deceptive of the mood of those beneath it.

"Captain," Rom said, "forgive me, but I never knew Captain Skyheart very well, aside from his reputation. What was he like?"

"His reputation would lead you to believe he was a fearsome man," Cyan said, smiling. "The infamous warrior, the Crimson Captain. Perhaps the best swordsman in the world. Although not completely untrue, he was far from fearsome. Though I am glad I never faced him in battle. He was a man of peace, really. People often forget that. He avoided conflict whenever he could, even when others would think it inevitable."

"You respected him, Captain?"

"Immensely."

"I must say, I heard whispers of his bad attributes."

Cyan laughed. "No doubt, Laike was an arrogant and frivolous man with terrible time keeping skills, a non-existent sense of direction and absolutely no leadership qualities. Half the time he was drunk and the other half he was asleep. He certainly never followed more than a third of the orders he was given, and that's being generous. However, nobody – no matter how much they hate him – could dispute his skill with a sword or his penchant for improvisation. So yes, I respect him despite his bad attributes. Maybe even because of them."

"And what of his treachery?" Rom asked.

Cyan sighed. He thought of the question for a long while. By the time he answered they had left the town.

"I'm sure he had his reasons," Cyan said.

Rom squirmed inside himself at the Captain's words. Surely such thoughts were treason, perhaps even blasphemy. If words were against Thieron then they must also have been against Thiera. He would have to pray for Cyan's soul when next he had the chance.

"If you don't mind my saying so, Captain," Rom said, "but Captain Skyheart didn't exactly appear worthy of the title."

"Before his promotion I'm sure I agreed with you," Cyan said. "There's more to being a Captain than swordsmanship and Laike didn't really have the temperament for such a responsibility. Some say that a Captain's duty is to the President, others to Thiera. I don't know what Laike thought and I suppose I never will now. He certainly didn't believe either of those. However, he proved himself to be a better Captain than I am."

"Captain!" Rom said, stopping. "How can you say such a thing?"

Cyan turned, looked at Rom and smiled lightly. "Laike never lost a man."

Rom thought of how many men had been lost since his time in the Third Division. Almost an entire division of men over the years and Cyan had been leading the division for many years before Rom joined. Indeed, Rom was only promoted to Lieutenant because the man before him died in battle. He pondered how such doom was possible. It then dawned on him what a feat it was to have never lost a man.

They continued walking.

"How did Captain Skyheart become a captain?" Rom asked.

"That's a story nobody quite knows. I've heard many speculations. Laike always claimed that everybody above him was dead. However, he was twenty one when he became a captain those three years ago. I find it hard to believe that there was nobody more qualified. DeFlare himself was certainly more experienced and was always held in high esteem."

"I knew Lieutenant DeFlare well," Rom said. "He certainly had conflicting feelings towards Captain Skyheart. I think they met somewhere between respect and despair."

"Is that so strange?" Cyan said. "All Lieutenants must have mixed feelings about their Captains."

"I would never question you, Captain! Your wisdom is absolute!"

Cyan laughed. "I'm just a man, Rom. You'll come to realise that soon enough."

Rom ran his fingers up and down his right lapel. "For all his notoriety there certainly is a lot of mystery surrounding Captain Skyheart."

Cyan smiled. "That there is. Yet I don't think Laike would have had it any other way. It's an immortal memory, perhaps even earned. That's a heavy burden to bear and one I can only imagine him as capable of carrying."

The conversation died and Rom pondered the Captain's musings. He had only met Captain Skyheart once or twice and found him impenetrable and unknowable. As such he could only form an opinion of him using his reputation and DeFlare's opinion of him; a skilled man, but something of a degenerate, perhaps even a dilettante. Rom found it hard to either like or respect him. However, Cyan seemed to believe Skyheart to have been honourable, if dishonoured. The Captain's judgement was good enough for Rom.

It wasn't long before they passed through something that looked to have once been a market. The sellers had left their carts and goods there in fear after the invasion of Genko. Clearly their lives were more important.

'Strange days indeed,' Cyan thought.

Not long after, they reached the zenith of a hill. A trail of trees led to a grassy plain and there, on the cliff above the ocean, stood Genko. Now occupied by the Mandran army. Despite the bright day and the abundance of metal on display, it didn't shimmer.

"Shall we enter?" Rom asked.

"No, we'll wait here until night and enter under cover of darkness. It's a long wait, no doubt, but it's favourable to facing the entire Mandran Occupation Force."

Rom nodded and they waited.

*

High in Thieron's Monument the newly appointed Commander Emaina Skyheart planned Thieron's defence from the Mandran army. He employed the tactics he thought his father would have approved of. However, his father never had to plan a defence. He had no idea if he was doing as his father would have wished.

He would have liked to have been able to ask his father what should be done. Indeed, he prayed that night for that very guidance, thinking perhaps his father would come to him in a dream. But nothing of the like happened.

Still, he was a Skyheart and even if that name meant little to the present generation, those previous revelled in it.

He sometimes doubted that the defence was possible. Then he decided, possible or not, it was irrelevant. He had to believe in it. It was his duty as Commander.

Chapter Thirteen

There had not been nearly enough berries for the town, however at least they weren't poisoned. The children were the most in need of nourishment so the berries were given to them, although Paccon gave a considerable quantity of his to Franklin.

The town was divided on the story of the disappearing fruit. Some believed it to be true after the wave of legends from the forest and these were peculiar days on the Southern Continent. The rest of the town thought Myri and Carre to be playing an elaborate prank, out of character though it was. Whatever was true, something was not quite right.

It was turning out to be an uneventful night. The Mayor had no further news from the Northern Continent and Celisso appeared to be giving Port Fair a rare moment of respite. The townsfolk accepted it, albeit questioningly; whenever Celisso's wrath went unfelt it meant that it would soon be released even more forcefully than usual.

Paccon stirred in his bed and opened his eyes. Something was wrong. Something about his person. It was as if there was a missing entity, a small piece of him had been displaced. He reached for the most obvious place – his top pocket. Alas, Franklin wasn't there.

"Franklin," he hissed, careful not wake Myri.

He rose and rolled out of bed. He looked underneath to no avail. His breath became frantic as he realised what he would have to do. He would have to go outside. Alone. In the dark. To look for his remaining fragment of his island. His past life. His home.

The thought awoke memories of his last adventure; fishing alone for the first time. The storm became fiercer in his mind with the roaring thunder and the bolts of lightning thrown from the raging heavens above. But, even that time he wasn't completely alone. Franklin had been a faithful companion and one Paccon could forever rely upon.

He waved the thoughts away and clenched his fists. He padded towards the door as silently as he knew how, ever watchful of the sleeping Myri.

It was a humid night, as they often were in Port Fair and the air felt stale, thick as if there was no freshness to it. The moon created unfeasible shapes in the square. Shadows which were not. Light that could not be. He wondered how much of it was in his imagination and how much he was truly seeing.

He exhaled slowly and took one slow step forward. The images remained but were no longer the vicious figures they had once been. He forced a weak smile.

It was impossible for him to know where Franklin had gone; he was no tracker and even had he been, in the darkness who could find any clues? Despite the unanswerable question, he found himself drawn towards the forest. On such a mysterious night, the birth-place of mystery was the only logical place to endeavour.

His steps towards the forest were barely noticeable. He tried his best to ignore the changing shadows around him, but each time he looked away they reached out to him. Eventually, after little progress, he closed his eyes and ran in the direction of the forest entrance. At many points he almost tripped, but a feral waving of his arms kept him balanced. Soon he felt the brush of bushes stroking his face. He opened his eyes and gave a thankful sigh, between pants of breath, to find he had reached the forest.

He peered into the mystical land. It looked different at night. The vibrant colours had shadowed into a collage of navy, black and deep purples. Yet, still, the beauty was undeniable - though beauty is not synonymous with safety.

Paccon stayed at the entrance for a while, trying to convince himself there was nothing inside that would hurt him. He witnessed no movement. He was in danger of over-thinking the situation and he knew this, but every thought made entering the forest harder. He closed his eyes once more and tried to take a step forward only to find his legs wouldn't work. He opened his eyes.

"Franklin needs me," he said. He took some deep breaths and felt something inside himself push him beneath the threshold of the forest. The following steps were voluntary.

He was walking the same path he had taken with Myri and Carre; safety in familiarity. Though, the darkness didn't allow for very much acquaintance.

He shivered and came to an abrupt stop as the silence was broken by a distant crunch. His breathing quickened along with the pounding of his heart. He tried to calm down by convincing himself he had trodden on a twig and it snapped under his weight, but just as he was beginning to believe this he heard the same noise again. He shivered once more.

The noise would surely lead to Franklin, but he was unsure he wished to be led there anymore. Perhaps that night's events hadn't been such a good idea after all...

"I've come this far," he whispered. "I can't go back without Franklin."

Decidedly more stealthily than before, he crept towards where he believed the noise to be coming from, ever surprised at his own bravery. He knelt behind a bush and observed.

The noise was emanating from a silhouette, sat, leaning against the apple tree. Despite having no features in the nightshade Paccon saw it to be particularly dishevelled, but definitely human. One limb approached the top of the silhouette and the crunch shot through the forest again.

From the corner of his eye, Paccon saw a diminutive shadow crawling towards the figure.

"Franklin," Paccon whispered.

Franklin continued towards the figure and climbed onto one of its legs.

"Well, what have we here?" the silhouette said in a flamboyant, though male, voice. He picked up Franklin and held him before his featureless face. The other arm swung towards the face and the crunch sounded again.

Paccon had to act. Once more he was pushed from inside and stumbled into the clearing.

"That's Franklin! Leave him alone!" Paccon shouted. The man, clearly surprised, though failing to find the high pitched voice of the child threatening, looked at Paccon with a slight turn of his head.

"Hello," he said.

"Leave Franklin alone."

"My pleasure," said the man, placing Franklin on the ground. The turtle clumsily made its way back to his rightful owner. He had had far too many adventures lately. Paccon knelt and picked his pet up.

"Don't ever do that again!" he said, waving a finger. It looked to him as if Franklin nodded. He placed him in his top pocket. Then he looked at the man. "What are you eating?"

"Apples."

"They're the town's apples. You should give them back."

"Town?" the man said. "Oh, yes, of course there's a town. I should have known that."

Paccon paused and shuffled on his feet. "Where are the rest?"

"Behind the tree," the man said, standing. "I'll show you if you want." He gestured with a hand to where he claimed the apples were.

"I don't trust you," Paccon said, staying where we was.

"I won't hurt you."

"I don't believe you."

"Fine," the man said, sitting back down. "Leave me alone then, you're disturbing my supper." He took another bite.

Paccon took a few steps forward. At this distance he could make out the features of the man's face. He didn't look all that threatening. In fact, he looked a little effeminate. The soft features weren't so far away from Myri's.

"You won't hurt me?" Paccon asked.

"I won't even touch you."

"Okay," Paccon said.

"Okay?"

"Okay."

The man rose, took another bite of the apple and threw the core away. He gestured for Paccon to follow him and they walked around the tree.

The man had not been lying. Behind the tree was a large bounty of apples, matching Paccon in height and outdoing him comfortably in width and breadth.

"I've been stockpiling them," the man said. "I was going to leave them to ferment and make cider." He paused and said dreamily, "But, somehow, I feel as if I'm missing out a few steps of the process."

Paccon looked up at him, mouth agape. "There are so many of them."

"I was going to make a lot of cider," he said. "Then again, if there's a town I suppose I can spare the apples. I shouldn't need homemade cider if there's a town, should I?"

He looked at Paccon and the boy shrugged.

"That's a very large hat you're wearing," said the man. "Was it expensive?"

"My Mama made it."

"Oh. I suppose she's in town looking for you."

89

"No."

"No?"

"No. I don't live in town. Well, I do, for the moment anyway. I shouldn't though."

The man scratched the scratched the back of his head.

"I see," he said. "I think. Where is your mother then?"

"On my island."

The man sighed. "It's far too late at night to be having these in-depth conversations. Well, without alcohol anyway."

Paccon yawned. "I'm tired," he said.

"I suppose I should take you back into town," the man said. "We can come back for the apples tomorrow, okay?"

"Okay," Paccon said, yawning.

"Good," the man said. He scratched the back of his head. "Now, which way is this town?"

They emerged from the forest to find the entire town looking for Paccon. Myri ran towards him and lifted him in an embrace.

"There you are," she said. "I was so worried."

She gave the man a look of animosity. The man noticed that the rest of the town were looking at him in the same way. He scratched the back of his head.

"Franklin went missing," Paccon said. "But it's okay, I found him." He pushed himself away from Myri's shoulder, interrupting her glare. He looked her in the eyes. "I didn't mean to worry you."

"It's okay, Paccon," she said softly, holding him closer once more.

The Mayor took a step towards the man, pointing a walking stick that the town had never seen before. "Who are you, stranger?"

"Why, isn't it obvious?" the man said smiling. "I'm Captain Laike Skyheart, of course."

Chapter Fourteen

The moon was hard in the sky that night. Diminishing light defended its position in existence against the ever growing darkness, thankful that no clouds had rolled in to reinforce the enemy of lustre. The luminescence cut through the cold night air, lengthening itself in the reflection formed by the sea.

In this ambience, the two men wrapped their coats around them as they hung close to the walls of Genko. They circled round the occupied city to enter behind what was once the palace. It was a long way to the ocean below were they to fall from the cliff. A fall all too familiar to one who was their former kinsmen. Although, he was nowhere to be able to warn against the experience, they had sense enough to not want to re-enact it themselves.

Cyan leant heavily into the wall of the palace, as much pulling himself along with his arms as he was walking. Rom did the same; it seemed to make as much sense as any other technique. The ground beneath was unstable and each small movement threatened the disaster of bringing the entire cliff down. Yet the Thieronians remained calm, as their precarious place in the world often required them to.

When they finally entered the city proper, they crouched by the stairs of the palace to decide the next course of action.

"Where do you think we should look?" Rom asked.

"We should retrace Laike's steps," Cyan said. "The most typical place for him to go would be an inn. We'll look there first."

"We'll have to make ourselves known."

"That shouldn't be a problem now that we're in the city. Mandra wouldn't let Thieronians in at the gates, but now we're in it could be to our advantage. We'll be the closest that the Genkoans have to an ally and we'll be willing to play that part."

Rom nodded.

The pair moved silently through the city, not even shadows. Had they been seen they would not have been thought to be human.

Soon, they found an inn and entered, Cyan leading the way. As they passed the threshold they changed from silent unnoticeable visages to soldiers of Thieron, receiving at least a passing glance from all in the establishment. It was a small inn, filled to capacity. The wooden features were beginning to wear and the passing of time had begun to show on the patrons' faces. In the far corner, a group on Mandran soldiers were growing increasingly inebriated and the more sensible drinkers had moved away from them.

Cyan and Rom's steps synchronised as they approached the bar through the haze of pipe smoke. Cyan leaned towards the barman and asked for two beers. Once they had been served they sat on stools at the bar and drank, wordlessly, observing those around them.

The Mandrans were playing a game Cyan didn't recognise. As he understood it, they acted out the mannerisms of a famous person and the other players had to guess who it was. They were loud and clearly drunk enough already.

Cyan turned back to the bar and noticed the barman looking at him.

"Thieronians, eh?" he said.

Cyan nodded.

"We're getting a lot of you in here recently. Although, a lot of oddities have occurred here over the past few days."

"I can imagine," Cyan said. "You seem to be doing good business about it, though."

"I can't argue with that. I don't take kindly to the Mandrans invading, but I won't refuse their money. I'm a businessman after all."

"This Thieronian you had in the other day. Did he say much?"

The barman frowned. "How did you know there was just one?"

"Because I know of only one Thieronian who would seek out a drink was it not part of his mission."

The barman glanced at the Mandrans. "We can't talk here." He gestured with his head for Cyan and Rom to follow him and then took them through a wooden door which led into a stock room. They sat at a small table and the barman continued.

"Captain Skyheart came in here a few days ago. I knew who he was, who wouldn't? I didn't ask why he was here, but I imagine you already know. He had a few whiskeys and asked me some questions. It was before noon and nobody else was in (truth be told, I opened especially for him). I answered freely. All the time he was asking about this old man, said he'd been taken by some soldiers and he wanted to find him. I told him to look around the palace dungeon, although I knew of no such man. He thanked me, had a few more drinks, and left, not showing any signs of drink."

"What else can you tell us?" Cyan asked.

"Nothing much. I did see a rather queer event during the invasion, though."

Cyan gestured for the barman to continue but he remained silent. "If you tell us you could save a great many lives."

"Lives," said the barman. "What are lives to me? I have my own, that's life enough for one man. No, what I need is something to improve my *quality* of life. Make me a little more comfortable."

Cyan sighed and threw a small bag of gold coins onto the table. The barman smiled and tucked it away. "So, as I was saying, I saw a rather peculiar event during the invasion. The Captain and the fellow he was with were fighting by the cliff. It looked to be over some jewel to me."

Cyan and Rom exchanged a glance.

"The Captain lost his balance on the cliff after a Mandran ship fired at it. He fell and threw the jewel to the other man, but he couldn't reach it and it fell in the sea after the Captain. I watched this other man for a little while after, despairing he was. Whether it was over the jewel or the Captain I couldn't say."

Rom looked to Cyan. "So that's it?" he said. "It's over. The Diamandé's lost to the sea."

"Not necessarily," said a moving shadow in the corner of the room. It rose and a man in a tri-cornered hat, elaborate leather coat, white shirt, black trousers and brown leather boots stepped into the light. He was a man approaching fifty with a grizzled face and heavy stubble. He sat at the table with the other men. Now that he sat in the clearer light Cyan noticed that what he thought was a shadow over the man's left eye was, in fact, an eye patch. At the sight of the man the barman made a hasty exit.

"My apologies," the man said. "But men in my position must resort to extraordinary lengths to find information."

"Who are you?" Cyan asked.

"Captain Lafere Swift. I suppose that makes us equals."

"I've heard of you," Cyan said. "You're a pirate."

"We're all pirates," said Swift. "Only, some of us have it as our job title."

"What do you know about the Diamandé?"

"Not a thing. However, if it has fallen into the sea, as the barman suggests, then it may well have found its way into the Southern Drift."

"Southern Drift?" Rom said.

"At this time of year a meander forms in the ocean. The tip of this meander is the sea near Genko. This snakes down to the south-western side of the Southern Continent. The meander is known as the Southern Drift. Were anything to have been caught in it, it is not unreasonable to suggest, or unknown to happen, that it could have washed up somewhere on the Southern Continent."

"Why are you telling us this?" Cyan asked.

Swift leaned forward, further in the light. Cyan looked at his remaining eye. The green iris showed signs of lust and effervescence yet to be extinguished. A strand of brown hair flopped in front of it and Swift brushed it back behind his ear.

"I've had my fill of Genko," he said. "I want to travel and I require a crew, but to acquire a crew I must first find a temporary one so that I can port somewhere where I can find one more permanent."

"You want us to help you get to the Southern Continent?" Cyan said.

"Indeed. It seems to be the solution to both of our problems. We both need to get the Southern Continent, and neither my*self* nor your*selves* can get there alone. If we pool our resources I'd imagine we could be there by tomorrow."

"Where's your ship?"

Swift grimaced. "This is the problem I have. There is a dock in the city, full of ships, yet I own not a one of them. However, pirate that I am, I am not averse to taking one (call it commandeering if the thought of stealing offends you). I just need a way to get past the guards."

"These are Mandran ships?"

"Not just Mandran ships. *Heavily guarded* Mandran ships, perhaps twenty men guarding each vessel. However, before me sit two Thieronian soldiers; one a Captain, one a Lieutenant. I've heard that a Thieronian Captain is worth ten of any other warrior. I'd conclude that a Lieutenant is worth at least seven. I've been crossing blades my whole life and I'd say I'm good for three. That makes twenty by my maths..." He paused and seemed to count it out in his mind once more. "Yes, twenty! We're a perfect match for any of those ships and we'd be fools not to try. So, Thieronians, what say you?" With this final question he pounded the table triumphantly.

"A rough plan," Cyan said. "Although it is the best we currently have."

Swift leaned forward again and Rom caught a whiff of his stench. He had clearly not washed for some time and the reek of alcohol was strong on him. It was made worse by having been mixed with the potent odour of something that Rom couldn't quite identify (nor did he want to).

Swift smiled revealing a set of inexplicably white teeth. "Naturally we'll need to dispense of the Mandran soldiers in the bar. Having seen you enter here some time ago I'd imagine they plan to apprehend you upon your leaving."

"There's a lot of blood to be shed in this plan of yours," Rom said.

"Yes there is. But, gentlemen, look closely and you shall see that none of that blood is ours."

Cyan leaned back in his chair. He thought of Operation Shell and how no Thieronian blood was meant to be shed. However, that was far from how it had transpired. There was little to say that this plan would fare any better, yet there was something about Captain Swift that he found strangely compelling. Yes he was arrogant, clearly drunk and dishevelled in appearance, but in Cyan's experience the best men were.

Rom looked to Cyan. "What do you think, Captain? Can we trust a pirate?"

Cyan paused and looked at Swift. "I think we can trust *this* pirate."

Swift smiled.

"We'd be stealing a ship," Rom said.

"A Mandran ship," Cyan said. "I believe that to be in the service of Thieron."

Swift's smile grew wider. "Spoken like a true pirate!" he roared.

The trio rose and entered the bar together. Swift had been correct in his assumption that the Mandran soldiers would anticipate their return. The soldiers confronted them in the now empty bar, swords drawn.

"Ha!" Swift roared. "You wait to do battle with a Captain and Lieutenant of Thieron, teamed with Captain Lafere Swift, the greatest pirate to ever have lived, and you send not for reinforcements? Ha! I say, ha!"

Swift drew from his black leather scabbard a rusted and dull cutlass. Cyan and Rom exchanged concerned glances.

"It's quite alright," Swift said, anticipating their reaction. "The old girl's seen better days but she works far better than she has any right to."

He pointed his sword at the Mandrans as he heard the Thieronians behind him draw their katanas with a duet of metal leaving wood. Swift smiled and lunged at the Mandrans. The Thieronians followed, Cyan immediately cutting down one soldier with a downwards strike. He blocked an attack from another and pushed him away.

Rom's first attack was blocked by a soldier who fell backwards, silly with drink. As he rose, Rom sliced at his chest and he fell once more, never to rise.

Swift was trading quick blows with a particularly clumsy soldier. The pirate displayed impressive footwork before becoming bored of the encounter and lunging for the soldier's heart. He found it and the soldier fell. He turned and immediately parried an attack from the largest of the soldiers. The Mandran pushed hard with his broadsword, but Swift kicked him away and swung at his neck. He missed and stumbled towards him, his blade finding his opponent's stomach by sheer luck.

Meanwhile, Cyan was fending off two soldiers, trading alternate strikes with them. It was reminiscent of a training exercise he was used to doing with the less experienced members of the Third Division. Upon seeing Rom struggling with, what looked to be, the most skilled of the soldiers, he struck them both down and rushed to his Lieutenant's aid. He swung his sword and the back of the man and found the tip of his katana slicing through the man's neck. It was a result he had not planned, but it left the Mandran decidedly dead and he fell to the floor, head just about attached.

"Thank you, Captain," Rom said breathlessly.

Cyan nodded and turned to Swift. "We should go."

Swift gestured towards the door and the men disappeared from the smoke-filled bar into the street of the black night. They turned to head to the dock. Swift and Rom began to run.

"I'm not thinking," Cyan said to himself. "Wait!" he called to the others.

"We must go, Captain!" Swift said. "It won't be long before the Mandrans flood the streets with troops."

"He's right, Captain," Rom said. "We may be able to defeat small groups such as that, but against many we would surely fall."

"I need to open the gates for the Genkoans," Cyan said. "Wait for me here. If too many Mandrans come, head for the docks without me."

With that he dissolved into the night.

It wasn't long before the Mandrans started attacking. It was unorganised at first; maverick soldiers charged them, one or two at a time, only to be felled by Swift and Rom's superior skill. Soon though, officers arrived and organised the attacks. Some came with spears, the preferred weapon of Mandra. However, even this was little trouble for the pair.

The clash of steel on steel rang throughout Genko. Soon, more soldiers would be on their way.

Cyan reached the gate and marvelled at the size of it. It was twice the height of the walls of Thieron, though that meant nothing. However, he knew it was also of considerable thickness. This was tonnes upon tonnes of reinforced metal that stood before him.

"Perhaps I should have thought of a plan before I got here," he said to himself. "Everything has a weak spot. I just need to discover what it is."

"We have to go!" Swift called above the wailing weapons. "There are too many of them!"

"Not without the Captain!" Rom shouted.

With that, a roar of might came from the direction of Cyan's work, followed by a crash of metal and a disorientating flash of light.

Cyan was with them and cut down the men attacking them.

"The Genkoans shouldn't have trouble entering the city now," he said. "We must go."

They ran through the now clear streets towards the edge of the moonlit cliff. Cyan stopped and sank at an effigy his eyes could not release.

Before him, Lieutenant Alrous DeFlare hung from a gallows, though from the injuries to his body it was clear he had been killed before he was hung from the structure.

"Alrous," Cyan said. He sheathed his sword and stroked the face of his compatriot.

"This should not be," Rom said.

"That it should not."

Cyan drew his sword and cut DeFlare down. Then, he gently rolled the body off of the cliff and watched it disappear into the water far below.

"You're with Laike now," Cyan whispered. He rose, his eyes closed. When he opened them Rom observed on the Captain a look of surprising peace.

"We must go now," Swift said. "Before they have a chance to gather their troops."

"Yes," Cyan said. "My apologies. However, I could not allow the death of one so close to me to be the spectre it had become."

"There is no need for an apology," Swift said.

Together, they made their way down the slope to the docks. It was there they were met by a well-planned ambush, approaching twenty men.

They looked at each other before diving towards their opponents.

After the skirmish the wood of the dock was soaked and congested with blood. Had it been a brighter night they would have seen that the water below them was stained with the crimson of their enemies.

The sound of their boots was choked as they boarded the nearest ship. Cyan was glad to find it unmanned – far too much blood had been spilt that night as it was. He failed to remember a night as malevolent as that in all his years, except the escape from Pale Castle.

The moon he once thought of as forever smiling, seemed to mourn with a thousand stars for tear drops.

Nobody spoke until they were out at sea.

"Captain," Rom said, "how did you open the gate?"

The image of the gate, thrown from its wrought iron hinges shot through Cyan's mind. "The Mandrans left some explosives nearby. I think I may have used rather too much judging by the force it produced."

"How careless of them," Rom said.

"Careless? There is a rather more unsettling alternative Rom."

"Captain?"

"They wanted the gate open."

Chapter Fifteen

They spent the night gathering the apples that Skyheart had been stockpiling. He was reluctant to relinquish them when he found out there was no alcohol in the town, but, eventually, seceded when Carre pointed out that he had no way of fermenting them and would have to wait a long while for them even if he did. Though still he insisted on them being known as *his* apples.

He said nothing of his journey or Operation Shell, nor did the towns-people ask. It seemed to him that he was unwelcome, though he wasn't completely surprised. He knew very little of the Southern Continent but he was well aware of the Mineral Wars and the part Thieron, not to mention his father, played. He also knew that they refused to let go of their past. Was that something the Old Man had said? He couldn't quite remember, but the sentiment had ominous undertones typical of that particular acquaintance.

He was offered nowhere to sleep, except by Paccon, though Myri with-drew the offer. She seemed to blame Skyheart for Paccon's disappearance, rather than credit him with the boy's return.

Spurned and cast off into the night, Skyheart slept on the pier. It wasn't the most comfortable night he had ever spent, though he had once claimed to have slept in an iron maiden. When confronted with the statement that such a night would have killed him, the Captain claimed he had drunk a considerable amount that night, so the experience was slightly dubious. It may have been a bed of nails, having lain on his stomach, naturally.

Yet, that night's sleeping arrangements suited him fine. Until it began to rain. He sighed. He would have been asleep by then had he something to drink.

Eventually day came and the clouds parted, revealing a glorious sun which destroyed any evidence of rain. When the townsfolk saw just how wet Skyheart was, a rumour started that he had absent-mindedly wandered off the edge of the pier and fallen in the sea. When he explained what had really happened, he was accused of 'trying to save face'. On his way back into town he sneered, saying, "Well played weather."

It was at that point he ran into the Mayor. Skyheart wondered how a man with such authority could be so small. Then again, he supposed President Kylar wasn't particularly tall, although he didn't ever recall seeing the President stand. He was interrupted in his thoughts by the Mayor.

"Hello, Captain," he said. "I trust you slept well."

"I'm sure you'll hear about it from one of the denizens soon enough," Skyheart said with a grimace.

The Mayor seemed not to hear him and Skyheart realised he was looking out at sea. "Glad to hear it," he said, turning back to the Captain. "I don't suppose I could speak with you in my office, could I?"

"Well, I haven't got anything pressing that needs attending to."

The Mayor led him through the Town Hall and into his office. Skyheart found the room cramped, although he supposed it was similar in size to his own. He surmised that the fact he hardly entered his office meant it remained free from clutter; unlike the Mayor's, which was so full Skyheart was surprised when he actually found a chair to sit in.

"I suppose our town seems a little quaint to a man such as yourself," the Mayor said.

"It looks different during the day," Skyheart replied with the most subtle of smiles.

The Mayor's face became grave and he gave the Captain a look of undeterminable motive. "I'm sure you've noticed we have not given you the warmest of welcomes, Captain. For this, I can only apologise. However, the Skyheart name, along with the entire Northern Continent, is synonymous with a part of Port Fair's past we have, so far, been unable to leave behind. Indeed, we know you very well and what you represent. We know of your ill-fated mission to Genko (fear not Captain, no more shall be said of it) and we are concerned. Please, forgive me Captain, but I must inquire; why are you here?"

Skyheart leaned back in his chair, forcing it back upon its hind legs. He pushed it too far and felt a sharp sensation of dread shoot through him as the chair, Captain still perched upon it, tumbled backwards, only to be caught by the wall. He placed the chair back on the number of legs it was designed for use with and leaned forward.

"I assure you, Mayor," he said. "I have found myself here completely by accident. You've nothing to fear from me. I fell in the ocean during the invasion of Genko and was washed up nearby."

"I suppose you'll want to be getting back?"

"Certainly not," Skyheart laughed. "It was always my intention to leave the Northern Continent, admittedly, more gracefully than transpired, however it seems to have worked out for the best."

"This I understand. But the town fears your presence will bring more soldiers. I'm sure you can see this is considerably undesirable."

"Please," Skyheart said, smiling. "The reaction the town gave me last night upon hearing my name suggested one thing; the world thought me dead. Believe me Mayor; your town is quite safe."

The Mayor gave him a similar look as before. Skyheart ignored it as the realisation came upon him that he was experiencing an all-too-familiar nausea. His right hand had begun to tremble slightly, though he felt as if he still had some semblance of control over it, unlike before. He took a few, discreet, deep breaths.

"Unfortunately, your presence is still an issue," the Mayor said with a troubled face. "The fact is you are still another mouth to feed and, as I'm sure you have inferred from our reaction to the apples you so graciously gifted us with last night, we are very low on food."

"I always thought the Southern Continent was shipped food by the surrounding islands."

"Indeed, it usually is. Recently, however, the sea monster Celisso has made his kingdom in our waters and no shipping vessels can pass him."

"And were someone to dispatch of said monster?"

"We know nobody of that skill."

"You do as of last night."

The Mayor's eyes widened and mouth dropped agape, just enough to notice. Skyheart smiled and waited for a reply.

"With all due respect, Captain, I hardly believe that even you are a match for such a vicious creature."

"Mayor," Skyheart said. "I'm Captain Laike Skyheart of Thieron's Division Four – the most skilled swordsman in the world. I think I can kill a fish."

"You're not the first man to make such an arrogant suggestion," the Mayor said. "There are those honoured in the Remembrance Garden who thought the same, and one in a private burial ground. You'd be wise not to try."

Skyheart rose. "Be that as it may I am not a wise man. I am an adventurer. And, as an adventurer, it is my sworn duty to rid you of such a troublesome beast."

The Mayor smiled. "You really think you can do it, don't you?"

Skyheart nodded and the Mayor rose.

"Well, this certainly is a happy coincidence."

The Mayor started leading him from the Town Hall into the square.

"I, uh... thought you didn't believe I could do it," Skyheart said.

"I don't. But even if Celisso kills you it's one less mouth to feed."

A ringing had begun in Skyheart's ears and the Mayor's words distorted into a harsh fade. His shaking had worsened and he felt as if he was suffocating with sweat. The light of the day was burning his eyes and soon he was on his knees looking up at a crowd he could just make out; red figures against the hard, white sun.

He fell further.

Darkness.

Doctor Gainsborough rushed through the door carrying the Captain and a crowd formed on the threshold. Myri was glad she had dressed when she had otherwise her fellow residents of Port Fair would have found her in a decidedly improper condition. She watched in horror as they placed the unconscious Skyheart on her bed.

"What's going on?" she said, summoning the most indignant voice she could muster, but her words sounded more curious than oppositional.

"He's severely ill," the Doctor replied, checking the Captain's rapid, bursting pulse.

"But why is he in my house?"

The Mayor appeared in the doorway after pushing his way through the crowd. "We voted. Your house is the best place to put him."

"When do I get my vote?"

"It's too late for that I'm afraid," the Doctor said. "Moving the patient again is too much of a risk. I was reluctant to move him the first time, but he'll be unconscious for a few days. It's best he's somewhere comfortable."

"A few days?" Myri asked. "Where am I supposed to sleep?"

"I'm sure that you and Paccon could *both* fit in the spare bed," the Mayor said.

The Doctor made his way to the door and the crowd dispersed. He turned to Myri. "Keep his fluids up and if his fever gets worse, send for me immediately."

He left with the Mayor and the door closed, leaving Myri alone with the son of the man whose decisions killed her father. The decisions that led to her mother taking her own life. Commander Skyheart – murderer by extension. And how many had this son killed? Many, so the stories told, though in his weakened, unconscious state, he looked deceptively harmless. Then again, she supposed he didn't look much like a murderer when he was awake either. Take away the crimson coat and obsidian black sword and he could have been anyone. She curled up in her chair and observed him as he squirmed in some fever induced dream.

Paccon entered from the garden and stopped in the doorway as he noticed the comatose Captain. He slowly turned his head to the preoccupied Myri and back to Skyheart. He approached the Captain and sat on the bed with him. He withdrew sharply and ran over to Myri as the Captain writhed violently. Paccon clutched at her and she soothed him.

"I thought you said he couldn't stay here," he said. His voice muffled as he plunged his face deeper into Myri's being.

"I've been over-ruled."

"Is he okay?"

"He's very sick."

"Will he be okay?"

"I don't know." She thought of adding "Hopefully not" before she noticed Paccon looking up at her with tears in his eyes. The look of sorrow on the boy's face silenced her malicious thoughts. Instead she said, "He'll be fine. After all, he's Captain Laike Skyheart."

He receded further inside himself searching for whatever festering soul was causing that interminable heat. He was drowning in the hot air around him, or his own sweat. If only it would dry, his skin would cool. Yet, he had no such luck.

He lurched forward into the darkness, not so much walking as his vision had left his body behind. Though, when he turned there was no body (his or otherwise) there.

Could any of this be said to have happened?

Only to himself and even that audience seemed unfeasibly large.

She sighed as she rubbed his forehead with the damp cloth. His fever was getting worse, she was sure of that. His face contorted to an expression of pain and he showed no signs of waking.

"What's wrong with him?" Paccon asked.

"I don't know," Myri said. "The Doctor didn't say."

Paccon sat next to her. "You don't like him, do you?"

Myri didn't answer.

His father woke him. The bearded man with features similar to his own, if a little harder, smiled upon his son, before looking out across the wastelands they found themselves in.

Laike hated nights like that one. He was sweating more than he could ever remember doing and he was certain it was suffocating him. He thrashed with his limbs, desperate to feel the air against his skin but it was no use. The air was thick and miasmic; a viscous fluid that would keep him breathing, only without letting him know it.

He rose and stood next to his father. They both looked north to the ashen black tower, seemingly draining all light from the scene. How many days' walk was it now? He couldn't be sure, but he knew they would get there eventually.

Knowing he and his father would sleep no longer, he kicked out the fire, though it rid him of no discomfort. He looked to the old man in the elaborate green coat, not so dissimilar to his own crimson one, for solace. His father smiled. He looked old.

"It's a long way, isn't it?" the Commander said.

"Yes, Dad."

"We should start moving soon."

"I'm ready now."

"It can wait a little while."

"You just say when."

"Are you sure you're ready?"

"Yes, Dad."

Commander Zenedin Skyheart nodded and on they went with laboured steps.

He tried to remove from his mind how old his father looked. His once blond hair was now a fierce grey and, though his physique was as muscular as ever, he had started to slow. Laike didn't want to think of his father as in decline. Yet, there he was, marching on beside him, struggling. Laike rested a hand on his father's shoulder and smiled. His father smiled back, though the smile was different from how it used to be, as was Laike's. Far from the wry amusement that Laike's smiles usually denoted, the smile they shared merely served as a shield to ward off sorrow.

On the father and son wandered together – towards the black tower.

Paccon had taken over the duty of caring for the Captain. He didn't bring the subject up with Myri again. She'd been quiet since he arrived.

Skyheart's fever was no worse, but no better. Certainly, he was far from the grip of an imminent recovery. Paccon propped the Captain's head up on the pillows and tried to cool him with the damp cloth.

He noticed Myri stir and wake in the morning light. Upon seeing the Captain she turned away.

At any other time he was sure he would have marvelled at the size of the tower. Obsidian black, it stood piercing the sky above with ease. Yet, he found himself looking at it in rather a blasé manner.

The heat amazed him far more. Surely living most of his life in a desert should have conditioned him for this? Apparently not. He sighed and paused in his thoughts for a few moments, contemplating whether or not to take his coat off. Upon seeing his father keep his on, he decided to do the same. Instead, he fanned himself with the lapels but felt no relief.

The thought of how he and his father arrived in the wastes entered his mind. He asked his father.

"It's best not to ask those kinds of questions sometimes," he said. "It's not like you to care about those things, Laike."

He thought about that for a long time. He'd always thought of himself as having a lot of questions. He supposed he kept them to himself mainly. He waved the thoughts from his mind and reached inside his coat in search of a bottle of brown liquor, but he found nothing.

"Disappointing," he said, though his father seemed not to hear.

Every so often Laike got the feeling that they weren't actually getting any closer to the tower. He imagined that may have just been because they were so far away. With such a large distance to travel each step would hardly have made a difference.

He looked at his father struggling, but didn't say anything.

"You don't look well, Laike," his father said.

"I'm just dehydrated," he replied. "Or thereabouts."

His father nodded but said nothing.

The moon rose, casting the shadow of the tower over the men. Laike was now sure that they were no closer, as if each step served to make him only more tired. Though he didn't mind; he was spending time with his father. They were long overdue with their arrival, but still, hurrying seemed needless.

"Are we as far away as I think we are?" Laike said.

"How far away do you think we are?"

"Very far away."

"Well, we're certainly far away. I doubt we're as far away as you think, though."

"I hope you're right."

"So do I."

"Why are we going there?"

His father said something as an answer that Laike didn't quite hear, but he felt no need to pursue it any further. Perhaps the fact that there was an answer was enough for him.

The Doctor put his hand to Skyheart's forehead only to find his fever had worsened. The sheets of the bed were soaked through with sweat but he had nothing to put in their place.

Myri sat next to him.

"Is he any better?" she asked

"Quite the opposite. His fever's worse. I never expected him to be in such a bad condition for two days."

"Will he recover?"

"The possibility is less likely with each passing second."

"He could die?"

"It's very likely."

"What's wrong with him?"

"A multitude of things. He's very weak from his time in the ocean and he's experiencing violent withdrawal symptoms. But most of all, he's just tired." He paused for a time. "So, he could die. Then again, that wouldn't be so bad, would it?"

Myri said nothing.

"Laike?" his father said that night around the fire.

"Yes, Dad?"

"Why did you let me get so old?"

"I didn't have much choice in the matter."

"Neither did I."

"It's not so bad, is it?"

His father didn't answer for a long time. Then he lay down and said, "We should sleep."

But Laike didn't sleep. He tried and at one point thought he did, as the sun rose but he didn't witness it. However, his tiredness suggested he had spent the night awake.

His father awoke. "It's not far now," he said.

Laike stood and looked at the tower. It still looked to be an eternity away. "If you say so."

"One day you'll agree with something I say."

"Are you sure about that?"

"Not completely."

They smiled familiarly at each other and began walking once more.

He could feel dehydration tightening its hold on him. His mouth and throat were raw with dryness; relief was nowhere to be found. He licked his lips as if to dampen them but only succeeded in making himself more aware of the situation. He smiled at his unfortunate circumstance; blighted by heat he ventured onwards, pushing his suffering from his mind. Unhindered by worry he looked to his father who was walking laboriously and ungracefully across the cracked wasteland.

Laike noticed that the ground beneath him had become decidedly more uneven. Upon inspection he noticed a myriad of footprints. Whether they were all from the same person, he could not tell, though they all looked similar in size and pattern. To become so worked into the rock the owner must have walked out there frequently and for long periods of time. Laike pointed them out to his father.

"Of course there are footprints," he replied. "She's been out here looking for us."

The image of his mother shot through his mind.

"Mum's there?"

"This has been a wasted journey if she isn't," his father said.

It hadn't occurred to Laike that his mother would be there. It hadn't occurred to him that anyone would be there.

Paccon watched as the Captain breathed softly in his sleep. His chest rose and fell the slightest of amounts every few seconds. In the time between, Paccon feared that he didn't have the strength for another and he had breathed his last. But each time there was at least one more. After some time their breathing patterns synchronised.

"The Mayor said the Captain's going to kill Celisso," Paccon said to Myri.

"He has to get better first," she replied quietly.

"Will he?"

"He might."

"I think he will."

Myri said nothing.

"He's always got one more breath left," Paccon continued. "Even when I think he doesn't."

"People can surprise you like that," she said.

Paccon looked up at her, trying to decipher whether she was agreeing or disagreeing with him. She wore no expression.

"How did you do it?" he asked his father in the bright noon.

"Do what?"

"Send those men to their deaths."

"Oh," his father paused. "Well, I just ordered them go, like I used to be ordered."

"Did it get any easier?"

"It never got harder. I suppose that was something."

"How did you deal with it?"

Zenedin stopped walking and examined his son. Laike could feel his eyes on his face, invading and excavating him.

"I suppose I just dealt with it," he said. "There wasn't much else to it. You know. You deal with it too." He started walking again.

Laike said nothing and didn't move. His shaking had started again, though not as fervently as before. He followed his father as he had so many times before.

"Can I ask *you* a question?" his father said.

"I've been asking you questions all this time; you may as well ask me a few."

"Why did you do it?

"Do what?"

"Steal the Diamandé."

"Oh." Laike thought about it as they walked. He thought of saying that he didn't take kindly to the Assembly's threats. But something within him told him that was just an excuse. He didn't answer until sunset, when his father told him he needn't reply.

"I suppose," Laike said, "that I just couldn't do what I was doing anymore."

His father stopped and looked at him in the same way he had before. "You look tired," he told him, as if Laike had said nothing at all.

"I am tired," Laike said in a voice that was more like his as a child.

"You rest here for a while," his father said. "I'm going to go on ahead." He turned to the tower and started walking. "Catch me up when you're ready."

Laike sat down and watched his father walk away. A few minutes later Laike lay down as his father had faded into the horizon. But he was out there somewhere, waiting for Laike, and he would be there, waiting for him at the tower.

Laike closed his eyes.

He felt a light rain falling.

It was then he knew...

He'd never be ready.

Chapter Sixteen

The ship drifted lazily through the ocean, cutting through waves with the slightest of efforts. The sea was a lullaby to the three men aboard, although Captain Swift was more at ease than the two men from the desert city. Slowly though, they were finding themselves at peace.

"I could get used to this," Rom said.

"Relaxing, isn't it?" Swift replied, steering the ship from the bridge, not that much was needed. "Even in a storm, I'm never more at peace than out here."

Cyan, sitting on the steps leading to the bridge, wasn't paying much attention to the conversation. His thoughts had turned to the Diamandé. If it wasn't in Genko was there really much chance it was on the Southern Continent? Swift had been saying that the Southern Drift was close, however they had yet to find it. Could the Diamandé really have been carried to it so easily? Certainly it seemed far more likely that it had sunk. Even if it *had* arrived on the Southern Continent, who was to say somebody hadn't taken it for themselves or it hadn't been washed up on some obscure shore never to be found?

The entire situation, as with so many recently, depended on so many variables. He was almost certain the jewel would never be found. He would never return to Thieron and his homeland would be invaded or crushed by the Mandrans. Yet, he seemed not to mind and that was what bothered him the most. When had he grown so world weary so as to no longer care about the fate of his home? Upon the news of Captain Thean's death? When he had heard he would never see his good friend Laike Skyheart again? Perhaps at the grave of Myst or Lieutenant DeFlare. Maybe before any of these. The doubt that he had ever cared was becoming more deeply planted in his mind.

The thought was strangely comforting.

Of course, he couldn't share these thoughts with Rom. The young Lieutenant still wore the expression of certain determination, his mind never straying from his duties. To even contemplate Thieron's demise was treason to him. Or so it would seem.

Cyan hoped his Lieutenant wasn't quite that naïve.

Rom looked up from the deck to Swift. "Are we near the Southern Drift?"

"I'm sure it's around here somewhere," the pirate said.

"Would it not be faster to sail to the Southern Continent unaided, rather than spending time to locate the drift?"

Swift paused. He rolled his one eye before focusing it on Rom. "It's around here somewhere."

"I just feel as if we're wasting valuable time."

Cyan rose. "Relax, Rom. It's one thing to follow orders, but to rush through them will never end well."

"But Thieron is in worsening danger with each passing moment."

Cyan placed his hand warmly on Rom's shoulder. "We have time, Rom.

The Genkoans have yet to attack and the Mandrans are far from ready to move."

"I thought you said that the Genkoans wouldn't get through the gates."

"They most probably won't. However, the attack will definitely slow the Mandran advance."

"Yet time is still of the essence," Rom said.

Cyan smiled. "We have as much time as life sees fit."

"I don't understand."

"I'm not sure that I do completely. It's something Captain Thean said to me once."

"I've heard the saying," Swift said. "I always thought it to mean 'You can only do what there is to be done'."

"And what is there to be done?" Rom asked.

"You know the answer to that," Cyan said.

"We can find the Diamandé," Rom said, looking far out to sea.

Cyan sighed inside himself. Rom did still believe. So be it. It was better to have a Lieutenant with a cause than one who was blindly following his Captain. Though, when the realisation came, Cyan knew it would make things far more complicated.

Swift looked from the helm to his crew. They weren't natural seafarers; however they knew how to follow orders. Unfortunately, as soon as they reached the Southern Continent he would once more be without a crew. Still, at least he was at sea for the time being.

He could feel himself sobering for the first time in days. He found it somewhat pleasant. The days he spent in a drunken haze often troubled him. He supposed he may have done something truly unforgivable and not have known it. Though, this time, he seemed to have done something halfway honourable, albeit not altogether selfless.

He took a deep breath of the fresh salty air and smiled. The ship creaked in the water – he always took that as a good sign, it meant the ship and seas were communicating. How he longed to be out there forever, but he would have to make port all too soon. Then how long would he have to wait to be at one with his love again?

He thought back to the longest time he spent on land: the three years he had spent imprisoned in Pale Castle. He was to be executed on the first day of his fifth year. They had executed his crew some time before just to see his reaction; they went disappointed – there was none. He was supposed to have been driven mad by his time awaiting his death, though it seemed only to consolidate his love of life and his love of the sea; the prospect of seeing which was what had kept him sane.

He grinned when he thought of his escape. He would admit that it wasn't as daring as another he heard of, though his was far from cowardly.

His thoughts returned to the present and he noticed Captain Cyan looking at him. He had a far off appearance to his eyes, as if he was thinking of a distant memory. Something told Swift that he, too, had been inside Pale Castle. It was something one could never lose or hide.

Rom pondered on his Captain's earlier musings. To suggest that they need not concern themselves with Thieron's fate was a thought Rom struggled to comprehend. Then again, it certainly made for easy living. But comfort was insignificant to a man in his position, a man who was responsible for the many citizens of Thieron. The most comforting thought available to him was that he had Cyan to share the burden with.

It was then that the feeling of being carried swept over the ship.

"There!" Swift said triumphantly. "The Southern Drift."

The ship drifted with slow purpose towards the south. All three men smiled gently.

*

A restless breeze pulled itself over them, blanketing them into an unknowable slumber. The mystery eluded each of them, for none tried to learn and in that act of dissidence they made an ally of ignorance as they made a friend of the breeze. For now they knew a nothing so absolute that it was doubtful that they had ever known anything at all. An assurance so cold even snow couldn't have fallen.

The sun gazed down upon them. Any other audience would have been warmed or moved. Not them. Only the coldest and most stoical of all beings could have been said to ignore the performance; which was exactly what they did, unwittingly.

The sea, so close but not altogether near, sighed as the endless tides landed against the cliff and left, landed against the cliff and left. Still they didn't move and solace was not given to that most sacred of spirits.

All went wanting.

They lay there, outside the gates of Genko, some in red, most in blue, never to know, feel, see, hear, smell or taste anything again; or at least not in the way they had grown so accustomed to in life. Some said they would ride the breeze, or waves, whichever was more to their liking, to be part of the planet forever.

The many remaining Mandrans, their red armour now an even more shocking vermillion with the drying blood of their enemies, moved between the dead Genkoan soldiers, performing a swift coup-de-gras straight to the heart. Some gathered their own dead to bury after they were given their ceremonial rights.

Yet still there was more killing to come.

When would they be ordered to march on Thieron? Not now, but soon enough.

And even then, would the killing end?

*

Night had fallen, though only one of the men on the ship slept. The two Captains were very much awake on deck. Swift, although not needed to steer, was never far from the helm, so much so he looked out of place anywhere else. Cyan leaned upon the railing of the bridge. He had said it was to keep

108

Swift company however he had yet to say a word since.

"This is taking longer than I expected," he said, finally.

"The drift begins to wane at this time of the summer," Swift said. "By the time autumn arrives it will be completely gone. Still, it's faster than sailing unaided."

"It's been a short summer this year."

"There are a few weeks left, maybe."

"Sometimes I feel as though the summers are getting shorter every year."

Cyan sighed and slumped heavily over the railing. His eyes drifted to the reflected moon, swaying listlessly over the waves. He lifted his head to look at the sky-bound counterpart, only for it, reflection as well, to disappear behind a cloud as black as the night itself.

"Or perhaps I'm just getting old," he said.

"You're a man who's seen a lot," Swift said. "Seasons pale when compared to a life, or even a year. In the end only the most eventful will remain in our minds. This summer will seem long by the time the season is over."

"You believe there's more to come?"

"The world will be a very different place before the leaves turn brown."

"For the better, I hope. Though I fear that's unlikely."

"We can hope," Swift said.

As silence returned, Cyan thought of a man he considered to still be out at sea. Somewhere out there was Laike Skyheart – a sad but strangely comforting thought at the same time. His friend was with him, just not as he once was.

The breeze strengthened, pushing the ship onwards.

"The breeze is thick tonight," Swift said.

"That it is," said Cyan.

"The dead are unsettled."

"Or there are new recruits."

"That's the most unsettling thing of all," Swift said.

"I'd have thought being part of the breeze would be peaceful."

"Most would yearn to be alive once more for a while, surely."

"I suppose that's mournful."

Swift smiled lightly. "I thought Thieronians believed in Thiera, not in the love of the planet."

"Most do," Cyan said. "But as you say, I'm a man who's seen a lot. I can't say any god or deity had a lot to do with it. I think I'd prefer it if they didn't. The good parts of life seem all the more spectacular thinking that they just are. The bad parts seem more bearable knowing that an omnipotent entity didn't allow them to happen, they just... did."

The clouds were parted by the breeze and the moon returned to light their way.

"I think that means they want us to get their safely," Swift said.

"Yes," Cyan said. "I suppose it does."

*

The new day brought disturbing news of Genko's easy defeat. How, exactly, such a massacre had occurred was still something of a mystery, although they could rest assured that it had definitely happened – the most disturbing news of all.

The sky reigned red over Thieron that morning as it so often did when they received horrifying news. The thick desert air hung even closer than usual, the suffocating sultriness allowing not a being to escape. Although summer was fading into autumn, the days just seemed to be getting hotter.

Away from the sun, though not the heat, in the impenetrable darkness of the President's Office, Commander Skyheart scratched at the beginnings of his beard. "Certainly, this is unsettling news. That the Genkoans bought us so little time is nothing short of tragic. However, isn't their defeat something we had anticipated?"

"Commander Skyheart speaks the truth," General Wraste said. "Although, what we are lamenting is not so much the defeat as the ease of it. Their force is – was, sorry – far greater than ours and yet they seem to have barely dented the Mandran numbers."

"Indeed," an Assembly member said, "this news means we must still fight the Mandrans on two fronts."

"We are no better off than before Operation Shell," said another.

"Yet surely no worse!" exclaimed the Commander.

"No worse?" an Assembly member said. "May I remind you, Commander, that we have no captains? Thean and Skyheart, along with their Lieutenants are confirmed dead. Cyan and Rom have disappeared since the news of the skirmish in Genko – presumed dead – and you have been promoted. Do not misunderstand, we are pleased with your work as Commander so far and know you would gladly enter combat if necessary. The loss of your traitor brother is, perhaps, to our advantage, yet the death of Thean alone is damning. Without Cyan and Rom..."

"We do not know for sure that they are dead," said the President.

"Sir," said General Wraste. "You don't mean to say that you think they may have survived such an onslaught?"

The President said nothing.

"We must consider our options," an Assembly member said.

"So far," said another, "we have considered battle. The President still holds out some hope for the return of the Diamandé. What other options are there?"

"Evacuation," said another.

"Evacuation?" Commander Skyheart shouted. "You'd dare suggest that everyone in Thieron run away from an enemy in past generations we have scoffed at?"

"These aren't past generations, Commander."

"I could never dishonour the Skyheart name by ordering, or even allowing, so cowardly a retreat."

"There is more at stake here than a family name, Commander. Besides, I believe the Skyheart name is tarnished beyond repair."

The Commander stepped back in line with General Wraste, snarling. He shrank inside himself.

"I'm afraid I have to agree with the Commander," the General said. "Evacuation is not an option. Aside from it being cowardly, the logistics make it impossible. Firstly, we would need to convince every citizen of Thieron to leave behind their possessions and homes. We would then need to find a way to get everyone through the desert. Even if were able to do this, where would we go?"

The Assembly looked between each other as the realisation of Wraste's words dawned on them. The President leaned forward on the table.

"Ready the troops," he said. "We will defend our home to the death and hope that Cyan and Rom return with the Diamandé, if they are alive. Thiera be with us."

*

With the light of the sun, Rom emerged from the lower deck and the sight put Cyan in a better mood. The Captain had yet to sleep, though the sunlight itself rejuvenated him. So there was only a slight possibility they would find the Diamandé, it was still a possibility.

Rom was also in a good humour. With his sleep came a renewed determination to do, at least, all he could. Though, he doubted he would know when his limit had been reached.

Swift smiled at the sight of his contented crew. The ship was approaching the horizon where, eventually, they would see their destination. And after that? Who knew?

Onwards, the sea carried them. Destiny awaited.

Chapter Seventeen

He awoke, not suddenly as he usually did, but in waves, as if consciousness was an incoming tide that he had been caught in. Eventually, his eyes opened and he looked around the dark room he was in. He noticed, in the bed beside him, the woman who had refused him a place to sleep and the boy he had met in the forest. The woman stirred with a gentle purr and turned in her sleep, now facing Skyheart. He couldn't remember the last time he saw such soft features. He imagined even his looked masculine in comparison.

An image of the black tower shot through his mind at the sight of her dark hair.

"Strange," he said quietly, "I don't usually dream."

He rose, finding that his shaking was giving him a brief moment of respite, although his nausea was still as potent as ever. It was then he realised that he had been stripped, most likely to calm his fever. He stumbled aimlessly through the darkness of the small house for a few minutes before finding his clothes on a chair by his bed. He sighed, annoyed at himself for not looking there first, and dressed.

He approached the door and left in silence.

The cool night breeze greeted him gently, helping dispel any remaining sleepiness from him. The moon smiled placidly, cutting through the navy of the sky. The air he inhaled invigorated his being. How well rested he was, yet he imagined that was to be expected after the amount of time he had slept. How long that was he didn't quite know, though the moon seemed to be nearing a new phase, so he knew it was more than just one night. Perhaps he had dreamed in real time. It seemed unlikely. However, it was unusual for him to dream at all, to dream in real time on the rare occasions when he did didn't seem so unreasonable. If this was the case, he had been asleep for around four days.

'Rather excessive,' he thought. Then again, he always had been a heavy sleeper.

Onwards, he walked into the night. He knew not where he was going, Port Fair was still very unfamiliar to him, but he continued on, sure he would find a tranquil place to rest. A part of him argued that he had rested quite enough over the past few days, however there was little else to do. It was too beautiful a night to train.

He had hoped that the fresh night air would relieve him of his malady, though he had no such luck. Only one thing would end this sickness and that was, as yet, unobtainable. Of course, he would have to honour his promise to the Mayor and kill Celisso; he had to, if he was to be satiated. Then again, he refused to do it without an appropriately sized audience and, of course, a few days getting used to his surroundings. He still knew little of Port Fair and Celisso, too, was a mystery. What kind of warrior would he be if he mindlessly, cavalierly, dove into battle with a creature he knew nothing about?

He admitted to himself that this was just an excuse to shirk his duties, but the people of Port Fair needn't know that. He'd just been involved in the extremely dangerous Operation Shell. He'd nearly died. As far as the Captain was concerned he deserved a short rest. Anyway, he'd kill Celisso soon enough, he just wished to do it on his own terms. That wasn't so unreasonable, was it?

Myri woke with a start. She opened her eyes greeted by the painfully bright morning light and Paccon shaking her wildly. He was saying something but in her groggy state she failed to understand the slur of words. Then, noticing the empty bed beside her, his words suddenly made perfect sense.

"The Captain's gone!"

She rose as speedily as she could manage, realising she had to tell the Mayor. She grabbed Paccon and the pair rushed outside. The square was busier than she had expected. She had slept later than she first thought. What she had assumed was dawn was actually closer to mid-morning.

'I need to stop sleeping so late,' she thought. 'I've got responsibilities now that I'm looking after Paccon. What if it had been him to go missing?'

They burst into the Mayor's office, visibly startling the old man inside. Myri took a few seconds to gather her breath before saying excitedly quickly, "The Captain's gone!"

Slowly, a look of realisation took hold of the Mayor's face. It seemed to Myri as if it started at the top of his head and worked its way down. First his forehead creased into small ridges, next his eyebrows narrowed and dug in close to the bridge of his nose. Then his eyes widened, glowing, followed by the fluttering of his nostrils and growing of his cheeks. When Myri finally took in his mouth she realised he was smiling the widest smile she had seen on him.

"He's gone?" the Mayor said. "That means he's awake. The Captain's awake," he said more excitedly. "The Captain's awake." He hurriedly opened his office window and, leaning out, he shouted, "The Captain's awake!"

The square burst into a frenzy of understanding happiness. Each denizen present repeated the phrase and rushed to the window.

"We don't know where he is," the Mayor said. "As soon as we find him we can be rid of Celisso!"

The Mayor needed not remind them of the incentive. Indeed, such a large consequence of the Captain's arrival was always present in their minds. But, it was only with the Mayor's words that the town divided themselves and went in search for the Captain.

The Mayor turned back to Myri and Paccon. "Thank you, Myri. You've been a huge help, despite the fact that you had every reason not to be. And you, Paccon; from what I hear from Doctor Gainsborough, you've been Captain Skyheart's personal carer."

Paccon blushed; even under the shade of his hat the colour was visible. "I'm going to look for him," he said to Myri. She nodded, allowing him to go and watched as he ran from the Town Hall out into the square.

"Doctor Gainsborough tells me you have rather mixed feelings about the Captain," the Mayor said.

Myri didn't reply.

"It's understandable," he continued. "I think we all do to an extent. We can't dismiss the past completely. We all have a tale of loss from the Mineral Wars." He looked a picture on his desk of a woman Myri didn't know. She was in a wedding dress. "He may bring great things to Port Fair."

Myri could feel tears building up behind her eyes. Oh, such familiarity to a feeling would have been pleasing were it a happier emotion that was evoking it. She managed to keep her tears inside by clenching her fists and taking some deep breaths.

'Why must people always speak of the past to me?' she thought.

"I should help look for him," she said, leaving, although she fervently hoped that she would not be the one to find him.

From his position under a lone cherry blossom tree, a few feet from the sand of the beach, he could hear quite a commotion. However, being halfway between sleep and wakefulness, he paid it no heed. He needed not concern himself with the matter anyway, his position was quite secure; a perfectly obscure place that only one so cunning as the Crimson Captain himself would think to look, and he was confident that Port Fair was home to nobody quite so shrewd.

Although, after the sound of the excited residents continued for some minutes he, disconcertedly, opened his eyes. He deduced that, by the position of the sun in the sky, it was nearing mid-day. Undoubtedly, it was his awakening that was causing the disorder, but that had happened when the hours were still dark. That gentle-featured, dark haired woman must have slept late.

"It seems she can rival me in the game of slumber," he said to himself. "Well, I won't deny her the competition." He smiled and closed his eyes once more. With the soft lullaby of the tide and the comforting warmth of the sun, the Captain was soon cradled in sleep once more.

Paccon watched as the adults around him dispersed in different directions about the town. He failed to understand why they would search there; surely the Captain was somewhere considerably more beautiful. That meant he was either in the forest or at the beach.

Still in the square, Paccon pondered the options. The Captain had already been in the forest, so he could have found his way there far easier. However, perhaps a man who longed for adventure, such as he, would go somewhere he had yet to experience. The beach seemed to Paccon to be the obvious place to search; after all, the sea called to all adventurers.

Just as he was giving up on ever making a decision, he felt a tickling coming from inside his shirt pocket as Franklin clambered to poke his head from the top. Paccon held his right hand to the pocket and the baby turtle crawled onto his palm.

"Are you going to help find the Captain?" Paccon asked.

It seemed to the imaginative young boy that Franklin nodded in reply, though whether this was just his imagination or Franklin was actually nodding, Paccon wasn't sure. Nevertheless, the boy placed Franklin on the ground and watched as the turtle crawled towards the beach at surprising speed. Paccon followed his pet, confident he would lead him to Captain Skyheart. After all, it wouldn't be the first time.

After a few minutes of following Franklin, Paccon neared the beach. While the turtle looked to need a moment to decide on which way to go (its head slowly and repetitively swung from left to right), Paccon played with the sand. It was different from the sand on his island, coarser and darker but not altogether unpleasant. It still ran comfortably between his fingers. He still preferred the sand on his island though.

"I wonder how Mama is," he said absent-mindedly, not aware of having spoken aloud. He noticed that Franklin had chosen to go left and was waiting for him with a look that, had a human been wearing it, he was sure would have expressed annoyance. "Sorry," he said, following dutifully.

He had always wondered if Franklin's seeming understanding of him was his imagination or if he and Franklin really did share a connection. He supposed the idea wasn't so far-fetched. Humans could understand each other and animals could understand each other. Was it so unreasonable that a human and an animal, especially ones that spent as much time together as Paccon and Franklin, could understand each other?

His thoughts were interrupted by sounds of thrashing some way out at sea. He stopped and looked as Celisso whipped his tail wildly. The mindless beating sent explosions of saltwater high in the air, dispersing into droplets, and falling as light rain on the beast's kingdom. At least it brought no rain on land that day.

Paccon realised his distraction had allowed Franklin to get some way ahead. The boy ran, hoping to catch his pet up, almost tripping in the soft sand. When he eventually fell, the soft ground cushioned him adequately and he rose again.

Franklin led him to a part of the beach he didn't recognise. The land had started to curve around, almost creating a cove, and the grass on the landing had grown longer. A lone tree with pink blossoms stood on the grass. The trunk had a kink in it, as if an artist had drawn it with two sharp brushstrokes. He was sure that there was a figure lying beneath it, though it was quite a distance away.

"Well done, Franklin," Paccon said, picking up the turtle he was sure was smiling self-indulgently. He put his pet back in his rightful pocket and ran towards the tree, holding onto the brim of his hat to make certain it wasn't blown away.

It was, indeed, Captain Skyheart sleeping beneath the tree. Paccon had never known anyone who slept quite as much as the Captain (although he only really knew his mother and Myri). It seemed to the boy that it was all the Captain had done since he arrived in Port Fair. He knelt and poked him lightly in the chest.

Captain Skyheart, who had never appreciated being woken, no matter how important, pressing or necessary the reason, upon realising what was happening, groaned and, facing the brave soul who had taken it upon him or her-self to poke him so vigorously in the chest, opened his eyes with a scowl. When he noticed it was the boy from the forest he softened slightly.

"How typical of me to hide somewhere a child would look," the Captain said.

"Actually, Franklin found you."

"Franklin?"

"My pet turtle."

The Captain's scowl became a smile. "I don't recall ever thinking like a turtle before."

"Why are you hiding?" the boy asked.

"Because they're going to ask me to kill Celisso."

"And you don't want to?"

"Not yet."

"Why?"

"Well..." the Captain paused. "You wouldn't understand."

"Okay," Paccon said, more acceptingly than the Captain had expected. Skyheart closed his eyes and smiled, pleased that his ploy had worked.

Paccon lay next to and in the same manner as Skyheart. He rested his head on his palms and cocked one leg, resting it on the knee of his other which was in an upright position with the foot flat on the ground. He wasn't sure he would have called it comfortable, but, seeing the Captain at peace in such a similar manner, he assumed it was the done thing. Indeed, it must have been more familiar to a contortionist than a child or a captain.

"I'm afraid I've forgotten your name," the Captain said dreamily.

"Paccon."

"Paccon. I like that."

"Thanks." Even this one syllable was a struggle, for the boy was smiling so widely at the compliment his lips were stretched too far apart to form even the simplest syllable.

"You're not from Port Fair are you?"

"No. I live on an island with Mama. Where are you from?"

"Thieron."

"Where's that?"

Skyheart gestured lazily with a hand as if to say, "Who knows?"

Paccon sighed. "So you're lost too."

"Quite the opposite," Skyheart laughed. His lips curled into a contented smile. "I'm right where I want to be."

"I thought you went on adventures."

Skyheart opened his right eye and rolled it around to look at Paccon. He closed it again without saying anything.

The boy rose to his knees.

"Could you take me home?"

"You know the way into town better than I."

"I meant *home*. To my island."

Skyheart fell limp. "Oh." He sat up and placed his right hand in the inside pocket of his coat. He withdrew a discoloured piece of paper. Well, it had once been 'one piece' but, since his time drifting towards the Southern Continent in the ocean, it had fallen apart and become 'some pieces' of paper. He laid them out on the grass he had flattened in his sleep and, after some reshuffling of various pieces, he said, "I think that's how the world looks... vaguely. Which one's your island?"

Paccon surveyed the map for some time, not recognising any of the tiny islands surrounding the Southern Continent. Then he pointed sharply at an island just off the north-eastern coast.

"There!" he said excitedly. "That's my island."

"Oh," Skyheart said, grimacing. "Well, I suppose I'll have to take you home."

"When?"

"Soon. Well, soon enough," Skyheart said. "Or at least, eventually. I'm very busy, you know."

"But you'll take me home?"

"Almost definitely."

Paccon thought it was a strange way of saying 'most definitely' but hugged the Captain nonetheless. Skyheart sat stiffly before prying the boy from him.

"Will you come back into town now?" Paccon asked.

"Not right now," Skyheart said. "I'm meditating."

But Paccon was already gone.

Skyheart sighed. "Just when I've found peace... I can't exert myself just yet, lest my shaking start again. Adventure can wait, just a little while at least." And with that he slept.

It was dark when the boy returned and the townsfolk were gathered in the square listing the places that they had searched. No attention was paid to Paccon, except by Myri. While the rest of the town told the Mayor where the Captain wasn't, Myri greeted Paccon with a warm hug.

"You were gone for ages," she said softly. "I was starting to get a little worried."

"I found the Captain," he whispered.

Myri pulled away from him and stared into his eyes. "Where?"

"Under the tree by the beach. He says he's meditating."

Myri smiled and walked over to the Mayor. Paccon watched from the crowd.

"Paccon's found the 'hero'," she said.

"Where?" the Mayor asked.

"Under the cherry blossom tree near the beach. Sleeping, of course."

The Mayor's face contorted to a level of anger she had never seen on him before.

"Arrogant wretch," he said. "Let's go and wake him."

"Not now, Mayor. It's been a long day for everyone. Let's wait until tomorrow."

The Mayor sighed. "Yes. Perhaps you're right." He snorted harshly. "I almost hope Celisso *does* kill him now. Hopefully they'll kill each other. That would solve all of our problems."

"No it wouldn't!" Paccon shouted, separating himself from the crowd. "Captain Skyheart's going to take me home."

"Home..." Myri said in a breath, without meaning to. She clutched her hands to her chest as if trying to stop her heart from escaping.

"He'll save us," Paccon said. "He just needs a little encouragement."

The Mayor smiled, his fury extinguished at the hope of the boy. "Perhaps you're right, Paccon."

The night went by unnoticed by all but her. She sat, curled like a feline, on the garden step, gazing at the moon, although the cloudy sky only allowed for passing glimpses.

She shivered and wrapped the blanket around her more tightly. She tucked her bare feet underneath her, trying to keep warm but failing. Still, she didn't want to go inside. She wouldn't sleep.

A firefly glowed on one of the graves at the end of the garden, illuminating death.

Myri thought of the dead fleetingly before the firefly rose and hovered over to her. It spiralled around her, leaving a short trail of light behind it. Then it left.

"My mind's elsewhere," she said.

Celisso's roar cut through the night and a light rain began to fall. She rose and went inside.

Before returning to bed she observed her temporary son, asleep. She stroked his face gently and he smiled.

"Dreaming of home?" she said. "Aren't we all?"

She lay in bed and faced the boy. When she closed her eyes she didn't sleep, though she did have the feeling of dreaming. A feeling that didn't go away.

Skyheart awoke to a familiar poking in his chest. When he was suitably annoyed and sure he could not sleep through such a persistent disturbance, he opened his eyes to the bright day. Paccon was kneeling next to him once more.

"Weren't you just here?" Skyheart said.

"That was a whole day ago, silly."

"I've slept for a whole day," Skyheart said through the curve of a smile. Admittedly, it wasn't the first time he'd achieved such a feat and it had been his aim, however upon hearing of the accomplishment he couldn't help but be proud.

It was then he looked behind Paccon.

He had brought the entire town with him. The woman who had refused him a bed for the night was standing at the front of the crowd with the Mayor.

'Well played, boy,' he thought.

The Mayor stepped forward. "We were wondering if you were planning on slaying Celisso today."

"Actually Mayor, I'm glad you're here. I was just about to go looking for you. These shipments that Celisso is blocking; he's eaten from them before, which is why they've been stopped?"

"That is correct."

"And what exactly is in these shipments?"

"Well, food: bread, fruits, vegetables, meat, some fish." He paused.

Skyheart thought of the list. He hadn't eaten for a while, however he wasn't hungry. No, his nausea had quite destroyed his appetite. He doubted that he could have digested anything solid anyway.

The Mayor continued. "Of course, there are the luxuries too. We often receive alcohol..."

"Alcohol!" Skyheart repeated out-loud, involuntarily. Realising he was unable to mask his motive, he leapt to his feet. "Mayor," he said. "Gather some bait and meet me at the pier. I require the rest of the town as audience." He paused, hoping to build tension. "Today, Celisso dies!"

Myri rolled her eyes at the Captain's arrogance, however the rest of the town seemed rather taken in. With nothing better to do, she went with her fellow residents to gather the bait and meet Skyheart at the pier.

They gathered the only bait, and food, they had. A small expedition party ventured into the forest to fetch apples from the 'enchanted' apple tree while the rest of the town collected the remaining apples that Skyheart had given them.

There were whispers that this was an unnecessary risk. Some suggested that if Skyheart failed then they had lost all of the food they had and would still have Celisso to deal with. An enraged Celisso. One man even insinuated that the Captain was most likely running away from Port Fair at that very moment. It was then pointed out to him that Skyheart was far too lazy to run away and death was probably favourable to him when compared with the effort of escaping.

This point of view was proven correct when they arrived at the pier, greeted by a resting Skyheart. He had taken the inconvenient position of lying in the centre of the structure. This was made all the more troublesome by his decision to lie across the pier as opposed to along. The citizens now had to step over him with their heavy loads of apples, grumbling as to why he couldn't help.

When the bait was properly set at the end of the pier, Myri approached the Captain and moved her right leg to kick him in the ribs. Skyheart's hand shot to her calf and her heart fluttered in his gentle, yet firm, grasp.

"I was meditating," he said. He opened one eye and looked at Myri. Her emerald eyes glimmered in the sun, though her face was shadowed by her dark hair. "Also, that's not a very nice way of being woken."

He released her leg and Myri placed her hands on the curve of her hips. "Well the bait's set," she said angrily. "Go on, kill Celisso."

119

Skyheart smiled and closed his eyes once more. "When the time's right."

"And when is that?"

"When Celisso decides." He opened his eyes and rose. Spotting a palm tree, he swaggered off the pier and moved to lie beneath it. "Wake me when it's coming," he said, waving a hand back to them as he walked away.

"Unbelievable," Myri said under her breath.

The town waited eagerly on the beach, peering out to sea. Many hours passed and still Celisso refused to approach. The beast preferred meat, but they knew when it was hungry enough it would eat apples. However, it would take a long time for Celisso to reach such a stage of hunger.

They waited in expectant silence. Nobody dared speak for fear of stifling Celisso or, perhaps even less desirable, waking the Captain prematurely.

Paccon stood at the base of the pier with the other children. Myri hadn't seen him interact with them before. She imagined that the shared anticipation had eroded to them the fact that the boy in the tall straw hat wasn't from around there. She smiled involuntarily.

She turned her head and looked to the Captain. Was he really the fearsome Crimson Captain; the man who defeated a whole garrison of soldiers at Pale Castle? He seemed far too lazy and self-involved to be the doer of such deeds. Surely the stories had made more of him than he really was.

She watched as he slept peacefully, barely even breathing. How different it was from before. The delirium induced coma seemed as if it belonged to a different man. Not even two days had passed since he awoke, yet he seemed so much more serene. Nevertheless, he still spent most of his time asleep. That could hardly be said to be a recovery.

Myri became annoyed with herself that the arrogant boy of a man was so often on her mind. Was he so intriguing? Certainly not. Although, as she tried to think of something else, her gaze failed to be drawn from him.

A whisper weaved throughout the audience and a murmur grew. Myri turned her head out to the sea. The water ruffled with surf and spray snaking towards the shore.

"Celisso's coming!" one of the children shouted.

A gargantuan, blood-red fin cut through the sea skin.

Some had made the approach to wake the Captain, but, upon seeing he had already sat up, stopped. He rose from his seated position under the palm tree and stretched his arms, yawning. When he was satisfied that he was awake enough he drew Cendré and began a slow walk to the pier.

He swaggered past Myri, Cendré slung across his shoulder, wry smile strewn across his face. His footsteps were soft, unsurprisingly light-footed for so slender a man. He swaggered through the gathered children who parted exactly in half, clearing his route to the pier. Once he passed, Paccon retook his position in the centre of the group.

The Captain's feet clicked loudly on the wooden boards of the pier; each step seemingly taking forever with Skyheart's slow pace. Each step was that much closer to a metronome beat.

After what seemed like an eternity Skyheart reached the end of the pier, standing in between the edge and the apples, as if it was his duty to guard them. He scratched the back of his head absent-mindedly as Celisso continued nearer.

The town had grown silent once more, watching expectantly as Celisso bore closer in its endless advance towards the Captain. It passed through their minds that the complacent attitude of the Captain would cause his own death. However, it also occurred to them that his arrogance seemed almost well-founded.

"Who ever heard of a duel in the middle of the afternoon?" Skyheart said to himself.

Celisso burst through the surface of the water, just one foot away from the Captain. Towering above Skyheart, the beast roared.

No clouds came.

The obsidian black blade of Cendré left Skyheart's shoulder, singing with soprano pitch as it sliced through the air. The crimson ribbons tied to the hilt stiffened with momentum.

Cendré tore cleanly through the serpent's scales, flesh and bone. The release of the captive veins caused pressurised blood to spurt wildly from the severed beast. Although the sword was not long enough to cut all the way through Celisso, the force with which it was swung ripped the remaining distance of tissue from the monster.

The top of Celisso's now disjoined body slid from the bottom half, crashing into the sea as the tail so often had. The force caused a wave to rise, soaking the Captain.

"I suppose I should have expected that," he said to himself.

He sheathed the saltwater washed Cendré and began the slow walk back to the beach.

The town watched, still in silence, amazed and bemused at the feat they had just witnessed. The ease with which he had slain the beast was surely impossible, yet what they had just seen was undeniably real.

The Captain's boot-clad feet returned to the beach, sending up wisps of sand with each step as he made, once more, for the palm tree. He lay in the shade, though not as he had earlier. His head used the curved trunk as a pillow, while his hands rested on his chest and his legs lay out straight.

This would just be a nap.

The town feasted that night under the full moon. The shipments had arrived in the early evening and the residents worked together cooking the huge meal on which they gorged after so long surviving on berries and, more recently, apples.

Skyheart took no part in the preparations, nor did he eat at the feast. He sat alone on the beach, resting as usual. He became aware of a presence and found the Mayor standing next to him, holding a bottle of a deep blue liquid. He gestured with it towards the Captain.

"What's this?" Skyheart said, taking the bottle.

"It's a wine made from a rare form of grape. It comes from one of the islands just south of here."

"You had me at 'wine'," Skyheart said, removing the cork and taking a large swig. He coughed after swallowing, the fierce alcohol taking him quite by surprise.

"How is it?" the Mayor asked.

"Crude, tart and rough," the Captain replied. "But it's certainly potent, so it's not without its charms."

The Mayor smiled. "I'll leave you to your reunion."

Skyheart gave his usual casual salute as the old gentleman returned to the feast.

He took in more of the primitive wine, his old friend refreshment gradually extinguishing his nausea. He lay back, at peace. No doubt he would eventually become bored there over time, but for now he was perfectly calm in a way he didn't recall ever knowing in Thieron. A day would come when he would adventure again, but it had yet to arrive.

He heard the percussive movement of sand next to him as the woman who had refused him sleeping arrangements sat down. The woman who had tried to wake him with a kick on the pier. The woman with the gentle features, dark hair and emerald eyes.

"Thank you," she said.

Skyheart smiled. "You don't need to thank me."

He offered her some of the wine by thrusting the bottle at her. She accepted, took a small swig and handed the bottle back, failing to suppress a cough. "They keep making this stronger," she said.

Skyheart's smile grew slightly wider.

"So you're going to take Paccon home?" she said.

"Soon enough."

"Sounds like an adventure."

"Yes," he said. "I suppose it does."

His voice dropped, not with the usual inflection his words usually held, but with something more solemn. Myri thought of inquiring further but decided against it.

"Well, I'm sure Paccon will come and find you in the next few days," she said.

"I'll be around, I should imagine."

She walked away as the Captain took a large swig of wine. He looked to the moon smiling high above the sea.

"Strange, how it does that," he said to himself.

"Strange how what does what?" a voice behind him said.

Skyheart jumped and turned his head to see Paccon. He calmed himself by taking another sip if wine.

The boy sat next to him. "I knew you'd kill Celisso."

"So did I."

"You sleep a lot, though," Paccon said, laughing just a little. "Why do you sleep so much?"

"Days are long," Skyheart said. "I like to break them down into smaller, more manageable days."

Paccon didn't really understand. "Can I call you Laike?"

"Certainly not!" Skyheart said incredulously.

"Why not?"

"It's not the done thing. You may call me 'Captain' or 'Captain Skyheart'."

"Okay.

Paccon's acceptance melted Skyheart's anger.

"Tell me, Paccon," he said. "What's her name?" He pointed to the woman with the emerald eyes.

"Myri," Paccon said, slightly confused as to how he could not know her name after spending so much time together. Then again, the Captain had been unconscious for much of that time.

"Myri," Skyheart repeated. He took another large sip of wine and lay down.

This night would wash over him.

Chapter Eighteen

The residents of Port Fair rested over the next few days, but none more so than Captain Skyheart. He could be found under the cherry blossom tree, sipping the crude wine. It had taken time, but he was growing fond of the beverage, unsophisticated though it was. It did a fine job of keeping his nausea at bay.

The townsfolk didn't bother him; he had earned his rest in their eyes. Had he wanted to he could have stayed there, unhindered by work or duty, for the rest of his days and it seemed to be a very real possibility. As he lay there, the warmth of the sun penetrating through his skin and mixing with the warmth of the alcohol within him, he found in himself not the yearning for adventure that had always been raging so fervently within his being, but a peace. Something he could never have in Thieron, unwelcome by his superiors as he was. Yet, in Port Fair, it seemed welcome was exactly what he was, hailed as a hero and a saviour, despite the history of the town.

He gave a satisfied groan as he stirred and his mind wandered further from the waking world.

Myri watched from the door, smiling, as Paccon fed Franklin a large leaf in the garden. The baby turtle didn't seem particularly interested. However, as the boy persisted, Franklin's will began to wane and eventually he ate the leaf, if just to be left alone. At least, that's how it seemed to Myri. She thought it unlikely that a turtle could have such motives or reasoning abilities.

"Where's Captain Skyheart?" Paccon asked. "He hasn't been in town for days."

Myri took a few moments to reply. Over the past few days she had become increasingly annoyed at herself for her conduct at the feast when she had drunkenly commended Skyheart. Admittedly, he wasn't what she had expected. He was not the bloodthirsty, violent Crimson Captain from the stories. Instead he was; lazy, frivolous, drunken, devious and, above all, insufferably arrogant. Put simply he was utterly deplorable. She imagined that her momentary lapse in her stance was a combination of the drink and the Captain's charm. Although she would have liked to deny him this trait, she found she could not. But still, even if he had saved the town, he had yet to uphold his promise to Paccon.

"He's probably under the cherry blossom tree," Myri said, not really paying attention to her words.

"Is he going to take me home soon?"

The prospect of Paccon leaving shot through her with a sharp stinging sensation, bringing her senses back around into the conversation. "I think he might need a little encouragement."

"Like with Celisso?"

Myri nodded and knelt next to her painfully temporarily-adopted son. "Just like with Celisso."

The metronome beat of the tapping on his ribs was beginning to rouse him. The unbearable possibility of waking fully caused his right arm to shield his eyes. No daylight would reach him if he had any say in the matter.

The beat quickened. The once gentle tapping became a violent poke (or as violent as a poke can be) and he felt himself steadily waking.

'Surely nothing can be this urgent,' Skyheart thought. 'Who could possibly wish me such trauma?'

Upon realising his ability to string coherent sentences together in his head, and thusly his wakefulness, he groaned piteously, removed his arm from his face and, reluctantly, opened his eyes. He was far too awake to ignore this intruder.

"That's quite enough of that," he said. Before him he saw the gentle featured, emerald eyed woman. What had Paccon said her name was? After not finding the name in his mind, he sat up, trying to dispel the last remaining iota of sleep from his system. "How can I help?" he said, reading her expression and knowing instantly that this was not a social visit. Indeed, she seemed not to want to be there with him at all, as if it was her duty to merely endure him. Had she grown resentful of him once more already? Oh, what a temperamental woman this one was.

"When are you going to take Paccon home?" she asked.

"That's rather direct," Skyheart said, reaching for the bottle of wine.

"When are you going to take Paccon home?"

"I've literally just killed a sea monster."

"That was three days ago!"

"Can we not live on past glories for at least a week?" Skyheart said, smiling. He moved the bottle to his lips and, just as he was about to drink from it, Myri snatched it from him.

"No more of this until you agree to take Paccon home," she said, waving the bottle around expressively, spilling droplets of the precious liquid.

Skyheart's smile widened. So she had one bottle, no matter – he had a stash of many bottles behind the tree. He had stockpiled the wine, as he had the apples, so he didn't have to keep going into town for supplies. He rolled over to fetch a bottle from the stash.

His smile fell from his lips at the sight.

Gone.

All of them.

He sat up sharply and looked at Myri. 'My, she's a cunning one,' he thought.

She smiled slyly.

"I'll leave you here to think about it," she said.

He watched as she walked away. He needed to think clearly. What could she have done with them? Of course, her advantage of having a far superior knowledge of the town could only work against him.

Oh, if that nausea were to assault him again, how could he bear it?

He would have to strike a deal.

He rose and ran after her, taking his place at her side before decreasing his pace to a walk.

"That was rather unnecessary," Skyheart said.

"I disagree. I think it was completely necessary."

"But why the wine?" he groaned in as high a pitch of voice as he could ever remember talking in.

"Because I refuse to negotiate with a drunk."

"Why? We're notoriously easy to negotiate with! Just give us more alcohol and we'll do anything."

"Usually that would be true," Myri said. "However, the more *you* drink the more reasons you come up with to shirk your responsibilities."

"Getting Paccon home is hardly my responsibility."

"You made a promise to a hopeful young boy. You have a duty as a man, no, as a *human* to keep it."

Skyheart flared inside. His humanity had never been called into question before. Indeed, he took particular exception to being insinuated as being 'inhuman'. He stepped in her path and faced her. They both stopped walking.

"Whether it is my responsibility or not is irrelevant, "Skyheart said. "I shall take him in my own time."

"I'd suggest taking him before your withdrawal symptoms strike you down again. It will be ever so hard to lead while you're unconscious." She walked past him forcing Skyheart to turn and follow.

"Had I preventative medicine then my consciousness would be assured," he said.

"And yet you spend all of your time asleep."

"Well that's just part of my genius."

"Genius?" Myri laughed.

"Yes, genius," Skyheart said indignantly. "Do you know of any other as skilled with a sword as I am?"

"No, but I know far more reputable characters with far more reputable occupations."

"This seems to have changed from a negotiation to a personal attack on me."

Myri stopped and turned to face Skyheart. "Paccon needs to be taken home," she said softly. "If you knew him like I did you'd care for him in the same way. If you had even an ounce of decency you'd take him and if you were a good man you'd have already done it. Now, I know you didn't come to Port Fair to solve our problems, however Paccon saved you from death while you were unconscious and you've yet to repay him."

Skyheart thought of the interminable dream, though by that point only the ominous black tower and the sight of his aged father remained. He sighed and watched as she approached the town. He followed, thinking of what she had said.

'I suppose I can only lie around drinking for so long before it becomes tiresome,' he thought. 'This could be quite a quest. Who knows, more may be on the way.'

They entered the square together, the Captain's mouth curling into a smile.

"Very well," he said quietly. "I'll take him."

He held out his hand to take the bottle from her. When she didn't hand it to him he scratched the back of his head as if it were part of the same motion.

"I'm really very thirsty," he said.

She surveyed the more-than-slightly-effeminate man before her. She observed in his eyes something she had not noticed earlier – she supposed it might have been mistaken for honesty.

"Promise me you'll take Paccon home," she said.

"I just said..."

"Promise."

"Fine. I promise," he said, snatching the bottle from her.

"You'd better start planning the route," Myri said. "We're leaving tomorrow."

"Oh, I did that long ago," Skyheart said gleefully. The second half of Myri's utterance he didn't hear until she started walking towards her house. "Wait," he said, walking after her. "What do you mean 'we'?"

She turned to him with a smile not dissimilar to his own. "You didn't think I'd trust you alone with Paccon, did you?"

"But you'll slow me down!"

"Be ready at dawn," she said, closing the door.

Skyheart stopped and smiled. "I seem to have found myself on an adventure," he said.

He downed the remainder of the wine. There was that yearning for adventure - it still lived in him. It had just taken the assurance of a new exploit to regain his enthusiasm for it. Invigorated by the prospects the next day would bring, he smiled wider. He then left to gather the supplies he would need for the adventure and, with the route he had devised, what an adventure it would be.

He woke with a start after a swift, sharp blow to the right side of his rib cage. He was becoming quite frustrated by the constant waking from the residents of Port Fair. Then again, he imagined that this would be the last one he would have to endure.

His eyes opened to the pale light of dawn and the face of Myri above him. She looked typically furious at him, though he had come to expect some level of annoyance in her, and had woken him by kicking him in the same manner she had attempted to administer on the pier.

"Get off of my fiancé's grave," she said through gritted teeth.

The back of Skyheart's neck burned with internal heat. He leapt to his feet in shame. It was dark when he had decided where to sleep that night and had failed to realise he was on a grave. In fact, quite how he had ended up in Myri's garden was a mystery to him too. He thought of explaining himself to her, but decided this was a situation not best served by words. He picked up the bag of supplies he had gathered.

"Sorry," he said. "I, uh, didn't know."

Myri softened visibly. She removed the flattened flowers that Skyheart had slept on and replaced them with some fresh ones.

"I'll be back in a few days," she said, stroking the grass, beneath which her fiancé lay.

Skyheart considered the three graves. He thought the garden a strange place to put a constant reminder of death; however it seemed to comfort Myri. These southerners were truly a strange people to the Captain's mind. It wasn't so much that they couldn't let go of their past, but that they made no effort to.

The two passed through the house and into the square where Paccon awaited them; eager, though clearly tired. It was a combination of feelings that Skyheart could empathise with. He failed to remember when last he woke at dawn.

Skyheart watched with the boy as Myri said goodbye to the Mayor and Carre. She kept this mercifully brief.

When she returned to them, Skyheart, confident that Myri had forgotten (or at least forgiven) his earlier indiscretion, held out the bag of provisions. "You can carry this."

"Why me?" she said.

"The reasons are many," Skyheart replied. "I need my hands free as point-man. I also need to be able to draw my sword should danger arise. Paccon can't carry the bag for obvious reasons. This leaves you – the woman who wanted to leave today."

"Fine," Myri said, snatching the bag from him. With that they entered the forest under the insipid sky as the dawn brightened into day.

Skyheart's heart fluttered. His adventure had finally begun.

Myri walked, holding Paccon's hand, a few feet behind the Captain. Even when on a journey his pace seemed leisurely, however, having to carry the supplies, Myri was thankful for this. She knew this was a pace she could keep.

Paccon gripped her hand tightly. As the morning progressed he gradually became more awake and more aware of his surroundings. He thought of how intimidated he had been by the forest on the night he met Skyheart. It seemed different during the day; mystical, recalling memories of his day there with Myri and Carre. However, today was even more magical – the first step on his reunion with his mother and his triumphant return home. He smiled broadly.

Skyheart, supercilious swagger intact, led them through the forest, confident for once that he was going in the right direction. Every so often he discreetly sipped from the bottle of wine he was housing in the inside pocket of his crimson leather coat. He wasn't exactly sparing with it, although he would hardly run out. The bag Myri was carrying was full of wine; he couldn't risk running dry, lest his withdrawal symptoms return. He didn't want a repeat of his state from a few days ago, nor did he wish to relive the delirium he experienced in the cave. He shuddered at the thought.

No more than a mile after passing the apple tree they came to a crossroads. Skyheart began to turn left onto the dirt trail.

"Wait," Myri said. "That's the Mountain Path."

"Your point?" Skyheart said.

"You want to walk the Flat Path, surely."

"That will take us two days longer."

"But it's safer."

"You've nothing to fear, Myri," he said, taking her gently and smiling. "After all, I'm Captain Laike Skyheart." He let go and began walking again.

Paccon looked up at Myri, noticing her gaze never left the Captain. "Are we going?" he asked.

"Of course," she replied, still looking after Skyheart.

They began walking again. Strangely, Myri felt inexplicably reassured.

Chapter Nineteen

The path led them to the base of the mountain by nightfall. In the distance, the endless mountain range grimaced against the luminescence of the moon. The starless sky gave no mind to the three travellers who now rested beneath it.

Skyheart pieced together the map in front of him and surveyed it, measuring out distances with his hands. Myri wrapped Paccon tighter in his blankets before taking her place next to Skyheart.

"How far do you think a hand is in real measurement?" he asked her. She replied with a look he was more used to receiving from DeFlare. "Well, we've travelled half a hand, including fingers. So we've travelled a palm. Then again, I do have exceptionally long fingers. In fact it could be three quarters of a hand for a lesser-fingered person. Indeed, I'd imagine it would be a whole hand for Paccon, however if we measure the journey in Paccon's hands it will seem considerably longer. The seven and a half hands we have yet to travel would be fifteen hands."

He looked at Myri only to find she had fallen asleep. He wrapped a blanket around her, his hands circling around her to the small of her back. He supposed she was an attractive woman and this thought had come to him sober. However, she couldn't be trusted – she was far too cunning.

He leaned over her to the bag of provisions. She breathed lightly on his cheek and he smiled. Carefully, he removed two bottles of wine (one for the night, one for the next day) and sat back in his rightful position.

He'd never been one for sleeping unprotected from the sky. He wished there was a tree nearby, however, this, apparently, was too much to ask for. With no shelter he sipped restfully from the bottle, hoping to drink himself to sleep.

A gust of wind picked up the pieces of the map he had, as yet, neglected to put away. He watched, powerless, as the world floated away from him.

'No problem,' he thought. 'I just need to go north until I reach North Port. The forest is to the south, so it's easy enough to follow.'

'And when the forest is no longer in sight?' said another voice from within him.

He sighed, rose and took a large swig of wine. He would not sleep that night.

Certainly, the map had been scattered, however the wind had been blowing back to the forest. He found one piece caught in a bush at the entrance. He picked it up only to find it was the square containing Thieron. A piece of the map and an important one at that, but it was obsolete on that particular journey. Still, he put it in his inside pocket and continued further into the woods.

After a few minutes of walking he came upon two more pieces. They were stabbed through by thorns, as if the map was not marred enough by years of folding and unfolding, along with the running ink from the days he spent in the Southern Drift. He removed them, not as carefully as he should have done, ripping them further. One was a picture of the Shadow Isles, a group of islands to the far south-west of the planet. An interesting place, yet ultimately useless to him. The other piece was of Port Fair. Admittedly, closer to the area he wanted, however one that was already well established in his mind.

Gradually realising the fruitlessness of his current endeavour, he took a large swig of wine. More fearful of Myri's reaction to his losing the map than he was of getting lost at some point on the journey, he ventured further into the woods.

Hours had passed and he had found a few more pieces; Genko, Paccon's island, North Port and part of the mountains. Far more useful than what he already had, but singularly useless without the rest of the Southern Continent. However, upon arriving at a small clearing he believed his luck was about to change. The clearing housed a lake and, in the lake, were several pieces of the map. Aware that the longer they were soaking the more the ink would run, he hurriedly fished them out. After saving the segments from their watery doom he discovered his efforts had been wasted. The ink hadn't been washed from the paper, yet he almost wished it had. All of the pieces were of ocean.

"Fitting," he said humourlessly. He sighed and began his walk back to the mountains.

Myri woke at dawn to find the Captain approaching from the forest. His swagger was rather less pronounced than usual and from his face had been removed the wry smile that he looked so naked without. Despite these changes in his essence he was unmistakable in the crimson coat he so proudly wore. As he neared Myri the swagger became ostentatious once more and the smile slowly crept across his lips.

"Where have you been?" she asked.

"I went to look for breakfast," Skyheart said. "However, the thoughtless denizens of your oh-so-beloved town seem to have plundered and pillaged every morsel the forest has to offer."

Before Myri had a chance to reply, the Captain gently shook Paccon awake. The well-rested boy suggested leaving immediately. To Myri's surprise the Captain agreed.

The trail spiralled around the southernmost mountain in much the same way as the path to the Coliseum in Mandra. The three walked on uncomplainingly in the same formation as the day before, although Skyheart was gradually putting more distance between him and his companions. He couldn't go wrong just yet; the only way to go was follow the trail to the top of the mountain, then cross the Ice-Bridge to the next mountain and follow that trail down. Hopefully, after that the road to North Port would be obvious. He could keep Myri from finding out about the loss of the map by maintaining this distance and keeping rest stops to as short a time as possible (against his nature though it was).

They rested at noon to a horizon of effervescent allure. The sun stood atop the zenith of one of the northern mountains, causing the peaked snow to glimmer and sheen. Soon, however, the lustrous orb began its descent. Would they ever know such perfect vividness again?

"It only lasted a moment." said Paccon.

"Can one wish for any more?" the Captain said.

Myri moved her gaze from the horizon to Skyheart. His face wore an expression of awestruck respect. In those few moments he was not the swaggering, arrogant swordsman, but a man admiring the art of nature. How different it was from what he usually knew.

Skyheart tilted his head to Myri. The light from the far-off snow glinted in the corner of her left eye. The Captain smiled as the emerald rings invaded and ravaged his very being.

"We should carry on," he said gently, his eyes endlessly meeting hers. "We may see many more images on our journey, godless though we stand. Horizons shall greet our every move and stars shall sing in the night sky merely to lullaby us to sleep. May the sweet scent of the cherry blossom follow us wherever we go, and may the unhindered grass meet each fall of our feet. Yes, we shall see many unforgettable effigies on this adventure. Indeed," he looked away from Myri and back to the horizon, causing her breath to escape from the very centre of her chest, setting upon her the very need to gasp in silently the mountain air, "some may, very well, always and already be with us."

He smiled in the same way he always did, although Myri observed in it a softness she had never noticed before, as if his lips had become yielding to a caress. He glanced at her once more before continuing up the spiralling path.

A warmth emanated from somewhere in her chest. She failed to place the feeling exactly or the culpable function causing it. Yet as it waved through her she felt a sudden peace as she had on the view of the horizon. She smiled weakly to herself – not a smile of happiness, nor one to fight off sadness, but one that found itself on her full red lips, upon the appreciation of the warmth within her.

She felt a tugging at her dress.

"He's getting ahead," Paccon said.

"Yes. Let's go," Myri said in such a voice that she could hardly have been said to have spoken a word.

She took Paccon's hand and the pair followed after the Captain.

The noon experience had been rather more sobering to him than he had been expecting. In fact, those skylines usually intoxicated him further. As the horizon had the opposite effect to his expectation, the speed of which he was drinking increased. When he realised he was running low and couldn't get any more until Myri was asleep, he slowed once more. It was more a preventative medicine anyway. He imagined being half drunk on a mountain trail was less than wise.

The cold air was starting to cut through his skin and he became aware that, if they travelled much higher on that day, they would be sleeping in the bitter cold. He halted and sat, waiting for his companions to reach him.

A few minutes later they arrived.

"I can still see Port Fair," Paccon said. They had circled back round to the south face. "We haven't come very far."

"We've come quite far," Skyheart said. "It's just that we've been going up for a while. Anyway, Port Fair is quite small now."

"How far have we come?" Myri asked.

"A hand and a half," Skyheart replied, immediately. "I checked whilst you were catching up."

Myri smiled. The decidedly unprofessional unit of measurement 'hand' evoked in her a good humour that seemed a little unfounded. However, amateurish though it was, it appeared to be working.

"Well," she said, still smiling, "perhaps you'd like to press on? We can make that hand and a half a whole two hands before night falls."

"Actually, I thought we'd rest here tonight. If we sleep much further up we'll freeze to death, sorry for the morbidity. We can move quickly tomorrow, reach the peak and cross the Ice-Bridge before descending the north mountain and sleeping at the bottom. Then we can continue to North Port the next day."

'Uncharacteristically cautious,' Myri thought, 'though it does have his hallmark laziness.'

"But it's still light," Paccon said.

"Well, we don't have to sleep straight away," Skyheart said, untying the bag from Myri's hip. From it he removed a loaf of bread; the crust was beginning to go stale, but as he tore it in three he discovered that the inside had kept fine. He passed a piece to Paccon who quickly began to eat it, his teeth ripping each bite from its compatriot of the loaf.

"You'll want to walk wrapped in blankets tomorrow," Skyheart said to Myri as he handed her a share of bread.

She nodded and picked delicately at the food, eating far more elegantly than the occasion warranted.

The sunset came sooner than they had expected. As the sun fell beneath the far mountains, giant teeth in the air, the sky turned a deep violet. Though soon, as with the noon, the moment was gone and darkness fell upon the Southern Continent. Paccon was asleep soon after, followed hastily by Myri. Skyheart discarded his empty bottle and replaced it with another full one from the bag.

Though Myri had fallen asleep quickly it was a light sleep that had been broken easily. She shuffled into a seated position and saw the Captain sitting on the edge of the track, drinking, his legs dangling from the trail.

"You should be asleep," Skyheart said. "We've a difficult day tomorrow."

"You should get some sleep too," Myri said.

"I will," Skyheart said, taking a sip of wine, "soon enough."

Myri clambered closer to him, though she stayed some way from the edge, still wrapped in her blanket. "It's a beautiful moon."

"I suppose."

"You don't think so?"

"I've always found such pale light to be rather eerie. Though, I must admit that it complements the mountains well." He passed her the bottle of wine, though she declined. He moved it back to his mouth and took a large sip.

"Where will you go next?" she asked.

Skyheart smiled and leaned back slightly. "I'm not sure. Perhaps the Shadow Isles."

"The Shadow Isles?"

"It's a small group of islands to the south west. The Shadus people live there. A strange group with supposed mystical abilities. I was once told that they control darkness, but I doubt it's true. I've always wondered, though. Other than that, they say that we have yet to discover some continents. Maybe I'll try to find them. The Southern and Northern Continents are so very small... the planet must be somewhat bigger than all that." He paused and looked at Myri. "I suppose it's back to Port Fair for you?"

"There are certain forces keeping me there," she said in a calm voice, bordering on sorrowfulness.

Skyheart paused for the briefest of moments and then looked away. "I'm sorry about your fiancé."

Myri smiled weakly as if to convey appreciation, though she would rather have not entered into the conversation at all.

Skyheart took another swig of wine. "How did he die?"

"Celisso."

"Oh."

"He tried to kill it..."

"You don't have to explain."

The pair became silent.

The cold air assaulted Myri and she wrapped the blanket tighter around her. Skyheart had yet to notice the cold. The alcohol was either warming him or numbing him. Either way he was happy enough.

After a few minutes more of silence, Myri, wordlessly, returned to the camp to sleep. Captain Skyheart finished his drink and soon followed.

They woke at dawn to a loveless vista. The sky lay above them, ashen black with cloud. The morning had more in common with night than the day of which it belonged.

"Oh dear," Skyheart said. He sighed and rose with slow reluctance, shaking Myri and Paccon gently from their slumber. The two less experienced adventurers kept their blankets around them as they began the ascension.

Skyheart stayed close to Myri and Paccon, knowing that this would be the most difficult day they had faced. He was proven right when the snow began to fall heavily with a thick wind blowing against them. He smiled with arrogant joy.

Stoically, the woman and child ventured onwards, led by this Captain from the north. Myri's thoughts lay burdensomely on her. A thick miasma had wrapped itself around her heart, replacing the warmth from the day before. Still, she struggled through the falling snow.

Paccon had said little on the adventure thus far. But what had he to say? All he knew was that he was on his way home to see Mama. Franklin was safe enough in his top pocket. Upon hearing the news that this part of the journey would be increasingly cold, Paccon had padded the pocket with some cloth he had with him in order to keep the baby turtle warm. Though, there was no denying the treacherousness of the journey.

They were beginning to slow, something that Skyheart had expected. As the depth of the snow rose higher they were forced to take larger, more cumbersome, steps. He took Myri by the hand, not hearing her protests against the roar of the blizzard, and began to drag the two through the ever deepening snow.

Soon, the cold began to cut through even the alcohol-warmed Captain, yet he refused to falter. The challenge even caused a smile to break out across his face, although he was careful not to let Myri see this as he was certain anyone but himself would have seen it as out of place, or even disrespectful. However, his irrepressible light-heartedness and good cheer remained, untainted, even as the blizzard raged with a far more determined level of intensity, as if to wipe the smile from his face.

Myri could feel herself beginning to become faint. The combination of the physical exertion, mental and emotional exhaustion and her falling body temperature was causing her to fail. She stumbled onwards, unaware of her wild unchecked movements. She opened her eyes, oblivious to having closed them, and found Skyheart was holding her to him as opposed to merely holding her hand as before. She also noticed that the Captain was carrying Paccon in his free arm. She imagined this was wise as the snow was nearing the height of boy's head.

She hadn't noticed just how tall the Captain was until that moment. Even against the torrent of white adversity he stood a whole head above her. Despite such observations she felt a slight objection to having been held so close to him without being consulted, though she was in no state to protest.

Myri stumbled, falling through a vast quantity of snow and landing on her knees, grazing them on the rocky ground. As soon as she could be sure what had happened, the Captain was knelt next to her, helping her up. He placed her on his back, before carrying Paccon in his right arm once more. She struggled to hold onto him as she weakened, however, every so often, he would stabilize her by lifting her, placing his left hand under he left thigh. Again, she would have objected to this under any other circumstances.

At various points she thought she heard the Captain speak, although she couldn't make out what he said as his voice was masked by the blizzard. But every time he spoke he shook Paccon gently, so she imagined it was to do with keeping the boy awake. Indeed, even she was struggling to stay awake and her head was nearing the Captain's shoulder - a resting place for the weary, growing ever more so.

Her head drooped, losing her battle against the wearisome situation. Her dark hair lay down the Captain's chest and comfort washed over her as the blanket on her back meshed with the Captain's warmth, finally assuaging her.

Then came the caressing lift of her thigh. The Captain turned his head and whispered in her ear. "Come now, I'm doing all the work here."

She could tell by the sound of his voice that he was smiling. Surely this precariousness didn't amuse him. She turned her head to him, affirming her suspicion as truth. His idiosyncratic wry smile was as present as ever on his face. It disappeared from her sight, though ostensibly remained, as he turned his head back up the trail. She lifted her head from the makeshift pillow and looked on in the same way.

She wondered how such a slight man could manage to carry both her and the boy whilst traversing the immersive snow. Certainly he couldn't be that strong. Then she remembered the obsidian black blade in his right hand tearing through the body of Celisso. No matter how sharp the blade was there had to be some strength behind the strike. To move so fast required an exertion of muscle, and yet on this man, muscle she could barely find.

Amongst the white mass she thought she could see a small area of black in the distance. She thought she must be imagining it. Or perhaps imagining herself imagining it, for the entire situation seemed so unreal she questioned the existence of the whole affair at times. But as they continued, the black area grew, until it was right next to them. She began to tap the Captain on his shoulder to bring it to his attention, but she desisted when she noticed he was already approaching it.

They entered into the blackness to discover a small cave. It crossed Skyheart's mind that perhaps 'cave' was too grand a word and 'alcove' was closer to the truth, or at least less of a lie. He placed Myri and Paccon as far back in the niche as he could and made sure they were both awake. Despite their weariness they soon became more lucid. He reached into the bag and handed the pair some cured meat with some more of the bread from before. As they were eating he placed the blankets around them.

"How much longer will it go on?" Myri asked, pulling Paccon closer to share her body warmth with him.

"I'm not sure," Skyheart replied. He sighed. "My plan hasn't worked at all, has it?"

"There were a lot of places where it could go wrong."

"That," Skyheart said, pausing as he removed the cork from his most recent bottle of wine, "is why it is a good plan."

He smiled at her and took a swig. He passed another bottle to Myri which she only accepted after his persistent gesturing with it at her.

"Why don't you get under the blankets?" Myri said. "You must be cold too."

Skyheart's smile widened. "As enticing as that offer is, I have to scout ahead. I want to see how far from the Ice-Bridge we are." He began to walk to the alcove entrance. "Don't fall asleep and be sure to drink the wine, it will warm you." He stopped on the threshold, the snow pulling the outside world from them. "Oh," he said and turned with his hips, tilting his head at Myri, "don't let Paccon drink too much of the wine. We don't want him ending up like me now, do we?" He smiled again, gave his usual casual salute and took a step outside, disappearing into the swirling, tumultuous mess of white.

She didn't comment on the inappropriateness of some of the Captain's comments. Now wasn't the time. She wrapped herself around Paccon, trying to end his shivering, yet he was as frozen as the mountain. She kissed his head, although his hat got in the way.

"Thank you," he said weakly.

"I didn't do anything," Myri said.

Paccon replied with such a benevolent and frail voice that it was impossible for annoyance to penetrate through her eternal worry for him. "I wasn't talking to you."

Of course, it was no problem for him. After all, he was Captain Laike Skyheart of Thieron's Division Four. What match was snow for the Crimson Captain? Besides, it had to stop eventually. Further and further he pushed his way through the eternal land of white, gradually making his way to the top of the mountain. Slowly though he moved, his pace was decidedly faster than when he was weighed down with his companions. Then again, he always did have a leisurely stride.

He used his body weight to push through the wall of snow, hoping that by clearing a path his return journey would be easier. He sipped at the wine on his way through, fuelling himself.

He reached the top of the mountain faster than he had anticipated. Alas, there was the Ice-Bridge; a natural sheet of ice leading from the southern mountain to one of the northern mountains. Had the day been brighter he imagined it would have sparkled against the luminous sun. Even on that darkest of days it had majesty Skyheart couldn't remember being witness to anywhere else on the planet.

He smiled and walked over to the bridge. He placed a foot on it and pressed down a few times. It seemed sturdy enough and not quite as slippery as he had expected, although he was sure he would hear some objection from Myri when the time came to cross. Of course, it was brilliantly daring – cavalier some may have said – and it was a rather long way to the end of the bridge. Even if the weather was clear when they began their crossing there was no guarantee it would stay that way. But there was nothing he could do about that, short of finding another way around and that would never do. How could he live such a disgrace down?

He took one large swig of wine and smiled. Then he turned to journey back to the niche where Myri and Paccon awaited his return.

Myri had been struggling to stay awake since the Captain left. The combination of the wine and warmth from Paccon and the blankets was intoxicating, instigating a somnolent wave over her, though her duty to keep Paccon awake prevented her from surrendering to the realm of sleep.

"Are you warm yet?" she asked the boy.

"Yes," he replied. "I wish the Captain was here."

"So do I."

"Will he be much longer?"

"I don't know."

"I'm tired."

"Stay awake."

"I will."

She pulled him closer, giving him her warmth.

They peered up from the blankets as a figure appeared in the entryway to their sanctuary. The remnant of humanity had faded into the shadow of the cave, causing its silhouette to weave into the darkness, only noticeable as it stood against the canvas of falling snow outside. It had something resting on what would have been a shoulder had it been human. It moved its free hand in some form of wild gesture propelling the image from obscurity into humanity, as it tore itself from the shadow and became, unmistakably, him.

Captain Laike Skyheart of Thieron's Division Four stood before them, the famed Crimson Captain, black blade of Cendré slung across his shoulder, wry smile strewn across his face, as with his free left hand he gave his usual casual salute. Yes, he of such complacent, arrogant, unassailable confidence had returned and, in that moment, Myri and Paccon felt a potent wakefulness engulf them.

"It's not far," he said nonchalantly, as he walked further into the alcove. "I suggest moving as soon as the blizzard stops."

They looked at him, too awestruck to say a word.

"You're probably warm enough to sleep now," he continued, taking a place, alone, in the darkest corner of the cave. He lay down with his head resting on his palms and his right leg on his left, propped up by the foot, flat on the ground.

He was the only of the three who slept.

She woke him more gently than she had before, stroking his face in a pleasing caress, rousing him slowly. He opened his eyes but did not speak. The blizzard had stopped – he learned this by the absence of wailing wind and then confirmed it as his eyes drifted to the cave entrance to reveal as clear a night as he could remember. The cloudless sky – webbing in a collage of blacks, purples and blues – exonerated the moon as the only source of light, save for the far away stars.

The Captain rose and met Myri's eyes.

"Ready?" she asked him.

He nodded and the three left the shelter, venturing into the moonlit night.

Skyheart's tracks had not remained after so many hours of falling snow. Once more he was forced to clear a path with his body. Myri and Paccon followed in the gap he cut. Their progress was creeping and stayed that way as the snow became increasingly difficult to displace as it froze the closer they got to the peak of the mountain. Still, Skyheart led them and they made progress nonetheless.

Paccon followed in silent awe at the feat of strength and determination he was witness to. He hoped he would grow up to be a similar man to the Captain and yet he found himself hoping that he would also be very different from the Captain, as if there was something about the man he loved, but would loathe to find as a characteristic in himself. What it was he couldn't say.

Myri kept her distance from Skyheart, allowing Paccon to walk ahead of her. She watched as the more-than-slightly-effeminate man struggled through the amassed snow. It seemed a shame to destroy it. The frozen snow captured the pale moonlight so vividly that a part of her felt as though it should stay there as a testament to nature's elegance. Though still he pushed through with his usual theatrical quality. She wasn't sure for whose benefit that was.

Skyheart had been correct – the bridge did sparkle. In the moonlight the ice held a thousand constellations of stars from every angle it could be looked upon. He smiled and turned to his companions, gesturing towards it with both arms.

"Behold," he said, "the Ice-Bridge!"

"We're crossing this?" Myri asked.

"Of course."

She walked up to it, knelt and wiped her hand across the surface. She turned, still kneeling, and held the hand to the Captain to reveal water. "It's melting," she said.

Skyheart scratched the back of his head. It wasn't out of the question that the bridge would be melting. Although it was still bitingly cold he surmised it could have been above freezing temperature. "That's just condensation," he said and then he paused. "From the snow."

"It's melting Captain! We need to go back and take the Flat Path."

"Out of the question. If there's another blizzard we'll freeze to death." He walked over and stood on the bridge, masking a slip into some wild gesture of triumph. "See," he said, "perfectly safe."

"I'll find another way," Myri pleaded. "Just let me see the map."

Skyheart's eyes widened and he turned his back on her. "It's perfectly safe, Myri." He began walking. "Stay behind me. If I fall and die at least you'll have fair warning." He said this with a laugh that made Myri shiver as it faded with his distance. In her horror she reacted too late to prevent Paccon from following. She had little choice and decided to do the same.

Of course, he knew it was melting. Truth be told he had been expecting it. Despite the slippery surface of the Ice-Bridge he made unhindered progress. Somehow his swagger seemed to aid his balance, although the science of this he couldn't quite grasp. His ease of progress made him ponder Myri's less-than-adventurous attitude to the current task. As if anything would go wrong.

Then the ice cracked beneath him.

It snaked past him and up the bridge to both ends with the whispering sound he had always associated with death.

"Captain!" Myri called.

"It's quite alright," Skyheart said. "It's a supportive fault."

He grimaced and took another step, knowing the consequence of the action long before it happened – but there was nothing else for him to do.

The ice shattered into a million diamond lights as they stood in the black night sky.

The diamonds fell, with the adventurers, into the eternal sea of black.

Chapter Twenty

Gradually, he came to as the wet patch on his face widened. Paccon opened his eyes to find Franklin licking him awake. He picked the baby turtle up and placed him in his pocket. How he'd survived the fall he had no idea.

The boy sat up and witnessed the Captain pulling Myri to her feet. They stood in the pool of light laid out by the moon in a hole in the natural roof of what Paccon would have called a cave.

"You colossal imbecile!" Myri screamed at the Captain. "You could have killed us all!"

"And yet I didn't," he replied, his smiling growing into a homage of ghoulishness in the pale light.

"I told you we should have gone around."

"How could we possibly have done that?"

"By looking at the map; something you didn't even consider."

"Well it's too late for that now."

"It can tell us where we are."

"I sincerely doubt that."

"Let me look at the map."

"Certainly not."

"Why not?"

"Because I lost it two days ago," Skyheart said, rather more amicably than he had intended, though it had the desired effect of ending Myri's tirade.

Myri sat down and looked at Paccon. "Are you okay?"

The boy nodded.

"Well at least we're all unharmed," she said.

"Yes, the veritable silver lining to this ashen black storm cloud," Skyheart said drily.

Suddenly, Skyheart's face became grave. Clearly in a panic, he leapt towards the provisions bag and opened it. When he saw the bottles were unharmed he let out a loud sigh of relief.

"What now?" Myri asked.

"We carry on," Skyheart said.

"How?"

"We walk through this cave. It should be easy enough. The cavern only goes in two directions, if we can't get out one way we'll try the other."

Paccon rose enthusiastically, although Myri needed rather more inspiration after such a large loss of morale. Still, she rose and the Captain led them down the cavernous path.

It wasn't long before the hole letting in the light counted for nothing and they were walking in total blackness. Skyheart had grown to hate caves and caverns after his last experience with one, however at least this time he had alcohol to keep away his delirium (or drink himself into an altogether more pleasant one). Despite not being alone, he may as well have been. Paccon had never been particularly prolix and Myri, in her fury, was best avoided lest she berate Skyheart once more.

He took a large swig of wine and ventured further into the darkness. He was unaware of where he was placing his feet with each step, yet he still walked with that oh-so unique of gaits. It seemed to help on the Ice-Bridge; not that that ended particularly well, but his swagger was nothing to do with that. He hoped.

The sound of Myri and Paccon's steps behind him gave the Captain little strength. He was sure, had he been alone, he would have at least reached North Port by now. Then again, if it wasn't for the woman and child he wouldn't have been on this interminable trip, but under the cherry blossom tree, sleeping. And what was that calling to him from inside his being? Adventure, something unplanned. That temperamental woman had insisted on this journey being planned meticulously and then she alternated at being impressed and incandescent at him. He then remembered that he hadn't so much planned the journey as chosen a route he thought would be the most perilous. He had tried to make it somewhat of a quest, but Myri, along with her decidedly unadventurous spirit, wasn't making that the easiest of tasks.

"Can you even see?" Myri asked.

"Almost," Skyheart said, before feeling the air rush from his lungs as he walked into a wall. He felt around only to find it was a dead end. He sighed and turned around. "We need to go the other way."

"I thought you said that this would be easy."

"Well Myri, I'm sorry, but I'm not familiar with this particular cavernous mountain."

Skyheart began to walk past her before feeling her hand gently grasp his arm.

"I know you'll get us out," she said.

He smiled a smile that nobody saw and then started back the way they had come. Myri and Paccon followed closer than they had before.

They walked in the dark nothingness of the cavern and in that cavern they found solace, for in a nothing with others as company, solace was all there was to find. The moonlight from the hole they once rested under cut through the darkness gifting them the comfort of light, but as they passed the vision diminished, yet the feeling remained.

On they went through the swirling blackness. Could they ever know true light once more? Surely after living in such perfect gloom lustre would forever be a stranger. Yet, soon light was seen by the travellers again.

High in the mountain wall the moonlight cut through the blackness, revealing a great hall had been carved into the cavern. Black rock had created all there was in the room. A large table stood in the centre with chairs all around it. To the head of the room a tall staircase led to a throne, large enough to fit three men in.

Skyheart scratched the back of his head before approaching the table. He ran his hand across it – the black stone felt somewhat more akin to marble than the rough rock of the mountain.

"Where are we?" Myri asked appearing next to him.

"This is where the Mandrans operated from during the Mineral wars," he replied. "Although, I never realised that they made it this far south. I was under the impression that only Thieron made it to the southern mountains." He paused. "Unless..."

He climbed upon the table and walked along to find himself directly in the light of the moon.

"Unless what?" Myri asked, holding Paccon close.

"I think we're further north than I think we are," Skyheart said, smiling. Upon the realisation of just what he had said he scratched the back of his head. "That is to say, I thought we were in one of the southern mountains, which at some point we were, but we've walked into one of the northern ones. So we're where we would have been had the Ice-Bridge not collapsed. In fact, we've probably saved some time thanks to our rather-too-speedy descent."

Myri looked at him quizzically. "You actually know what you're talking about, don't you?"

Skyheart laughed lightly. "It happens every so often, somewhere in the hazy state between sobriety and wisely drunk."

He took a victorious swig of wine.

"You're lucky there's nothing left for the Mandrans to take," he continued, jumping from the table to the floor. "They'd have a convenient base here, were they to return."

He looked back to Myri who said nothing. It seemed to him as if her eyes were made of a thin liquid, or as if a thin liquid was covering them. Though, Skyheart supposed it was just the pallid light of the moon, or her tiredness.

"It would be better if we rested once we were outside," he said. "More comfortable too."

He smiled weakly before carrying on through the mountain.

He knew where the path would lead them, somewhere his original path would have avoided. Unfortunately, there was no way around it now and his destination was inevitable: a place that the map had shown as more mountains, but he knew better.

His reticence was, however, mixed with intrigue. The place that they were headed was shrouded in mysticism. What would he meet there? Nothing, surely. Just as in the past, albeit the past of another man.

Myri wanted nothing more than to sleep. After leaving the great hall and being thrown into darkness again, a wave of weariness had overcome her. The Captain seemed confident that they would rest soon enough though, and who knew more about resting than him?

Soon he was proved correct and they once more found themselves outside, with soft grass beneath them. Night was beginning to give way to day, but the tired adventurers cared not for time. Now all they wanted to do was sleep.

And sleep they did.

Chapter Twenty One

They woke, closer to noon than dawn, to a glorious day. They sat in favour of the sun as they ate a small, yet nourishing, breakfast before continuing on their journey.

Skyheart had woken with a peculiar nausea, far removed from the withdrawal sickness he had become so accustomed to in Port Fair. He had a distinct rotting feeling inside his stomach, as if he was digesting himself. It all made sense when he remembered where he was.

The meadow was much as the Old Man had described it. A collage of flowers housing every species and colour, each more vivid than could be found anywhere else on the planet. In the sun of the late morning they looked to have been planted by a benevolent deity. Each was so precise in height and placement that no human could have even conceived planting them there. The flowers danced in a light breeze that seemed to engulf the entire meadow, stretching far passed the horizon.

Skyheart scratched the back of his head and took a swig of wine. He looked at Myri who was gazing out over the vista.

"The resting ground of Divos," she said within a breath. "He was god of joy to our people, but he died here in the Mineral Wars. Or so the story goes." She composed herself only to succumb to the beauty once more. "I never thought that I'd see it."

Skyheart shuffled on his feet and drank once more from the bottle of wine.

"What's wrong?" Myri asked.

"The presence of gods has never sat well with me," he said. "A fallen god is all the more unsettling."

Myri observed on the Captain an expression she had never seen on a grown man. His eyes expressed such awestruck intensity that they had about them the aura of a new-born child – amazed at each sight his eyes beheld. She had never expected such a gaze from a man so well-versed in the world. Yet, around his eyes stood a mark of fear and uncertainty. His face was paling quickly, his skin becoming so translucent so as to reveal the complex vascular structure beneath. Surely this was not the man who smiled arrogantly when faced with danger, the man who swaggered complacently towards near certain death. His lips had become a purple colour, as if bruised or deprived of oxygen. He had more in common, in those moments, with a drowning victim than Captain Laike Skyheart of Thieron's Division Four.

She stroked his arm gently, startling him. He turned to her and the colour began to return to his face. He smiled, uncommitted, before looking out to the meadow once more. He pointed out to the vista as Paccon chased a butterfly through the flowers, laughing. Myri smiled with all her gentle features.

"I've never seen him so happy," she said.

Skyheart drank some more wine but didn't reply.

"How much further do you think we have to go?"

"A few hands still," he said in a ghostly quiet voice. Myri didn't smile; the unit of measurement held no humour in that voice. It was the voice of a stranger and one she didn't wish to know at that.

Paccon came bounding through the tall flowers, only visible for his hat poking above the blossoms.

"Let's go!" he said excitedly, grabbing Myri by the hand and dragging her into the flowers. She smiled and allowed herself to be led.

Skyheart followed reluctantly.

He had seen it as soon as he had woken; saying nothing to his companions, for they would not see it for some time. A cherry blossom tree, in the midst of a magnificent bloom, stood near the centremost point of the meadow. The trunk had grown crooked, as if by design, with the pink and white blossoms becoming a flourishing mane over the perfect specimen of nature.

Under normal circumstances this would have been a welcome sight, a place for him to sleep and drink merrily. However, under the glory of the tree, amongst the vivid blooms of the flowers, were two visages out of place in the natural canvas. There stood two dull colours. Man-made colours.

One a dark blue.

One a white.

Both covering an area of black.

He took his usual place at the front of the procession. Whether this was because of what he had seen he didn't know, however the desire to do so was ravaging him so forcefully that there was little else. His presence seemed not to deprive Paccon and Myri of any of their joy in the meadow. And so it shouldn't. If the god of joy lay there, surely that place was the only to have joy still and forevermore.

The tree grew larger in his eyes as the distance to it decreased. Indeed, the presence of gods had never been a good omen for him.

A hand caressed his shoulder lightly with the gentlest of touches and embers glowed with new life somewhere within his chest. Yet his nausea remained. The touch ceased his walking and he turned to see Myri. She held to her chest a tall flower with fuchsia petals, which had grown out in the shape of a six pointed star. The stamen protruded outwards on thin receptacles. The vivid green stalk had grown long and tall.

"You should have this," she said smiling. "There aren't any crimson ones."

She laced the stalk through the ever unused button-holes of his crimson leather coat. The stalk trailed all the way to his hip with the head of the flower poking from the top most button-hole.

"Now you'll always remember our adventure together," she said, her smile widening.

"Thank you," Skyheart said, smiling back courteously. Though, as they resumed walking, the miasmic angst of what was to come fervently wrapped around his mind and heart, gripping them intently. As hard as he tried to wash this worry from himself, it stayed, ransacking him of all zeal. His nausea flared as the unmistakable glint of steel came into view and Skyheart stalled.

The white and blue apparitions were approaching.

"Are they people?" Myri asked.

"Keep going to North Port," Skyheart replied. "I'll either reach you soon or..."

"Captain, what's happening?"

"It would seem my past has caught up with me," he said, drawing Cendré and resting it on his shoulder.

"Captain..." she said, stretching her right arm to him. He met her gaze, stopping her.

The blue of his eyes had become like ice, as cold and as hard as death. As he looked at her she fought the urge to shiver. Yet in his gaze was a darkness unknown to her and, as the smiled crept across his face, so was the man. Unknown and unknowable.

Despite the vividness of the meadow her eyes glowed. Surely they should have seemed dull in comparison and yet it was the meadow that dulled beside her. Her dark hair, black as Cendré itself, hang limply by her face, trailing down her chest which was rising and falling as she breathed. He watched as she took Paccon's hand, the boy silent as ever.

Wordlessly they parted.

What death would meet them here?

She led Paccon through the flowers inattentively, uncaring of the direction. She didn't realise she was crying. The boy struggled to match her pace, but her hand stabilized him, stopping him from tripping.

"He'll be okay," Paccon said.

"What?" Myri replied, unconscious of having spoken.

"He'll be okay. You don't need to worry about him."

"How do you know?" she said, her tears falling more forcefully.

"He's Captain Laike Skyheart."

The three men stood in godless silence as the wind died to obscurity and the flowers ended their dance of eternity.

Skyheart remained in his passive stance; sword slung over his shoulder, seemingly unready for combat, regardless of his former comrades pointing their swords at him. At their distance the gesture was rather unthreatening, as if they were posturing more out of protocol than malice.

He could still see the cherry blossom tree, in the shadow of which his reluctant adversaries had once stood. In the moment, even that seemed passive – the image that normally would have enticed Skyheart towards it, almost lustfully, instead evoked nothing from within him.

Cyan appeared no different than ever. His remote friend, quietly aging, drawing little attention to himself, filling the world with subtle heroism. Though now, with his sword pointed at the Thieronian traitor, his strong physique faded, distorted by age – grudgingly lingering in his sense of duty.

When had Skyheart last seen Rom? He couldn't remember. All events that had transpired on the Northern Continent seemed an endless age ago. But the young Lieutenant, rivalling even Skyheart for youth, did not falter in the same manner as his Captain. He wore an expression of decided intensity and, although his posture looked rather half-hearted, Skyheart knew he was ready to kill. Indeed, even now he only hesitated for the sake of his Captain.

Skyheart scratched the back of his head and sighed, breaking the silence. "Must we point swords at each other?" he said.

Cyan smiled and sheathed his sword. "It does seem rather juvenile, doesn't it?"

The Captains both looked at Rom who reluctantly sheathed his sword.

"We weren't expecting to find *you*, Laike," Cyan said.

"No?" replied Skyheart.

Cyan shook his head. "We thought you were dead."

Skyheart smiled. "No hell can hold me."

Cyan smiled back. "Quite. Where exactly are we, Laike? This meadow isn't on any map."

"This is the resting place of a fallen or forgotten god," Skyheart said. A curious feeling swept over him as he spoke the words of the Old Man.

"The gods aren't faring well these days," Cyan said.

"Gods only fare as well as their subjects, and we are in resolute damnation."

Cyan nodded knowingly.

Rom shuffled uncomfortably. The solemn voices of the two Captains were so uncharacteristic that he struggled at times to listen. This haunting speech of the Crimson Captain betrayed his reputation. He almost spoke wisely.

"Tell me, Ryden," Skyheart said, "if you thought I was dead, then why are you here?"

"We came in search of the Diamandé."

"Surely DeFlare told you it sank."

"DeFlare's dead," Cyan said, more sharply than he had intended.

The ill-fated news shot through Skyheart, turning his blood into flames before cooling into the pit of his nauseous stomach. For some moments he struggled to breathe, but gave no sign of this. When he regained control of this aspect of his being, the fresh air gave him no relief; instead it turned to festering demise in his lungs. The acid inside him spewed, catching his heart at intervals. The acerbic discomfort called out for him to drink and calm himself, but his mind refused this urge. His head lightened and he found himself taking a step backwards for stability. In these brief delirious moments he wished to be struck down by either of the men facing him.

Lieutenant Alrous DeFlare was dead; the man with whom he had shared the majority of his adventures and, while DeFlare had not always approved of his actions, he had always been there to witness them. While the Captain had always kept DeFlare at some distance he had always thought him to be a vital part of his exploits, a vital part of Division Four and an even more vital part of himself.

He couldn't help but feel that DeFlare's death belonged to him.

The devastating revelation that the Diamandé was lost forever hung heavily on Cyan's heart, endlessly threatening to drag it down into some unfathomable region of his being, never to be found again. This was not just the end for Thieron, but for himself and Rom. The Assembly had said not to return with failure. With this failure there was very likely no Thieron to return to. How could he continue to live with such dishonour?

Rom glared vengefully at the man who had doomed Thieron – with death making roots in his mind. He considered drawing his sword and felling the Crimson Captain then, the harbinger of destruction that he was, though he realised with Skyheart's speed the only man to die in that encounter would be Rom himself. Dead men cannot avenge the fallen. He would have to wait.

"How?" Skyheart said in barely a whisper, though his sorrow seemed to carry the word to Cyan.

"He was executed after the Mandrans took control of Genko. We buried him at sea, thinking he would want to be with you."

"Thean and Okain?"

"Executed in Mandra. Their bodies are still there."

Skyheart's nausea flared, rising and engulfing his entire heart. The corroding organ screamed with displeasure, squirming in the cage of bone in which it was encased. The rest of his being cried out to collapse, though he could not oblige as each muscle became tense with pain. An intense ache worked its way through him – finally leaving as he tightened his grip on Cendré.

Thean's death had come not only as a profound sadness but also a traumatic shock. The old Captain had lived for so many years and was so talented a warrior that Skyheart had expected him to live forever. Skyheart had often tried to shake that naivety from himself, however with Thean's continued longevity it was hard to relieve the childish thought. Though now, fate had done it for him.

"Why did you do it Laike?" Cyan asked.

"I suppose that I just couldn't do what I was doing anymore," Skyheart mumbled.

"Sorry?"

"It was the only escape I could think to manufacture," Skyheart said more clearly. "Aside from quietly disappearing."

"More ostentatious heroics were in order," Cyan said, nodding. "Perhaps under different circumstances you could have had your wish at nobody's expense."

Lieutenant Rom could wait no longer. Was his Captain truly going to merely talk to this traitor? He drew his sword and thrust the tip in the direction of the far-off Skyheart in a far more threatening manner than before.

"Captain!" he said. "Let's kill this evil renegade now and be done with it! Thieron must be avenged!"

"Silence! Insolent fool!" Cyan roared at the young Lieutenant, causing Rom to drop his sword and fall to the ground in shame.

"My apologies," Rom said quietly.

"Evil," Cyan repeated from Rom's speech. "A warrior of your skill thoughtlessly throwing around words like 'evil'. Pathetic."

"But he betrayed us, Captain!" Rom pleaded.

"And so he is evil? Who decided that Thieron is so benevolent?"

Rom looked up at his Captain before hanging his head limply from his neck.

"This is war, Lieutenant," Skyheart said. "Merely two sides with differing opinions. If our enemies are evil in our minds then you can be sure that we are evil in theirs. Were any of us so benevolent, would we have entered into a war? If war is evil are not its inhabitants? Even morals belong only to their owner."

"Well spoken, Laike," Cyan said.

"Thank you, Ryden," Skyheart said with his usual casual salute.

"So you feel righteous enough to condemn an entire nation for your own freedom," Rom said, "using only the war as an excuse?"

"Silence yourself, Rom," Cyan said more calmly than before. "The answers to these questions will not please you."

Rom followed Cyan's advice. He rose and sheathed his sword, regaining his stoic position next to his Captain once more.

"Those people you were travelling with," Cyan said. "Who are they?"

"A woman from a port town and a boy from one of the surrounding islands. I'm escorting him home," Skyheart replied.

"Anything for an adventure," Cyan said, smiling. "He is what I think he is, isn't he?"

"The hat would suggest so," Skyheart replied. "Also, he has a young turtle with him that doesn't need water. Come to think of it, we had quite a fall in the mountains that we shouldn't have survived. I assume that's all his doing."

"I thought that they culled all of the mages."

"It would appear that they missed one, at least. I doubt he even knows he is one."

The comrades-come-enemies shared in the godless silence once more.

It was long into the afternoon now and day was beginning to darken, though they still had some time until night was complete in its preparation. As the sun lingered before setting, the sky painted itself into a violent fuchsia and the slanted light cast the warriors' shadows long in the meadow. Skyheart was standing in Cyan's by this time, despite the considerable distance between them. Behind Skyheart, the mountains stood tall and strong, but he was vulnerable between the inescapable landscape and the inescapable encounter.

The sweet scent of the flowers betrayed the putrid odour of death he should have been aware of. Indeed, on any other day as that one, he was sure he would have done.

"Must we really do this?" Skyheart said.

"I'm afraid so, Laike," Cyan replied.

"I've only killed one man with a name to me. I'd really rather not make it three."

Rom moved as if to speak, but stopped short of actually speaking.

"Is there no freedom in death?" Cyan said.

Skyheart smiled sorrowfully. "So you know about Myst."

"Why did you kill him?"

"He wanted me to join him in a glory that, at the time, I couldn't allow due to my obligations as a Captain of Thieron. Strangely, one of the few times my responsibilities bared any weight on me. Nor could I allow for him to meet glory alone. I offered him freedom, which he could not accept due to his pride. Thusly, we settled on a different freedom, one we had discussed long ago.

"I felt that death. As I have felt all the ones before, and since I have felt a thousand more. I have felt so many deaths that my own shall hardly be known to me, as a gentle breath in a squall. And still, my demise shall be absolute – swallowed by a smiling oblivion and thrust into a silent doom."

He held the flower that Myri had laced through his coat limply in his hand.

"And there, even this flower shall wilt, once so vibrant to be ignorant of what death is. But these petals shall fall and the flower shall rot, just as man.

"The man knows his demise lies directly before him, or perhaps upon him – for even now the chest struggles to rise for air – but does he scream? I've never known him to. His dignity stifles it to a sigh, so wearisome of the entire event he has grown. He doesn't see his life in his eyes, for he has been seeing it there for his entire life and has no need of a recollection. And he doesn't scream, because he knows, maybe it isn't all that bad. After all, everything always works out.

"But what if he dies by the fall of a sword? As the flower loses its petals the man can but hope for a clean cut, a sharp blade and that his head falls on a comfortable terrain wearing a flattering expression. Leaving not with a scream, but a sigh.

"What does the sun care for the loss of this man? Not a ray. For the man has been left to ride the breeze or waves as he wishes, joined by the petals as the flower disperses – with a gentle unheard sigh of its own. What doom is this? Only in the sense that it shall last forever. And what of oblivion? Only in the sense that one can never truly know the breeze, for both the air and the water are forever moving – the ebb of the planet is forever faceless, though benevolent it smiles, leading us. For the land is not owned by us – we are nurtured by it.

"And if there is a deity – for whether there is or is not will always be a point of contention – is irrelevant. The planet, if not its inhabitants, is wise enough to decide on the correct course and any god (that exists or existed or never existed or shall come into existence) would never be understood by our imperfect breed. So we shall throw our understanding to the breeze with our dead and trust in the planet. For perhaps we are better off without gods if all we are to do is war in their names. No, I'd rather trust the endless tide of life we have failed to comprehend. We shall know that in our existence there is no mysticism, and that is the most mystic thing of all."

"Yet each death still pains us greatly," Cyan said, bowing his head solemnly.

"Yet each death still pains us greatly," said Skyheart.

As if aware of Skyheart's speech, the breeze began again, heralding the end of sunset and the birth of night. As the moon came to its throne, a lone cherry blossom was blown gently from the tree and carried with the free dead to Skyheart's hand. He held the blossom admiringly before freeing it once more. As if it was a butterfly, it glided towards the mountains.

"They say," began Rom, "that a captain of Thieron is worth ten of any other warrior and a lieutenant seven. They also say that you're worth more than any other captain. Think that you can stretch to a captain and a lieutenant, Captain Skyheart?"

"I'd rather not find out," Skyheart replied.

"I'm afraid we have to, Laike," Cyan said. "The breeze is calling for company."

The two men still in the employ of the Thieronian army drew their swords. Skyheart scratched the back of his head and sighed. Cendré remained resting on his shoulder.

She'd lit a fire for the simple reason that when he approached she wanted him to know that they were there. It was too warm for her to sleep with the fire, or perhaps her thoughts were what prevented her from sleeping. Or maybe it was just his absence.

Paccon had drifted off almost immediately. How, Myri had no idea.

From the camp she looked back to where they had come from, though the swirling darkness showed no sign of the Captain's presence or the inevitability of his arrival.

Could he have died? She knew not and yet the prospect seemed decidedly intangible. Surely there would have been some sign of it. Though, when Kote had passed, the planet paid no attention, nor did it give any indication. She imagined that it was the same when her parents had died.

Still, the road showed not a wisp of crimson. She brought her legs close to her chest and wrapped her blanket around her. The night was not as warm as she had thought.

Skyheart had a distinct advantage in the darkness and one he had no wish to possess at that. Cendré reflected no light from the moon, making Skyheart practically invisible. Though, he had yet to unleash a strike. He was using his superior speed to elude the strikes of his opponents.

Of course, he could distinguish his assailants far easier. The steel of their katanas shone with the lustre of the moon. The white coat of Captain Cyan beamed. Indeed, Skyheart could have ended this battle long ago, had he the mind to. However, killing had never been the most natural of his instincts and to end the lives of three he knew personally at his young age seemed somewhat unjust. No matter how philosophical he tried to be about death, he failed to justify causing it. For all the freedom in death, was there none in life?

As if in answer two strikes came from either side of him. He parried them both, realising he was surrounded and could not escape. How they had gotten so close without him noticing them was, at first, a mystery. Then he realised Cyan had removed his captain's coat and the two men had kept their swords sheathed until the very last moment when they had struck. A clever ploy and

150

one that would have worked against anyone else, but this was Captain Laike Skyheart.

He had no time to marvel at Cyan and Rom's ruse as a slew of attacks came from all around him. He parried them, unable to unleash one of his own. Then again, he had no wish to.

Cyan and Rom were certainly a formidable pair, far more of a duo than Skyheart and DeFlare had ever been. Where the upper-ranks of Division Four had very much been separate entities, their Third Division counterparts were, in battle at least, as one. They exchanged no words, instead reading each other's movements and acting accordingly.

Even alone, Rom was considered deadly. Certainly he was heralded as the best warrior of the Thieronian Lieutenants and, although no match for any of the Captains, could outwit even the most tactically minded of his peers. Skyheart thought back to a swordsmanship contest in Thieron where he witnessed Rom feign two attacks against Okain only to return to the original feint and follow through with as hard a strike as Skyheart had ever seen.

That wasn't to say that Rom had no weaknesses. He relied heavily on patterns; complex patterns, but patterns nonetheless. However, to know each part of the pattern took considerable wit and, when faced with two men, full comprehension of Rom's patterns was near impossible. Rom's second weakness was his strength. He was not as strong as DeFlare and when his strikes were parried he left himself open for attack by having his sword knocked some distance from a defensive position.

Skyheart thought back to his duel with DeFlare in Genko. How the Captain had struggled to defend against those heavy blows. He couldn't remember when last he fought a man so strong.

Cyan posed threats that only a Thieronian Captain could. Each strike of his that Skyheart parried made Skyheart's body ache. Each attack was so unexpected that they could have been considered arbitrary, yet each was so well placed and swung with such conviction they could only be strokes of a master-plan. But for all this planning, the speed of his opponent allowed not for a blow to land. Indeed, in such a small arena of combat as they had trapped Skyheart into (he was now fully caught in between the Captain and Lieutenant with almost no room to move at all) his speed should have counted for nothing. Still, each of their movements seemed sluggish when compared with the blur of his sword arm.

Somehow, unknown even to him, Skyheart made his escape from his surrounded position – though still his opponents rained down upon him with strikes. But with more room he could now evade their strikes as opposed to parrying them.

The blades of their swords as they cut through the air sang out with crying whistles. The two blades caught the languid reflection of the moon as they sliced through the blackness, almost as if two gargantuan dragonflies flew through the meadow, chasing something unknowable to an onlooker.

The realisation had come to Skyheart some time ago, though he had been trying to subdue the thought, albeit fruitlessly. He had hoped that he could deny the thought as being the truth, yet as he fought further into the night he struggled to shake the feeling from himself. The concept made him ache far more than the strikes of Cyan. The acidic miasma tightened around his heart as his mind set afire. He could no longer disaffirm the notion.

If he was to survive this, he would have to kill at least one of his attackers.

He was neither surprised nor horrified when the idea of letting them kill him entered his mind. It would certainly have resolved his quandary of which one of them to kill. However, he had a duty to Myri and Paccon – a duty to live. Yet, in those moments of introspection he found himself wishing he could shirk that responsibility as he had so many before. How easy it would have been to let one of them fell him. Was his life really any more important than Cyan or Rom's? Even to him the answer was not an outright 'yes'. Yet desire is a fickle interest and, equal to his desire to shirk his responsibilities, was his desire to gaze into those emerald eyes once more and finish this adventure, even, and this was becoming increasingly probable, if it was his last.

The question he found himself asking was this: who could he live with killing – Cyan or Rom?

The answer was harrowingly obvious.

The moon rolled out from behind the obscurity of a cloud, bathing the meadow in eerie light. With this, the gift of vision, the men ceased in their contest of death.

"You're not trying, Laike," Cyan said.

"I've made my feelings on the situation perfectly clear," Skyheart said.

"I wouldn't have entered into this malevolent process was it not necessary."

"I realise that."

"And you still refuse to kill?"

Skyheart said nothing.

"Very well," Cyan continued. "Can a man have a duty to a dead nation?"

Skyheart smiled. "Some of us have not duties to living ones."

Cyan smiled. "Quite." He looked at the frowning Rom. Clearly the Lieutenant had only stopped in his attempts to kill Skyheart because his Captain had. Cyan sighed inside himself. When would this young man learn to think his own thoughts? He looked once more to Skyheart and stretched out his free left hand. "The best of luck, Laike."

Skyheart smiled warmly and took his friend's hand in his. "Save your luck for yourself, Ryden."

They parted ways with that briefest of exchanges. When Cyan turned back to wave once more to his ex-comrade, he received Skyheart's usual casual salute.

"I'm confused, Captain," Rom said. "Should not someone's blood have been spilt?"

"Rom," Cyan replied. "Captain Laike Skyheart is a difficult man to kill and an even more difficult man to be killed by. As a man who has shirked nearly every responsibility given to him, he has only killed when absolutely necessary – strange, for such a frivolous man. He is sagacious in ways I shall never fully understand and he combines this with pretentiousness that most could only find antagonistic. I suppose he decided not to kill us as we had no chance of killing him. We should be grateful. For although we have not a home to return to; we may roam, as he has decided to."

He turned to look at the Lieutenant only to find he was gone.

He turned further and found Rom running silently, sword poised to kill – towards Skyheart.

Cyan opened his mouth to send a warning, to who he wasn't sure, but found only a gasp in his throat.

Rom's pace quickened.

'And now, Captain Skyheart,' Rom thought, 'disgrace of mankind, traitor to Thieron – you shall die by my sword. My Captain, blinded by undeserved respect for you, fails to bring down his sword to cleave your head or to order me to do the same. Well, if he has forgotten his duty, I, as his Lieutenant, must remind him, for as a Lieutenant of Thieron I have a duty to my Captain.

'Forgive me for my insubordination, Captain Cyan. I assure you – it is nothing less than essential.'

His sword, held behind him, clipped the stems of the flowers as he ran, creating the sound of a caught rudder – though Skyheart was aware of his approaching attack long before then. He had never expected Rom to merely walk away. One so inexperienced could never hope to forget his Captain's duties and his own to ensure the completion of those duties. How could a Lieutenant of Thieron, bound by ancient laws of rank and loyalty to so many, understand the complexities of allowing a traitor to live?

Skyheart grimaced. How cruel life was for allowing his earlier prediction to be correct. Lieutenant Rom would not cease in this battle until either he or Skyheart was dead.

So be it.

Neither Rom nor Cyan saw Skyheart move, but at one moment he had his back turned to them, walking to meet the woman and child he had been travelling with, Cendré resting lazily on his shoulder, and in the next he was behind Rom, Cendré at his side, dripping with blood as crimson as his coat, looking soberly at Cyan – some distance away.

It took some time for Rom to fall such was the strike from Captain Skyheart. The shock of the speed of the movement had struck Rom with a temporary rigamortis and an instantaneous death. He eventually fell when Skyheart sheathed Cendré, the dead Lieutenant flattening a small area of flowers he lay upon.

"I'm so sorry," Skyheart said in a sorrowful breath.

The two Captains met by the body of their dead comrade. They bowed their heads, partly out of respect and partly to hide their solemn expressions from one another.

"Thank you for keeping him intact," Cyan said.

Skyheart nodded. "Where will you go now?"

"To place Rom with DeFlare."

He looked at Skyheart revealing tearless eyes. The sight of such stoicism was almost more melancholic than the situation itself.

"We will meet again, Laike," Cyan continued. "And then we shall end this. However, I will allow you to finish your adventure with only two named dead on your conscience."

Skyheart nodded in gratitude and watched as Cyan placed Rom over his shoulder.

"We'll meet at the sea," Cyan said. "All of us – captains and lieutenants alike. We'll all roam together on those endless tides. The three divisions, together."

"There are four divisions," Skyheart said.

"No," Cyan said. "Emaina's not like us."

They parted and Skyheart watched as Cyan shrank into the darkness of the mountains.

"No," Skyheart said. "Emaina's not like us at all."

Chapter Twenty Two

Their figures seemed to appear with the dawn, although one could be certain that they were there long before then. The desert heat reinforced them – shimmering air doubling their already staggering numbers.

Yet still they hoped to defeat them.

And the question rose: why did the Mandrans not advance?

In the President's Office on the highest floor of the Monument, the highest ranks of Thieron surveyed the future battleground.

The Commander, as pale as his associates, whispered to himself. "Why don't they move?"

With this, he wished he hadn't spoken as the Mandrans began their advance.

Chapter Twenty Three

The sun rose red the next morning, though the sky remained its pale blue of dawn. Captain Skyheart wished for the day to turn grey and rain. Such pleasantries as good weather were unwelcome, juxtaposed against the events of the night before.

He drank from the wine bottle, slowly but continuously, as he lay on his side, cradled in her sleeping arms. He had been relieved to find her asleep, for in her slumber he faced no questions and the absence of questions left no answers to be spoken. No mention of the dead.

Her gentle breath caressed the back of his neck, cooling him on that warmest of mornings. Though that was all it did. Oh, how he wished for her to exhale solace.

She woke, as peacefully as she ever had, as peacefully as she had ever slept. Discovering the Captain in her arms delivered her to a plain of comfort, though he felt as unlike Skyheart as one could. Holding him there, she realised how small he was as he suckled on the wine. She began to stroke his hair, running her fingers softly through the dull blonde locks before he wrapped her hand in his and placed it around him once more, as if her arm was a blanket.

He shuffled backwards, further into her embrace. She fought the urge to tighten her grip, wishing to feel him against her, and instead simply moved closer to him.

They lay there for some time in that motionless silence and only moved once Paccon awoke. Skyheart rose to rummage through the bag and pulled out more bread and meat. He gave a portion each to Myri and Paccon but ate none himself. Once the small breakfast was eaten they moved north wordlessly, on the dirt trail that Myri had suggested long ago.

The trail gave the impression of having once been a glorious plain, for on both sides of the now dirt was an area of lush grassland, once one. But as time had gone on and travellers used the route near-constantly, the grass had been worn down creating a natural trail over many years. Had Myri been brave enough to speak she would have called it a 'desire path'. Yet on such a day desire seemed so far removed she could not bring herself to say the word. Even thinking it seemed sacrilegious, though even that seemed out of place.

They walked in a way they never had before. With her left hand, Myri held Paccon's hand and she had wrapped her right arm around Skyheart's left, her head resting limply on his shoulder with her hair draped down his chest. Skyheart's pace was far quicker than usual, so fast that Paccon almost had to run to keep up. After some time like this Myri decided to carry Paccon.

Skyheart seemed not to notice any change the day brought. Though for the entire journey he stood in favour of the sun, not a ray beamed consolation onto him. He may as well have been a shadow walking alone in a dark hall, though master-less shadows have a habit of becoming unbound. Indeed, even with Myri hanging from him as if to stop him from disappearing, he had the sensation of shattering; his shards ignored by the breeze. How could one so esteemed by the sun be so scorned by its earthly counterpart?

In the early afternoon the sea town of North Port came into view. It was so small it could hardly have been said to have been a town, then again, village wasn't quite the correct term either. A few white stone buildings were grouped together with terracotta tiled roofs. A small wooden dock was positioned on the edge of the town, housing a few fishing boats and a much larger ship.

"That's a Mandran ship," Skyheart said.

Myri, amazed that the Captain had not only spoken but in his own voice too, struggled to find any words to reply with. For so long she had been silent, her mouth seemed to be a separate entity rather than her own body part.

"Are they invading?" she finally said.

"No. The Mandran Navy is one vast in numbers and those numbers are used to full effect at every opportunity. An invading force would be far larger."

Skyheart thought back to the Mandran invasion of Genko. It now seemed so long ago he doubted it was he who had experienced what was in his memory. The hundreds of ships firing cannon shot from far out at sea before docking and charging, running past DeFlare and himself. He could no longer comprehend his surprise as the first shot destroyed part of the palace, crushing the Empress in the process.

"What's the plan?" Myri asked.

"Plan?" Skyheart laughed. "There's no plan. Although, I should like a closer look at that ship."

"Why Captain Skyheart, you almost sounded dutiful," she said, smiling.

Skyheart gave her a devious look that was more the Captain impersonating himself than *being* himself. Myri tried to convince herself that the look was genuine; the cavalier Captain would have been welcome on such a day. Before she managed to coax herself into the belief, the Captain started towards North Port.

The ship was certainly structurally sound, not that Skyheart had the most expansive knowledge of sea-travel. The ship would work - he knew that much, though still he walked the deck pretending to inspect the vessel. Eventually he walked to where Myri and Paccon were standing, by the mast.

"Well, it's certainly in ship-shape," he said. "Which is good; I do so abhor an out of shape ship." He smiled, thinking how droll he was.

"What do you suggest we do?" Myri asked. "Wait for the captain?"

"Skyheart laughed. "I'm Captain enough for this vessel (I've already got the title, after all). We'll take it for our own. I've some experience at sea."

This wasn't a lie in the strictest meaning of the word. Skyheart had experience at sea in the sense that he'd spent many days in the ocean drifting towards the Southern Continent. However, he had no idea about the workings of a ship.

"Is that so Captain Skyheart?" said a voice from the bridge. "And how do you plan on taking my ship?"

Skyheart looked to the bridge. A one-eyed man in a black tri-corner hat with long brown hair, a white shirt and black trousers stood, lounged over the helm. He had removed his long black coat because of the day's heat.

"Captain Lafere Swift, I presume," Skyheart said, smiling.

Swift bowed flamboyantly in reply with a smile every bit as wry as Skyheart's.

"Captain Swift?" Myri pondered.

"The famous pirate," Skyheart replied. "He's almost as notorious as I am. Some call him the 'Captain Skyheart of the seas'."

"I try to play down the comparison," Swift said. "Though it seems in you I've met my equal."

"Strange," Skyheart said, smiling, "I don't think I've ever met an equal before."

Swift smiled and began walking down the steps to the deck. "Last I heard of you, you were dead."

"Last I heard of *you*, you were awaiting execution at Pale Castle."

"Alas, I escaped. But now I find myself in the worst of all quandaries: without a crew and destination."

"I can give you both, if you're willing."

"Oh, I'm willing. But can you follow an order?"

"Not a one."

"Then you're in good company."

The two men laughed so similarly that Myri wasn't entirely sure how to react. But before she knew it, Skyheart and Swift had moved to the bridge and the ship had set sail.

"We're close now, Paccon," she said.

The boy smiled. "You hear that, Franklin?" he said, removing the turtle from his pocket. "We'll see Mama again soon."

The sea was kind to them, granting them a safe passage on gentle waves, though Swift insisted that the channel was instantly changeable and treacherous by turns; however Skyheart had yet to see evidence of this. He was also surprised at how little work there was to do on-board. He had always imagined being aboard a ship would consist of endlessly knotting rope (although to what end, he wasn't sure) and taking orders from a fearsome rodent of a captain. But Swift seemed relaxed and, almost, charming.

"Lonely, isn't it?" Swift said.

"I'm sorry?"

"So few in a crew – it's lonely."

"I don't know any different, I'm afraid."

"I suppose not. Then again, on land you're used to small groups I'd imagine."

"What's your point?"

158

"Point?" Swift said, looking out at the horizon ponderously. "I'm not entirely sure that I have one."

Skyheart took a large swig of wine. "I know that feeling all too well."

Although the waves grew larger in the afternoon they posed no threat. On the deck, Paccon bounded up and down with excitement as his reunion with his home and mother neared ever closer. Skyheart smiled – had he ever been that excited as a child? Certainly not after his father... well, there was no use thinking of that just yet.

His eyes drifted to the bow where Myri stood gazing out over the ocean; an alluring figurehead leading the ship safely through the waters. She turned to him and smiled. He replied with his usual casual salute.

Yes, surely there would be malevolent times ahead, when he would be forced to face Cyan and decide between raising the named dead to three or to die himself. Certainly, inside of him there was a longing to discover what had become of the Northern Continent and this curiosity had yet to wane. But, for now, he would enjoy his adventure and the company he found himself in, for there was little else that could give him such pleasure.

Soon, the island came into view and Paccon's excitement grew more uncontrollable. He laughed with joy as home swelled in his eyes.

"Mama!" he called. "I'm home!"

Swift turned to Skyheart. "Imagine the celebrations when we land," he laughed.

"Truly it will be a delight to behold," Skyheart said, the warmth of triumph emanating from within his chest.

They anchored, still some way out, and entered one of the smaller row-boats. Swift, as captain, had taken it upon himself to row, allowing Skyheart to observe the island as they approached. It was certainly small, then again, this was a man used to the vast expanses of the Northern Continent where the sea was seldom seen.

A long dormant volcano towered some way into the sky. Around the base of it were grouped many exotic trees and, although Skyheart could not quite make the bearings out, he knew they held many tropical fruits, the likes of which he had never tasted. The sand was as white as the snow on the mountains they had traversed those few days ago. Close to the trees were a few scattered rocks and pebbles near a hut, easily large enough for two to live in.

Though, what was that feeling he was gripped by?

He looked to Myri, sitting next to him. She too was surveying the island, though far from wearing the triumphant expression of a finished adventure, she seemed... solemn.

Skyheart pondered this. What was more gratifying than a successful adventure? Other than the beginning of one he couldn't think. Yet, even as he ran through these thoughts, a lone tear ran from her left eye.

Did she feel it too?

He wiped the tear from her face with his thumb. Startled, she turned to him and smiled weakly. He fought the urge to hold her, what good what it do? Then, before he realised, she plunged her face into his chest as the boat docked on the sand.

"Mama!" Paccon shouted heartily as he disembarked. He ran towards the hut, oblivious to the weeping Myri.

Skyheart could feel the tears seeping through to his skin. Why must such radiant eyes be forced to express such sorrow? He lifted her chin gently in order to look at her, though as her eyes met the level of his, she looked down. In as smooth a motion as he had ever used, he wiped the remaining tears from her face. Myri blinked rapidly, removing the watery blur before meeting his eyes.

"He's not mine anymore, is he?" she said.

Skyheart could feel his insides squirming.

"He's not mine anymore," she repeated. "Or maybe he never was. The breeze is so thick these days, so heavy, that it's hard to tell who's who. But to have a child – even for so short a time – one can begin to see through the haze. And now he's gone, so quickly so as to thicken the mist. The tears don't help." She paused and wiped them from her eyes. "But to have a child; this is something I will never fully know. I will never be lovingly called 'Mama' as he called her – even in her absence." She smiled weakly, staring down at her hands, resting in her lap. "I'm alone again. And to think it happened so unceremoniously."

Skyheart's hands wrapped themselves around hers and pulled her closer to him. His nose nestled in her hair while his lips rested gently by her ear.

"You're not alone," he whispered.

She turned to him, their noses meeting side by side. Their lips were the shortest of distances from each other, yet it seemed insurmountable.

"Yes I am," she said. "You'll leave... or die." She rested her forehead on his. "And that's if I even wanted you to stay. How can I? Kote's still so fresh."

"I won't die."

"You die every night." She started crying again. As the two were so close, the tears wetted Skyheart's cheeks too. Yet, neither of them wiped them away. "I'm not allowed to feel like this."

Her emerald eyes, drenched with tears, remained as vibrant as ever, perhaps even more so. The suns of her irises, eclipsed partially by her pupils, sparkled lightly in the daylight. Tragedy would surely befall the world if those eyes ceased to shine.

"You've adventures to have anyway," she said, stroking the flower she gave him in the meadow.

Skyheart opened his mouth to speak but remained silent when he heard the voice of the forgotten Swift.

"This is an awfully quiet reunion," he said from the shore, out of earshot at the volume Myri and Skyheart had been talking.

Of course, Swift was correct. For all Paccon's excitement and joyful noisemaking on the ship, they could hear sounds from neither the boy nor his mother. Even the birds in the trees refused to sing.

"Paccon," Myri whispered, rising. She gracelessly fell from the boat and sped to the hut.

Skyheart watched, each of her utterances chanting sombrely in his head.

The sea whispered for him to follow, but as he tried he found his current position all the more alluring. Only when Swift grabbed him did he follow the water's order.

They stood in the doorway – for the sadness of the hut was so thick that only those with true, cutting determination could enter. Seemingly, only the boy possessed this attribute.

He was knelt next to his greying mother. The skin; so translucent so as to give no sign of life ever having inhabited the body. The figure; now so thin as to reveal the skeletal structure beneath. The expression she wore was one of peace, though the face appeared not to belong to her. Blood had congealed in her hair, giving it the texture and look of a red, fibrous sinew.

"Mama..." Paccon whispered, shaking her gently. "Mama..." He shook her once more. Surely, even the weariest of the sleeping dead could be woken if only the loving living were willing to try.

Slowly, Myri entered and took the boy in her arms. His silent tears dampened the shoulder of her dress and worked their way through to her skin. She shuddered with each convulsive sob of the boy. If only he would make a sound. Eventually, she rose and led him outside.

Skyheart and Swift remained in the doorway, before Swift could take no more and began heading back to the sea to feel the only solace he knew.

"So many without a home these days," Skyheart lamented.

He entered the hut and knelt next to this woman, to whom he was unknown. Even he merely knew her as 'Mama'. When had he last seen a dead body, the life not ended by the hands of man? He couldn't remember.

"Just one more for the breeze," he said. "Or perhaps you'd prefer the tides. Whichever – you're already there now, aren't you?"

He turned and left only to find Swift waiting for him by the door. It is equally possible that Swift wasn't waiting for him at all. Indeed, his expression was so vacant it seemed he had tried to return to the ship only to be halted by his own thoughts. Even as Skyheart inspected him, Swift appeared to do battle with them.

"I don't suppose you've a shovel?" Skyheart said.

"I'm afraid not," Swift said, shaking himself back into the conscious world. "There's not an awful lot of digging to be done out at sea."

"I'd imagine not."

The Captains tried to laugh, however the severity of the situation allowed them only to smile half-heartedly. Wordlessly, they walked some way up the beach and started digging with their hands.

He had always felt like a small child in her arms, yet, in the heat of the day in the shade of a fruit tree, he felt even smaller than usual. More like a new-born baby, but, small as he was, he felt strong. Myri tightened her embrace of him as his crying intensified.

It had been a colourless day. Only now did she realise this. Despite the heat, the sun was white in the sky, not its usual gold. The sky was cloudless, but not blue – a pale grey was perhaps closer to the truth. The sea, reflecting the colour of the above, was a disdainful monochrome. The entire world had faded to sepia.

"I'll be able to talk to her won't I?" Paccon said. "So she knows I miss her and she's always on my mind."

"Of course you can."

"And I'll hear her, but I have to really listen."

"That's right."

"And she's always there."

"Yes," Myri said, in her gentle tones. "She's always there."

She watched as the Captains dug. Such flamboyant and frivolous men doing such demanding labour seemed strange, yet the Captains simply persevered with the task. How long had Skyheart been this uncomplaining worker?

Paccon sobbed again and pushed himself further into her embrace, sure that there was consolation there if only he could go far enough to find it. As far as he pushed himself and as tight as Myri held, relief eluded him.

"Does it get easier?" he asked between his violent sobs.

Myri said nothing.

Skyheart rose, pulling himself from the hole carefully, so as not to force any sand to fall back into the hole. Fortifying the sand with water had helped to some extent, however it was still less stable than he desired.

Skyheart slowly walked back to the hut, flinching just the smallest of amounts at what was to come. After entering, he knelt next to Paccon's mother and slid his arms under her back. The chill of her body worked its way through his skin, travelling to the deepest sanctum of his bones. He shivered. Could he ever know warmth again?

He rose and left the hut, entering the domain of the afternoon sun. Even that failed to penetrate through the cold that currently gripped him. His nausea would have been welcome compared to that. With each sand cushioned step it worsened and soon the frozen blood inhabited his entire being.

After what seemed like an eternity he reached the grave and, with Swift's help, he lowered the dead woman in.

"What are you thinking?" Swift asked, as Skyheart looked longingly out at sea.

Skyheart turned to Swift. "I sincerely hope I never have to dig another grave."

Swift nodded before the Captains both sighed and began filling the grave with sand once more.

At sunset the four were gathered around the grave, the cooing sea lulling the day into sleep. Paccon's tears had stopped some time ago, yet his eyes contained all the signs of a boy who was about to cry. He could feel that familiar itching behind his eyes, but nothing came, despite the fact he thought this was a more appropriate time to cry. He stood there, clinging desperately to Myri's hand. Would this day never end?

Swift had taken it upon himself to make a monument carved from wood. It read:

'Mama,
Never as far as we think.'

Swift placed the small wooden stake holding the sign into the sand. The three adults hid their suspicion that the tide would eventually carry the message away; however Myri imagined that Paccon felt the same way. She surmised whether the message was there or not was irrelevant, the sentiment always would be.

It was then Paccon asked to be alone. The adults obliged.

It was some time before he actually spoke, not that he was unsure of what to say. It was more that he wanted to be certain that everything was said and everything was heard.

The shadows were at their longest as he said: "I came so far to see you but you weren't here. That's okay. I know you're somewhere. I'll always talk to you, because Myri said you'll hear me and you'll reply if I listen really hard. But I'm listening now and I can't hear you. Maybe I need more practice."

He removed Franklin from his pocket. The turtle seemed to wear the same expression as the boy – one of weary sorrow. They'd have cried were they not so tired.

"Franklin," he said. "I'm leaving you here, in case Mama comes back."

The turtle pulled his head back slightly as if in confusion.

"I know you'll be okay," Paccon said to Franklin. "Because when Mama comes back you'll have company. Even before then she'll be around, just not how she used to be." He put Franklin down.

"Mama," he said, no longer able to look his pet in the eyes. "I had such an adventure coming to find you. Maybe I'll tell you about it someday." He turned to the sea.

"I love you, Mama."

Skyheart and Myri sat beneath one of the trees and watched as Swift returned to the row boat. Skyheart looked at Myri, though her attention was fixed on Paccon.

"Strange, "Skyheart said, "we've been in favour for the sun for so long I wasn't expecting this."

"It certainly was an adventure," Myri replied.

"It's not over yet."

Myri turned to him. "What do you mean?"

"Well, I wouldn't be much of a hero if I didn't take you and Paccon home now, would I?"

"But the Northern Continent..."

"Is in shambles whether I return immediately or not."

Myri turned back to the image of Paccon at his mother's grave. "I suppose I've got my son back now, haven't I?" But somehow the words brought no solace.

By the time night fell they were back out at sea under a starless sky. The scorned moon lay behind a thick black cloud that resolved never to move. The sea remained as quietly calm as it had earlier in the day. Skyheart, now at the helm as Swift slept in his cabin, was glad of this. As long as the waves were gentle he had some hope of keeping control, though Swift had insisted that these waters were instantly changeable and Skyheart must be prepared to do battle with them at any time. At that moment however, it seemed to be more of a warning for caution than a necessary order.

Myri emerged from the lower level and climbed the steps to the bridge. Her movements were slow and tired.

"Paccon's asleep," she said. "That boy could sleep through anything." She slumped over the railing next to Skyheart. "It's a miserable night."

"It was a miserable day," Skyheart replied.

For a time they said nothing, the only sound came from the crooning sea, rocking the ship gently. They shared in the silence, gloried in it and in those moments they were one. Skyheart wished to live in that wordless serenity forevermore. But, eventually, it was broken.

"I'm sorry," Myri said.

"Whatever for?"

"For wasting your time with this fruitless endeavour."

"'Fruitless'? I haven't had an adventure like this in some time. The journey alone was worth the toil." The image of Rom's corpse floated through his mind. "Although, that's not to say it wasn't without its tragedy. But you could hardly have helped that."

She considered asking him of the night in the meadow but thought better of it. Once more the silence washed over them. She stared over the rail to see the sea before them. It had gained the colour it was lacking during the day, taking on the deep purple of the night. It had more in common with a passage of silk than water.

"He's so like me," she said. The utterance had the volume of a whisper but the force of a cry. "No, he's not as lucky as I am. He's lost everything and in his loss I have gained him. Why must I always benefit from the dead?"

Skyheart said nothing.

"The pain must be worse for him. After all, he knew his mother. I have no memories of my parents. It's not so much a pain for me as a dull ache. How can you miss what you never knew? Perhaps I'm lucky – I've less love to lose."

"You've lost more than most, Myri," Skyheart said. "Even by the Southern Continent's standards. Paccon's an extreme case, though not without his luck. He's still got you. Never think your sorrow is unfounded. So few so young have lost a fiancé."

"Kote?" she whispered.

The breeze gently helped the ship along.

It took Skyheart several moments to realise she was sobbing.

"Captain," Myri said, "why?" Her sobbing overcame her and she took a moment to compose herself. "Why did you appear?"

Skyheart said nothing.

"Ever since you arrived, it's all been just so easy; something it never should have been."

Such was her sorrow she bent over the rail for support with her convulsive wails. Yet, not a sound she made.

Skyheart released the helm.

"Paccon needs you," he said, lacing his arms around her, "and while you may appreciate his company, you are far from benefitting from the dead. You are taking up the responsibilities that they no longer have the power to do."

The ship rocked on the buoyant sea.

Myri turned to him, her hands cradling themselves to his chest. "And what about you?" she asked.

He pulled her closer to him, shrinking to her height while she rose to meet his. Their lips made the briefest of caresses.

A giant wave forced the ship high above the water. The ship crashed back down throwing Skyheart and Myri from one another.

"Skyheart!" roared Swift's shouting voice as he stumbled from the cabin. "Get back to the helm!"

Skyheart launched himself in the direction of the wheel, unable to walk as the increasingly violent waves continued to assault the ship.

A wave that dwarfed even the first reared before the ship. Unaware of this, Swift pulled himself up to the bridge and grabbed the helm, knowing it would take the strength of two men to navigate their way through this torment.

Trying not to shrink from the ever nearing behemoth, Skyheart called for Myri to hold onto something as he found himself unable to locate her.

The colossal wave dove onto the ship, washing from the deck anything not securely fastened. How Skyheart and Swift had managed to stay aboard they had no idea.

"Myri!" Skyheart called.

No reply came.

There was no sight of her on deck.

"She must have fallen overboard!" Swift growled over the squall. "Get her! Now!"

With that he grabbed the scruff of Skyheart's neck and threw the unbalanced man over the side of the ship, before placing both hands on the wheel.

It had come as a shock to Skyheart – suddenly finding himself underwater. However, he had no time to panic. Some way from him he saw a figure that looked vaguely human, getting ever further away from him. Thrashing with all his limbs he made for this effigy, hoping it was Myri. As he neared he saw it was her, but she was unconscious, sinking towards the sea floor. He clasped one of her arms in his hand before heading back to the surface of the water,

Swift had stabilised the ship and managed to follow Skyheart's position with near-impossible accuracy. As Skyheart emerged with Myri, Swift hauled them aboard before returning to the bridge.

Skyheart laid Myri on the deck. She was pale, almost grey, and showed no signs of breathing. Desperately he tried to force the water from her lungs to no avail.

"Captain?" Paccon said from the door to the lower levels.

"Get back below, Paccon," Skyheart said, trying to force some semblance of life back into Myri. He looked and Paccon was gone.

Confident they were safe for the time being, Swift appeared by Skyheart and tried many of the same techniques as the Thieronian. When he stopped he said something that Skyheart couldn't make out. Skyheart took up his attempts again.

He finally realised when Swift placed a hand on his shoulder.

"She's gone."

Chapter Twenty Four

The rest of the night was spent in the silent haze that only death can create. Seemingly that shadow, so familiar to Skyheart by this point in his life, followed them with a viscous crawl, darkening all that it passed over. The moon, still in its solitary retreat behind the thick black clouds, bared no heed to the sorrow on the tides beneath. The waves had calmed, tired from their earlier aggression.

Skyheart was sat next to her lifeless body, cradling her head in his lap. He took large swigs of wine at various intervals. He stroked her hair; he couldn't say why, then again, nobody was asking.

"We've taken a lot of damage," Swift said softly. "The furthest we can make is North Port and even that will be a stretch."

Skyheart nodded. "That should suffice," he said. The manner in which he spoke was so typical of the Captain that Swift was taken aback.

"You seem... contented," he said.

Skyheart looked at him and shrugged. "Just one more soul reporting for duty with the breeze. Besides," he stood up and took a swig of wine, "it's all part of the adventure."

The boy knelt beside him looked up at Skyheart. Then he looked back at Myri. He stroked her hair as if to wake her. Paccon was more reserved than he had been on his island, however, a lone tear managed to work its way from his eye and crawled down his cheek.

"It's okay to be sad," Swift said, placing a hand on Paccon's shoulder.

Paccon nodded. "I know," he said before turning his head to Captain Skyheart. The Crimson Captain was lapping up the remainder of wine in the bottle. He threw the empty container overboard and rummaged in the bag for another. Upon finding one he turned to Paccon and the boy spoke again. "I don't think I like adventures."

"They have their downsides," Skyheart said, removing the cork.

Swift turned away from them and slowly returned to the bridge. His steps were laboured as he walked up the few stairs. He had hardly known the woman, though still he felt nauseous at her death. He imagined it was sympathy for Skyheart and Paccon, then again – he barely knew them either. Perhaps that's just what death does.

He gripped the helm firmly and once more began steering through the buoyant seas. This was his place.

Paccon was surprised that he had shed so few tears. But after crying so much at the death of his biological mother it was hard to conjure up any more for the surrogate, though he would have liked nothing more. He reached to his pocket for Franklin, only to be reminded by the emptiness that he had left him on his island. He didn't regret it so much as he felt remorse over the decision. He couldn't take his home with him everywhere he went. Although, how could he find home anywhere now?

To Skyheart, the plan from here was obvious – back to Port Fair and then... well, he shuddered at the mere thought of it. No need to think of it just yet, he'd experience it soon enough. He looked to Paccon, the boy who had lost two mothers in one day, and sighed. Where did he fit into the Captain's plan? Unfortunately, he could only come part of the way.

They made port at dawn under a blanket of grey clouds.

"Autumn's on the way," Swift said.

"It always is," Skyheart replied, tying the bag of alcohol to his hip. "Except when it's here, then it's always trying to leave. Then when it's gone it's on the way again."

He lifted Myri and rested her over his shoulder in a way people were more accustomed to seeing him with Cendré.

"That's a haunting image," Swift said.

Skyheart sighed. "I'm not planning on making this a particularly long trip."

"And with the boy?" Swift gestured towards Paccon who was staring listlessly out at sea.

Skyheart turned and looked at the boy for a while before replying. "Well, maybe it will be slightly longer than I envisioned."

"Perhaps you should cover her with something. So he doesn't have to look at her for the whole journey."

"Somehow I feel that will be kinder to both of us," Skyheart said, placing her body gently on the deck once more. He entered the Captain's Quarters and closed the door behind him.

From where Swift was standing, at the entrance to the landing ramp, he thought he could hear Paccon muttering to himself. He considered leaving the boy alone, but, curiosity suitably piqued, he made his was over and leaned on the railing with him.

"Who are you talking to?" Swift asked.

"Myri and Mama."

"Did they say anything?"

Paccon shook his head. "I don't think I'm listening hard enough."

"You'll get the hang of it." He smiled at the boy.

Silence invaded the deck of the ship for a few brief moments, until Skyheart came crashing from the Captain's Quarters holding a black cloth. He proceeded to wrap Myri in it.

"Is Captain Skyheart okay?" Paccon whispered.

"I'm not entirely sure," Swift replied.

"Do you think he's used to death?"

"I don't think anyone is used to death."

"Oh," Paccon said. He paused. "Will I ever see you again?"

"I'll be around," Swift said, smiling. "If ever you see a ship listing lazily over the horizon that will be me. I might even be the first man to go up there." He pointed upwards.

"The sky?"

"Certainly. I've always thought of it as a higher up sea."

168

"Do you really think you'll get there?"

"Who knows?" Swift said, looking at the boy out of the corner of his remaining eye. "I'm quite the pioneer, you know."

They both smiled.

Skyheart rose, Myri placed over his right shoulder. With his free left hand he drank from a bottle. After the long swig his hand fell limply by his side and he smiled at Paccon.

"Come on, Paccon," he said. "It's time to go."

Paccon looked sorrowfully down at the deck and Swift saw Skyheart's smile fade.

Skyheart turned and looked out over the path they would be taking. How different it would be without her. He turned back towards Swift and Paccon. He gave the pirate his usual casual salute.

"It's been a pleasure," Skyheart said. Then he paused and said quietly, "for the most part."

"You take care," Swift said.

"I'll try my best," Skyheart said, smiling. He took a swig of wine. "Though, it's not in my nature. Where are you headed?"

"I'll be around."

Paccon roused and looked up. He walked up to Skyheart and, wordlessly, they parted with Swift.

"Where are we going?" the boy asked.

"Port Fair," Skyheart said.

"To bury Myri?"

"Yes."

"With her family?"

"Yes."

"Where are we going after that?"

"You have to stay there, to keep Myri company. Which is a shame really – I would so love the company."

"Where are you going?" Paccon asked.

Skyheart didn't answer. Instead he sipped from the wine bottle and threw it away. Then he took another from the bag. His steps were heavy, though not altogether slow. However his swagger was not as pronounced as usual.

When had he last slept? Certainly not since they rested after escaping the mountains. How many days ago that was he couldn't be sure. The sun had seemed to rise and fall so many times the previous day that it could hardly have said to have been a day at all; so much as it was a solar episode.

He took another large swig of wine. It burned his gullet on the way down and he smiled at the familiarity. What comfort numbness was, and yet solace wasn't what he found.

Paccon struggled to keep up. Hunger ravaged his stomach, though he didn't complain. He didn't feel as if he could have eaten anyway. Food would only have served to make him more nauseous at the closeness of death recently and the taste would have been lost on him. It all would have been a waste.

He tripped, increasing his pace to stay with the Captain, but he didn't fall.

Still, it was enough to make him more cautious of where he was treading. Skyheart appeared not to notice, deep in thought as he was, and neither spoke, stopped or slowed. Paccon felt the convulsions of an oncoming stream of tears but somehow managed to keep them inside, instead sobbing gently in his throat.

It was only now that Paccon realised they were walking on the same path as they had taken upon their exit from the meadow. He could see the mountains in the distance, piercing the clouds as if to banish them and allow the sun to prevail. As yet, they seemed to be failing. The route looked different on the return journey; then again it wasn't only the direction that had been altered. So much had changed the road was comparatively similar.

Then why did he feel so lost?

Skyheart shifted her weight on his shoulder and then he drank. It irked him to treat her as some common object but the cold emanating from her and seeping into him made it difficult to treat her as human. He thought that inhuman of himself, yet it helped his mood. To carry a corpse was something that irked him more than treating a corpse badly.

He sighed. Had he ever had a plan then this was definitely not part of it.

His mind wandered to when he held her to him on the mountain. Her warmth. Her breath tickling his neck. His heartbeat synchronising with hers.

"Best not to think about that," he whispered to himself. He took a drink and, more out of instinct than consciousness, turned to find Paccon had fallen some way behind. He waited. When they boy caught up he apologised.

"It's okay," Paccon said.

"I was daydreaming," Skyheart said. "I should have been paying attention. I'm sorry."

"It's okay," Paccon said. His eyes looked to have welled with tears. He blinked rapidly to get rid of them.

"Would you like to rest?"

The boy nodded and they sat at the side of the path.

Skyheart placed Myri's body next to him and took a large sip of wine. He looked back the way they had come and could still see the coast. He supposed it was noon by now, though it was still too cloudy to be certain. If he was right it was taking far longer than he had imagined.

"I can slow down when we start again," Skyheart said absent-mindedly.

"I can keep up," Paccon said, trying not to look at Myri. But, eventually, his will faded and his eyes drifted to their human cargo, though the shape she once held was distorted or destroyed by the cloth she was wrapped in. "How long can we rest for?"

"Not too long; it's best to rest at night."

"Okay. It's a long way isn't it?"

"Yes, we should start moving soon."

"I'm ready now."

"It can wait a little while."

"You just say when."

"Are you sure you're ready?"

Paccon nodded.

170

They rose and continued.

As the sun finally slid from the cloudy haze of the sky, obscuring the Southern Continent into further darkness, they came to where the path met the meadow. Skyheart stopped without meaning to and looked upon the fateful place. It was much as it had been before, though now the flowers did not so much dance in the breeze as they were pushed by it – the restless dead wishing to make their presence known.

"Calm yourself," Skyheart said. "There's no reason to get excited; you've eternity to whisper through." He bowed his head for a moment, forgetting the load on his shoulder. Unfortunately, that moment was all too fleeting. "How softly we are reminded, though how violent the memory."

Paccon was somewhere between the realms of wakefulness and sleep. He staggered towards the Captain and fell to his knees. He lay down.

Skyheart placed Myri on the ground and took a blanket from the bag. He wrapped Paccon in it.

"You can sleep now," he said. But the boy was already asleep. Skyheart stood and took a bottle from the bag. He removed the cork with his teeth and spat it away. He wandered into the meadow.

"I'm pushing him too hard," he said. "But what else can I do? This is emotional enough without the stopping. Each time I rest my mind is brought back round to the trauma. Don't misunderstand, I don't wish to be rid of the boy, but... you were right. He's so like you. His solemn nature with brief moments of bliss. His compassion. His strength. It's all you. You understand, don't you?"

No answer came.

Skyheart drank.

"How like you," Skyheart said dryly. He looked to the flower Myri had given him there. It was still laced through the button-holes of his crimson coat. The fuchsia was beginning to fade and turn to brown with the wilting process. "So even memories are resolved to die these days. How typical."

He drank.

He turned and began to leave the meadow.

The breeze picked up and a lone cherry blossom drifted past him. He caught it in his free right hand before letting it float away again. The sweet smell of it was intoxicating and subtly familiar, though not entirely the same as the scent the tree or blossoms usually were.

The breeze whispered after him with a mournful sigh of a name he was seldom called. Skyheart didn't hear, though. His thoughts were too loud in his head. Such was the night.

When he had returned to Paccon and Myri he lay down, but his loud thoughts refused to leave him alone. How could one relax with such monotonous wailing inside oneself?

"And sleep used to come so naturally to me," he said. "So naturally in fact that the waking world was a veritable stranger. Then again," he sat up and took a sip of wine, "everything else is different now. I should have expected this."

He sighed, leaned back on his arms and looked to the horizon.

He drank as he watched the sun rise, placidly and pleasantly drunk; though he was sober enough to look at, sober enough in his speech and movements in fact, so experienced was he in the dance of drink.

The light woke Paccon, working its way through his eyelids, rousing him from his tempestuous slumber. He groaned and opened his eyes, hugging the blanket for warmth. It smelt of Myri. He unwrapped himself from it and sobbed a little while Skyheart was still turned away.

"Are you ready to go?" the Captain asked.

"Yes," Paccon said quietly.

Skyheart rose limply and placed Myri on his shoulder once more. He began walking up the path.

"Are we not going through the meadow?" Paccon asked.

Skyheart stopped. "No," he said, not looking at the boy. "Myri wanted to go this way." He turned to Paccon and smiled. "Besides, it's all part of the adventure." He started walking again. "New routes and all that."

Paccon followed, fists clenched, trying to make sense of the situation. How could the Captain remain so good-humoured when she would never move, breathe, or smile upon either of them ever again? Was he truly so self-centred that it didn't affect him? Then what of those long moments of silence? To have thoughts so profound so as to be almost completely unaware of his travelling companion must have been a relief – an escape even. But how could he think of anything but Myri? And why did he smile so freely?

Paccon tried talking to her, but she didn't answer.

He tried talking to his mother, but she didn't answer.

He sobbed as he walked. The Captain didn't notice.

By late afternoon they had made quite some progress. Skyheart surmised they had less than a day's walk ahead of them, though Paccon was becoming weary and the Captain had slowed to the boy's pace.

The sun descended, bruising the horizon with the darkness of night. Paccon's eyes closed involuntarily and he fell into the Captain. Skyheart considered carrying him, but decided he was carrying enough as it was. He laid the boy on the ground, placing Myri next to him, and wrapped the boy once more in the blanket.

He also tried to sleep, but his heavy heart bade him no comfort.

He sat up and drank, companionless. Night began to swell around him, though the darkness was minimal with so many stars in the sky. The moon smiled mockingly at him, the largest it had been for some time. Even the breeze kept its distance, scorning the Captain. After all, was it not because of him that the breeze had a new recruit?

"These thoughts hold no solace," he said, drinking; though even the wine held no escape from the thoughts. "The blame is mine; that is all there is to it!" he cried, standing and waving his arms frantically. "So if the breeze wishes to spurn me it has every right to!" He calmed and sighed. "Have I not made it so much more plentiful?"

He drank from the bottle aggressively and sat back down with a heavy thud.

He stopped, thinking he heard a voice behind him and turned to see whose it was. But only two bodies in no state to talk where lying behind him. He supposed he merely imagined it, or his own voice had become so unfamiliar to him that he could no longer recognise it.

"Aren't we nervous tonight?" he said, sounding far more like himself. He drank once more.

It could hardly have been said to have been a place. An impenetrable black stood, swirling around him and the two women lying before him. Were there two of them? There were, in the sense that there were two figures, although they were almost identical. The pettiest of differences was that one was further along in the process than the other. Where the younger still held some colour, the older had become completely translucent; starved of life for so long that the living were a different species. The younger still held some resemblance to her former self but would soon be as much a stranger as the elder.

Had they meant the same to him? In a way, although he had only fully cried for one. A boy so young could only express so much sorrow.

The swirling darkness whispered to him like the sea. It gently washed over the women. Soon it would carry them away.

He wished it would, for with all the horror the apparition held he couldn't look away from the two women he had loved so fervently.

"You can leave now," he said as the darkness washed over them once more. "I'll be okay."

But they stayed, deaf to his pleas.

From the darkness, the younger one rose limply, with all life gone. Each bone creaked with dead effort as she greyed into obscurity.

And to think her eyes were once so vibrant.

Paccon awoke into a land not so dissimilar from the dream. The waltzing darkness of the night greeted him, suggesting he had not long been asleep. His eyes had had yet to adjust to the light, but he thought he could see something lying before him.

Something like a face.

Her face.

Her face; grown so lucid so as to rival his mother's in the worsened state of his imagination. A stranger to him. A stranger to the world.

Her eyes; open and vacant, listless to haunting effect.

The boy shrieked, tears bursting from his eyes as captives from a poorly guarded prison. Oh, how he had wanted to keep them inside, but in that moment restraint had been a mystery to him. To deny himself the luxury of relief would have been an unbearable affliction and, above all, an exercise in futility.

Captain Skyheart appeared beside him and pulled the boy into a loving embrace.

173

"It's okay," the Captain said, "the cloth just worked loose."

Paccon felt the Captain leave him, accompanied by the noise of gentle shuffling. When he had courage enough to look, he saw that Skyheart had covered Myri's face.

"There," he said, smiling at the boy, "it's all better now."

"No it's not," Paccon said quietly. "It's not better and it's not okay. Not now or ever. She's gone and she's not coming back. She's not on the breeze and if she is she doesn't care about us anymore. That's why she doesn't answer." He paused for a long time, breathing indolently. "But you don't even care."

"Please don't do this," Skyheart sighed.

"You smile and drink like nothing happened. You ignore me and walk as if you're on your own."

"It's because I can't deal with this..."

"I lost Myri too!"

Paccon's shout reverberated through the night, resonating with righteous truth.

Skyheart turned away and stared at the moon. He shuddered. The boy was right... and after all that time he had spent as if he was alone. He felt the tension leaving his body, though he had not known it was there. He thought for a moment that he might cry, but the feeling passed. He supposed the revelation of company had lifted some of the burden.

"I'm sorry Paccon," he said softly. "I've been ever so absent-minded recently. I suppose... I suppose I wasn't ready for her to die. Then again, that doesn't change anything. Perhaps I should be used to death by now."

"Did you love her?" Paccon asked, his eyes drifting lazily to the left.

"Who's to say really? I don't think it's quite as simple as that." He turned to Paccon and approached him. "Are you going back to sleep?"

The boy shook his head. "I'm ready to go."

Skyheart smiled sympathetically and helped the boy up with an outstretched hand. He picked up Myri and carried her in both of his arms across his waist.

The boy stayed close as they walked the rest of the way. He felt no need to hold back any more tears. He felt no need to shed them.

"How much further have we got left to go?" Paccon asked.

"A hand," Skyheart replied smiling. "Maybe two of your hands."

Paccon smiled. "We're close."

"Yes, we're very close," Skyheart said, smile widening as he forced from his mind what was to come. He felt the boy clutch at his coat and, together, they wandered further into the night.

Carre had woken early that morning under a wavering sun. She rose from disturbing dreams she had no memory of into the vaporous day; miasmic at its core, coagulating at its outskirts. To move she had to cut through the air. Yet, despite the thickness, the day was cool.

The sun rose a weak white over Port Fair, warming the sky into a deep violet. A small cloud strolled past until it gradually faded into nothingness.

The sea murmured pleasantly, reflecting the sun above.

Carre, standing on the sand of the beach, found her thoughts turning to Myri. She'd be back soon, surely – then she'd have someone to spend these mysterious moments with.

She noticed the stranger in the white leather coat standing just a few feet from her. He'd arrived in Port Fair a few days ago with his dead comrade whom he buried at sea. He kept to himself and didn't bother anyone so the town agreed to let him stay. Carre couldn't escape the feeling that there was something slightly familiar about him.

His expression suggested to Carre that he was engulfed in thoughts similar to her own; however, he seemed rather more serene than her. He was almost philosophical. She imagined that had come with his age, learned in the trials of life she had yet to face. She wondered if the reward was worth the grief.

"Perplexing days we find ourselves in," he said, without looking at her.

"I'm sure they'll clear up soon enough," Carre replied. "Or, at least, I hope they will."

"Any news from the Northern Continent?"

"Very little," she said, "and what there is I'd rather not know."

"Wouldn't that be easy?" He smiled solemnly and, for a moment, Carre felt that she knew him. But the feeling was fleeting, as was the smile, and the man returned to being a stranger. He looked away to some recess of the sky meant only for those who had the mind to search for it. Carre tried to follow his eyes but found her gaze falling far out at sea.

"I used to come here as a child," she said dreamily. "I used to find it soothed me, but now the sea means something very different to me. Curious, how our perception of the world changes as we mature."

"Very. As a child I longed to be an adult for I believed it would give my life significance. But, upon becoming a man I felt more insignificant than ever – lost in an ocean of maturity with a forever outgoing tide. The sensation intensified as I got older." He paused for so long that Carre noticed a new age to him. "It seems I've never been the present; only the past or future. It's awe inspiring what an abstract concept can do to a man."

"Unsettling, isn't it?"

"Torturously so, and yet I've never been less than comfortable."

Carre turned to him with her hands pressed her chest. "I'm not sure I understand."

"Not to worry. I'm not entirely sure that I do. I think that I'm trying to say that everything always works out."

"Really?"

"I think so."

"How can anyone know what they think anymore?" she said, turning to gaze out at sea once more.

"All will become clear," she heard in the man's voice. "It always does."

"I hope so," she said, turning, only to find he was gone.

"Carre?" said a rather more familiar voice behind her. She turned and saw the Mayor with the gravest of faces. "Are you okay?"

"I was talking to the stranger... but he left without me noticing."

"People have a habit of doing that," the Mayor said. He looked away from her for a few brief moments before meeting her eyes once more. "I'm afraid I have some bad news."

But over his shoulder she had already seen it.

The return of Paccon and Captain Skyheart, holding a body covered in a black sheet.

"Myri," she tried to say but found no breath to speak.

"I'm so sorry," the Captain said in a whisper that inexplicably reached Carre.

She fell to her knees, her heart screeching doom from within her. How long for the din to shatter her completely? Paccon wrapped his arms around her, not giving her breaking soul a chance to come apart. The woman returned his embrace.

"Any mother for an orphan," Skyheart said sympathetically, though he went unheard.

They laid her to rest in her garden in a grave between her parents and Kote, in the hope that she could finally know them and find him. Little was said. The more Skyheart experienced death the less he found there was to say about it. Instead he left a small monument to her, carved from wood:

'Myri Harmoire,
May you know on the breeze
the happiness you could not in life.'

He placed it upon the mound of freshly upturned soil and wished he had some flowers to give. He clutched at the flower she had given him, but left it where it was.

He looked at the subdued faces around him. The gathering was small, only consisting of those present on the beach – the Mayor would break the news to the rest of the town later that day. The Mayor, although clearly moved by the loss of Myri, seemed at peace with it. Skyheart imagined he had seen this sort of occurrence a lot during the Mineral Wars. This was just another bad tiding from a man of the Northern Continent. The Captain hoped he would never become that well acquainted with death, though he couldn't shake the feeling he was already on that path.

Carre had composed herself. Skyheart thought that unsettling; to show only the briefest moment of grief at the passing of one so dear to her (one so dear to him), was that not cold? After all, she had the chance to mourn. She had not the burden of blame, nor had she the task of returning the body to the planet. All was done. Then again, he supposed it wasn't his place to wish her sorrow. She had a lifetime to mourn yet.

Paccon was typically stoical. So young and already passed on to his third mother. Skyheart wondered how old the boy was. Six, maybe? Though he was certainly short for his age, mature as he was. He thought maybe solemn was a better description than mature, however the two seemed connected, so he left it as it was in his mind. He longed for the boy to smile – to have a chance to smile – as he had fleetingly during the night.

Still, with the sadness of the situation, he couldn't help but wish that one of them would have some outpouring of emotion. Even the most subtle of tears would suffice. But none came.

"And so," he said, turning from each of the small congregation, "we bury yet another of our own, though we show no remorse. So be it."

"The grief is not ours to show, Captain," Carre replied. "It is yours."

Skyheart smiled, yet the curl of his mouth lacked its usual wry arrogance. It seemed that it simply crawled across his face because it was time to, as an incoming tide, and, like the waves of that tide, it faded soon after. He scratched the back of his head lazily and tilted his head towards Carre.

"I fear I've many more grievances to come in the next few days, within the next hour even. Were I to release my anguish now I may not be able to go on." He stroked his hair from his face, revealing icy blue eyes. His smile returned. "Still," he said, "I knew Myri far less well than the rest of you. In such a way I am cursed." He paused. "And there I was thinking there was nothing to be said."

"Would you like to be alone with her?" Carre asked.

Skyheart shook his head and allowed himself to smile again. "No. It's time for me to leave. Were I to stay I would feel the desire to stay forever."

"Must you go?"

Skyheart nodded and knelt before Paccon. "You understand, don't you?"

The boy nodded.

"I'd stay if I could, but events have transpired in such a way that I must return to the Northern Continent."

"You won't be back, will you?" the boy asked.

"I don't think I'll be in any condition to."

The boy fell into an embrace with the Captain. Skyheart whispered something to the boy that Carre couldn't hear. When they parted Carre saw that Paccon's eyes were drenched in tears.

Skyheart rose. "Well, goodbye all," he said. "You shan't be seeing me again."

He turned and began a slow walk back to the house. His usual swagger was present, yet, far from the supercilious confidence Carre had once imagined it denoted, she saw the tremor of an efface man.

"Wait," she called.

Skyheart turned.

"Won't you need this?" she said, holding up the bag full of wine he had, not so long ago, untied from his hip.

He waved his hand in a negative motion. "I don't think that will be much help this time."

And with that he left.

Carre turned to Paccon. He had stopped crying; in fact he almost looked at peace. She gently asked him what the Captain had whispered to him.

"He said, as I get older, I'll find out a lot about myself and what I discover within me will forever connect me to those I've lost – especially Mama. I wonder what that means."

He tugged at the brim of his tall pointed hat and pulled it further down onto his head, shielding his eyes from the sun.

The two Captains met by the cherry blossom tree. The sun, now just past its dawning position, cut a hole in the sapphire sky. The whisper of the sea and cooing of the breeze merged into one, combining into an overture of tranquillity.

They looked at each other with severe expressions, the tails of their coats fluttering in the wind.

"I hoped you wouldn't be here," Skyheart said.

"I hoped you wouldn't come," Cyan replied. "Or at least, not so soon. I planned to be gone by the time you returned." He paused. "How did your adventure end?"

"Fruitlessly," Skyheart said. "Though, I've come to expect that of late." He scratched the back of his head. "Is this really necessary?"

Cyan sighed and ran his fingers through his greying hair.

"Invariably, Laike," he said, taking a few steps forward and placing his hand on the hilt of his katana. "I think... I think I've always feared death, no matter how pleasant I've tried to make it seem to myself. I used to think the uncertainty was what terrified me – but what's uncertain about it? It's the only certainty I can think of. Yet, I've never thought of my death as inevitable. But, here it is. Do you fear death, Laike?"

Skyheart shrugged.

"You're allowed to be vulnerable, Laike; we're friends."

"I don't think that friends kill each other, Ryden."

Cyan sighed. "No, I suppose they don't. Unfortunately these are extreme circumstances and friendship must be put aside." He drew his sword and moved his left leg backwards, lifting his katana above his head – ready for both attack and defence.

"Please, let's not do this, Ryden," Skyheart said. "Killing Rom was hard enough."

"You were a good captain, Laike," said Cyan. "You did your duty for the most part, contrary to popular opinion. You only ever lost one man and that was DeFlare. Even then you were incapacitated. That's far better than I can say for myself. Now come, do your duty again."

Skyheart tilted his head and looked out to sea. The sun lengthened in its reflection making the day seem brighter than it was. Soon, the lustre became too much for Skyheart and he looked back to Cyan. As beautiful as the vista was, it held no answers.

He drew Cendré and rested the black blade on his shoulder.

"Whoever lives," said Cyan "collects Thean and Okain – to put them with their comrades."

"So we can meet on the endless tides."

Cendré's ribbons danced, synchronised with the Captains' coats, creating waves of their own.

"Forgive me, Laike," Cyan said. "But, either way, I'll never have another chance to ask. Your speed; it's Cendré isn't it?"

"The finer points of the phenomenon elude me," Skyheart said. "Though,

178

as I understand it, the sword calls upon the power of the planet and distorts everybody's perception of time, except my own."

"So you only appear faster?"

Skyheart shrugged. "I suppose that the most accurate explanation is that far from making me faster, it makes the universe slower. Besides," he said, smiling, "you're stalling."

Cyan smiled. "Very well. I see no point in wasting any more time."

He moved first and, though only a twitch, it was enough to spark the charge from Skyheart. He found himself surprised that he could follow the Crimson Captain's movement – he never had been able to before. Though, as Cyan sliced downwards, he found himself moving slower than ever and the weapon stayed raised above his head.

Skyheart reached him.

Cendré cut through his chest, but there was no pain. There was no sensation at all. The ashen black blade simply washed through him. There was no cooing voice calling him to other side, no bright light or great epiphany of peace. There was only that all-encompassing metanarrative and one he had forbade himself to know in any detail in life, but, in death, there was little else for him to know. It came quickly, but with no more force than as if he had merely drifted into sleep.

Darkness.

Skyheart rested Cendré on his shoulder, standing not two paces behind where Cyan once had. The overture had ended and a symphony of silence had taken its place.

"Will this wakefulness ever end?" he said as a familiar ship appeared on the horizon.

Chapter Twenty Five

Around this time, a rumour, shrouded in mystery, as they so often are, roamed the Northern Continent. It spoke of two infamous men, both thought dead, besieging Mandra. One, a pirate, fought bravely, deftly killing many Mandran soldiers, though he was overshadowed by his accomplice: a man in a crimson coat. His long blonde hair became a mane as he moved swiftly from man to man, cutting each down without so much as a strike in retaliation.

Despite their clear talent for killing, both men seemed to despair in it.

There were some who said that they did it simply for the adventure. Others said it was revenge that led them to do it. However, most said they went to Mandra to retrieve two fallen comrades.

Well, that's just what some people say.

A new day was dawning as they docked in Genko's port and Skyheart had started shaking once more. His nausea was the worst it had ever been. He had begun to fear he may collapse again, though he suspected his symptoms had been heightened by the events of the past few days, along with the anticipation of those to come.

A thin rain greeted them and, somewhere, many miles away, thunder roared. Although fine, the rain was persistent enough to soak Skyheart's hair through, darkening it to a dull golden colour. As the rain seeped into his skin he could feel a distinct chill reach even the deepest of his bones. The wilting flower in his coat looked to the ground as if to shield itself from the rain.

"I suppose this means autumn's here," Swift said, lowering the landing ramp.

"You didn't have to take me here," Skyheart said.

"I know."

"I do appreciate it though."

"I know," Swift said, smiling. "Are you sure you don't want me to come any further with you?"

"I'd certainly like the company," Skyheart said. "Though I fear there may be a few too many Mandran soldiers around who won't appreciate you being alive."

"Will they react so well to you?"

Skyheart smiled. "I shouldn't imagine so."

"You look as if you're ailing, Laike."

Skyheart knew exactly what Swift meant. He could see his own paper thin skin on his hand, so pale so as to almost be able to see each heartbeat work its way around his body.

"I need to go alone," he said.

Swift nodded and Skyheart turned, beginning to leave.

"I won't say 'goodbye'," he continued. "I've said it far too much recently."

"Will you be back?" Swift called after him.

Skyheart stopped and turned with his hips to face Swift. "I'll be around," he said, smiling.

He disembarked from the ship and watched as Swift sailed away on a ship that should have been too cumbersome for one man. However, he seemed to manage with ease.

Skyheart walked from the dock up the hill to the cliff where he had once, reluctantly, fought DeFlare. He sighed. The memory seemed so long ago he wondered if it had really happened. The rain made it that much murkier. But, before the Captain, stood a wooden gallows – once used to make an example of Lieutenant DeFlare. Now it stood as a monument to commemorate the graveness of the days.

He looked out to the sea beyond the structure and saw Swift's ship listing lazily over the horizon. He supposed his comrades were out there, somewhere, too. In his weakened state the thought caused him to grip the wooden framework for stability.

"Well we certainly had some adventures together, didn't we?" Skyheart said, smiling weakly. "Not that you were too keen on having most of them. You just wanted to get along with life. I suppose that was fair enough, sensible really. But I think you enjoyed it when we got going.

"I never thought of you as a lieutenant, far from it. In many ways you were more of a captain than I was. You certainly did more work, anyway. I always looked to you for guidance, whether you knew it or not, and I think I turned to you far more than you ever turned to me. Every so often I needed to know I was doing the right thing. I could do with you now, really.

"I had quite an adventure once we parted, perhaps my greatest. Maybe I'll tell you about it someday.

"Forgive me... please," his voice fell to a whisper. "I know my treachery was against more than just Thieron. But I didn't think of it in that way. It's difficult to manufacture freedom, especially when you know not what freedom is.

"I'm not supposed to be saying any more goodbyes. But, you should be a fair exception." He sighed and released the gallows. "Goodbye, Alrous."

He was disturbed by approaching footsteps from the awakening city. Slowly, he turned and saw a group of six Mandran soldiers, armed with spears, creeping towards him. He looked at them, each in turn, inching through the worsening rain; all as drenched as him. He once more became aware of his shaking and scratched the back of his head. As his hand fell back down to his side he spoke.

"Cannot a man mourn in peace?"

"A man? Yes. You, Captain Skyheart, cannot," one Mandran spoke. "By all accounts you should be the one being mourned."

"Even now there are those who mourn his existence," one growled.

"What of our dead? Who is to mourn them? Our dead who lie in the sands of your desert city, with not a soul to say a comforting word."

"So you have already marched on Thieron," Skyheart said. "You mean to say I am too late?"

No reply came.

Skyheart's eyes flitted between the men. "How did you fare?"

"He wants an account of the battle now," said a soldier.

"It's irrelevant," said another. "Why should a traitor need to know of his motherland? You mean to say you have remorse for your actions?"

"More curiosity than remorse," Skyheart said. "I wish to know what consequences I have set in motion."

"Enough of this. Let us kill him and avenge our fallen brothers!"

They readied their spears.

"These days hold too many dead already," Skyheart said. "Can you not feel how thick the breeze is? One can hardly move against it."

"Draw your sword! I'll not kill an unarmed man."

"Must anyone die?"

"Ready yourself, coward!"

"Is it not obvious what will happen?"

Silence fell upon the men with a gust of wind, blowing Skyheart's drenched hair to the right. With the breeze came a brown leaf, crumbling against time, floating with the tide of air. A crowd had begun to gather. Soaked in both curiosity and rain. Why they wished to see more bloodshed, Skyheart couldn't imagine.

Starting at his shoulder, he flicked a forceful energy of will down his right arm, ceasing his trembling.

"You're not going to want to see this," he whispered.

The breeze dissipated and the dead leaf slowly danced towards the ground. It swayed in opposing directions, forced down and diverted by droplets of rain. Eventually, it landed on the cold grey brickwork of the city of Genko.

The six Mandran soldiers hit the ground in synchrony with the leaf.

Nobody saw Skyheart draw his sword, let alone move. Yet, there he stood, just two paces behind the bodies of his opponents, the obsidian black blade of Cendré resting on his shoulder. Gradually the rain washed their blood from the surface.

He sighed and, with his free left hand, wiped the rain from his face. He sheathed Cendré.

The crowd dispersed without a sound, the padding of their footsteps shrouded by the crashing of the falling rain.

"You," Skyheart called to a passing man in grey garbs. He walked with a fresh hunch, shuffling away from the eyes of the world. "What news have you of Thieron?"

The man stopped and looked at Skyheart with an expression somewhere between fear and begrudging acceptance of life.

"Best you see for yourself," he said bitterly, but still he did not leave. "You have another question."

"Yes. There was an old man imprisoned here for... something. Is he still here?"

"Oh, him," said the man disinterestedly. "No, he left a few days ago. The Mandrans made quite a spectacle of freeing him. They never explained why." He turned and walked towards his house.

"Thank you," Skyheart said, though the man paid him no mind.

He was granted an apathetic passage through the city by the remaining Genkoans and came upon only a few soldiers, who gave him much the same treatment as the citizens. He had expected such scorn from Thieronians, but their enemies too? Perhaps treachery is unforgivable to all, no matter on whose side one stands. Or maybe people don't take kindly to the dead returning to life.

Soon he reached the gate, or where the gate once stood. All that was left of it now as a jagged hole burnt in singed black metal. Beside the hole, a man in an elaborate red uniform stood, staring at Skyheart.

"So, the dead walk," he said. "I'd always hoped we'd meet. Didn't you?"

Skyheart scratched the back of his head. "It's difficult to wish to meet a man whose existence is a mystery to you."

"I am General Tegus. Supreme Commander of the Mandran Armed Forces."

Skyheart shrugged and looked distractedly at a boy on the side of the street. The boy peered at the ground dejectedly before looking at the Captain. He said nothing.

"I take it you're here to free the people," Tegus said.

Skyheart's attention turned to the General. "I'm not sure what I'm here for."

"You don't mean to be these people's liberator?"

"And how many more would have to die for that, I wonder."

Thunder blared somewhere to the east and Skyheart's shaking returned. Resiliently, he shuffled on his feet as rain fell as a sheet upon him.

Tegus laughed. "You mean to do nothing?" Excitedly, he approached Skyheart. "Forgive me, but that is fortuitous news indeed." His arms waved in wild gesticulations. "I'm sure you can imagine my fear when I heard you had arrived. The mighty Crimson Captain, back from the dead, returned to exact his murderous vengeance on Mandra!" He circled the Captain as he spoke, rather closer than Skyheart was comfortable with. "Though, to find you mean to do nothing is something of a disappointment, albeit a welcome and relieving one." He stopped in front of Skyheart but did not face him. "Yet, it intrigues me..." His eyes met Skyheart's. "As Premier Statesman of New Mandra, formerly Genko, I invite you, Captain Laike Skyheart of Thieron's Fourth Division, to join me at the palace. You would be a most welcome guest."

"Actually," Skyheart said, "it's Division Four. Besides, I must be going."

"To what end, Captain? What you journey towards will not disappear simply for taking rest. You are soaked through! And surely you desire to know what has transpired since your departure?"

"I must be going."

Tegus sighed. "I would loathe to be forced to make the killing begin again, Captain. Have not enough died?"

183

Skyheart weakened and fell to a slouch. He exhaled a long, weary breath. When he tried to regain his strength he found something had carried it away.

"Very well," he said.

"Splendid!" Tegus said, taking Skyheart's shoulder in his hand and turning him back towards the inner-city. "We have much to discuss."

The young boy shivered against the cold and thought of returning home, what home there was left. There would be nobody there; just cold uninviting stone. He resolved to stay in the rain. The result would be much the same, either way.

He bathed luxuriously yet uneasily as his clothes dried. The great stone basin he found himself in had clearly been taken and carved from the mountains of Mandra. How much of those peaks had they destroyed in the name of spectacle? At least he was warm. There was some comfort in that, though he could not shake the feeling that he should have been on his way.

The room was large, though other than that it was unlike the rest of the palace. The walls had been panelled with a light wood, as opposed to the favoured marble, and the floor was lazily shined obsidian. Such a large room with so little in it was unsettling to say the least. It led him to wonder why spectacle had been placed before practicality. However, he knew this to be a common folly.

He finished his thoughts and rose, drying himself with a towel. Then he dressed. He had washed with a cherry blossom scent infused into the water and they had apparently washed his clothes with a similar perfume. Now dry, the leather coat felt more like it was his than in previous days. He doubted it had ever truly dried from his time in the ocean, yet it showed no signs of wear. Lastly, he placed his scabbard in his belt. Why they had not disarmed him he couldn't say, though he certainly had no lethal intent. But surely it was standard practice to disarm an enemy, unless Tegus had specifically asked that Cendré remain with him.

He waved the thoughts away. Whatever the reason it was irrelevant. He had no desire to use Cendré.

He left the bathroom and was led by an attendant down a corridor (far more in keeping with the rest of the palace) to a small bedroom. He had no intention of sleeping, but as his head fell upon the pillow he was met by darkness.

He awoke from his dreamless sleep to find his nausea and shaking gone, though something disturbed him. He had slept; was that not wrong of him? How contemptible to allow oneself to slumber after all that had happened and with so much more left to come. With her body in the ground so many miles away, over a vast ocean and her soul on the breeze so close to him – yet he had slept. Perhaps he was taking the situation too lightly, exhaustion beating down on him until he could care for nothing other than the act of closing his eyes.

He sat up and was met by a mirror, revealing to him a face that looked much more like his normal self than he was expecting. Where his skin had been silk thin it had become a healthier colour. Though the most obvious change was that he was smiling.

"No more of this melancholia then?" he said to himself. "Very well; I'll not be the one to argue with that. So, well rested and contented both, I suppose it's time I rise. I've kept Tegus waiting long enough."

He slid from the bed, his black boots meeting the floor with a satisfying click. He stood and made for the door.

The same attendant who led him to the quarters took him to a room far more familiar to Skyheart, the Throne Room. Before him, in the far wall, was the unrepaired hole, through which one could see a glorious day – cloudless as the summer had been. The boulder that had been worked loose by the cannons of war still blighted the room. Tegus, standing by this, touched it in admiration.

"You're quite the heavy sleeper," he said, smiling at Skyheart. "You've slept for a whole day and not for the first time I hear."

Tegus walked towards the Captain, his footsteps echoing loudly throughout the marble room. "It's a strange feeling, victory. Indeed, this room was once the very embodiment of what Mandra fought against. But now, as New Mandra, this eastern province shall thrive with western significance. As we speak, Mandran rock from the mountains is on its way here to furnish, not only the palace, but the city."

His eyes fell upon Skyheart's coat. "Your flower's dead. Perhaps we could provide you with another?"

Skyheart peered down at the colourless lily. The protruding stamen had fallen from the flower long ago and the petals looked to go the same way in the near future. The stalk was brittle with dehydration and cracked as he moved.

"This one shall suffice, thank you," he said with that familiar wry smile,

"Are you sure? We have some spectacular Mandran roses from our mountains. They might not be quite as weather resistant as the desert plants that you're used to, but I assure you the colours are quite striking."

"I'm quite sure."

"Very well," Tegus said, shrugging. "I must say, you seem far better than yesterday."

"In what respect?"

"In all respects. But enough small talk. I promised to recount what happened since you disappeared. Although, with your vigour returned, perhaps you'd rather kill me and liberate New Mandra?"

"I've already told you that's not why I'm here."

"Well," Tegus said, "it's not in my nature to pry, so I won't. Anyway, it's all academic by this point – there's not much you can do, especially without drawing your sword. It would seem even you are no threat to the Mandran Empire. But, I speak irrelevance.

"You wish to know of the events since your departure to... wherever it is you've been. As I've said, I won't pry. I'll not bore you with details, as it is I'm sure you'll want to be on your way quickly and it's not my place to obstruct you.

"I'll get the most awkward piece of information out in the open first, which is useful as, chronologically, that is its rightful place. The battle for Genko ended soon after your disappearance, or death as it was then known, and I began to survey the city. On my travels I came upon a strange scene: a dejected Thieronian, not much older than yourself, had engaged in a standoff with some of my soldiers, only, he refused to attack them! I admit, my curiosity was piqued at this and I approached to find out more. Of course, I knew he was a Thieronian Lieutenant right away, your Lieutenant in fact (I had the pleasure of watching your body fall from the cliff from one of the invading ships. That pleasure has now diminished somewhat with your return, however at the time I was, shall we say, overjoyed at the sight of the crimson coat plunging lethally into the cascading waters beneath. To be part of such a magnificent campaign that would kill the Crimson Captain would have been such an achievement...). Not only did I know who he was, but I knew why he was there.

"Just as I was leaving Mandra I heard of the arrival of two envoys from Thieron. Of course, I was suspicious. You Thieronians are devious people (I mean to cause no offence – indeed it is one of your greatest strengths) and are not to be trusted in any circumstance, not least in times of war. I was told that these men from the desert had come to seek peace with Mandra, a not so un-noble sentiment I suppose, though I must admit I had a rather striking image of the pair grovelling at the Queen's feet in my mind. Unfortunately, I had to leave soon after hearing this news in order to be part of our attack. As it transpired I was right to be suspicious. I was informed not long after the battle that the two envoys had given the Queen the Diamandé, or a poor imitation of it, that fooled her not for a second. Of course, we didn't need the *real* one either. With our surprise attack mounted our victory was assured.

"With knowledge of Thieronians in Mandra, despite their motives (at the time) being a mystery to me, it was clear that your Lieutenant and yourself were here to strike a similar bargain with the Genkoans. Clearly, you were playing us off against one another: a brave plan, but ultimately unwise.

"I pretended to your Lieutenant that I knew not of your death, to see how he would react upon having to admit your demise to himself. He was lacklustre to say the least. Of course, this was needlessly antagonistic of me, yet I could not help myself and, for that, I apologise. However, after enough provocation the Lieutenant managed to rouse some emotion. This emotion was rage. He swung at me with his sword, intent to kill burning in his eyes! Though, as you can see, this was fruitless and my soldiers executed him before he could reach me. I later berated these men for killing him in such unceremonious circumstances. I would have preferred something more public, though I was rather relieved to find myself alive."

Tegus smiled and waited for Skyheart to reply. But the Captain remained placidly contented and Tegus was left wanting. Tegus had hoped for a similar rage to that of DeFlare's, though with no guards around, a rather more vocal aggression would have been preferred. But Skyheart moved only to scratch the back of his head and said nothing.

"I won't lie to you, Captain," Tegus said. "Your reaction, or lack thereof, surprises me."

Skyheart smiled. "Well, General, I already knew that DeFlare was dead. That the Mandrans killed him is no surprise and I long suspected that you had witnessed this."

"But does your bosom not swell with pride that he died trying to fell me; his enemy?"

"Actually, I'm rather ashamed of him for not succeeding in killing an opponent who needs to have others fight for him."

A sharp pain cut through Tegus and he stalled. For the briefest of moments he thought that Skyheart had covered the entire length of the room and struck him, impossible though it seemed. However, the Captain still stood placidly far down the other end of the room. The pain soon faded and dissolved into a heat that encompassed the General's entire body. He clenched his fist and broke into a deep scowl.

"No offence intended, of course," Skyheart said, smiling.

"Of course," Tegus snarled. He took a few seconds to calm himself before continuing. "Well, now I'll tell you something you don't know. It was I who ordered the Lieutenant to be hung from the gallows. It seemed only right to display to the people what would happen to those of them who stood in our way."

"General," Skyheart sighed. "I came here to discover what happened on the Northern Continent during my absence, not to discuss my dead subordinate. If you've called me here just to talk about DeFlare I fear you've wasted my time and yours."

Tegus smiled revealing two rows of perfect teeth, the canines making particularly strong impressions.

"Very well," he said. "Enough of the Lieutenant. Though I must say, I think it shameful to be so blasé about the death of so close a colleague. But, if you insist...

"Our next move was to predict what Thieron would do next. Of course their options were thoroughly limited. They had three choices: strengthen their defences, retrieve the Diamandé or join forces with the returning Genkoan frontline. In a way they did all three and, in another way, they did none.

"We had, and have, no interest in the Diamandé. Aside from having defeated the enemy that posed the greatest threat to us, Mandra has no wish to put any faith in magic, especially magic from Thieronian mythology. Add to this the fact that the entire Mandran Navy witnessed said jewel plunge into the ocean and you have a strong case for not attempting to retrieve the Diamandé.

"By far the biggest threat to us at this time was the remaining Genkoan army. The entire frontline was intact posing, at least, a minor threat to us. Thieron is so far away, we knew that they would never attack and, as long as they were mounting their defences, we had nothing to fear from them. In their search for the Diamandé they would send a small force and one that would avoid detection at that. But the Genkoans had numbers. Don't misunderstand, Captain. Their numbers were nowhere near ours. But, were they to incite the citizens of the city to attack us too, then we would be at a significant disadvantage. Our only hope was to fight them outside the city, where there was enough room to make our numbers count.

"It was here we were met by a problem; we knew not how to open the gate. As I'm sure you know the gates of Genko run on electricity. The finer points of the operation elude us as do the mysteries of electricity itself. Mandra has no need for such power, but our pride was beginning to get in our way.

"In anticipation of the Genkoan assault, we tried to convince the Genkoan people to open the gates for us, promising riches to anyone who would aid us. We were met by silence and antipathy. As an act of goodwill we freed a prisoner from the dungeon of the palace. 'Look!' I said, 'We, the Mandran government, set free a Genkoan. Help us and you too will be free forevermore!' It was an old man we set free, no threat to us. No threat to anyone. We thought by releasing a pitiable character we would attract more attention from the people. However, once more the Genkoans reacted poorly. We later found out the Old Man wasn't Genkoan...

"When rewards and affection failed we moved onto torture and despair, promising we would end the subjects' suffering once the gates were open. But these are hardy and loyal people who refused to succumb to us. Many died.

"It then became clear to us that force would have to be the opener of the gate. We gathered all the explosives we could with every intention of blasting the gate from its hinges. However, upon acquiring such a vast amount of explosives a thought came to me: would it not be suspicious if we, the new occupying force, destroyed our main defence? To admit to the Genkoans that the city had become a cage would have been to admit defeat. Far from coaxing them into an assault it would discourage them – helping them realise it was a trap.

"Fortunately, (and believe me Captain, it was little more than fortune) Thieron solved our problem. It would appear that the small force, two men to be precise, sent to find the Diamandé had agreed to make sure that the gates would not stand in the way of the Genkoan force and decimated the gates for us. Of course, warriors that they were, these men (accompanied by a pirate of some notoriety) dispensed with a large number of my soldiers too. Quite how three men killed so many armed men while escaping unscathed is a mystery to me, but I know what happened and I'll not question it.

"With the gate gone we made light work of the Genkoans in the field just before the city. But that was to be expected. After the battle we buried our dead, not that there were many – though still there were more than I hoped for. We then allowed the Genkoans to bury their dead.

"All threat to the newest corner of the Mandran Empire had dissipated and Genko became New Mandra. We then rebuilt our forces in both the east and west. I'm sure you know to what end."

Tegus smiled and stopped, though his smile diminished once he saw Skyheart was just as calm as before.

"And what happened when you reached Thieron?" the Captain asked.

Tegus smiled again with a flash of that dagger of a canine. "Best you see for yourself."

Skyheart smiled in reply sending the sharp pain to shoot through Tegus again. Once he was certain he was still alive he scowled.

"Are you not incensed?" he growled. "Are you not incandescent with rage? We gathered our entire armed forces with the sole purpose of destroying your homeland! Whether or not we were successful is irrelevant! You cannot allow this act of aggression to go unpunished!"

He drew a rapier from the scabbard at his side and three guards entered the room.

"I am your enemy, Captain Skyheart! You are Thieronian and I am Mandran. The times dictate that we engage in a fight to the death!"

"I'll not be dictated to by time or man," Skyheart said calmly, though he wore an expression of mild irritation. "Those who lay dead in the desert will not be revived by my cutting you and your guards down, nor will it revive DeFlare or the other companions I have lost. That you seek glory by killing me, or being killed by me, I suppose is some form of flattery, but I shall neither thank you or oblige you in this. The breeze is thick enough as it is and the endless tides are restless with heavy waves. I'll certainly commit no more to either."

Tegus sneered and sheathed his sword. He waved the guards away and they left. He watched, fists clenched, sweat forming on his brow and upper lip as Skyheart scratched the back of his head.

"You're a coward, Skyheart," he said. "But I should expect nothing less from a man who would betray his own country."

"We don't own the land," Skyheart replied, "the land nurtures us and all of the land is connected, perhaps not on the surface, but is it not all part of the same planet? To draw lines and make enemies because of those lines holds no benefit. I'll have no part of it. I'll have no enemies."

He smiled and with that he left.

Chapter Twenty Six

His departure from New Mandra led him to a field of blossoming flowers. Autumn dew trickled from their petals down their stalks, glistening in the morning light. The ground beneath, so fertile from the many dead, held enough nutrients for the flowers to survive in even the harshest of winters.

Flowers raised on man's flesh.

Skyheart retched at the thought, but thankfully had nothing in his stomach to expel. For death to create such a vibrant pasture disturbed him. Had he found himself upon a dry cracked plain or desert he would have been far more at ease. Though was there not hope in the view? That a battle could breed this spring-like life, this natural monument to those that had died, held some comfort. Did it not?

Skyheart shook his head. "Had there been no battle there would be no need for a monument. Would that not be better?"

He paused and sighed.

"Could I have stopped this had I been here? This – perhaps, but only by replacing it with other deaths." He smiled weakly. "I wonder if that's true."

Walking through the field evoked memories of the meadow. They were similar to look at, he admitted that to himself, though there were no other similarities. Each brought forth almost opposing emotions. To walk the meadow was to know true serenity; a place of near religious revelation, yet to be alone in that as a personal revelation. That wasn't to say one couldn't be uneasy there – to be so close to the feeling of something so significant so as to define one's very own existence could make even the most self-sure visitor shudder with obscurity. But, the beauty of the place would always quiet that unease and make a friend of it.

However, to walk the field he was now in, one could know no friends. One would find a stranger in himself and the planet, and so the Captain did. He drifted through, but was neither a part of it or apart from it. Each possibility seemed unbearable and it was upon realising this that he realised both were true. He embraced that, pulling it inside himself where he knew the glow would burst around the edges of his eclipsing heart.

As his trailing foot landed on the ground outside of the field the feeling left him and relief entered as he sighed. That the epiphany escaped him soothed him. Whether it had been an authentic feeling or one he had manufactured to make it through, he couldn't decide. But when he turned and looked upon the field once more, he saw not what he had seen before; the joyous monument to a needless battle. No, he saw a mass grave, with not individual flowers, but a giant bouquet of them.

"So, the planet itself mourns your passing," he said. "High praise indeed." He looked away in the direction he would soon be walking and sighed heavily. "Though for the planet to lament our foolishness should be symbol enough for it not to happen again. Yet, I doubt we've learned."

As he wandered, leaving the place behind, he tried to remove death from his mind.

He roamed the land he had travelled many times and had once known, to find it different from before. Armies of men had burned and ravaged it, so much so that he had little hope for his destination. If he was easily lost on the road when the land seemed familiar, then navigation was now almost impossible. Yet he drifted over the land, no longer aware that it had once been more, for he had seen so much since he returned to the Northern Continent that the questions had built until he may as well have not returned at all.

However, soon enough he reached a small town that was all too familiar. Deserted, it stood stoically against the armies of east and west, until now, when only the armies of west remained and the town had nothing left to defend, yet still a world of war to defend against.

The ground was swamped with rainwater, as it was when last he was there, though now the air was dry. As the wind gently blew he noticed the faint smell of smoke from a dying fire. Or a fire long dead.

At the side of the road that his feet sank into with each careless step, were two swords he had planted there. Vines had started to climb their way to the hilts, unhindered by the rusting blades. Despite the sun they did not glimmer.

Skyheart smiled and continued on his way.

The plains had been scarred by the many feet that fell upon it in the previous month. The Genkoan army had marched west only to retreat in order to take back their city. The Mandran army then marched to Thieron only to return to New Mandra. Yet still of Thieron's fate the Captain could but surmise.

When night fell he slept.

When day came he woke and rose.

Though the sun had risen, the sky remained bruised in patches where the blue and violet merged to create this late dawn of autumn morning. By noon the bruises had faded and Captain Skyheart reached the outskirts of the Thieronian desert.

Although New Mandra had seen the first storm of autumn, the desert had yet to see any rain. Dunes had begun to form with the late-year winds, but the rains would not reach until winter and even then they would be mercilessly brief.

He ventured through them, determined to discover the consequences of his actions on what was once his homeland – though it had certainly never felt so. Of course, the knowledge of the deaths of DeFlare and the Captains along with their subordinates did not make for the most optimistic of thoughts and predictions. Furthermore, his sympathy for the President and the Assembly had waned to non-existence upon the threat of execution, no matter how long ago that was. What of his old friend Reed the barkeep? What of the leaderless Division Four?

What of his brother?

So deep was the Captain in thought that he was negligent to the presence of another. That one so often on his mind...

"Strange," the watcher said, startling Skyheart, "the planet told me you were alive, but I didn't believe it."

Skyheart examined the Old Man only to find him no different than before.

"Strange indeed," the Old Man continued. "I saw your fall, you know; from the barred window of my cell. Quite a fall. Had I known you had the Diamandé I may have let you free me..."

Skyheart looked away from the Old Man towards a small flow of sand trickling down a dune. It clustered near the bottom, only to be dispersed by a small gust of wind. He looked back to the Old Man.

"You know of the Diamandé?" Skyheart asked.

"Of course," the Old Man said. "Who else would the planet confide in? The existence of the defence mechanism has long been known to me. Listen," he fell to a whisper and gestured with his index finger for the Captain to be quiet. "Can you hear it?"

Skyheart slowed and softened in his breathing. The thick breeze motioned past with a whisper, but no... not a whisper. A moan.

The Captain nodded. "The planet's in pain."

"Very perceptive," the Old Man said, smiling. "It doesn't like what we're doing to each other; all this war. It's making a new defence against any more pain. Hopefully we'll learn this time. It lost one in the Diamandé, though the other remains resolutely safe."

"Cendré..." Skyheart whispered.

The Old Man nodded. "Of course, you knew that already. It's basic Thieronian mythology, although the cause is somewhat different; far from a goddess it was the planet that bestowed it upon us. Thankfully it fell into your hands – someone who would use it only reluctantly and maybe not even then."

"Then why make it a weapon?"

"That I don't know," the Old Man said. "Maybe to display to us just what we are."

Skyheart said nothing.

"Not that it chose you," the Old Man said. "That's a burden too great even for you. It's just the way it worked out." He smiled solemnly. "Then again, I suppose a new defence is nothing to get excited about – it can't be good news for us, can it?"

Skyheart sighed. "I went there."

"I'm sorry?"

"The meadow."

"You *did*?" The Old Man approached eagerly. "What met you there?"

"Beauty," Skyheart said. "Followed by death." He caressed the lily Myri gave him. "Then silence."

"I would expect nothing less," the Old Man said. "I should so like to see it again. Alas, some things can never be."

Skyheart said nothing. Instead, he observed as the Old Man inspected him with those ancient grey eyes, becoming ever greyer. The Captain didn't move. The gaze wouldn't allow him to. All he could do was stand and be watched.

"You've changed," the Old Man eventually said. "Not that you'd have me know it. But you're definitely different. You discovered something, only to have lost it. You knew peace."

Skyheart looked away but said nothing.

"Very well, you needn't tell me," the Old Man continued. "I should find these things out for myself."

"Have you been as far as Thieron?" Skyheart asked, turning his head to the west.

"Yes."

"And?"

"Best you see for yourself."

The breeze stopped and, with it, so did the planet's moaning. So sudden was the silence that the two men looked sceptically at each other. With no warning the ground began to tremble violently, collapsing sand dunes with whimsical explosions. The two men steadied themselves with difficulty. They were thrown from the ground several times, struggling not to be drowned by the desert.

A mighty roar sounded far away, though not so far as to be indistinguishable. With that the earthquake ended.

Skyheart gathered the breath that the event had stolen from him and picked the Old Man up from the ground. The Old Man wiped sand from himself.

"So the new defence is born," he looked at Skyheart with a severe expression. "That's bad news for you. It means it doesn't need Cendré anymore."

"That's quite alright," Skyheart said with a smile. "I don't plan on needing Cendré anymore either."

"Well," the Old Man said, "all that's left to do now is to wait and see what the defence actually *is*. Whatever it is, it sounds alive."

"I'm afraid I must be going," Skyheart said. "The new defence is of little consequence to me, I fear."

"Fair enough, and far better than I deserve," the Old Man said. "But, true to form, I must ask you this: have you an answer to my original question?"

Skyheart smiled. "I've no time for unworthy ideologies, Old Man. No matter how pertinent they may be to my situation."

The Old Man smiled. "Nor do I," he said.

Skyheart turned in the direction of Thieron and began to walk away.

"Be cautious, Captain!" the Old Man called after him. "Danger may await you!"

Skyheart stopped and turned back to him. "Danger? Now wouldn't that be an adventure?"

And with that he left.

The Old Man watched as the Captain's silhouette shrank in the distance, disappearing against an ever growing horizon. The Old Man scratched at his beard and pondered the conversation. Then he smiled.

"Farewell, Captain Skyheart," he said, before leaving in the direction of the roar.

Chapter Twenty Seven

The desert sands swirled and danced in the cooling afternoon. In the distance, the tower of gold once known as 'The Monument' lay shattered on the ground, with the rest of the city fallen and destroyed around it. Despite the sun, the vast corpse of metal did not shine, as if in acknowledgement of Thieron's demise.

Motionless bodies (all in the black uniforms of Thieron) lay strewn across the sand, their blood thickening the desert into a sinuous crimson sludge. Though one man walked through. His coat, the same colour as the bloody sand creaked with shifting leather, disturbing the silence of the scene. His footsteps lifted sand, discolouring it further, with a wordless stroke. So many times he had walked familiar vistas that he shed not a tear. That this was once his homeland and these his countrymen, mattered not to him. What did pain him was that they were human and that they were now dead. They had once breathed, spoke, laughed, cried and so many other things that not a one of them would do again.

Or, perhaps just one of them would, though not for long.

In the corner of his eye, Skyheart saw a figure trying to rise. A bearded man in an elaborate green coat looked up at him. Blood seeped from his stomach, drenching the hilt of the short-sword he had used to commit ritual suicide. He coughed weakly and his skin paled further. He tried to lift a hand to wipe the viscous red liquid from his mouth but had not the strength to do so. Captain Skyheart knelt down and wiped the blood away for him.

"Hello, brother," he said gently, as one so dear to him often had.

"Oh, you're alive are you?" the Commander spat. "Escape from hell did you?

"No, hell can hold me."

Emaina sneered. "I suppose I should commend you for coming back. It's more than most traitors would do. Or is it the ultimate insult?"

Emaina stopped and the brothers' eyes met.

"When did this happen?" Laike asked.

"Days ago. I can't remember how many. Each seemed so long that I barely remember life before the Mandrans arrived. We held them off for as long as we could, but they broke into the city... and then this."

"Why did they leave you?"

Emaina sneered once more. "They thought that I was something to do with you. The humanity that they weren't completely wrong..." He sighed. "After the battle I wandered the desert looking for those I knew, to bury them. I found Wraste first; he was cut down trying to escape.

"The Assembly were all together. They looked to have tried to bargain their way out with the little gold Thieron had. But it was left alone, stained with their blood. Mandra wanted only our destruction. Even the gold of the Monument lies untouched.

"They beheaded President Kylar to show their troops victory. Then they buried the few dead they had and left ours to rot in the desert heat."

Emaina met his brother's look. "You could have stopped this."

Laike stood, scratched the back of his head and looked away.

"I'm not sure about that," he said, though Emaina seemed not to hear.

"I suppose even you felt the earthquake earlier," Emaina said, "and then that roar... I wonder what it was."

"Nothing you need to worry about," Laike said.

Emaina looked down at the sword penetrating him. He smiled morbidly.

"No, I suppose not," he said.

Laike turned and looked at him. "You look like Dad," he said.

"One of us has to."

"I had a dream about him."

"Oh?"

"He looked old."

"Well," Emaina said, "he would be now."

"We were walking towards a black tower in a wasteland. Mum was waiting for us there, but we never got there. Well, Dad might have done. He left me behind."

Emaina gave Laike a curious look. "I didn't know you thought about him like that," he said.

"I did love him; as a father. Just not as a commander." Laike looked away, but his brother maintained his gaze. "Why do you think he did it?"

"Could you live with what he did? I know I couldn't... Sending all those men to their deaths." Emaina looked at the battlefield around him. "Luckily I won't have to. Much in the same way."

"But Mum as well..."

"Maybe he couldn't bear to be without her."

"And so two children have to raise themselves," Laike looked at his brother. "Why leave us?"

Emaina winced. Then he shrugged. "Why do you ask me questions that you know I can't answer? I'm Commander of Thieron, not a prophet."

Laike turned away.

The sun was beginning to set and the sky had faded to the colour of an autumn leaf. The golden horizon deepened as the breeze whispered through the desert. Sky and sand, regal gold both, could have been one.

"Well," Laike said, "I suppose we're all Mandran now."

Emaina didn't answer, but Laike thought he heard an all too familiar sigh. He thought of turning to look once more upon his brother, but couldn't bring himself to do it.

"Goodbye Emaina," he whispered.

He drew Cendré and rested the obsidian black blade on his shoulder.

"Come now Cendré. There is nothing left to keep us here in this world of war. We've experienced all we must and, perhaps, more than we deserved. We were touched by war more than most, but we were lucky enough to know love.

"We are now finally free. We shall ride on the breeze, fall from the eternal heavens and swim on endless tides."

He smiled.

He and his trusted sword turned to fine black ash and drifted from the battlefield.

Where Captain Laike Skyheart had once stood, a wilted grey flower fell, only to be caught by the breeze and softly carried away.

Lightning Source UK Ltd.
Milton Keynes UK
UKOW03f0008180914

238717UK00001B/104/P